LETHAL PREY

ALSO BY JOHN SANDFORD

Rules of Prey
Shadow Prey
Eyes of Prey
Silent Prey
Winter Prey
Night Prey
Mind Prey
Sudden Prey
Secret Prey
Certain Prey
Easy Prey
Chosen Prey
Mortal Prey
Naked Prey
Hidden Prey
Broken Prey
Invisible Prey
Phantom Prey
Wicked Prey
Storm Prey
Buried Prey
Stolen Prey
Silken Prey
Field of Prey
Gathering Prey
Extreme Prey
Golden Prey
Twisted Prey
Neon Prey
Masked Prey
Ocean Prey
Righteous Prey
Judgment Prey
Toxic Prey

KIDD NOVELS

The Fool's Run
The Empress File
The Devil's Code
The Hanged Man's Song

VIRGIL FLOWERS NOVELS

Dark of the Moon
Heat Lightning
Rough Country
Bad Blood
Shock Wave
Mad River
Storm Front
Deadline
Escape Clause
Deep Freeze
Holy Ghost
Bloody Genius

LETTY DAVENPORT NOVELS

The Investigator
Dark Angel

STAND-ALONE NOVELS

Saturn Run (with Ctein)
The Night Crew
Dead Watch

BY JOHN SANDFORD AND MICHELE COOK

Uncaged
Outrage
Rampage

JOHN SANDFORD

LETHAL PREY

G. P. PUTNAM'S SONS
NEW YORK

=

PUTNAM
— EST. 1838 —

G. P. Putnam's Sons
Publishers Since 1838
an imprint of Penguin Random House LLC
1745 Broadway, New York, NY 10019
penguinrandomhouse.com

Title page photograph by zef art/Shutterstock

Library of Congress Cataloging-in-Publication Data

Names: Sandford, John, 1944 February 23– author.
Title: Lethal prey / John Sandford.
Description: New York : G. P. Putnam's Sons, 2025.
Identifiers: LCCN 2024052243 (print) | LCCN 2024052244 (ebook) |
ISBN 9780593718407 (hardcover) | ISBN 9780593718421 (ebook)
Subjects: LCGFT: Detective and mystery fiction. | Thrillers (Fiction) | Novels.
Classification: LCC PS3569.A516 L48 2025 (print) | LCC PS3569.A516 (ebook) |
DDC 813/.54—dc23/eng/20241118
LC record available at https://lccn.loc.gov/2024052243
LC ebook record available at https://lccn.loc.gov/2024052244

Printed in the United States of America
1st Printing

The authorized representative in the EU for product safety and compliance is Penguin Random House Ireland, Morrison Chambers, 32 Nassau Street, Dublin D02 YH68, Ireland. https://eu-contact.penguin.ie.

AUTHOR'S NOTE

As with most novels, this is a work of fiction. In this case, all but one of the characters are completely fictitious. The exception is the attorney Earl Gray, who appears in the final pages of this work. Gray is an actual Twin Cities defense attorney, and for many years a man of much interest to local reporters, among whom I was once one. He has graciously agreed to defend our killer.

LETHAL PREY

1

BACK IN THE DAY—2003

Nine o'clock, a dazzling moon outside the window, a shrill whistle for a werewolf.

Amanda Fisk stood by the door, listening, teeth bared. There was no doubt about it: the little bitch was getting it on with Timothy.

She had tracked Timothy from his apartment—his ex had gotten the house—across St. Paul and downtown, right to Bee. She'd seen the blonde open the door, and her arms going up around Timothy's neck.

They'd disappeared back toward the stairway. She'd given them some time, and followed, using her own key to get in the building.

Now, with her mind clear and hard as a diamond, Fisk walked down to the cafeteria and through to the executive dining room. She felt as though she had a hand in her back, pushing her along. She got a knife from the serving cart, and as she was walking out, noticed the box of kitchen gloves. She took two, pulled them on, and continued back to her small office. As she walked, she got a whiff of . . . buttered popcorn? Was there somebody else in the building, somebody she didn't know about?

She didn't think so, but she did a swift recon, looking for light, movement, sound. Nothing. She went back to her office. Smelled the popcorn again. Couldn't find the source, but it seemed to be lingering around an unoccupied copy room. Didn't actually worry her, but it seemed curious.

She continued on. She had no plan, but then, as a law school graduate, she understood both the merits of meticulous planning and the merits of spontaneity. This was time for the latter; that was demonstrated by the serendipitous discovery of the nonslip latex gloves.

In her office, she locked the door, sat in her office chair in the semidark, and tested the point of the knife. As expected, the knife was dull. No matter, she had the time. The ledge under the windowsill was rough red brick, and, whetting rapidly and with anger, she groomed the table knife to a fine murderous point.

And she calculated.

The lovebirds would not be leaving together. Timothy Carlson had arrived in his Porsche 911, and the bitch had her Subaru in the parking lot. When the knife was ready, Fisk walked back to the VP's outer office, where the pair had gone to use the soft leather couch. She waited two spaces down, inside an unlocked conference room, the door cracked open just enough to see. The anger clawed at her throat, and she struggled to control her breathing. Timothy didn't know it yet, but she was already planning the wedding. They'd been dating for a year, and an idiot blonde named Doris wasn't going to sidetrack her plans.

There in the conference room, she didn't have to wait long. With Timothy, unfortunately, you *never* had to wait long.

And Timothy, laughing, possibly a bit abashed, as he should be, left first, checked his fly, said goodbye through the open doorway one last time. He walked along the dark corridor to the stairs, down the stairs, and out.

DORIS GRANDFELT STEPPED out two or three minutes later, peered nearsightedly around, and then, barefoot and bare-assed, carrying her underpants, skirt, shoes, a shoulder bag, and what appeared to be a handful of Kleenex, scurried down the hallway to the ladies' room.

Fisk followed, her senses tuned to any possible interference or interruption, but the building, except for the two of them, and the scent of buttered popcorn, was empty. The knife was light in her hand, ready.

She stopped outside the restroom, kicked off her shoes, listening, then pulled open the door and peeked. Grandfelt was in one of the toilet stalls. Fisk stepped inside, eased the door shut, then tiptoed silently across the tacky cold tile to one side of the booths.

Perhaps there was a change in air pressure, or perhaps the prospective victim simply had excellent hearing, but Grandfelt blurted, "Hello? Someone there?"

Fisk stood unmoving, and Grandfelt listened, then continued whatever she was doing in the stall. The toilet flushed, and after a minute, Grandfelt pulled the door open, stepped out, fully dressed, and walked to the line of sinks that faced the booths.

Not quite perfect for a murder, but good enough. When Grandfelt reached for the soap dispenser, Fisk stepped out quickly, coming up from behind. Grandfelt's eyes snapped up to the mirror, too late, Fisk stuck the knife in the other woman's back, striking hard, the blade penetrating past the spine and into the heart.

Grandfelt recoiled, bent, shrieked once, and turned, and Fisk stabbed her again and again and again and the blue eyes were looking up at her and she stabbed her and stabbed her eyes and throat . . .

She wasn't quite sure how long she was there, but whenever it was that she came back to the world, Grandfelt was not only dead, she was a mess. How did her blouse get ripped open, who tore off the lacy black bra? Fisk had no memory of it, but . . . it must have been her. And she had blood on her, *all over her*, blood almost up to her elbows, and covering her blouse, jacket, and slacks.

She listened, heard nothing. If someone came . . . she still had the knife, and now, she noticed, she was bleeding from a cut on her hand. How that had happened, she didn't know.

Here she was, with a dead body on her hands. It felt like a risk, but not a large one, and had a feeling to it: she could run the table here. She stepped outside the restroom and into her shoes, looked around. Her purse was still in her office. She went that way, to get it, realized she was still carrying the knife, and when she got her purse, fumbled it inside and slung the purse over her arm.

She walked back down to the cafeteria, dug around, and found a box of black plastic garbage bags in a cabinet, and a pack of brown paper towels. She carried them to the restroom.

On the way, she noticed, for the first time, a feeling of wetness on her arms and chest and stomach: Grandfelt's blood. That had to be dealt with, but not yet.

Back at the restroom, in her bare feet again, she set the purse aside and went to work. Grandfelt, not a large woman, she jammed into two overlapping garbage bags. Fisk spent another five minutes scrubbing up the blood on the restroom floor—probably didn't get it all, but if there was a tiny speck here or there, the janitors would get it, and never know.

She shoved the bloody paper towels into the bags with Grandfelt, took a minute to wash her own hands and arms, cleared off a slash of blood on her left cheek. Her clothes were saturated with blood, but it was less visible than it might be. She was wearing her work clothes, a dark blue jacket and dark blue slacks, over a pale blue blouse. The blood was evident on the blouse, but not so much on her jacket and slacks, especially not in dim light. And she could button the jacket: that was all good.

She buttoned the jacket, checked her hair, rinsed the blood out of the sink, took a last look around, dragged the bags to the door, listened.

All clear. She got her purse, put her shoes back on, and dragged the bags down the dimly lit hallway to the elevator, gripping Grandfelt's arms through the plastic. She took the load to the first floor, then to the back door. She pushed the bags through the door to the top of the steps, let the door close behind her, hurried out to the street, where she'd left her car. She drove it around to the back door, picked up the garbage bags—heavy, but not too heavy—staggered out to the car and dropped the body in the trunk.

Now what? Rather, now where?

She thought for a moment and came up with just the right spot. Minutes from the parking lot, and she knew it well, having grown up only a few blocks away. As she drove, she made a mental list: leave the body, but get all the other crap out of the sacks—the towels, the shoulder bag, the shoes. An ID, if there was one in the bag, would instantly identify the body, and might somehow identify the scene of the crime. The knife was in there: must get rid of it right away.

What about Grandfelt's car, still in the parking lot? She considered that, as she pulled into Shawnee Park. If she had time . . .

The police might believe that Grandfelt was murdered in the building, but more likely would believe that she'd been picked up by somebody and taken away to be murdered. After all, there was no evidence of a murder in the building. She'd have to get rid of the garbage bags and be careful about it.

Shawnee Park was tucked in a kind of armpit where I-494 met I-94 in Woodbury, east of St. Paul. She checked the few lighted windows in the surrounding neighborhood but saw no movement. Still wary, watchful, she stripped the body out of the sacks and threw everything else into one of them. As she was doing that, she noticed Timothy's Nike tennis shoes in the trunk, thought a minute, then pulled them on over her loafers. The ground was damp, no reason to leave small female footprints if you don't have to.

That done, and fueled by adrenaline, she dragged Grandfelt out of the car, humped the body a hundred yards across the playing fields to a line of trees, pushed back into them, and dumped it. Hurrying back to the car, she got inside, saw the purse sitting on the passenger seat, and the glimmer of the knife handle.

She picked it up, stepped out of the car again, stuck the knife in the ground, pushed it as far down as she could, and then stepped on it, to get it that last inch down in the soft earth.

Drive carefully, she thought, on the way out of the park, neither too fast nor too slow, and with confidence. She'd done so well, this was no time to blow it.

Grandfelt's car.

She didn't drive back to the murder scene, but she got close, parked on the street a block away. She dug in the garbage bag, found car keys in the dead woman's purse, and walked to Grandfelt's car; blood was drying on her blouse, and she could feel it crinkling against her skin, raising goose bumps. She drove the Subaru six blocks and left it a block from a still-open bar that everybody, including Fisk, referred to as a meat rack.

She sat for a moment, watching and listening, got out, locked the Subaru with the fob, and walked through the night to her own vehicle.

She could smell the blood on herself. Feel the lucid rays of the full moon cool on her face and arms. Perfect.

2

BACK IN THE DAY

The next night, the moon was fat and full and creamy in a faultlessly clear, liquid sky The silvery stream of illumination poked through the parkside trees, leaving a sharply defined pattern on the ground, like spots on a dalmatian. Out in the open, around the softball diamonds, the light was bright enough to read a newspaper.

Brandon and Alice Parkinson were walking their kinky-haired gray labradoodle, Lloyd, on a grassy ramble along the edges of Shawnee Park. A retractable leash allowed the dog to dash into the trees and tangle himself in brush, but no matter, the Parkinsons were not in a hurry. They enjoyed the warming spring evenings, the air as soft as a cashmere blanket, a relief from the cold edges of a recently departed Minnesota winter.

Alice was back from Chicago, a visit to her parents. She'd taken the Empire Builder train to and from St. Paul. She was still afraid to fly after the 9/11 terrorist attacks on the World Trade Center and the

Pentagon two years earlier. As a side benefit, she felt confident in transporting six ounces of primo weed back from Chicago, where her mother had a tight connection with a dealer. She would not have been confident bringing it back through O'Hare's airport security.

As they walked, they could hear the faint but unmistakable sound of Britney Spears singing "Oops! I Did It Again," which must have been coming through an open window somewhere in the neighborhood, another sure sign of spring. Brandon carried a flashlight, the better to untangle the dog when that became necessary. He flicked it off and on as they walked along the line of trees at the far edge of the playing fields.

Lloyd checked out a dried pile of dog poop. Alice pulled him away and said to Brandon, "Stop hogging the J, for cripes sakes."

Brandon passed the joint, Alice took a toke, held her breath for a few steps, let the aromatic smoke filter slowly out her nose. Alice was a believer in the slow nose exhale, that the sensitive nasal linings transmitted the THC more rapidly to the brain, made the high stronger and more resonant.

She passed the joint back and they ambled on, letting the dog lead. They'd been talking about their teenaged daughter, Shona, who was showing an intense interest in a particular boy in school. Brandon called him "the rat" because of his distinctly ratlike appearance, a thin face with a prominent nose and a pointed chin on which the kid was attempting to grow a beard.

"That's really unkind," Alice said, reaching a point in her stoneage where everything went mellow. "He can't help his appearance."

"Of course he can," Brandon said. "He even dresses like a rat."

"That's true," Alice conceded. Brandon passed the J and Alice took a contemplative toke and passed it back. As she exhaled, she said, in a squeaky voice, "I'd prefer not to have any ratlike grandchildren, if I can avoid it. Especially not when Shona's in tenth grade."

LLOYD HAD DRIFTED deeper into the trees and was pulling at the leash. "He's tangled up again, goddamnit," Brandon said, pecking at the joint.

"Gimme some light, I'll get it." As Brandon shined the flashlight back into the trees, Alice pushed a branch aside, following the leash to the dog. When she got to him, she stopped. Looked. Looked again, into the bright puddle of moonlight. "Brand! What the heck is that? What the heck is it?"

She swiveled back, dragging the dog behind her. She hugged Brandon around his waist. "It looks like . . ."

Brandon, who'd played high school football back in the late '70s, knew no fear. He stepped into the trees, Alice behind him, holding on to his belt, and turned the flashlight toward a white lump.

The woman had been butchered.

She lay on her back, half upside down in a depression in the damp earth. She was mostly nude. She'd been ripped from sternum to pelvic bone, stabbed multiple times in the face and eyes, neck, and upper chest. Her body was a ghastly pale lump in the now sepulchral light of the moon. And he could smell her: a butcher shop odor, mixed with a fecal stink.

Brandon said, "Oh, fuck me," turned away, backtracked, and vomited on Alice's shoes.

After discovering the body, the couple, stoned to the gills and panicked, crashed through the brush and trees, dragged the frightened dog into the open, and ran toward the house where Britney had been singing her song, now replaced by the Backstreet Boys with "I Want It That Way."

They were running for what they thought might be their lives, between the ballfields, to a parking lot. There, stopping to catch their breath, they called 9-1-1. Ten minutes later, they led a squadron of Woodbury cops back into the trees and the body.

After a quick survey of the murder scene—a mutilated young woman with blond hair, half-wrapped in a silky blood-soaked blouse and beige skirt—the cops called the Bureau of Criminal Apprehension in St. Paul and asked that a crime scene crew and investigators be sent over immediately.

3

BACK IN THE DAY

The morning after the body was discovered, two very large BCA investigators, both new to the organization, stood back and watched. Their names were Jenkins and Shrake. They had first names, of course, but nobody used them. Jenkins had been a homicide investigator for the city of Minneapolis before moving to the BCA. Shrake had been an investigator for the city of Duluth.

Although both were smart, hard-nosed cops with enough experience to become cynical about the possibility of progress in human nature, none of the big guns at the BCA trusted them to work a high-profile, media-sensitive investigation like that of the murder of Doris Grandfelt. She was the prime example of the Hot Blonde Syndrome: if you want to keep your murder quiet, kill a Black woman. Or a Mexican or a Palestinian.

You do not kill hot blondes, whose ghastly deaths make the top of the ten o'clock broadcasts, and get away with it.

Unless you do, of course.

In which case, the Jenkinses and Shrakes of the business will be brought in when it's too late to do any good, hopefully to take the blame for the lack of results.

THE TWO NEW investigators had known each other from police department golf events and were becoming friends, as they eased into the chill waters of the BCA. They were allowed to go to the scene of the murder, and ask questions, as long as they didn't get too close. Shrake caught a crime scene investigator sitting on a bench behind a softball backstop, eating a cheese sandwich, and said to Jenkins, "He'll speak to us if we're nice."

"Or we could beat it out of him," Jenkins said.

"I like the concept, but I want him healthy enough to talk."

All they knew about the CSI was that his name was Larry. They sat on either side of Larry, who looked at them warily and asked, through a mouthful of cheddar cheese, "Wut?"

"Tell us about it, Lare," Jenkins said, leaning close. He was perhaps a hundred pounds heavier than Larry, most of it muscle, so Larry swallowed and told them.

The scene, he said, had been frozen for a hundred yards around, but not before a half-dozen Woodbury cars had come and gone, followed by four more BCA vehicles that tracked over the earlier tracks. The crime scene investigation had begun the night before under portable lights, but nothing was disturbed until morning, when the scene was fully sunlit.

"We're about to move the body over to the medical examiner. We did the inch-by-inch stuff around the body and now we need to see what's under it."

"What have you detected?" Shrake asked.

"We may have some footprints."

"Footprints?"

"Maybe."

"Will that amount to anything, Lare?"

"Uh . . . who knows?"

JENKINS AND SHRAKE hung around the investigation when they could get away from their own routine assignments, picking up bits and pieces of the BCA investigative culture. The woman, they were told, had been dead for roughly thirty-six hours by the time the medical examiner got to her. Investigators believed she'd been killed the night before she'd been found, which would have been a Wednesday night. She wasn't killed earlier than that, because she'd been at work on Wednesday. She hadn't been killed later than that because she hadn't shown up for work Thursday morning.

"That's some fancy detectin', right there," Shrake observed.

SHE WASN'T KILLED in daylight hours, because the park was somewhat busy and there was a neighborhood on its south side, making it difficult to drive across the open playing fields in daylight without being seen. The body could have been carried—the victim was small—but a vehicle delivery seemed more likely.

The murder weapon had been sharp, with a blade that was narrow but inflexible, something like a boning knife. If the knife had been a penknife with a three- or four-inch blade, then the murder could have been spontaneous. But it wasn't a penknife. The blade was long enough that it would have been awkward to routinely carry, except in a sheath. That meant, investigators believed, that the murder had been planned, and the knife deliberately carried to that end.

"Unless it wasn't planned," Jenkins said. "I had a guy, stoned on some kinda weird shit, stab a guy outside a taco shop with a knife he found on the sidewalk like one minute before. Unfortunately for him, he was standing under a video camera when he did it. No previous contact between the two, no motive . . . the stabber wasn't even a religious nut and was from out of town. We never would have caught him without the video. He was identified by his mom, who saw him on TV."

THE CRIME SCENE crew determined that the murder had been committed elsewhere, but found multiple foot tracks around the dump site. The killer had been wearing size ten-and-a-half Nike Air Force 1's.

"What size are your Nike Air Force 1's?" Jenkins asked Shrake.

"Fourteen."

"Okay, you didn't do it."

No identifying material remained on the body, with one exception—a dry-cleaning tag on the hem of the woman's skirt. BCA investigators quickly identified the victim as Doris Grandfelt, an accountant at Bee Accounting Corp., with headquarters in the Lowertown section of St. Paul.

The identification was confirmed by the victim's twin sister, Lara Grandfelt. Bee Accounting was a twelve- to fifteen-minute drive from the park, depending on traffic. Grandfelt's car was found a few blocks away from Bee, near a bar known as a meeting place for singles. There was no blood in the car. A once-over at Bee Accounting found no sign of the attack there.

Although Grandfelt had been a pretty, vivacious woman, none of the bar employees remembered seeing her there the night she was murdered. A presumption developed: Grandfelt had been grabbed after work, on the street, probably on her way to the bar, and had been taken somewhere else and was killed, wherever that was.

"That's possible," Shrake said.

"If unlikely," Jenkins observed. "I've been there a few times. There are always people on the sidewalk when the place is open."

"You ever get lucky?"

"One time I thought I had, but it turned out a week later, I hadn't."

"What happened? I mean, you didn't . . ."

"I don't want to talk about it."

THE MEDICAL EXAMINER found that the victim had had a sexual encounter before her death. A rape kit was done and the DNA results were preserved forever in the BCA's computers. The perpetrator—or, at least, the last man to have sex with her—had not used a condom, nor had he made any effort to avoid leaving traces of himself.

The autopsy revealed that Grandfelt had engaged in sexual activity at least twice the day of her death, and that the first case of intercourse involved a condom that used a spermicidal lubricant. Traces of the lubricant were recovered from deep in her vagina, but no DNA was recovered from that first sexual contact. There was no way to determine whether the sexual contacts were with one man, or with two different men.

Some investigators questioned the idea that she'd been raped, because there'd been no vaginal bruising or tears, or signs of an involuntary, violent penetration. The investigators couldn't tell whether the woman had fought against an attacker. She had none of his blood on her fists or in her mouth, and none of his skin under her fingernails.

One of the investigators, a woman named Maria Jimenez, told Shrake, "Doris had some muscle. She grew up on a farm down by Lakeville, threw hay, worked out here in the Cities. No ligature marks, no sign she was tied up, no signs of resistance. Nothing. I don't believe she was raped."

"You're smarter than you look," Shrake said.

"What?" Fists on her hips.

"Wait. That didn't come out right. You're smart. And you look great. Really great."

"Go away, bozo."

THE ATTACK SEQUENCE was developed by the male investigators, who argued that Grandfelt had been raped and stabbed between eighteen and twenty-one times, in what appeared to be a psychotic frenzy. Most of the stab wounds were in the areas of her face, chest, and throat, with two more in each of her eyes. One wound went through her back and into her heart.

A psychologist employed by the BCA suggested that the eye wounds, which were postmortem, were intended to keep the dead woman from seeing her killer in death. The cops took that with a grain of salt the size of a basketball.

Sometime after she was dead and her arteries had stopped

pumping out blood, she'd been cut open, and some of her internal organs dragged around with the knife blade.

The killer was nuts.

"We can all agree on that," Jenkins told Shrake, who nodded.

GRANDFELT SHARED AN apartment with another Bee employee, a woman named Stephanie Brady. Brady had been away, in a Duluth motel, consulting on a tax return. She was in Duluth for several nights before, and the day the body was found. She told the investigators that Grandfelt had not been involved in a steady sexual relationship, as far as she knew. She *had* been involved in a sexual relationship that ended the summer before, Brady said.

The man, named Jeremy Williams, had both an alibi and volunteered for a DNA test that indicated that he was not the last person to have had sex with Grandfelt. His alibi had been checked and found solid, if not perfect, which was good for Williams, because cops were suspicious of perfect alibis. Williams was an assistant coach at Cretin High School in St. Paul. He said he'd never visited Grandfelt at work and had never visited the park where the body was found. The investigators couldn't break that down.

There had been another relationship before Williams, which the BCA traced to a man named Clifton Howard (also incorrectly referred to in several reports as Howard Clifton), but he had moved to Seattle two years earlier, having broken off the relationship. He had established alibis there for the period around the murder and also volunteered for a DNA scrub.

Her twin, Lara, a bank employee in St. Paul, told investigators that

Doris had had an off-and-on sexual relationship in college with a boy named Christopher Schuler. She said that Schuler was "odd."

Schuler was found working in Salt Lake City as a waiter, and the restaurant staff confirmed that he had been working the night of the attack, and the days before and after. Schuler wrote an angry letter to Lara Grandfelt about pulling him into the case, and Grandfelt called him to apologize.

A review of Doris Grandfelt's employment status revealed that although she had graduated from Manifold College, a small church-linked school in southern Minnesota, with a major in accounting, she was not employed as a supervising accountant at Bee—she was more like a skilled clerk and was paid as a skilled clerk. Two dozen male Bee employees were interviewed and asked for DNA swabs, which they provided, to no effect.

Despite a low salary, Grandfelt dressed well, and had a collection of designer shoes—Chanel slingbacks, Louboutin stilettoes, Blahnik pumps, Gucci horsebit loafers. Jimenez, the investigator who didn't think Grandfelt had been raped, looked at the shoes and said, "She wasn't going to the state fair in these things. I smell money coming from somewhere."

Grandfelt's parents were affluent but provided no significant post-college support for their twin daughters, believing hard work would teach them the value of a dollar.

Further interviews with her roommate and with friends revealed that Grandfelt had an active club life in Minneapolis and was known by a number of bouncers and bartenders as a welcome regular. After doing the interviews, one of the investigators confidentially suggested that Grandfelt might have been involved with sex-for-pay, to fund the expensive wardrobe and clubbing lifestyle. There were hints that she was not unfamiliar with cocaine, although no signs of the drug were found in the autopsy or in her apartment.

When word of the sex-for-pay and cocaine discussion leaked to the Minneapolis *Star-Tribune*, Lara Grandfelt went ballistic and tried (unsuccessfully) to sue both the BCA and the paper for defamation. Can't defame a dead woman, she was told.

"What do you think?" Shrake asked Jenkins. "Was she on the corner?"

"Those shoes . . . there was no way she was buying them on her salary. She wasn't on the corner, though. Too conservative for that. Probably working for someone over on Hennepin, who'd set her up with dates, maybe provide some protection."

"Anybody talk to Minneapolis vice?"

"Jimenez called over, but they'd hadn't heard of her. Grandfelt, not Jimenez. Never been busted for anything. Not even a speeding ticket."

"We need a survey of Hennepin Avenue bartenders, see what they know."

"I could sign up for that. I'd need some expense money."

DORIS GRANDFELT, AS a clerk-level accountant, was responsible for overseeing the packaging and the signing in and out of confidential tax and financial information, using both FedEx and UPS couriers. She sometimes stayed after dark to do that. Eight different UPS and FedEx drivers were interviewed and eliminated as suspects.

In the days and weeks following the murder, frustrated BCA investigators were unable to find anyone who admitted having sex with the woman on the day she was killed, or any other day, other than acknowledged sexual partners. None of those admitted to having sex with her in the months before she was murdered.

In the end, the cops did 336 separate interviews. They had unidentified DNA; had evidence that the killer wore Nike Air Force 1's, size ten and a half, as did a million other American males; had evidence that the killer owned a knife with a blade at least six inches long of unknown make, but probably good quality—the knife hadn't bent or deflected when hitting bone. And they had a great collection of footwear, locked in an evidence room.

If there had been any reason to do a full forensic examination of the third-floor women's room in the first hours after the discovery of the body, investigators might have found stray blood cells that could have been traced to Grandfelt, and thus pinned down the scene of the crime. But there was no reason to do that, and after a few daily applications of restroom floor cleaner by the janitors, the possibility was gone.

There was never exactly a final conference about the murder, and the case didn't become "cold"—although it definitely became cool—but there was a big get-together at which all the investigators were invited, including Jenkins and Shrake.

Their opinions were not solicited, but Shrake gave them anyway.

"You oughta . . . we oughta . . . get every single ambulatory male client of Bee's, and every male Bee employee, and make them take DNA tests. Jenkins and I believe that we would at least find out who was having sex with her, that last time."

DNA tests were expensive, there were hundreds of male clients, blah blah blah. It wasn't done.

That was about it.

BACK IN THE DAY

In 2003, Lucas Davenport was being driven crazy by three kinds of people: computer programmers, actors, and accountants. He didn't yet yearn for the time when he'd been a cop, instead of a start-up business executive, but he was getting there.

On this particular day, in the Nick O' Time Coffee and Pastries Shoppe, it was actors who were up his ass.

He'd spent weeks writing scenarios for 9-1-1 training calls. Under his game plan, each 9-1-1 trainee would be seated in front of a computer, just as she would be in real life, and would take a prerecorded call: frightened people screaming for help. Each call would require the operators to make an appropriate response, guided by suggestions that would flash up on the computer screen.

Each operator response branched to another screaming reply by the caller, which branched to another response, depending on what the answer was. At more advanced levels, the operator would be dealing with three or four calls at once and would have no prompts, as would happen with a disaster of greater or lesser extent, like a school shooting, or a small-plane crash.

The whole sequence would be overseen by an instructor, based on training manuals also being written by Lucas.

Lucas wanted the calls to be vocal and realistic—that is, the trainee would have a set of headphones and a microphone. When a call came in, he or she would select an appropriate response and read it in the appropriate tone of voice.

He knew what he wanted, but the programmers explained in incomprehensible detail how difficult it was and why they should be paid more. Which drove him crazy. All he wanted to know was whether they could do it. They could, but they whined.

THE ACTORS WOULD provide the 9-1-1 calls with the appropriate amount of panic:

"My house is on fire!"

"There's a man in my house. He's got a gun!"

"My husband is hurting me! Here he comes . . ."

"My son has shot up and he's not breathing!"

Lucas had experience writing board games—based on historical battles and fantasy conflicts—and had put his entire savings into the new computer company, tentatively called Davenport Simulations.

He was paying the programmers and actors, all graduate students at the University of Minnesota, a pittance, along with stock options, which everyone, without exception, laughed off as improbable.

Hence the other major pain in his ass: the accountants.

————

SO THERE HE was in a booth in the Nick O' Time with two actors, both grad students, both female, both attractive, one white and blond, one Black and dark-haired, trying to explain to them why asking for a "somewhat Black" accent was not racist, but designed to elicit a certain kind of response from a trainee, who might or might not be racist.

"I don't want Mammy from *Gone with the Wind*, I want somebody who sounds like they live in North Minneapolis," he said. North Minneapolis was local code for "Black."

"Lots of white people in North Minneapolis," the white actor said, deliberately yanking his chain.

Lucas: "You know what I mean."

"It'd be less racist if you paid us more," the Black woman said.

"Tell me that when you cash in the stock options," Lucas said.

The two women laughed and the white woman said, "Yeah, right, remind me to do that."

The three of them were impatiently working through the whole cultural/racial conundrum when two large men, mid-thirties, muscular, wearing Polo golf shirts under sport coats, and khaki slacks, with World War Two haircuts, one of them snapping his chewing gum, came through the door. The one snapping gum had brilliant white teeth, which were actually implants, paid for by the state when his natural teeth had been knocked out by a woman wielding a flowerpot.

The men looked around, and Jenkins spotted Lucas, ambled over to the table, trailed by Shrake, checked the actors and asked Lucas, "Settin' up a salt 'n' pepper three-way?"

"Shut up, you fuckin' clown. We got serious business here," Lucas said. To the startled actors, "Don't pay any attention to him. He's a moron. Are we good? You understand where I'm coming from? It is a *racial* thing, but not racist. Not on our part."

"That sounds a little racist, whatever it is," Shrake said, without being asked.

"I do understand, but I've got to think about it," the Black woman said. She looked up at the two large men and then back at Lucas. "Who *are* these jerks?"

"Ooo, I like them spicy," the slightly smaller of the two large men said.

"I ought to kick your balls up around your collar," the actor said.

The blonde said, "Do it, Jackie." And to the slightly smaller man, "She's in karate."

The larger of the two large men: "So, uh, could we get some phone numbers?"

Lucas, rubbing his forehead with his fingers: "Jesus God. I'm just trying to get through life."

THE TWO MEN went to the counter to order coffee and scones, and the two actors left, agreeing that they would review the new scripts and call with any notes that they thought would improve them. They'd think about the "Black accent."

When the men came back, Lucas, who was not small, moved over so Jenkins could sit next to him, because Jenkins and Shrake would not both fit in the same side of a restaurant booth.

Jenkins said to Lucas, "This is my new partner up at the BCA.

Shrake. He's kind of an asshole, but he's willing to carry my lunch bucket."

"That's not the entire story," Shrake said, getting comfortable with his scone. He was not a tidy eater. "I hang out because I can supplement my income by playing golf with him."

Lucas said, "I've already heard about Shrake. There are rumors that you guys are working the Grandfelt murder and you're fucking it up."

"Who is this guy?" Shrake asked Jenkins.

"Used to be a big-deal homicide investigator in Minneapolis. Then this cute little hooker who was feeding him tips got caught by her pimp. He carved her up with a church key. Lucas sort of went off on the poor guy. The politicians got pissed and he was kicked out of the department. They claimed he used excessive force," Jenkins said. To Lucas: "Whatever happened to the chick?"

"Still looks like a jack-o'-lantern, a week after Halloween," Lucas said.

"Nasty. How about the pimp? He walking again?"

"I don't know. I don't check on him anymore," Lucas said. "I was told by a reliable source that he no longer needs diapers."

Shrake lifted a hand to be slapped, and said, "Testify!"

Lucas slapped. "So. You guys fuckin' it up?"

"Not us. We're going around talking to the least-likely suspects while the big guns get the real possibilities," Shrake said. "Not that there's much difference between the two groups."

"I heard the victim was a mess," Lucas said.

"Bad as it gets," Jenkins said. "The only thing I've seen that compares was back when I was on the street. A couple of kids drove an old MGB into a bridge abutment at eighty miles an hour. You couldn't tell which head went with which body. Grandfelt was like that . . . she was ripped to pieces."

"Tell me everything," Lucas said, realizing that he was more interested than he should be, as he was now a business executive and not a cop.

Jenkins told him the story in detail, and when he was done, Lucas asked, "You gonna catch whoever did it?"

Jenkins and Shrake glanced at each other, then they both shook their heads. "I don't think so. Whoever did this knew what they were doing," Shrake said. "He left us nothing to work with. We've taken a bunch of blood samples and they all go back to Grandfelt. No extraneous hair, no skin, no DNA. Grandfelt was playing games with a bunch of low-lifes over on the Hennepin strip, and had been for a while, so that's a problem, because it multiplies the possibilities."

"Don't think it was a low-life—or it might have been, but that's not the critical factor," Jenkins said. "The critical thing is, whoever did it is a psycho. I wouldn't be surprised if he'd done some other killings. This was not an ordinary thing."

"So you got nothing? Not even a hint of a motive?" Lucas asked.

Shrake sighed, and said, "You know, it could be sex, but I don't think so. Not money, either, because Grandfelt didn't have much. Jealousy? That's a possibility. But it might not be any of those. We found her car on the street near a meat rack, so it might be somebody who preys on blondes. Picked her up, took her somewhere quiet, fucked her and murdered her. No motive other than what the voices in his head were telling him to do. You know?"

Lucas nodded: "That makes it tough."

"Maybe impossible," Jenkins said. "I feel 'impossible' coming up like the sun in the morning, though the hotshots won't admit it.

They're saying they'll have the guy in a week. They're full of shit. I'd be surprised if they get him at all."

That was all Lucas knew about the Grandfelt murder at the time it happened.

Lucas stayed with the new company for three years, then sold all the stock in a management buyout financed by San Francisco venture capitalists. He became a dot-com multimillionaire and went back to being a cop, because what he really liked in life was chasing killers.

The actors and programmers, who had between five hundred (a janitor) and ten thousand (the lead programmer) stock options each, were cashed out at twenty-one dollars a share, which left them even more amazed than they were delighted, and they *were* delighted.

EVERY YEAR OR so after the murder, state investigators checked with public DNA databases for any DNA that correlated with the killer's. Nothing turned up, which led investigators to believe that the killer didn't care about his ancestry, and perhaps was at the end of his particular genetic line.

The BCA investigators also suffered through extended face-to-face contact with Lara Grandfelt, the twin, whom they unofficially classified as one of the biggest pains in the ass that they'd ever encountered.

The twin was smart, tough, and eventually affluent enough to hire private investigators and lawyers. She delivered a monthly telephone harangue to whichever investigator was unlucky enough to answer the phone, questioning whether it was stupidity, incompetence, or simple laziness that kept the BCA from finding the killer.

One investigator, often the butt of her accusations, admitted during lunch at the Parrot Café that he hated her. And then, after all of that, after all the shouting, after all accusations of incompetence, cupidity, cover-ups, and possible corruption, twenty-one full years after the murder . . . Lara Grandfelt threw gasoline on the case and set it on fire.

5

PRESENT DAY

Lucas was sprawled on a king-sized bed in the Holiday Inn Express on the outskirts of Marshalltown, Iowa, hands linked across his stomach, as he gloomily contemplated the blank screen of the television. Nothing on—nothing good. Dressed in boxer shorts, a tee-shirt, and dark blue athletic socks, he thought about getting off the bed to do some pushups, but he'd already done that and the carpet smelled funky.

Masturbation was a possibility, but he was an older guy now, and was saving himself for a double-header when he got back home.

He could go after the slow, extra fat bluebottle fly that was buzzing around the room, with a rolled-up newspaper, but that idea was both trivial and boring.

He had been reading a thriller novel that had annoyed him

with: (1) heroes who were bulletproof, and (2) repeated references to "flat-screen TVs."

He thought, "No, dummy, they're just TVs. There are millions of people living in the United States who wouldn't know what a non-flat-screen TV would even look like."

He confirmed both his annoyance and his boredom by looking up "flat-screen TVs" on his flat-screen telephone and found that old-style CRT TVs hadn't even been manufactured for fifteen years.

He got up and looked out the window. If he pressed his face against the cool glass, which he didn't, he could see a soybean field across a highway to the south. Straight ahead, a Menards, a Midwestern version of Home Depot. He was vaguely hungry and considered walking over to a Culver's diner for a piece of pie, but he really wasn't that hungry.

Or, he could walk over to Menards and look at building stuff and tools, which he had already done twice.

Lucas would be sixty years old at his next big birthday, still a few years away, but he had a depression gene, which had gotten on top of him a couple of times in his life, and which he feared. He'd been feeling melancholy for months. Not good. His adopted daughter, Letty, had almost died in a New Mexico case the year before, which had been profoundly disturbing. He thought about it too much.

And the years were going by. Unexpectedly, they never stopped. Not only did they not stop, they even seemed to have speeded up, one sloppy winter piling into the next, with only a sliver of summer between them.

He hadn't had any compelling jobs since one he'd shared with

Letty; mostly just chasing around after dirtballs, who, while they were sometimes dangerous, were not interesting in themselves.

Both Letty and his wife were telling him he had to find something besides chasing dirtballs. Find a hobby, they said. Try something arty, or musical. Write more games, as he'd done when he was younger. Take some money out of his investment accounts, which returned a reliable five percent, and see if he could blow the money up into something really large.

He didn't want to do any of that. He did like going over to Menards and looking at tools: he'd considered finding a congenial contractor and designing and building a spec house, just to see what he could do.

But what he really wanted was to chase down serious, intelligent, violent criminals instead of the dirtballs he'd been pursuing over the last year.

THE CASE THAT brought him to Marshalltown was one of those. Two outlaw brothers, the Bergstroms, Boy and Andy, were selling counterfeit vodka made from corn alcohol. The Marshals Service got involved because the brothers were both under indictment for passing counterfeit twenty-dollar bills, their previous business venture. When Secret Service agents had tried to arrest them, the brothers had shot their way past them, and escaped.

No one had been injured, but you couldn't let a couple of clodhoppers get away with that stuff.

The Bergstroms gave up on the twenties, which weren't all that good anyway, made with a scanner and printer that had the anti-counterfeiting chips cleansed by an Iowa State University hacker. The currency looked okay at a glance, but the paper it was printed on sucked, and a couple of months after their venture launched, every convenience store on the plains had been on the lookout for the crappy paper.

As criminals searching for another source of income, the Bergstroms had begun printing fake liquor labels and pasting them to recycled bottles, which they filled with corn alcohol and artificial flavors. They bought bulk alcohol out of the backdoor of Iowa corn-based distilleries that normally sold it to oil companies as a gasoline additive. They resold the rebottled booze to less-than-ethical alcohol distributors.

Their biggest problem, it turned out, was finding the bottles to hold the liquor.

The task force had drilled a few investigative dry holes—the Bergstroms were wandering around the Midwest in pickups ("one red, one blue" according to an alcohol supplier squeezed by Lucas) and were therefore hard to pin down.

In the end, an ATF agent named Clayton Vanes set up a fake Internet recycling company that bought and sold empty liquor bottles out of a storage unit in Clear Lake, Iowa. The storage unit was overseen by a rotating group of marshals, including Lucas.

Unfortunately, the Bergstroms hadn't shown up to buy the bottles themselves—they'd sent Jennifer (Jiminy) Katz, Boy Bergstrom's girlfriend, instead. Lucas sold her one thousand empty Stolichnaya bottles and she disappeared in her truck, now accompanied by an electronic tracker surreptitiously mounted on the rear axle.

They'd followed her to a rented farmhouse ten miles from Marshalltown, where the cops settled down to wait.

———

LUCAS WAS STILL looking out the window, at heat waves coming off the parking lot—it was hotter than hell outside, and so humid you could drown—still considering the possibilities, pie or tools, when his radio buzzed. He picked it up and Lanny Anderson, who was sitting in a hole on top of a knoll next to a stump in a clump of trees ten miles out of town, with a pair of binoculars, said, "Guys, we got a pickup."

An ATF agent, Mary McLeod, asked, "Red Silverado? Blue Silverado?"

"It's red. Not real shiny red, dusty red. But yeah, it's a Chevy."

"That's it, a thousand miles of gravel roads," McLeod said. "Guys . . . let's mount up."

Lucas was already pulling on his jeans. He added a long-sleeved shirt, clipped on his pistol, and picked up a cheap blue nylon windbreaker that read "U.S. MARSHAL," all caps, in six-inch-high yellow letters.

Anderson called back, "It's Boy Bergstrom and his old lady, no sign of Andy. They're out of the truck, walking up to the house."

"That's Andy's old lady in the house, I gotta believe he'll be coming in soon, they don't roam far apart," McLeod said. "We're heading for the parking lot."

Lucas got his gear bag and was out the door. Two other marshals, Turner and Weed, were in the hallway at the same time; altogether, including the guy in the hole on the hill, there were eight of them, four marshals, three ATF agents, and one Secret Service agent. If Andy Bergstrom showed up, they'd bust the house. If Boy Bergstrom tried to leave in the dusty red Chevy, they'd box him in on the road. A Bergstrom in the hand was worth two in the bush.

In the elevator, Weed said, "If I hadn't gotten out of that room, I'd probably have killed myself. I watched like two hundred clips of *The Big Bang Theory* on YouTube, and all I got out of it was that I'd like to jump the blonde."

"Eminently jumpable, I would say," Turner said. To Lucas: "What do you think?"

"I don't know what the hell you're talking about. Some kind of porn deal?"

"It's a famous TV show. Like *Friends*, but funny," Weed said. "Christ, Davenport, you gotta loosen up, man."

"I'm not feeling loose. I got a headache," Lucas said.

"Understandable. Things are getting tense."

"It's not a tension headache, it's a boredom headache."

"Worst kind," Turner said. "Maybe we'll have some fun, and it'll go away."

In the parking lot, seven of them loaded into four vehicles; Lucas rode with McLeod, an intense fortyish woman who saw a promotion in the Bergstrom investigation. She'd told Lucas, after a couple of drinks in a Marshalltown bar, that everything would be perfect if they got shot at, and got to shoot back, but nobody got hurt. "Getting shot at does wonders for your résumé," she said. "At least, in the ATF."

"Not so much in the Marshals Service," Lucas had said.

"Yeah, I know about you," she had said. "You don't duck. You zig when you should zag. You gotta be quicker."

"I'll try to remember that," Lucas had said.

SHE WAS ALREADY in the driver's seat of the Ford Expedition when Lucas got to the parking lot. She was cranked up, ready to go: "This is it," she said. "This is it."

"Easy," Lucas said. "We're not there yet. We can get both those assholes if we're patient."

"I know, I know, I know," she said, pounding on the steering wheel. She picked up her radio and said, "Everybody loaded up?"

"Jamal ran inside to buy some bottles of water, he'll be a minute," Weed radioed back.

THREE MINUTES LATER, they were rolling, on their way to a pre-scouted baseball field outside the tiny town of Ferguson, south of Marshalltown. The field was off the road, down a lane, and they could park where a row of oversized SUVs couldn't be seen; they'd be less than a mile from the target farmhouse. The trip was short and dusty, through an ocean of cornfields. The ballpark was empty, and they parked, got out of the vehicles, gathered to talk and go over the attack plan one last time.

They would wait until Andy Bergstrom showed up, then move.

Lucas and a Secret Service agent named Mark Kenyon would bail out of the convoy a half mile from the farmhouse, cross a barbed-wire fence, and walk through a cornfield and up a hill to the copse where Anderson was hidden with his binoculars. The three of them would circle around the hill to another cornfield that extended right up to the farmhouse's backyard, which included an old machine shed and the remnants of a barn—the barn's superstructure was gone, but the basement walls still stood.

They would sneak up behind the machine shed, if that seemed feasible, and act as a blocking force. The other five cops would approach from the front of the house, jamming up the driveway. They would talk to the people in the farmhouse with a bullhorn; and

McLeod would call the county sheriff's office to inform the sheriff of the operation.

When they were all again satisfied that they knew every minute of the plan—McLeod had taken them over it a half dozen times—they stood around.

"Christ, I didn't know Iowa could get this hot," said Jamal Barshim, looking up at the sun. "This is like the fuckin' Amazon."

They spent forty-five minutes sweating heavily, and then Anderson called: "Got a blue pickup."

"Load up," McLeod said.

Anderson, a few minutes later: "It's Andy. Boy is out on the porch with the women, now they're all going into the farmhouse."

McLeod: "Go."

LUCAS BAILED OUT of the Expedition, carrying a shotgun from his gear bag and a bottle of water, and Kenyon climbed out of the following Suburban, with an M4 and a bottle of water, and they waded through knee-high weeds in the ditch, carefully crossed the barbed-wire fence into the cornfield, and began walking through the eight-foot-high field corn toward the hill where Anderson was waiting. The corn might as well have been buttered, and yellow pollen stuck to their clothes and faces and slid down their necks, the green corn leaves cutting at their hands as they pushed through the field. The field was a half-mile wide and they could see nothing until they emerged from the far side.

The corn ended at the base of the small knoll. There was no fence, and no sight line to the farmhouse, so they scrambled up, a cow watching them from a pasture on the other side of the knoll, and at the top, in the middle of a stand of several scrubby trees, Anderson was eating a chicken sandwich and watching the house.

"Ready?" he asked. "You guys are sweating like pigs."

"Thanks for letting us know," Kenyon said. And, "Pigs don't sweat. They don't have sweat glands."

Anderson ignored that and said, "I haven't seen any movement since they went inside. I scouted a path down to that shed."

They followed him off the knoll, past the corner of the cow pasture, through another cornfield, where they were walking blind again, to emerge behind the machine shed. They crossed another fence. Anderson was carrying a shotgun, and he and Lucas pumped shells into the chambers of their guns, and Kenyon popped the charging handle on the M4.

Lucas called McLeod and said, "We're behind the machine shed, ready to go. Come on in."

"Moving now."

Lucas said, "Soon as they show up, Lanny, why don't you take the right side of the house, I'll move up behind the barn. Mark, you take the left side."

"Sounds good."

THEY HEARD THE trucks coming, saw the cloud of dust following them on the dry gravel, and Lucas flashed on the Lucinda Williams song "Car Wheels on a Gravel Road." The trucks burst into the driveway, blocking the two pickups. McLeod was out in a minute and on the bullhorn: "Boy Bergstrom, Andy Bergstrom, come out. We have officers in the back, you are surrounded. Come out with your hands up."

One minute later, a woman opened the back door and stuck her head out. Lucas, with the butt of the shotgun on his hip, stepped away from the barn so she could see him. She did, and pulled back inside and slammed the door.

Then came the boring part:

After twenty minutes of shouting back and forth, the Bergstroms came out with their hands in the air. They were cuffed, and though they said the women had no weapons, McLeod, Weed, and Lucas carefully entered the house, simultaneously, front and back, and found the two women in the kitchen, where they had been making bean-and-bacon soup in a large kettle. Steam was still coming out of the kettle and it smelled terrific.

Jiminy Katz saw Lucas and poked a finger at him: "You're the son-ofabitch who sold the bottles to us."

"I did," Lucas said. He rubbed his forehead. The headache had not gone away.

"That was a shitty thing to do," Katz said. "I trusted you. I thought you were a good-lookin' guy. I gave you five hundred dollars."

"If you write to the President, maybe he'll give it back," Lucas said. "Besides, you still got the bottles."

Katz gave him the finger.

McLeod: "You're both under arrest for aiding and abetting federal fugitives."

"Oh, fuck this," said the second woman, whose name they didn't know. She was looking at McLeod and had her back to Lucas as he came up, but when he got close, she spun and unexpectedly punched him in the mouth. She was fat, but had fast hands.

Lucas lurched back, then squared off with her, said, "I'm not embarrassed about hitting women, and I will," and showed her a fist, and she said, "Ah, screw it," and gave up.

They cuffed the women and McLeod took them out. Weed said, "She got your lip."

"Yeah. Cut it on my teeth."

McLeod, over her shoulder: "You zigged again."

THEY MADE THE arrests a few minutes after noon. Lucas did some perfunctory paperwork—the ATF was running the operation—and at three, he was in his Porsche Cayenne, headed north. He had blue ice in a cooler and took out a bag every once in a while and held it on his lip as he drove; in between icings, he could taste the salt in barely oozing blood. Marshalltown was almost due south of St. Paul, four hours away on I-35.

He called his wife, Weather, on the way, said, "Brace yourself, sweetheart, I'm on the way home."

"Big talk. We'll see if you can back it up."

ALL THE WAY to St. Paul, he nibbled and tongued his cut lip, making it worse, but he couldn't stop. At home, he didn't kiss Weather, a plastic surgeon, who told him that his lip wouldn't need surgery and gave him another blue ice. They were eating dinner with the kids, when he took a call from Elmer Henderson, junior U.S. senator from Minnesota.

"Senator," he said.

"Lucas. I got a job. I'd appreciate it if you'd take a look."

"I just got home from Iowa," Lucas said. "Is the job boring?"

"C'mon, man. And no, I don't think it will be. Necessarily."

Weather called across the table: "Some fat cat in trouble, Elmer?"

"Hi, Weather. No, not exactly . . . Well, sort of," Henderson said.

A CHANGE OF location:

As Lucas was driving north on I-35, BCA agent Virgil Flowers was standing on the tee at the dogleg fifteenth hole at the Mankato Golf Club, wondering if a seven wood was the right club, when his cell phone rang. His golfing partner, a ruddy farmer named Aaberg, who played in bib overalls and carried an 8 handicap, said, "I told you turn that thing off, you silly shit."

"I'm working," Virgil said. "I can't."

"Working on another snap hook, is what you're doing," Aaberg said.

The call was from Virgil's boss at the BCA. Virgil took it, listened, said, "Yeah, I can make it, but why? Why can't you tell me now? Who's going to be there? How did Lucas get involved? I thought he was in Iowa. Henderson? Really?"

Clusterfuck. He could feel it coming.

"Don't let the phone call affect your swing," Aaberg said, when Virgil had rung off. "I mean, that fairway is about as wide as my dick is long. You'll be lucky to find your ball with a chain saw."

Virgil drove the ball a hundred and eighty yards straight down the fairway, to the middle of the dogleg turn, watched it bounce and stop, and said, "I'm so pretty. I couldn't have done that better if I'd walked the ball out there and dropped it."

"You're still two down with four to play, my porcine friend," Aaberg said. "Let me up there."

"Make sure you get all the way through the swing," Virgil said. "Gotta fight that tendency to leave out to the right. And for God's sakes, don't hold your breath when you swing."

Aaberg left it out to the right. Golf balls will do what you fear.

6

Next day.

Blue skies, as the song said, smilin' at them. Warm, not hot, and dry as a potato chip.

Lucas parked a block over from the Lake of the Isles park, saw a familiar cream-colored Tahoe pull to the curb another block away, and waited until Virgil got out of his truck.

Virgil waved, took a sport coat off a back seat, pulled it on, and sauntered down the sidewalk. "What are we doing?"

"I don't know exactly," Lucas said, as they did the slap and knuckle-bump. "Henderson said something about consulting on the Doris Grandfelt murder. Were you around when that happened?"

"Still in the Army. I heard a lot about it when I got to the BCA," Virgil said. He leaned forward, looking at Lucas's face. "What happened to your lip? Weather bite you in a fit of blind passion?"

Lucas told him about busting the Bergstroms as they walked over to the lake, south of the Minneapolis downtown. They turned the corner toward a white house that looked like a wedding cake, three stories tall, each higher level set back from the one under it, crowned with a golden weather vane.

"That's gotta be it," Lucas said. "Henderson mentioned the weather vane."

"I'm thinking seriously about quitting," Virgil said, scuffing along. "The next book contract should be fairly large. Quitting money. I'll find out this fall. If this turns out to be bullshit, it could be the perfect excuse."

"You'd lose the state insurance," Lucas said. "That's like owning a gold mine when you have preschoolers. Those goddamn preschools are virus factories."

"Yeah, you keep telling me. Still, I'm one disconsolate cop." Virgil had twins, one of each.

"Big word for a shitkicker," Lucas said, "If not for a famous novelist."

LUCAS WAS A tall man, athletic, restless, heavy through the shoulders. Dark hair touched with gray, a businessman's cut, blue eyes, a hawk-like nose. A thin white scar crossed from his forehead to the cheek below his left eye, the result of a fishing accident, a thin wire leader snapping out of a log, slapping his face like a whip. He was wearing a summer-weight wool suit from Brioni, and a blue-green Hermès necktie that chimed with both his eyes and the suit, but not the scar. Despite being a cop, he was a fashion plate. If he wasn't quite handsome, women tended to like him.

He'd gotten a deputy U.S. Marshal's badge through sheer political pull. If a U.S. senator of either party developed a law enforcement problem, Lucas would do what he could to help out. Important people owed him, and when not working for a politician, he was allowed free rein to chase the assholes of his choice.

Virgil was as tall as Lucas, when they were both barefoot, and a bit taller in his alligator cowboy boots. He was hay-bale muscular, lanky, his blond hair worn too long for a cop. In addition to his job as a BCA agent, he was a three-time thriller novelist. His second novel had made it to the bottom of the *New York Times* paperback bestseller list, and the third one had gone to number six on the hardcover list and had hung on for three weeks. As a new author, he was still naïve enough not to be especially grateful; he thought he deserved it.

Virgil lived on a farm near Mankato, Minnesota, eighty miles southwest of the Twin Cities. Although his territory was generally southern Minnesota, he was sometimes pulled into the St. Paul headquarters for special assignments. His clearance rate for major crimes was the best in the BCA, which was especially notable because of the twisted, not to say bizarre, peculiar, grotesque, or outlandish crimes that happened in rural Minnesota.

Virgil was wearing jeans, a lightweight blue fishing shirt, and a button-front tan canvas jacket that wasn't quite a sport coat. The jacket had gaping pockets good for carrying notebooks and pens, and on occasion, a gun, though he didn't like guns.

TOGETHER THEY CLIMBED the wedding cake's exterior stairs, walked across a wide stone porch, where Lucas pressed a doorbell. As they waited, a slender man in a blue-striped seersucker summer suit climbed the stairs behind them, said, "Hey, guys," and Lucas asked, "Are you in on this? What's going on?"

"I don't know. The senator didn't tell me." Neil Mitford, chief weasel for Elmer Henderson. Both Lucas and Virgil had worked with Mitford on other cases and had found him to be cheerfully untrustworthy. He was also absolutely loyal to Henderson and knew more about politics than any sane person should.

Virgil looked at Lucas and said, "He probably knows. He lies a lot."

"True."

"A key requirement in my job," Mitford said. "Besides, if I didn't lie to you, somebody else would. Might as well get it out of the way."

"Also true," Lucas said. The way of the world.

"Did you push the doorbell?" Mitford asked. He pushed it again, and the door popped open. A short, slightly heavy woman in a gray dress said, "Good, you're here. I'm Marcia Wise, Lara's personal assistant. Come in. The others are waiting."

Virgil said, "Ah, man."

Lucas: "Could be interesting."

Virgil: "Could be stupid."

Mitford: "We got rich people, we got politicians, we got lawyers and cops. Probably gonna be both."

THE OTHERS WERE waiting in an oversized, overdecorated living room, white plaster walls decorated with oil paintings of unidentifiable landscapes, most featuring a piece of an ocean with a sailing ship, or a field with horses; colorful red/blue oriental carpets that weren't, but felt, ankle-deep; and mid-century furniture. Despite a plethora of chairs and sofas, the others were all on their feet holding glasses—a mocktail party with cranberry or orange juice. A tray of cheese and crackers sat on a side table.

Lucas picked out a woman who might have been fifteen years younger than he was, and decided she was Lara Grandfelt, because she carried the same flavor as the house, and the party seemed to rotate around her.

She was a little hefty but comfortable with it, had an unlined face with sharp, watchful blue eyes. She wore a middle-blue woman's business suit, almost a match for Lucas's own, and diamonds the size of macadamia nuts, one on each earlobe. She was holding two glasses full of juice, and handed one back to Wise, her personal assistant, when Wise led Lucas and Virgil into the room.

Lucas wondered briefly if Wise was another slightly less affluent Grandfelt sister, and Wise was her married name. She and Grandfelt were the same size and shape, same hairdos and color, their dress was different in color but similar in style, and Wise had diamonds in her ears as Grandfelt did, but with smaller stones. Henderson, the senator, said, "There you are. Virgil: why don't you come to work for me? I need somebody down south."

"You're looking summery, Senator," Virgil said. A polite Minnesota evasion for "go fuck yourself."

Henderson, a willowy blond known for his rapacious appetite for pretty women of all ages and races, as well as a cocaine habit that sometimes made him feel younger than he was, had been talking to a tall auburn-haired woman who Lucas didn't know, but who gave off attorney vibes. She had a long thin nose, long thin lips, and what looked like long legs under her dress, which was an intensely figured ankle-length crimson and black number that looked, to Lucas's fashion-trained eye, suspiciously like a Loro Piana. She wore a librarian's wire-rimmed glasses.

They were joined by Mitford, who said to Henderson, "The vice president is calling again."

"I'll talk to her later. She wants money and a bigger turnout in Washington County."

A BCA agent named Jon Duncan, who was Virgil's nominal boss, raised a glass of cranberry juice to Lucas and Virgil. He called, "You guys are looking great!" and Virgil said, "Yeah, no," a Wisconsin idiom he'd picked up while fishing in the Northwoods, for "go fuck yourself."

Duncan had been talking to Edie Lamb, U.S. Marshal for the District of Minnesota. Lamb was technically, but not actually, Lucas's boss. Lucas knew, and both Henderson and Lamb knew he knew, that Lamb was divorced because her husband had caught the senator and Mrs. Lamb, in Henderson's phrase, "buttering the biscuit" during a Christmas party at Henderson's mansion.

The shared knowledge may have brought Henderson, Lamb, and Lucas closer; or maybe not. Really, who knew?

Henderson was responsible for Lamb getting the U.S. Marshal's appointment, and for Lucas getting a deputy marshal's badge. Together they'd been involved in a number of tricky situations, some of which a non-cynical observer might have considered questionable, if not entirely reprehensible.

Two other women were talking in a corner: a young blonde in a dark blue suit who also gave off attorney vibes, and a short woman with flyaway brown hair, skeptical brown eyes, and a few extra wrinkles on her olive-complected face. She said, "Hey, Lucas."

Lucas knew Carla Benucci as a reporter for the St. Paul *Pioneer Press*. "You doing a story?" he asked.

"Not there anymore, I got bought out," she said. "I'm doing PR for Mason, Tono, Whitehead and Boone."

"I'm sorry," Lucas said.

Benucci shrugged: "Shit happens."

THE AUBURN-HAIRED WOMAN talking to Henderson took a final sip of cranberry juice and tapped the empty glass with a spoon to make it ring. "Everybody? We're all here. Time to work."

She introduced herself and the blonde: "I'm Tricia Boone, of Mason, Tono, Whitehead and Boone, and Michelle Cornell is an associate with our firm. We represent Lara Grandfelt." She reached out and touched the diamond-studded woman. "We're here to help Lara launch a long-delayed quest. I will let Lara tell you about it and say only that our firm is firmly behind her, whenever our legal services may be needed."

Grandfelt smiled, turned to look at everyone in the group, and said, "What we're going to do, is we're going to find the monster who killed my twin sister. That was more than twenty years ago now, and that's long enough to know he's roaming free."

Lucas scratched his forehead, an unconscious gesture of skepticism, and Grandfelt caught it. "Marshal Davenport doesn't think we'll get anywhere, but he doesn't know what we're going to do," she said.

Boone jumped back in: "Why don't we all sit down. I believe there are enough chairs."

They all did, and Grandfelt said to Boone, "You were going to fill in some background . . ."

Boone nodded. "Yes." She opened a file folder on her lap, cleared her throat, and said:

"Lara Grandfelt and her sister, Doris, both graduated from Minnesota colleges—actually, Lara was at the university—just before the turn of the century. Lara studied finance and economics, and Doris studied accounting at Manifold College in Northfield."

After graduation, she said, the sisters found jobs in the Twin Cities, Lara with U.S. Bank in their wealth management department, and Doris with a local accounting firm. Three years after graduation, Doris was brutally murdered, a murder that was never solved.

In the years between the murder and the present, Boone said, Lara left the bank to begin her own wealth management firm. "She has done very well with it. Lara's not ridiculously rich, but she's done very, very well. Is that correct, Lara?"

Grandfelt nodded and said, "Yes."

Boone said, "I'm reviewing all of this so that we're all on the same page, and so we know that the money involved in this project—I'm coming to that—was legitimately sourced. So. Lara has asked Mason, Tono, Whitehead and Boone to set up a project designed to investigate and find the perpetrator of the rape and murder of her sister, Doris."

"Neither Virgil nor I worked that case . . ." Lucas began.

"We know. We've done the research. You were starting your own company, Davenport Simulations, and Virgil was in the Army. The state Bureau of Criminal Apprehension handled the investigation," Boone said. "When you, Lucas, later went to the BCA, Lara told me, she spoke to you once about the lack of progress in the investigation. She got you to review the files . . . with no result."

"Yes, I remember it now." Lucas shrugged. "The BCA ran a good investigation, but there was nothing to go on. They never got to first base."

Boone said, "I understand. Lara, however, has been unable to escape the gravity of the murder. She can't escape the injustice of it."

"That's true," Grandfelt said, looking around at the crowd again.

"So she wants Virgil and me to reinvestigate, and Elmer and Edie and Jon are here to strong-arm us into it, if we need strong-arming." Lucas said.

"I wouldn't have chosen that precise phrase, but that captures the . . . substance . . . of it," Boone agreed.

"What are you going to do?" Virgil asked Grandfelt.

Before she could answer, Boone stepped in again. "Lara has directed our firm to post a five-million-dollar reward for information leading to the identification of the killer. The reward is to be made as a gift of gratitude to the person or persons who provide the information. If that passes muster with our tax people, and I'm told that it should, the gift will be tax-free. If somebody wins it, they'll get to keep the whole amount. Later today—and we've already prepared this—the reward will be posted on all the major true crime sites on the Internet."

Virgil said, "Wow!"

BOONE LAID OUT the details. She expected a lot of people would be digging into the case, and Michelle Cornell would be in charge of reviewing submissions by what Boone called the true crime researchers. Anything that seemed even slightly relevant would be forwarded to Lucas and Virgil.

Lucas, as a deputy federal marshal, and Virgil, as a BCA agent, would have the legal authority, together, to get almost anything that needed to be gotten, to kick down any doors that needed to be kicked.

"We have the complete investigative files from the BCA and Woodbury, every piece of paper they have, already in-house. We didn't steal them. That's absolutely legal under Minnesota law. If we find that they've held anything back, we will sue them," Boone told Lucas.

Lucas: "And you'll post them? The files?"

"Yes. Including the crime scene photos. Lara has seen them and wants them on the sites."

Grandfelt said, "I can't tell you how painful that was, seeing those photographs." Her lip trembled, but she kept her chin up. "I'm set on this. If you need anything from me—anything, day or night, you call. If for some reason I can't answer, my personal assistant will." She reached out and touched the woman in the gray suit. "Marcia Wise. She'll find me wherever I am. You will have personal numbers for both of us."

Virgil: "You will be stirring up a storm and you'll have no control over it."

"We will be *complying* with Lara's wishes, which are perfectly legal," Boone said, her voice gone sharp. "Frankly, we tried to talk her out of this, but she insisted. She is the client. The client does *not* have to accept our recommendations."

"So it's a done deal," Lucas said.

Grandfelt nodded and Boone said, "Yes, it is."

"Why now?" Lucas asked.

Grandfelt said, "I had . . . I'm having . . . a brush with breast cancer. I had a lumpectomy a month ago and I'm currently undergoing chemo. My doctors say I have an excellent chance of survival, but the whole death business . . . it came closer. I realized that one thing I had to do, if there was any way to do it, was find my sister's killer. This is what I came up with."

"Much of what you'll get will be flat-fucking-weird," Virgil said. "Excuse the language."

Boone steepled her fingers and smiled over them, showing some teeth. "We understand that, Virgil. I have to say, that's not our problem. It's yours."

Henderson, who was looking down at his phone, said, "C'mon, guys. Do it."

Lucas checked Virgil, who lifted his hands, palms up, in a "why not?" gesture, and Lucas said, "I can see problems. But it sounds interesting. For a while anyway. I don't want to plow through acres of made-up nonsense, but I'll look at anything that might be real. If a guy starts talking about UFOs, we're outa there."

Boone didn't care: "You can do anything you want. Totally up to you. If you need to travel, keep the receipts. There's an expenses fund. That will also pay for any legal support you need."

Virgil asked, "Is there a time limit on the award?"

Grandfelt said, "Yes. One year. After that, it goes to a range of animal welfare groups."

"I'm not going to investigate for a year, not with no possibility . . ." Lucas began.

Boone interrupted, "We expect most of the action to happen in the first month, perhaps in the first couple of weeks. If the killer isn't caught, we expect the attention will begin to dry up."

Lucas turned to Grandfelt. "You should know that we're not only gonna get true crime people, we'll get treasure hunters and scam artists and nutjobs and probably a few lawsuits. People could get hurt."

"Yes, Ms. Boone and I have talked about that. Extensively. We think the risk is small, and there's a sound basis behind what we're doing here," Grandfelt said. "It's called crowdsourcing. We'll not only have the true crime people working on it, but they have a network of volunteer researchers who know how to use the resources of the Internet, and artificial intelligence, and have extensive connections inside law enforcement. At all levels. A large group of intelligent, motivated people, thinking out of all the correct boxes, often find solutions to problems that so-called experts would never consider."

"And we'll take care of the lawsuits," Boone said. She'd been sitting, but now stood up and looked at Benucci, the former reporter.

"I think it's time for you to step in, Carla," she said. To Lucas and Virgil, she said, "Carla is our director of communications."

Lucas: "Why am I not surprised that you have one?"

"We're a large organization. She stays busy," Boone said.

"Her job would be to spread the news about this . . . bequest?" Virgil asked.

"Exactly. We figure to be coast-to-coast by tomorrow night," Boone said.

IN THE NEXT five minutes, Benucci laid out what she planned to do. She had links to several of the most-used true crime sites, and would drop the information releases, and the reward notice, that evening.

She'd been in touch with most of the major network morning shows, she said, and two had already agreed to do interviews. She was hoping for two or three more. "We think CNN, Fox, or MSNBC will bite for the evening round. Haven't heard back yet."

She said the five million, the unsolved murder, the rich twin, the online photos, they all made for great hooks.

"Lara and Tricia will sit for the interviews. I've laid out several talking points." She turned to the two women: "You, Lara and Tricia, should familiarize yourself with them. I've got files for both of you to review. Good stuff that will yank the talking heads straight into the story. Tomorrow morning we'll put you at Senator Henderson's media center. We'll bring in Gloria Martinez to do your hair and makeup."

"Why am I not surprised that you have a media center?" Lucas asked Henderson.

Henderson said, "Hey. Agree to do this and move on."

"How much did Lara contribute to the reelection fund?" Virgil asked.

"She has been quite generous, and we are looking forward to an even closer relationship in the future," Mitford said.

Benucci said to Boone and Grandfelt, "You'll need to get there early for the New York shows. The files contain the address of Senator Henderson's office and a complete timetable, which may change tomorrow if we make some of the evening shows. The media center isn't a big deal. A back room with a walnut desk, bunch of books, picture of Senator Henderson shaking hands with the President, and an American flag. A painting of something. Not sure what, abstract landscape, won't offend anyone. Good lights. We'll lose the President and the flag."

Boone smiled and said, "I'll do it, but I'm a little nervous. I don't do this kind of TV thing . . ."

"John Mason said you do. Good publicity for the firm and you're the best-looking partner we got. Some of the others . . ." Benucci faked a shudder. "All you and Lara have to do is say what I write and not audibly fart." To Lucas: "John Mason's the managing partner."

"I got that," Lucas said. "I actually know him a little. Unlikeable guy."

"Well, he's a lawyer," Benucci said. "He's the co-inventor of the pop-tort. Made a lot of money with it."

Lucas stood up, walked once around his bright red Eero Saarinen womb chair, looked from Henderson to Grandfelt to Boone: "Okay. I'm in." He turned to Virgil. "Where are you at?"

"I have my doubts, but I'll take a shot at it," Virgil said. "I'll probably have to move into a hotel up here, at least temporarily. Gonna be expensive."

"We'll cover the hotel, we'll cover all your expenses," Grandfelt said. "I believe your agent Duncan has already started a procedure to do that."

Duncan, who had been sitting quietly, said, "We're ready to go. Virgil, you just submit your expenses as you usually do . . . no problem."

Henderson said, "We're all set, then. It's an opportunity to do some good."

Benucci, former newsie: "Right. Lemme know when that happens."

7

Virgil called Lucas at eight o'clock the next morning. Weather had already gone to work, and the kids were at summer camp, so nobody was there to kill the phone except Lucas, who slept late. Virgil's name popped up on the screen, so instead of throwing the phone under the bed, he answered.

"What do you want?" Lucas asked.

"We're all over the goddamn network news. Our names are. They sorta fucked us."

"What?" Still sleepy.

"The Doris reward. Boone was on NBC and got pushed around and finally said we're running the investigation. She named us. She talked about you tracking the Vegas cannibal and shooting the 1919 killer, and about my testimony in the New York heroin sweep. She made it sound like we're Butch and Sundance. Like catching the killer is a sure thing."

Lucas sat up in bed, slightly more awake: "You're saying if they put that on the jacket of your next book, that'd be a bad thing?"

Moment of silence. Then, "Let me get back to you on that."

LUCAS WENT DOWNSTAIRS in his shorts, turned on the TV, and there it was.

The reward created the expected media hubbub and lit a fire on the true crime websites. Lucas went out to the website set up for the reward and read that the crime files were downloaded 31,461 times in the first two hours after the morning show interviews. The files themselves were all over Facebook and included the crime scene photos in all their gruesome detail.

Lucas called Boone as soon as the law offices opened: "What the hell? You gave them my name, and Virgil's?"

"We talked about it here at the office and thought we'd have more credibility if we mentioned the names of reputable law enforcement officers . . . who have a presence on the Internet," Boone said. "As you two do."

"You didn't even call me?"

"Senator Henderson suggested that it wouldn't be necessary. Or desirable," Boone said.

"Fuck that guy," Lucas said.

"No, I won't be doing that," Boone said.

Long pause.

"Uh-oh."

"I don't think we need to discuss the subject any further," Boone said.

"You better lock Michelle Cornell in a closet."

"Michelle has been spoken to," Boone said.

"Henderson is a child," Lucas said. "Smart, cynical, manipulative, influential and rich, but not totally in control of his sexual impulses. Listen, nobody mentioned my phone number or address or anything?"

"No, no, no, and we specifically emphasized that all inquiries should go through Michelle. My personal feeling is that a lot of these true crime hunters, the males anyway, may be sublimating something. We put up a picture of Michelle which we feel will tend to focus attention on her."

"That's good," Lucas said. "Especially if the killer is still living around here and he's insane and likes the idea of stabbing pretty, young blond women."

"Oh . . . no!"

Cornell's picture was taken down five minutes after Boone ended the call with Lucas.

MICHELLE CORNELL HERSELF called Lucas later in the morning, and again in the afternoon, to update him on the response.

"It's not slowing down," she said on the morning call. "If anything, downloads are picking up. Apparently, people have already shown up at the crime scene. The Woodbury police are talking about closing it off, but it *is* a public park."

"God bless them," Lucas said. "Has Lara been sued yet?"

"No, but it's early, and Doris's one-time boyfriend has been complaining about harassment."

"He's still local?" Lucas asked.

"He's a revered high school coach up in White Bear. Somebody got his cell phone number and posted it on one of the websites, along with his address, and now it's all over the place. He's gotten a lot of calls and some people showing up at his house and the high school. So, we could be hearing from him."

"I won't be," Lucas said. "That's you guys."

"What did you think of the files?" Cornwell asked.

"I haven't looked at them," Lucas said. "I went over them years ago and didn't see any obvious holes. I'm waiting for you to give me something specific to chew on."

"You'll get it, if it comes in. We haven't had much yet. Some requests for clarification of the rules for the reward."

"All right. Well, stay in touch." He rang off and went to mow the backyard. He was half done when he couldn't stand it any longer, went back inside, and began looking at true crime sites, which he'd never seen before.

He wasn't impressed, and after forty-five minutes, went back outside and finished mowing.

ON THE AFTERNOON call, Cornell said that the files had been downloaded more than a hundred thousand times, probably because of the controversial nature of the crime scene photos, the inclusion of which was being debated on most of the major cable news channels. Cornell said she'd had some suggestions about who the killer might be. "I'll be sending them to your email . . . now."

"I'm busy," Lucas said. "I'll look at them tonight. Or tomorrow."

"Lucas, Marshal Davenport, you've got to . . ."

"I'll get to them when I get to them," Lucas said. "I've got a broken storm window that I've got to take down to the hardware store. I need new covers for the air conditioner condensers. Winter's coming."

"It's August . . ."

"And winter's on the way and has been since June twentieth," Lucas said. "This is Minnesota. I'll look at your stuff when I can, but I will look at it."

VIRGIL CALLED AT five o'clock: "They have a hundred and sixty-one thousand downloads. They're breaking the Internet. I am forty-five thousand words into the fourth novel which will be make-or-break and I don't have time to waste. Have you heard anything substantial?"

"Not a thing, yet. Cornell sent me some names, people that the true-crimers think might be possible suspects, but it's all guesses and speculation. Too early, I think," Lucas said. "And c'mon. What does it take to write a novel? You sit on your ass for a couple hours a day and type? If you sleep eight hours, and type for two, that gives you fourteen hours to work the Doris case."

"Two hours? You're an ignoramus. All these downloads . . . what the hell is going on? I thought we'd get a bunch of emails. It turns out there are people scouting possible crime scene locations. The same places the BCA looked at when Doris was murdered, and didn't find anything."

"Ride with it," Lucas said. "With this assignment, you could probably ditch all the other routine shit you'd have to do out in the sticks. Get even more time to type."

Virgil was silent for a moment, thinking it over. Then he said, "Stay in touch."

———

FRANKIE, THE MOTHER of Virgil's twins, was doing the bills when Virgil rang off. They were sitting at the kitchen table in the farmhouse. Honus the Yellow Dog was lying halfway under the table, chewing on a dried bull penis. The twins, Alex and Willa, were at preschool in Mankato.

"You didn't really make it clear to him, that you were pissed about your names getting out," Frankie said. "You should have been a little more hard-nosed."

"Aw, it's not his fault," Virgil said. "He didn't do it. And he made a good point toward the end."

"What was that?"

"Listen and learn," Virgil said. He was back on his phone, calling his BCA boss, Jon Duncan, who worked late.

Duncan said, "They've got a picture of you on CNN. You and Lucas. You're on a witness stand and your hair is too long and you're wearing cowboy boots and a suit that looks like it came out of Sears Roebuck's sub-basement. Or Hitler's bunker. You look like the defendant."

Virgil: "What can I tell you? Grandfelt and her lawyers were supposed to get the publicity. They were supposed to sort out all the bullshit that comes in, and then if anything showed up, pass it along."

"That no longer seems to be the case."

"I know. Henderson and the governor are gonna be pissed if we don't get results they can take credit for. You're gonna have to take me off the books until this thing is over. I'm thinking at least a month. *At least*. Probably more."

Duncan: "What about your caseload?"

"Put Jimmy over in Rochester," Virgil said. "He knows the territory. Even better, I could get a rate for him at a motel in Mankato. I'll link him to the current files."

"I'll have to think about it," Duncan said.

"Or, you could get some guts up, and tell the governor to go fuck himself. Keeping in mind that Lara Grandfelt is a major moneyman. Woman."

"Let's agree that I won't be telling the governor to go fuck himself," Duncan said. "I'll figure out something. I'll cut you free. Let me know when you go full time on this."

"I'm full time now," Virgil said. "The Grandfelt files were downloaded a hundred and sixty thousand times, worldwide, as of now."

"My God!"

"Yeah."

VIRGIL RANG OFF, smiled a sneaky smile, and said to Frankie, "Done deal. I'm off for a month. I'll get another thirty thousand good words, and at that point, I'll be running for home."

"Unless Lucas manipulates you into taking the lead," Frankie said. "He sounds unhappy . . ."

"No chance of that." Virgil took a turn around the kitchen table, avoiding Honus's tail. He looked in the refrigerator, at nothing in particular, then closed it. "Isn't this the goddamnedest thing you ever heard of? Doris Grandfelt has been dead for more than twenty years."

"I think it's interesting," Frankie said, putting down her pen and setting the checkbook aside. Honus the Yellow Dog stopped chewing on his bull penis to look up at them. "In fact, I was going to download those files and see if I might come up with an idea or two. I could use the five million. I could build a full-sized heated dressage barn and ride all winter. You and Sam could practice pitching in there."

"Download the files twice and save a copy for me," Virgil said. "Listen: maybe you could handle my end of it. You've always been a cop groupie. You read true crime sites. You know about this stuff. I could start doing two-a-days on the book."

"Poor old Doris," Frankie said, shaking her head. "Pushing up sod for more than twenty years and you cops just don't care."

IF THE COPS didn't care, Amanda Fisk did.

The new publicity was astonishing, the ghost of Doris Grandfelt risen from the grave to haunt her. Switching from network news to cable news to streaming services to YouTube, she found it all over the place. Five million dollars didn't seem like *that* much anymore, but the reward and circumstances had gone viral.

Sure, five mil was a nice house, a nice car, no debt, money in the bank . . . but not so much that an entire city full of people should stampede into the search. Now, late in the evening, more than a hundred and seventy thousand people had downloaded the files. Of course, some of them were in Mumbai and Kiev, but still . . .

The photos were especially out there. Done on film, because digital hadn't been good enough back in the day. Most of the shots were in color, but they'd been backed up in black-and-white. Because some of it was shot at night, there was a whole file of black-and-white images taken with flash, which doubled the harshness.

In the black-and-whites, blood was black, instead of red, so Grandfelt's blood-clotted eyes were black holes, and her lips, painted with red lipstick, were black. Her face was white as paper, lashed with black streams of blood, and the green weeds, where her head lay, were as black in the photos as the blood, like Medusa hair.

Some vicious little pervert had made a cosplay mask of her face, had posted a death dance to TikTok, and had gotten more than a million hits, most of them from China.

THE PHOTOS WERE grim—the aesthetic aspect of them—but not exactly a nightmare, not for Fisk. There was a thrill to it, seeing it all over again, remembering. The bitch had gotten what she deserved.

As disturbing as the renewed investigation was, even more worrisome was the cops who were doing it—Davenport and Flowers. She'd never had either of them in court, but knew them by reputation. Flowers seemed to have x-ray vision when it came to solving crimes; Davenport seemed happy to shoot anyone involved. Neither was stupid and both were experienced.

The thrill *was* threaded with fear. The murder was more than twenty years in the rearview mirror, and now right back in her face. The awkward slippery blade had cut more than Doris Grandfelt: the scar was still there on Fisk's left hand; there might have been some blood left behind, possibly on the body.

If the Bureau of Criminal Apprehension had sampled that blood, then there would be a DNA record of it. That meant no ancestor search on Ancestry.com, because that site gave up matching information to law enforcement. It meant no job that might require a DNA search—no job with law enforcement or security or the military.

There was jeopardy, but how much was impossible to tell at this point. She needed to download the files, to see if the BCA was looking at more than one DNA profile.

The search and the reward would have to be carefully monitored. One thing to discover, if that were possible: what would happen if Lara Grandfelt died? Had she embedded the reward in her will? If she had not—there'd been no mention of it in the news stories—then her death might bring the whole hunt crashing down.

Though if Grandfelt were killed, a new hunt would begin. But this time, handled carefully, she'd leave no possible DNA evidence . . .

Something to think about.

She thought about it as she downloaded the files and began her research.

The next morning, Lucas was stirring unappetizing, sand-like protein into his breakfast oatmeal when his phone rang. The number was unknown, but that happened, so he picked up and said, "Yeah?"

A woman's voice: "Is this Marshal Davenport?"

"It is."

"This is Sergeant Leeann Carney over at Woodbury PD. You gotta get over here."

"What's going on?"

"You sorta need to see it," Carney said. Her voice had a whistle in it, as though she was breathing over a snaggletooth. "We got a boat-load of true crime people crawling around the Grandfelt crime scene and there have been some . . . conflicting opinions. I'm talking poten-tial assault."

"Is a boatload bigger or smaller than a buttload?"

Brief hesitation, then: "Smaller, but it's gonna be a buttload soon enough. The feeling is, since you're the guy in charge of this circus, you oughta see it."

Lucas: "I'm not really . . . Okay. Listen, are you there?"

"I am."

"I'll ask for you," Lucas said. "Leeann Carney."

"Yes. We'll be looking for you," Carney said. "Uh, what do you look like?"

"I'll be wearing jeans, a light blue golf shirt, a dark blue sport coat, and a Wild ballcap. Women tend to find me incredibly attractive."

"I'll look for the ballcap," Carney said. "You know, in case your animal attraction gets all clogged up."

OFF THE PHONE, Lucas ran a shot of cold tap water on the oatmeal, remembered to drop a half-handful of raisins into the mix, popped it in the microwave for two minutes, and called Virgil while he waited for the mess to heat up. Virgil was still at home, although it was already 10:30.

"I'm going over to the crime scene," Lucas said. "Meet me there. We'll get an idea of what's gonna happen. I'm told there's a whole bunch of true-crimers already there."

"I'm eighty miles away . . ."

"Yeah, I know. I haven't eaten breakfast yet. I printed out the files last night and I'll thumb through them while I eat, so . . . I'll be a while. We should get there about the same time, if you leave in the next few minutes," Lucas said.

"What are you having for breakfast?"

"You know—two eggs over easy, four strips of bacon, toast, orange juice," Lucas said. "Thinking I might have the last slice of coconut crème pie for dessert. Left over from last night."

"Right. I know about Weather's vegetarian diet kick," Virgil said. "You're having two celery sticks and half an avocado. With a glass of water."

"See you in an hour and a half?"

"See you there."

VIRGIL HAD BEEN working on the new novel—tentatively titled *Rock'n a Hard Place*, about a murderous country-rock band—since eight o'clock. He rang off, saved the manuscript to Microsoft's cloud and two separate flash drives. The window was open and he could hear the distant sound of a tractor doing something, maybe cutting hay, and a crow calling closer by.

He was barefoot, wearing a vintage Queen tee-shirt and blue nylon workout pants. He changed into an extra soft pair of jeans, a checked long-sleeved shirt, and leather walking shoes. Another pair of jeans, underwear, and two shirts went into a duffel bag along with his dopp kit. A shotgun, Apple laptop, a separate keyboard and mouse, a Garmin GPS receiver, Nikon Z7II camera with a couple of lenses, and binoculars went into a gear bag. An iPad would go on the passenger seat. He hauled it all out to his Tahoe.

He'd begun reading the Grandfelt files the night before, which Frankie had printed out in a near two-hour session. He stuck a partially marked-up printout in a canvas shoulder bag, along with his Glock and two magazines from the gun safe. He relocked the safe and pulled on his canvas not-quite-a-sport-coat, to go with the shoulder bag. That done, he cracked the cap on a Dos Equis, slipped it into a jacket pocket, put a Dog Star Ranch hat on his head and walked across the farmyard to the barn.

Frankie was out behind it, in a horse-manure-smelling round pen, lunging a horse named Rush. She was a short, busty woman wearing a white mannish shirt and black riding pants tucked into knee-high English riding boots. Rush was a tall brown rescue of unknown heritage that Frankie thought she could make into something. Honus the Yellow Dog was slumbering outside the pen.

Virgil put his forearms on the pole fence and shouted, "I gotta go. Up to Woodbury. You gotta pick up the kids at preschool."

"Wait!" Frankie slowed Rush to a walk, then led him over to Virgil. She was sweating, a pleasant salty summer scent. "Where?"

"Woodbury. Lucas called. Something's happening and he wants me to take a look. I could be a day or two."

"You get any work done?" she asked.

"Maybe twelve hundred words," Virgil said. "Not great, but not terrible. Needs work."

Frankie said, "I've been thinking about the sex scene from last night. It slows things down too much and it's not that interesting."

"I fixed that. Took out the foreplay."

"That's the part I would have left in. Anyway . . . you won't be back tonight?" she asked.

"Probably not. I'll be at the Radisson. I can catch the rest of the daily quota tonight. Three hundred words. Maybe put some of the foreplay back in." His daily quota was fifteen hundred good words, which editing would reduce to a thousand keepers.

They talked about scheduling—missing days and nights were still routine in the cop business—and Frankie climbed on the bottom rail of the fence to kiss him good-bye. As Virgil walked back to the Tahoe, Frankie started Rush again, circling him at a gallop, the horse moving like an elite athlete, the sound of his hooves sending Virgil off.

He pointed the truck mostly north, flipped the cap off the Dos Equis, put the bottle in the cupholder, said a brief prayer to St. Waylon, the protector of drivers against the evil eye of the highway patrol, and settled in for the ride.

AUGUST IS THE best month in Minnesota, though some argue for September. The drive through the farmland was pleasant, aside from a dozen windshield bugs, coming off the near flood-stage Minnesota River, their yellow spatters like flicks of custard on the glass. The bug guts tended to bake on in the summer heat and it would get hot later in the day. He carried Windex and a roll of paper towels for cleanups. Of course, the random grasshopper collisions of August were nothing compared to a heavy mayfly emergence, so-called because they usually hatched in June.

So Virgil went on, thinking about not much, taking in the countryside, occasionally flashing on the Grandfelt crime-scene photos he'd reviewed the night before. He soon enough found himself threading through the town of Shakopee and then onto I-494, which would take him around the southern side of the Twin Cities to the crime scene.

Take him around the Twin Cities slowly: half the metro area was overrun with orange traffic-warning barrels, marking out construction zones and piling up traffic.

———

HE CROSSED THE Mississippi, turned north, his iPad map app directing him off I-494, through a maze of tree-lined residential streets, past small houses that dated to the fifties and sixties, to Shawnee Park, in the suburban town of Woodbury. He spotted a jammed-up parking lot with twenty cars in it, three of them cop cars, and he rolled slowly that way.

The park, as he could see it from his truck, was a bowl with two baseball fields built into it, facing each other, with a shared outfield. A park building, probably for maintenance and possibly for bathrooms, was in front of him as he parked, and behind it, he could see a circular white wall that looked like it might be an outdoor hockey rink in the winter.

Across the playing fields, a line of tall trees—cottonwoods, aspens, what looked like box elders and maples—marked the edge of the playing fields, and behind the scrim of forest, sunlight sparkled off water.

As Virgil got out of his truck, a uniformed Woodbury cop walked over, checking Virgil's grille lights as he came, and asked, "You a cop?"

"BCA."

"Flowers?"

"Yeah."

"There was a big guy, named, I forget, maybe . . . Dubuque? He's a federal marshal, who said you'd be coming. He's in the woods over there, where those people are." He pointed.

Virgil thanked him, took a minute with the Windex and paper towels to clean up his windshield, then walked between the two softball diamonds toward the trees. Lucas was standing in a group of women, saw him coming, and broke away with apologies, which Virgil assumed were insincere.

Lucas, smiling: "Holy shit, you're not wearing a tee-shirt. And I saw you cleaning your windshield. Could you do mine?"

"No, but I could lend you my Windex," Virgil said. He looked toward the women. "Who are your friends?"

"The lead regiment of true-crimers. We got a problem," Lucas said.

"Yeah, I can see that," Virgil said. "They look like a bunch of rabbits nibbling on carrot sticks."

"I was thinking woodchucks and ears of corn. When you get closer, you'll see their hair is bristly, more like a woodchuck's than a rabbit's. Or, possibly, like a beaver's," Lucas said. "Be careful. I caught one woman asking me a question and she had a telephone sticking out of the top of her pocket. I could see the camera lens and I know damn well she was recording. She asked why we'd been sitting on our asses for twenty years, and I gave her two words—'We haven't'—and walked away."

"They're aggressive."

"I've met both aggressive and sneaky," Lucas said. "And, aggressive-sneaky. And I've only been here for fifteen minutes."

"Any . . . clues?" Virgil asked.

Lucas snorted and looked back at the clutch of women: "They wouldn't know a clue if one jumped up and bit them on their collective ass."

"Then what exactly are they . . ."

"They're looking for clicks on their websites," Lucas said. "Every one of them has a website and they live on clicks and followers. If they get enough clicks, they can get ads from true crime publishers. Some of them probably make upwards of eight hundred dollars a year. You and I are clickbait."

VIRGIL TURNED BACK toward the parking lot, waved a hand at it, and said, "I got a clue for you."

"I could use one."

"How'd you find the park?" Virgil asked.

"My phone app," Lucas said.

"That's how I found it. Without the app, I could have wandered around for an hour and never seen it," Virgil said. "The killer knew it was here. How'd he know that? How'd he know how to get back here, twenty years ago, in the dark, without an app?"

Lucas looked out at the street. "Good point. He either came from here, or he had some reason to come here. I thumbed through the file this morning and I didn't see any of your BCA guys saying that."

"I read some of it last night, and I didn't see anything either. What are we going to do about that? It's fourteen hundred pages, for God's sakes."

"Dunno." Lucas pointed to a blacktopped trail that led through a line of burr oaks: "There's an elementary school back there. Not far. Wonder if a schoolteacher could have done it?"

"We can talk about it," Virgil said.

"Here's another thing I was wondering," Lucas said. "The original investigation couldn't determine whether the body had been delivered to the dump site with a vehicle, because too many vehicles had been driven back and forth across the field before crime scene got here. Woodbury cops, mostly, and apparently the grass had been mowed recently, so there might have been tracks from the mowers . . .

Anyway, did the killer drive Doris across the field? If he did, it must have been way late at night. Why would he do that? There are places just as good, where he could have dumped her closer to a road."

"Another excellent question," Virgil said. "A guy brought that up in a report. Remember Louis Kelly, I think he retired probably ten years ago? He said nobody saw a vehicle in here that night. But if it was late enough . . ."

"Hard to black out a vehicle anymore," Lucas said.

"Maybe you could, back then," Virgil ventured.

Lucas: "Maybe it was a matter of luck. Nobody saw the vehicle because nobody saw the vehicle."

"That would be my guess," Virgil said, peering across the green playing fields and tan dirt of the infields. "If the murder was spontaneous, you might have had a killer who didn't think about it. He'd been to the park, knew about the trees and how to get to them, and he was panicked or scared and knew the details of this place, so . . . he brought her here."

"A baseball player?"

"Maybe the true-crimers would have some ideas."

"Don't ask," Lucas said.

One of the women broke out of the group and walked toward them. She was middle-aged, stocky, dressed in camo cargo slacks, a long-sleeved tan shirt, hiking boots, and a straw hat. She had spent time in the outdoors, and her face and hands carried a hard tan. She wore black plastic-rimmed sunglasses like the owner of an art gallery might wear, and, Virgil thought, Lucas was correct: she looked unnervingly like an oversized woodchuck. Or possibly a beaver, but he couldn't see her teeth to pick one.

"You aren't done with the interview, are you, Marshal?" she asked. Her voice had an edge to it, like the teeth of a saw.

Lucas said, "I'll be around, but I'm not real big on conversation, unless you've turned up information on the Grandfelt murder."

"Haven't been here long enough yet, but I will," she said. She turned to Virgil: "I know about you. You're that fuckin' Flowers."

Virgil, "Aw, for Christ's sakes."

"You'll see me around," the woman said. "My name is Anne Cash, Anne with an 'e.' My website is AnneCashInvestigations.com. It's the biggest and best true crime site on the Internet. You should take a look."

"We will," Virgil said.

She turned and took a step away, then turned back, brought her phone up before Lucas or Virgil could react, and took a picture of them together. "Thanks," she said.

"That's kinda rude," Virgil said to her back.

"Live with it," she said. "I'll have you up on my site in twenty minutes."

"Toldja," Lucas muttered.

"Gonna be a long day," Virgil said, looking over at the collection of women. On further inspection, he discovered three men among them. "Have you been to the murder scene?"

"I think so. As best I can tell. Is your GPS receiver in your gear bag?"

"It is."

"I only had my phone," Lucas said. "Let's get the GPS. We've got the location to three decimal points from the original investigation. I can get close, but I'm not sure I'm right on top of it."

"What's to see?"

"Well, nothing," Lucas said. "But you know, as long as we're here . . ."

Virgil got the GPS receiver and Lucas guided him around the group of women, who stayed back for a minute, but then followed them toward the trees and a major patch of raspberry canes. A narrow game path poked through the brush, and they took it back toward a substantial body of water.

"Battle Creek Lake," Lucas said. "Should have been called Battle Creek Slough."

"Or swamp," Virgil said. "That would be primo snapping turtle water back there. They're good eatin', so I'm told."

"I'll stick with snails," Lucas said. "Being of French heritage."

Virgil powered up the GPS receiver, when a woman called, "Davenport? Flowers?"

THEY TURNED AND saw a uniformed cop hurrying toward them, chevrons on her shirt sleeve. Lucas said, "Sergeant Carney?"

"That's me. I spoke to the city manager and they're calling around to the council and talking about making the park off-limits tomorrow." Carney was a thin woman with bony shoulders and a heart-shaped face, blue eyes, and a short blond ponytail. "We'll let them roam around this afternoon, but after that, it's entry by permission. That's if the council approves. Somebody's already cut branches off some of the trees . . ."

Virgil: "Why did they do that?"

"They're all making videos," Carney said. "Some of them with their phones, but some of them have these big Nikons and Sony cameras. The branches were in the way. They thought they were filming the murder scene, but they weren't. It's over this way."

They followed Carney along the narrow path into the trees, low branches swatting at their faces, raspberry canes scratching at their pants, trailed by a line of true-crimers. They passed a strong stench, and Carney said, "Somebody took a dump last night."

Lucas: "No kidding."

They went on, until Carney stopped and said, "It was right about here."

THERE WAS LITTLE to see but trees and brush. Virgil took out his GPS receiver, moved a dozen steps away to a spot with more open sky, and waited. A few yards back, the women were taking pictures and video of him, with a variety of cameras.

When Virgil had four satellites, he walked back to Lucas and Carney and said, "I think we're actually about ten yards that way." He nodded to the west, to a spot a few feet off the narrow trail, and they went that way and looked around. Still nothing to see except a clump of nettles.

The women closed in on them, and one of them took a small can from a pocket on her denim travel vest and quickly sprayed Day-Glo orange paint on a tree trunk.

Carney said, "Hey! Stop that."

"It wears off," the woman said. She turned to the other women and asked, "Anyone seen Bud?"

"He's coming, he had to run to the car." The speaker had a Sony camera mounted on a complicated upright handle that read "Small-Rig" on the front, and also mounted a Røde microphone. She pointed the camera at the woman who sprayed the tree and said, "You're live."

The painter turned to Lucas and said, "So this is the exact spot, Marshal, where, twenty-one years and ninety-eight days ago, Doris Grandfelt suffered an agonizing death at the hands of an unknown . . ."

Lucas turned his back and walked away, and the woman shouted, not looking at him but at the camera, "Marshal! Marshal! I'm talking to you."

Lucas, joined by Virgil, kept walking, and the camera tracked them.

"That'll be worth a few clicks," Virgil said.

"I don't want to get involved in any sensational YouTube shit," Lucas said. "We gotta take care, man."

They could hear Carney arguing with the women about the spray paint. A man hustled toward them with an instrument over his shoulder, a hand grip on one end and what looked like a basketball hoop on the other, with a video screen mounted in the middle. He was carrying it in a way that seemed designed to obscure exactly what it was. Lucas stepped in front of him and asked, "What's that thing?"

"Metal detector," the man grunted. He sidestepped Lucas, who let him go.

"Metal detector," Virgil mumbled as they walked away. "What the hell?"

Carney caught up with them at the cars: "Chief Bacon would like to talk to you guys, when you're done here."

"Where's he at? City hall?" Virgil asked.

"No, he's here somewhere, over in the other parking lot," Carney said. "I'll find him for you, but I won't stay around to listen. He's in a pissy mood."

"So are we," Lucas said.

———

BACON WAS A rotund man, maybe fifty, with salt-and-pepper hair and a red face. "I don't know whether I want you guys to come up with something or not. The council is all over me, bad publicity for the city and all that. It'd be nice to find the person who killed Doris, but there's a cost to it."

He went on for a while, on the one hand this, the other hand that, and when he turned away for a minute, to talk to another city cop, Virgil muttered to Lucas, "Let me handle this."

"What are you going to do?"

"Hit him with my justifications."

Virgil did that. When Bacon turned back to them, he said, "We know you guys have your daily concerns to keep up with, there's not a lot of investigation to be done here, we'll try to keep the focus on the BCA, we don't think this mission will amount to much, maybe a day or two, Miz Grandfelt's law office is handling the paperwork, blah blah blah . . ."

When he finished, Bacon said he appreciated all that, he'd leave an officer for crowd control, then got in his car and disappeared down the road.

"Well done," Lucas said. "But what's this?"

Carney was jogging toward them, across the softball outfields. "They found something with the metal detector," she said, as she came up. "I told them to leave it, but I don't think they will."

"Where is it?" Virgil asked.

"Right on the edge of the trees."

She pointed, they looked. The crowd of women and the three men had gathered in a tight huddle, bent over, looking at something in the dirt.

"Damnit," Lucas said. He led the way across the playing fields, the women turning to look at them as they got close. "Probably a bottle cap."

"WHAT IS IT?" Virgil asked. "You didn't touch anything?"

"We dug it up. Right below the surface," the metal detector man said. He held his hand out, showed them a nickel, sitting in his palm.

Lucas: "A nickel?"

"Yes. Amazed nobody found it before. It's a 1995, so the killer could have dropped it," said Anne Cash, the woman they'd spoken to earlier.

Virgil: "There's a path worn in the grass from people walking along the edge of the trees. It could have been dropped by anyone, anytime."

Another woman chipped in. "Its importance isn't what it is *in itself.* Its importance is, it demonstrates the negligence of the original investigation. This should have been found by the crime scene crew."

Lucas: "But it might have been dropped last week. Or anytime in the twenty-one years since the killing. Or the eight years before. It's meaningless. Or maybe you could use your blog to find out who might have had a 1995 nickel."

"No reason to get sarcastic," Cash said.

"Yes there is," Virgil said. "You're standing around looking at a nickel like it's the Kensington Runestone, and it's a fuckin' nickel."

Lucas elbowed him in the rib cage, and when Virgil looked at him,

Lucas nodded at the far edge of the group. Virgil turned that way and spotted a woman pointing a diminutive camera over the shoulder of the woman in front of her. "That 'fuckin'' will get us a few clicks," Lucas said. "Let's go get a Coke or something. Talk about this. You drive."

IN VIRGIL'S TRUCK, they talked about not much, because there wasn't yet much to talk about, until Lucas said, "I've got a big favor to ask."

"No."

"You don't know what I'm asking," Lucas said.

"I don't need to. If it's a big favor, I don't have time," Virgil said. "I've got a novel to finish."

"Look. For the next couple of weeks, you gotta do *some* work," Lucas said. "You can't just take the month off."

"*Some* work. A big favor sounds like a lot of work. But okay, spit it out."

"There's no point in both of us doing everything," Lucas said. "I'll be the liaison with the suits—Grandfelt, the lawyers, the politicians. I'll keep them quiet and satisfied that we're working. Daily updates. You be the main liaison with the true crime people."

"Jesus, Lucas, I . . ."

"You're a lot better at that kind of stuff than I am. You're more social. You've got a better line of bullshit. Look at the way you handled the police chief," Lucas said. "I can't do that—I sound like I'm lying. I don't have the patience to deal with the whack-a-doodles. You do it all the time, out there in the corn and beans. I mean, look at your friends. Johnson Johnson? I'm surprised he's not up here with a Grandfelt-sniffing dog."

Virgil shifted uncomfortably in the driver's seat. The comment about his friend Johnson Johnson had been true enough. "Look, I'll tell you, I gotta finish this novel on time. I gotta. It's gonna be my life, and to me, it's more important than Doris Grandfelt. I no longer have my heart in chasing assholes. I'm willing to work on Grandfelt, but I can't get all tangled up . . ."

"You don't have to get tangled up," Lucas said. "All you have to do is liaise."

"Is that a word?"

"You know what I mean. Don't like the true-crimers? Blow them off if you like," Lucas said. "But be the man. Let me take care of the suits, and you're the man the true-crimers call up when they need to."

Virgil thought about it for a minute, then nodded. "We can give it a try. If it starts eating me up, I might quit right in the middle of everything. Fuck Lara Grandfelt and her dead sister."

Lucas switched out of pitch mode, settled into the seat, and said, "Thank you."

THE PARROT CAFÉ was a BCA hangout, a low-rent café with decent burgers, mediocre fries, a piss-poor pie, acidic coffee, and an ever-present odor of brown gravy and pencil-thin sliced beef. Two old friends, Jenkins and Shrake, were pushing cheeseburgers into their faces. Jenkins did a fake double take when they walked in, and Virgil said, "You might know it," and Lucas said, "They're eating. There's a surprise."

Shrake, cued by Jenkins's double take, turned to look, and started laughing, bits of hamburger and cheese flaking off on his sport coat. "Sherlock and Holmes. You catch the guy yet?"

"We're making progress," Virgil said. "It'll take a week to nail it down."

"I heard you nailed down a month off, with pay," Shrake said.

"That much is true," Lucas said.

"Move your asses over," Virgil said.

The two extra-large men moved over in the booth, and Virgil and Lucas sat down. Virgil said to Lucas, "I oughta talk to Jon about getting these guys out to the park. They won't find anything, but they might get dates. They always need dates."

"Won't happen," Shrake said. "We've got a runner of our own to find."

A waiter named Jaxon came over and Lucas and Virgil ordered pie, banana crème and cherry, respectively, with Diet Coke and coffee, also respectively.

Virgil: "So you guys are looking . . ."

They were looking, Jenkins said, for a semi-outlaw biker who unloaded some bad Chinese fentanyl on his cousin, who subsequently died, albeit with a smile on his face.

Virgil: "Have you checked with the Sturgis cops?"

Jenkins looked open-mouthed at Shrake and said, with a sudden intake of breath, "Oh my God, he might be onto something."

Lucas: "Okay. You've looked in Sturgis."

"In fact, he just left Sturgis, on his way back here," Shrake said, checking his Apple iWatch. "Ask us how we know that."

"You're tracking his phone," Lucas said.

"We plan to box him up about the time he hits Coon Rapids,"

Jenkins said. "No reason for us to be sweating our butts around So-Dak." He pushed a french fry into his mouth and mumbled around it, "You guys actually find anything yet?"

The pie arrived, looking a little used.

"No, and we won't," Lucas said, poking a fork at Jenkins. "This is almost the biggest clown show I've been involved in, although, of course, that wouldn't apply to Virgie."

"That's the goddamned truth," Shrake said, shaking his head. "Did I ever tell you about this chick crawled up a furnace vent and Virgie . . ."

"About fifty times," Lucas said.

"So, about this Grandfelt thing," Jenkins said. "You got nothin'. You got no ideas, you got no moves that haven't been made, you got nothing but your dick in your hand . . ."

"One thing," Virgil said. "There were footprints around the scene, almost certainly made by whoever dumped the body. It's all in the files, I read about it last night. There was a tread pattern that over-lapped scrapes in the dirt apparently made by Grandfelt's shoes when she was dragged into the trees. Size ten-and-a-half Nikes . . ."

"We know about that, and that's not a clue," Shrake said. "Half the guys in the Twin Cities could have made them."

"Shut up for a minute, let me finish," Virgil said. "There were too many footprints. That's my opinion, not somebody else's. There were six clean footprints in the dirt around the body, including the one that crossed the scrapes. We got photographs of them all. They shouldn't have been there. The ground wasn't that wet at the time of the killing and when Lucas and I were back there this morning, I was hardly making any prints at all. And I've got heavy tread on my boots."

"You're saying the prints might have been deliberate?" Jenkins asked.

"I'm saying it's possible," Virgil said.

Lucas scratched his head, nodded, said, "It's possible."

"You know what you just did?" Jenkins asked Virgil. "You just peed on the only clue you had."

"Got the DNA," Lucas said.

Virgil: "If she was raped."

"There was a question about that at the time," Jenkins said. "The boys thought she was raped, and the girls didn't. The girls thought she was pushing pussy."

"I know," Virgil said. "But that possibility wasn't something that was talked about much. Maria Jimenez was death on rape but thought that Grandfelt's sexual contacts may have been voluntary."

"I remember," Shrake said. "That's about the same time Maria started suppressing her intense attraction for me."

"I do remember that, her suppressing it," Virgil said.

"If the sex was voluntary, I feel sorry for the guy who left the DNA behind. If you find him, his ass is going to prison for rape and murder," Jenkins said.

Shrake said, "Yeah," without sounding happy about it.

Lucas's phone buzzed, and he looked at the screen. "Sergeant Carney."

He answered, listened, and said, "We'll be right over. Don't let anybody touch it."

Jenkins, Shrake, and Virgil looked at him as he rang off. Virgil asked, "What?"

Lucas: "Finish your pie, author-boy. Carney says the metal detector guy might have found the murder weapon."

When they'd been at the park earlier in the day, there'd been a dozen true-crimers; now there were twice as many, standing in a bunch near the corner of a parking lot, with a half-dozen cops mixed in with them.

"They look like movie explorers digging up an Egyptian temple," Virgil said, as he eased the truck into the parking lot. And it was true. With a few exceptions, the crowd was dressed in vaguely military khaki and one of them was wearing an Aussie hat with an upturned brim on one side. "You think they found the knife?"

"I dunno what I think," Lucas said. "They're all the way across the field from the dump site."

They got out of the Tahoe and walked across the parking lot, where the man with the metal detector saw them coming and held up a transparent plastic bag with a table knife in it. "Found it right here by the edge of the parking lot," he said.

Virgil took the bag and held it up to the sky so he and Lucas could look at it.

A too-thin woman, who'd filmed them earlier in the day, said, "I'm Dahlia Blair. I was a witness to the discovery and so were a whole bunch of other people, including police officers. By the way, none of us touched the knife. Nothing has touched it except the inside of the evidence bag. If you look at the back of the knife, it says 'stainless steel,' but it's all pitted up, so it's been here for a while."

"Like twenty years," Anne Cash chipped in. She and a half-dozen other true-crimers were making videos.

Lucas, looking at the knife, and its sharp whetted point, muttered to Virgil, "They might have something."

"Yeah."

Lucas turned to the man with the metal detector and asked, "Why were you all the way over here?"

Blair began, "We deduced . . ."

"I want to talk to this guy," Lucas said, nodding at the guy with the metal detector.

The man grabbed at the spotlight. "We deduced, or deducted . . . deduced? that the reason there were no vehicle tracks that could be attributed to the killer is that he never drove a vehicle across the grass and that's why nobody saw him come or go," he said. "He pulled up to the parking lot, which was, at the time, surrounded by shrubbery, turned off his headlights, and carried the body across the outfield and into the trees. The neighbors here say kids sometimes park here, you know, romancing, so it's not unusual to have a car stopping in the night. Anyway, since nothing more was showing up around the body scene, I thought I'd scan around the parking lot. I was only at it for fifteen minutes, when this popped up."

His statement was filmed by everyone who had a camera, then one woman, who'd been at the front of the group with a big Canon, turned and casually walked around the crowd to the back of it, then began stepping away, walking backwards.

Virgil said, "So listen, we . . . what's your name?"

Dahlia Blair said, "Bud Light."

The man said, "Actually, my name is Charles Light."

"But everybody calls him Bud," Blair said.

Virgil continued to ignore her. "Okay, Charles, can you show us the exact spot . . ."

The woman who'd stepped around to the back of the crowd was now twenty-five yards away. She turned, then broke into a trot, heading toward the cars. Nobody noticed for a moment, then another woman shouted, "Jane! Jane! Wait!"

Another woman shouted, "She's gonna post! Wait, Jane . . ."

Half of the crowd stampeded after Jane, and Light laughed and said, "They're gonna have to move fast. Jane can run."

"How do they post from here?" Virgil asked. "On their phones?"

"Can't type fast enough on a phone," Light said. "They'll all start uploading vid to their iPads while they're typing up headlines and maybe a short story, then they'll post through Verizon or AT&T, or whatever they've got."

"But why the rush . . . who's gonna look . . ."

"There's a website called FirstStabAtIt.com—'first stab at it dot com'—that's like a true crime headline site," Charles explained. "You know, 'breaking news.' Whoever gets the first couple of headlines up there gets the clicks."

"Why aren't you guys running?" Lucas asked.

"Bud and I are associated with NebraskaTrue," Blair said. "That's our website. We'll have the full first-person report that everybody else will have to copy."

"Jesus," Virgil said. They watched more members of the troupe peeling away, headed toward individual vehicles.

"Anyway, you thought that there might be something left behind by the killer?" Virgil asked. "Then, shazam, like magic, you found the knife? That seems . . . curious."

"Very curious," Lucas agreed.

"What? You think I faked it?" Light was outraged, in an introverted way, his face turning pink behind his wire-rimmed glasses.

"Wouldn't necessarily have to be you," Lucas said. "Could be anyone looking for clicks. When we say this is a curious discovery, I mean it's outrageously curious. So curious we've never heard anything like it. Ever."

"Gotta be a first time for everything," Light ventured.

"No, there doesn't," Virgil said.

One of the remaining women, who hadn't stampeded, said, earnestly, "I'll tell you something, officers. I'm a longtime treasure hunter. I've got my own metal detector in my truck, I just haven't gotten it out yet. When Bud yelled, I went over to help dig out the knife. The piece of sod where the knife was buried was clean. Untouched. When you've got a little experience, you can tell. That knife was there a long time."

Virgil said, "Okay. So where's the spot?"

"We were careful about it. Ginny put a shot of red paint exactly one foot from the knife cut, and there's a yellow pencil pointing at it." Light pointed at a spot fifteen feet away, and they all looked and saw the pencil. "We moved everybody away so they wouldn't trample it."

Lucas said to Virgil, "Better get your crime scene people out here."

"I'll call them," Virgil said. He took out a red-backed Moleskine notebook and a pen and said, "Your name is Charles Light? L-i-g-h-t?"

"That's correct," Light said.

One of the non-stampeding women said, "That's why everybody calls him 'Bud.' You know . . ."

"Yeah, I get it. Bud Light. I can sympathize," Virgil said.

"I spec' you can—that whole fuckin' Flowers thing you got going," Light said.

Lucas snickered and Virgil said, "Shut up."

FOR THE NEXT half hour, nothing happened; Virgil kept the evidence bag with the knife, and most of the women had gone to their vehicles to post to their blogs and Substack newsletters, although a few hung close to Lucas and Virgil, and several others trampled through the dump scene with cameras. Then two members of the BCA's crime scene crew drove up in a Mustang convertible with the top down. When the driver got out of the car, he lingered by the front fender, admiring the mirror shine on the fire-engine red finish. Virgil walked over and said, "The car looks like your wife licked it."

"She does. I make her lick the entire car before breakfast every morning and then polish it with Q-tips."

"Good for you, happy to see that toxic masculinity still has a place in the world," Virgil said. "Here's the bag."

The crime scene guy held the bag up, then passed it to his companion, who pressed the plastic around the knife, squinting at it. After a minute he said, "What you have here is your basic Oneida cafeteria- or restaurant-grade stainless steel table knife. I will tell you more after I look at it through some glass, but it appears to have been crudely sharpened, possibly on a red rock. Or a brick. I can see little red grains in some of the sharpening grooves, and blood would have leached out a long time ago, so it's not blood. Whoever did it sharpened the edge fairly well, but mostly put a point on it. It fits our description of the murder weapon."

"So . . . it was intended as a stabbing weapon?" Virgil asked.

"Looks like, but it could cut, too."

Dahlia Blair, armed with her camera and microphone, had been standing behind Bud Light, twenty-five feet away, shooting over Light's shoulder. Lucas only noticed her when she broke away from the bushes, heading for the cars.

"We've been busted again," he said.

The crime scene guy with the bag said, "What?"

"You're gonna be in a movie," Lucas said.

Virgil wandered away, working his phone as Lucas explained about the true-crimers, and when Virgil came back, he looked around for cameras and microphones, then said quietly to Lucas, "Bee Accounting has a cafeteria. It ain't much, but that's what I got."

"We should go there," Lucas said. "It'll at least get us out of this shit show."

THEY DROVE SEPARATELY to the Bee building, found street parking, and when they were both on the street, Lucas looked around, then said, "Your big mouth is gonna get you in trouble, Virgie."

"What? What'd I say?"

"For one thing, you referred to that fuckin' nickel as a fuckin' nickel, on camera. And then that Blair woman was hiding behind

Light with her camera and microphone when you were talking to the crime scene guy. You know, about having his wife lick the car and making her polish it with Q-tips, how it's a good thing there was still toxic masculinity in the world."

"Aw, that won't . . ."

Lucas interrupted. "You really do live out in the sticks, don't you? You ever hear of social media?"

"You say cruder stuff than that . . ."

"Not on camera," Lucas said. "Listen: these people are dangerous, if a guy wants to keep a job."

"Fuck it. I'm gonna quit anyway," Virgil said.

"Don't do that. You're too good at this."

BEE ACCOUNTING WAS located in a remodeled early-twentieth-century warehouse, complete with worn limestone grotesques carved into the building's frieze. As they walked up to it, Lucas said, "Red brick. With tiny red grains."

"You plucked that observation right out of my brain."

The lobby was guarded by a friendly older man who sat behind a wooden counter to one side of a locked glass door that led into the interior. He was watching a Twins game on a computer.

Lucas and Virgil showed him their IDs and asked to speak to whomever was in charge of the cafeteria. The man, who was wearing a silver metal name tag that read "Terry," suggested that they speak first to the office manager, whom he paged. "You gonna bust somebody?" he asked, after making the call.

"Probably not," Lucas said. "That today's Twins game?"

"Yup. Not looking good."

"Better that I'm not watching it, then," Virgil said.

"Same with me, but I can't help myself," Terry said. "Six-zip in the third."

"Damn Yankees . . ."

A WOMAN PUSHED through the glass door, round-faced, middle-aged, sharp-eyed, with a pair of reading glasses hanging from a gold chain around her neck. "Officers?"

Lucas introduced them and she said, "You're the two who caught Judge Sand's killer. I saw you on television."

"We did," Virgil said.

"I hope we haven't killed anyone here?" She said it with a smile, but there was a question mark in her voice.

"We're looking into the Doris Grandfelt killing," Lucas said.

"Oh-em-gee," she said. "I read about the reward. Five million dollars?"

"Yes. Something's come up. We'd like to talk to whoever supervises your cafeteria."

"Well, okay . . . That's up on two."

They followed behind her through a room with three glass-faced offices and perhaps twenty thigh-high gray cubicles with people—five-to-one women—looking at computer terminals. She took them to an elevator, and they rode up one floor. As they did, the woman, who said her name was Hester Sweeney, asked what they were looking for.

Virgil said, "A table knife was found near the crime scene. We're interested in the silverware you use in the cafeteria."

She asked, "A metal knife?"

"Stainless steel . . ."

"Huh. Well, I'll introduce you to Marlys, who runs the lunchroom and the dining room. We have separate facilities for the regular employees and the executives. The only real silverware would be in the executive dining room, but I don't know how long that's been the case."

Lucas: "How long have you worked here?"

"Six years. Marlys has been here a little longer. I don't think there are many people left, who were here when Doris was killed. It's famous around here, of course, the killing is."

She took them to a lunchroom, a plain tile-floored open room with plastic-topped square tables, four orange or blue plastic molded chairs for each table, windows that looked at the former warehouse across the street. A line of coolers stood against one wall, with a plastic-topped counter that held baskets of plastic knives, forks and spoons, straws, napkins, along with packs of ketchup, mustard, mayonnaise, and salt and pepper. Three people were sitting at separate tables, eating sandwiches or soup, reading their phones and ignoring each other.

Marlys Jackson was a short Black woman, pretty and busy, her head in one of the coolers, a clipboard in her hand, the type who'd be doing four things at once. She was wearing black jeans with a deep-red blouse and had rings on six of her ten fingers.

When Sweeney introduced them, Jackson put her fists on her hips and said with a Texas accent, "I'll help any way I can, but we wouldn't have any silverware left from way back then. Let's go talk to Philip. He was here when Miz Grandfelt was killed."

Philip Wall was a dishwasher, a thin shaky white man with a gray ponytail and tattoos on his skinny forearms. He wore a transparent throw-away plastic apron and had a pack of Marlboros sitting on a sterilizing cabinet.

With Sweeney and Jackson listening in, he told Lucas and Virgil that the lunchroom never had anything but self-serve food—sandwiches, yogurt, drinks, granola bars, candy—with a few other items that could be heated in a couple of microwaves. "It's all been plastic throw-away utensils since I been here, except executive dining," he said. "I think the silverware was changed about, shoot, I dunno, maybe ten years ago? Same brand, Oneida stainless, different design."

"You don't have any of the old stuff around?"

Wall scratched the back of his head, thinking, then said, "You know . . . we might still have the picnic stuff."

"What's that?" Lucas asked.

"A long time ago, we used to have office picnics. The execs would take employees who'd done good work out to one of the parks," Wall said. "They'd, you know, play volleyball and croquet, or whatever, and they'd take food along and silverware, instead of plastic, because, you know, it was supposed to be kind of fancy, and they were executives. They had these big old wooden picnic baskets."

"You still have them?" Virgil asked.

"There used to be some in the old basement storage room, unless they got thrown away."

Lucas turned to Sweeney. "Can we go look?"

They could.

On the way to the basement, Lucas asked if any of the picnic excursions went to Shawnee Park.

"I don't know about that. I ain't an executive," Wall said.

The basement was a concrete hole under the building, with red-rusted steel beams and a lot of pipe and electrical conduits; it smelled of damp but seemed dry enough. Wall led the way to a metal door, pulled it open. The room behind the door was lined with wooden shelves, showing grime and cobwebs. "There you go," he said.

A half-dozen woven-wood picnic baskets were stacked on the shelves. Wall pulled one of them off. The basket had folding handles, both broken. Wall pushed them back, pulled open the top of the basket. Inside was a plastic box full of miscellaneous stainless silverware. He took the box out, opened it, and Lucas poked through it, found a knife, held it up.

Virgil took out his phone, called up a photo of the knife found in the park.

"Ah, boy," he said. "They're identical."

SWEENEY LED THE way back up a flight of stairs to the main lobby, made a call on her phone as she walked, talked for a few seconds, listened for a few more, and as they came into the lobby said, "Cory Donner would like to speak with you. He's the CEO."

Lucas was carrying the box of silverware, and said, "Sure."

Donner's office was on the fourth and top floor. The office was obviously designed for work with an efficient, not overly large desk, a long side table stacked with paper and manuals, a wall of books, a wall of filing cabinets, and two modest windows overlooking a lifeless intersection.

Donner stood when they came in, nodded at Sweeney, and shook hands with Lucas and Virgil. He was as tall as the two cops, but stooped, balding, with quick dark eyes. A suit jacket hung from a wall hook, and he was tieless, his shirtsleeves rolled up to his elbows.

"When I read about the reward, I worried that the murder would come back to haunt us," Donner said. "We've had several people try to push past our lobby, so they could 'investigate' the company."

"Did Hester tell you what we found?" Lucas asked.

"She said something about silverware—that you'd found the murder weapon and it matches some of ours."

"Some of your silverware way back when, not the current stuff," Virgil said. "When the murder occurred, we interviewed some people here. The BCA did."

"I know, I was one of them," Donner said. "I volunteered for a DNA test. The investigators did it, but nobody ever told me what they found out. Nothing, I guess. I did have a solid alibi for the time of the murder. Tell me what's happened now, to restart it all."

Lucas and Virgil took turns filling him in, and when they were done, he asked, "You're not certain that what you have is the actual murder weapon?"

"No, but unless somebody deliberately planted it, it looks likely," Virgil said. "I wouldn't put it past some of the treasure hunters we're dealing with, but how would they know the style of your silverware from more than twenty years ago, and then find a corroded knife that matches it, and have time to actually plant it?"

"Yes, that would be improbable," Donner said. He scratched a cheek, thinking about it. "I'll talk to my board about this, but I can tell you right now that we'll give you anything you want, cooperate any way we can." He hesitated again, then added, "That would be our general policy, but our attorneys might not completely agree. They might want some technical legal stuff done . . . Whatever, if they have a problem, I'll get them in touch with you or whoever you say."

They thanked him, and Virgil asked, "How many people had DNA tests done?"

"I'm not sure. One of the BCA investigators told me that they were asking for the tests from people who they had some reason to suspect, even if it was slight. He said that they were more interested in Doris's club activity than in her . . . her relationships in the company, since she didn't seem involved with anyone here. You know, sexually."

Lucas: "Was Doris pretty? Lively? Would she have caught the eye of guys working here?"

Donner shook his head, gave them a wry smile. "She was quite pretty, a blonde, athletic. You know." He glanced at Sweeney. "Boobs. If she was never going to be Miss America, she was attractive. But. There's a big 'but' here . . . that's a but with one 't.'"

Lucas: "That would be?"

"In the early 2000s, mmm, probably about the time she started working with us, we had quite the little sex scandal here. We had a married couple working for us, and there was a sexual problem involving our then CEO, Dick McCann. McCann, I think it's fair to say, was predatory. I was very junior at the time, not yet a partner, but everybody heard . . ."

"He jumped somebody's wife?"

"Uh, no. At the time, he might have gotten away with that," Donner said. "A wife. What he did was, to use your phrase, he jumped somebody's husband."

"Was Doris involved?" Virgil asked.

"Oh, no, no, but there was a terrific shock when this all started coming out. There was even a brawl down on the first floor, involving the wife and McCann. For several years after that, there was no hanky-panky at Bee Accounting. The partners at the time made it very explicit that if we had people getting friendly, they'd quickly be getting friendly at some other company. They told us that they would send us packing if we misbehaved, even if the misbehavior was consensual."

"Sounds a little harsh," Virgil said.

"Reputation is extremely important in this business," Donner said. "Clients want sober, industrious, cautious people working on their taxes and payrolls."

They talked for a few more minutes, and Donner told them they were welcome to take the silverware with them, for inspection by the BCA's crime lab.

ON THE WAY back down to the lobby, Sweeney said, "I hope we can hold all this confidentially, you know, like Cory said, the reputation . . ."

In the lobby, Lucas and Virgil stopped to put on their sunglasses and check with Terry the door guard on the Twins game—now seven-zip in the sixth. "We're toast," Terry said.

As they told Sweeney, they wouldn't be talking about what they found, but when Lucas and Virgil walked out through the front door, they were caught by Anne Cash and two other women, who were pointing cameras at them. When they were sure they had them both on video, the three women all panned their cameras over to the Bee Accounting sign above the door.

Cash called, "That's right. We followed you. What'd you find out, Marshal? What's in the box under your arm?"

Virgil: "Ah, fuck me."

Lucas: "You did it *again*."

10

Amanda Fisk drove her silver Mercedes SL550 too fast through the gym's curb cut, deliberately parked so the stripe for a parking space ran directly down the middle of the car: she hated door dings. Ding her doors and she might kill you.

She climbed out, brushed a cookie crumb off her blouse, and headed for the entrance. Fisk was of middle height for a woman, at five-seven, strongly built—Pilates three days a week, hard singles tennis two evenings. She had a straight nose and a long chin, gray-green eyes, thighs and calves beautifully rounded. She was naturally blond and pink-skinned, with hair falling down to her shoulder blades; Renoir (if he were still alive) would have given his left nut to get her as a model.

She pulled her sports duffel off the passenger seat, pushed through the gym door, waved her membership card at a card reader that beeped green and unlocked the interior door. Inside, she turned left to the women's locker room, where one of her oldest acquaintances—not exactly a friend—was emoting.

Emoting had been on Fisk's vocabulary calendar—*displaying emotion in an excited or theatrical manner*—so she had the word handy, and Rebecca Jones was definitely emoting.

Jones spotted Fisk and said, "Oh my God! Mandy! Have you heard about Bee?"

"Bee?"

"Bee! Those true crime people found a knife they say is the murder weapon, and it came from Bee's cafeteria!"

On a scale of one to ten, Fisk's emotional response ran from one to one-and-a-half. She said, "Really?" and used her key to open her locker.

"Doesn't that freak you out?" Jones demanded. "Weren't you there when Delores got murdered? There's five million bucks on the line!"

"Doris, not Delores. And I was," Fisk said. "I didn't know the woman—she was a clerk and I was in the legal department."

Jones, in her workout shorts and Athleta sports bra, innocent eyes wide, moved closer: "You must have known her at least a *little*."

"Actually, no," Fisk said, looking over her shoulder at the other woman. "We were all worried when she got killed, because we wondered if the killer might be somebody at Bee. The police were all over the place, but I guess they decided that she'd been hanging out with some rough people over on Hennepin Avenue. There'd been rumors that she'd been turning tricks for spending money. At the time, I couldn't have told you what she looked like."

"I read on True Crime Triple-X, about turning tricks," Jones said. "I heard her twin sister is threatening to sue anybody who says that!"

"Then don't say that; that's my official recommendation," Fisk said. Fisk was an assistant county attorney in the criminal division, which was appropriate, she sometimes thought, because technically, she was a criminal, even if never caught or convicted.

Other members of the Pilates class had been listening, and as Fisk began changing into her shorts and top, one of them said, "I didn't know you worked there."

"Right out of law school," Fisk said. "A nightmare of unrelieved boredom and miserable pay. Quit, and never looked back."

An older woman said, "Wasn't there some other sex scandal over there?"

"There was, I guess, before my time," Fisk said. "A gay thing, with the married CEO."

"Wow. Doesn't sound like an accounting firm."

"Why not?" Jones asked, eyes even wider. "Sex stuff goes on everywhere. My sister is a schoolteacher, and you should hear the stories she tells. You know there are teachers' bars, where teachers go to get drunk and laid?"

"Not in St. Paul . . ." said the older woman.

"Yes! Right here in St. Paul! You know what it's called? Randy's Brew House. Randy's. Isn't that a great tipoff?"

After some more chatter, Fisk said, "I'm gonna go stretch."

FISK HAD WORKED at Bee as a contracts attorney, and when she began looking for a way out, she was initially hired to work in the civil division of the Ramsey County Attorney's Office. Within a year, the county attorney shifted her over to the criminal division, where she quickly became a star. She never met a rapist she wasn't willing to burn at the stake.

When she finished her workout—she didn't look like it, but she was a brute, who absolutely murdered the kettle bells after the tough Pilates session—she called the office and told her immediate subordinate that she'd hurt her knee at Pilates. She'd talk to her husband about it, probably get a knee brace of some kind, and would be late getting back to work.

That done, she drove home to her pale-yellow mansion on St. Paul's fashionable Summit Avenue.

Fisk had two dogs; or rather, her husband did. Jack Russell terriers, who, if you didn't know better, you might think were perpetually on doggy amphetamines. They jumped and yapped and ran in circles, and outside, in the fenced yards, chased blue-and-orange rubber Chuckit! balls with a manic intensity, to the amusement of the pair of Belgian Malinois that lived on the other side of the chain link. The Malinois, also known as land sharks, looked upon the Jack Russells as potential hors d'oeuvres.

If Amanda Fisk had had her way, she might have heaved the little fuckers over the fence—she identified more with the Malinois than with the Jack Russells—but her husband would simply have bought more, and if he'd found out what she'd done, would have divorced her.

The marriage had never been on solid ground, although they'd managed to hang together for twenty years. Both had an essential streak of cruelty—valuable to both lawyers and surgeons—which created an unspoken understanding that new partners might be hard to find.

On the other hand, while Fisk was forty-eight and might eventually find someone, Dr. Timothy (not Tim) Carlson had slipped past sixty-five, and if they split, he might have to go it alone, without half or more of their accumulated wealth.

Timothy.

Fisk got a green drink from the refrigerator, a special blend of alfalfa, artichoke, and spirulina, with dashes of ashwagandha, shiitake mushroom, and St. John's wort. The drink may have counted for a certain level of her meanness, although she'd had a flinty soul from the time she was a child.

She sat in the breakfast nook, looking out the window at the city of St. Paul down the bluff, and thought about Timothy. She'd been thinking about him quite a lot the last two or three years. If there was one single thing about him that drove her berserk, it was the goddamn dogs.

TIMOTHY HAD TO be in the operating theater at six-thirty most mornings, leaving the house at six o'clock. He was up at five o'clock, efficient in his morning routine, showering, shaving, popping his blood-pressure pills, eating a breakfast of granola and orange juice while checking stock market futures and the *Wall Street Journal*. He'd be done with all that by five-forty, and then he'd go out in the back with the goddamn dogs and he'd bounce a Chuckit! ball off the back of the house so the dogs could do their acrobatic midair catches, thrilling both Timothy and the dogs.

It was the irregular thump of the ball against the house that drove her to the edge, and now, probably, over it. *Thump! Thump-thump* (both dogs!) *Thumpity-thump!* (Long pause; was he done?) *Thump!* No, he wasn't. This went on for twenty minutes before he brought the dogs in and left for work.

———

FISK FINISHED THE green drink, dropped the bottle in the garbage sack, walked around the dogs, who were ricocheting through the kitchen, got kitchen gloves and a sponge mop from the laundry cupboard, duct tape from the junk drawer in the kitchen, and the orange-and-blue Chuckit! ball launcher. The ball launcher was a plastic arm little more than two feet long with a cup at one end to hold a Chuckit! ball. Using the launcher, Timothy could heave a Chuckit! ball fifty or sixty yards through the air.

Wearing the gloves, she taped the ball launcher to the end of the mop handle and carried the handle and four Chuckit! balls up to the bedroom and out onto the narrow balcony, the dogs following behind. They were curious little fuckers.

There was a three-foot-wide sharply slanting eave under the balcony, meant to shelter the first floor's yellow siding from rain stains, with a gutter at the edge of the eave. Fisk reached through the balcony railing with a Chuckit! ball in her hand, put it on the shingles and let it roll down to the gutter. When it got there it was moving so fast that it shot off onto the backyard's flagstone patio.

Okay, that didn't work.

She looked left and right, but unless somebody was hiding in a hedge, nobody could see her. She extended the sponge end of the mop over the railing until it was flat on the shingles, then stooped and put a ball behind the sponge head. Leaning over the balcony, she eased the ball down to the gutter, and then into it.

Good. She added one more, then left the mop handle, with attached ball launcher, on the balcony, checked left and right again, and closed the balcony doors and told the dogs, "Shut the fuck up." Finally, she went into her closet and dug out a knee brace, in case anybody at the office was solicitous about the injured extremity, pulled it on, and headed back to work.

THE THING ABOUT Timothy.

Though they'd never spoken of it, Fisk knew, of course, that Timothy had been the last male to deposit DNA in Doris Grandfelt's waiting vagina. She also knew from reading the now-online Grandfelt investigation files that they did not have hers, from the cut on her hand.

Timothy hadn't murdered the woman, but if his sexual contact with Grandfelt became known, he most likely would be charged with murder, in her legal opinion. He also certainly knew that.

From a nonlegal point of view, Timothy's legal jeopardy wasn't the worst thing that could happen. Much worse, it might impoverish *her*. Fisk's work as a prosecutor covered their basic expenses for any given year, while Timothy's money bought the house, the cars, and stacked up a tidy amount in two different wildly successful hedge funds. He'd been doing that since the '90s.

From the outside, they looked small rich; from the inside, they were wealthy. A lot of that money would go away if he needed high-end legal talent to defend him in a murder trial, especially if that trial was followed with a lawsuit by Grandfelt's still-surviving parents.

(Fisk was familiar with a Twin Cities murder trial story in which the accused, a wealthy woman, had asked the Cities' best defense attorney how much of her fortune he'd take if she hired him. He'd replied, "All of it." Fisk believed the story to be true, because the woman had been acquitted and wound up living in a mobile home.)

Alternatively, if neither of the criminal or civil trials took place, and Timothy wasn't around to get his DNA tested, their accumulated fortune could be used to sustain quite a nice lifestyle on, say, the island of St. Thomas, in the U.S. Virgin Islands.

TIMOTHY GOT HOME between three-thirty and four o'clock on most days. Amanda got home between five and six. When she got home that night, he was in the kitchen and had just finished microwaving fast-food onion rings.

They didn't usually speak much, but this evening, she said, "You gotta come up to the bedroom and see what those goddamn dogs did."

"They're not goddamn dogs," he said, taking a bite out of a hot onion ring.

"Yes, they are, you gotta come up and look at this . . ."

She'd gotten up, she told him, at her usual time of seven-thirty. Because it looked like a nice day, she'd opened the balcony doors, and the little fuckers had rolled Chuckit! balls between the balusters that supported the railing. The balls were now stuck in a gutter.

"I tried to get them out," she said, "but I couldn't reach them. I could touch them, but not get them in the cup . . ."

At the balcony, she showed him the mop handle with the attached launcher arm. "See if you can reach. It's supposed to rain and this is the gutter we had the problem with."

He should have thought about it, but instead, he popped the last of the onion ring, took the mop from her, and bent over the balcony railing, reaching far over for the balls. When he was fully extended, she grabbed his belt and the back collar on his jacket and heaved him over.

Timothy screamed, "No!" and then he was gone, the scream truncated as he hit headfirst on the back patio, fifteen feet below the balcony. Fisk left the balcony doors open, and said to the bouncing dogs, "Go find Timothy! Where's Timothy?"

Out the back door, the dogs rushed over to his body, for a body it was: he'd crushed his skull *and* broken his neck, Fisk thought. She knelt beside him, careful not to get her pants in the widening pool of blood. She could see some brains, she thought. She hovered, just to make sure, and when satisfied that he was gone, she went back inside to call 9-1-1 and to start practicing her grief.

The grief would be a stretch for her, because Amanda Fisk was a psychopath, and didn't feel much at all about Timothy's departure from this mortal coil. But, she'd pull something together, grief-wise.

And though she was a lifelong psychopath with a taste for fresh blood, Timothy was only her sixth kill, and possibly not the last.

Doris Grandfelt had been number three, and, so far, the most gratifying.

SO THE COPS came, and then a medical examiner's investigator, who looked at the Chuckit! balls in the gutter, and two more on the patio near the body. He had the body bagged up and sent to the morgue.

The cops, who knew who Fisk was, were sympathetic, but not too, because they'd seen any number of dead bodies, and as long as they, the cops, weren't related to the body, they didn't much care.

She was eventually left alone: she had no close friends who might be inclined to come over and sympathize with her. She spent time with a garden hose, washing blood off the patio. Blood, she found, was not easily rinsed out of flagstone. The goddamn dogs, for once subdued, sat and watched.

That night, in her bed—she and Timothy slept in separate queen-sized beds in the same bedroom; Timothy liked having the dogs on the bed with him, and she didn't—she fell to sleep as quickly as she did on any other night, the dogs sitting on the other bed, staring at her.

Usually, she slept through dreams, and never remembered him. On this night, she kicked and twisted and sometimes groaned, and she remembered . . .

Don at the top of the stairs, on his way down, green plastic bowl in one hand, beer in the other. "I made some buttered popcorn for us. We can watch a movie."

11

Neither Virgil nor Lucas had mentioned to anyone outside the BCA that the knife found by the true-crimers was identical to the knives used in the Bee executive dining room at the time of Grandfelt's murder. Nevertheless, all the major true crime blogs had the story within hours of the discovery, with Charles Light's face smiling out at the readers, posed beside his metal detector.

Since the major media outlets were all monitoring the true crime sites, the news had gone everywhere by midafternoon.

"They were tipped off by somebody inside the company, or somebody inside the BCA," Lucas said. Virgil was sitting across from him, stocking feet up on the desk. "Had to be one or the other—I didn't see you making any phone calls."

They were in a temporary office at BCA headquarters in St. Paul. "I suspect it came from here," Virgil said, looking out the office window. "Not everybody here likes me and even more of them don't like you. Somebody's fucking with us, probably for their own amusement . . . though they're taking a hell of a risk. They could get their ass fired."

"Or it could have been from somebody at Bee. No way to know," Lucas said. He was sitting behind the borrowed desk, going through the true crime sites in a desultory way, and had made notes.

He finished, and Virgil asked, "Well? Who put the word out first?"

Lucas looked at his notes. "Anne Cash. She's the one who's been ragging on us the most and she was the one who talked to the *Star-Tribune*, which is where the tipster probably got her name. She had the break about the Bee silverware forty-five minutes after we walked out of the Bee building, and thirty minutes after we got here and talked to Jon. The other sites copied her."

THEY WERE STILL talking when Michelle Cornell called from the law office, and Lucas poked the speaker button on his phone: "Who found the knife?" she asked.

"Guy named Bud Light—real first name is Charles," Lucas said. "I don't know if it'll lead to anyone, but if it does, he's first in line for the money."

"Is it going to lead to anything? Lara is excited," Cornell said.

"We don't know—we'd need to talk to people who had access to the dining room, and the BCA has sent some investigators over to start doing that," Lucas said. "This is the first significant break they've had in twenty years, so they'll hop all over it."

"What are you guys doing?"

"Mostly listening to people talk," Lucas said. "We're supposed to be looking at tips and leads coming from you, and there haven't been any—the BCA is doing the up-front investigation."

"Everything I'm getting is crap," Cornell said. "I don't need your opinion to know that."

"Thanks for being a filter," Lucas said. "We both appreciate it."

WHEN CORNELL RANG off, Virgil took his feet off the desk and asked, "What are we doing?"

Lucas grimaced: "You know that big pile of shit we haven't been reading?"

"Not that! All fourteen hundred pages of it?"

"Yeah. We've got to read it now," Lucas said. "The whole drift has changed. I hope that knife wasn't a plant."

"Don't see how it could be," Virgil said.

"Neither do I."

"But if it is a plant, the dishwasher did it," Virgil said.

"Good thought, but unfortunately, it's not a plant."

They read the rest of the afternoon and into the early evening, and still hadn't gotten more than a third of the way though the files. Virgil took a call from a TV reporter named Daisy Jones, saying that she was about to interview Charles "Bud" Light, and she would like a comment from Virgil. "I already got one from Lucas, and I'd like to get one from you, too. Lucas said it would be okay," she lied.

"That's weird, since Lucas has been sitting six feet from me for the last three hours and hasn't taken any phone calls from TV reporters, including you."

Virgil held his phone out and Lucas said, "Hey, Daisy."

"Ah, shit," she said. "Anyway, give me a comment, Virgie."

"Okay, you ready?"

"I'm ready."

"No comment," Virgil said, and he hung up.

"We really ought to watch the interview," Lucas said.

"Anything's better than reading more of this," Virgil said, dropping a sheaf of printouts on the desktop.

DAISY JONES HAD the best police contacts in the Twin Cities and a way with man-in-the-street interviews. She even *liked* the man in the street, guys like Bud Light, and they liked Daisy back.

Light had done everything but polish his bald spot and the thin brown hair around it may have been battened down with Vaseline, because it sparkled in the TV lights. He was wearing a blue blazer with an unfortunately red-striped dress shirt and clashing blue-green paisley bow tie. He'd worn steel-rimmed spectacles when Lucas and Virgil had talked to him, but he'd taken them off for the television appearance and was squinting at Jones.

He was good at being interviewed.

"I thought, okay, let's think about this some more," he said. "The body was back in the trees, but I'd gone over that scene inch by inch and didn't find anything back there. Just outside the trees, where people walked, I found a nickel . . ."

Jones: "A nickel?"

"Yes. It was useless. It was a 1995, so it could have been dropped by the killer, but it could have been dropped anytime between '95 and last week."

"He's quoting us," Lucas said to Virgil.

"Without attribution," Virgil said.

". . . so I thought, where else would the killer have been? I decided he wouldn't have driven across the ballfields, because people would have seen him doing that from the houses around the park," Light continued. "More likely, he parked in the parking lot, and carried Doris Grandfelt's body to the trees. She was a small woman, her body weighed ninety-two pounds according to the medical examiner, and so . . . mmm . . . it was estimated that she probably weighed a hundred and five pounds when she was alive. Something around there. She'd bled out, lost all her blood, and a typical woman has a little over a gallon of blood in her body."

"How do you know all this?" Jones asked.

"Medical examiner's report, which is online, and the blood part, I googled." He seemed pleased with himself.

"Googled." Jones looked faintly amused. "So you speculated that the killer carried Doris Grandfelt across the ballfields . . ."

"Yes. I thought, if he was in a big hurry, who knows what he might have dropped around the parking lot. I was right—except that he didn't drop the knife, he hid it, by pushing it down into the ground. The butt end of the knife was a half-inch wide and no more than an eighth of an inch thick, so if you pressed it point down into the ground, nobody would ever see it. He was getting rid of evidence in case he got stopped by the police as he escaped the scene."

They talked about the knife, and how Light had extracted it from the ground without actually touching it himself. "Like picking up doggy poop."

Jones: "Doggy poop?"

"Yes. We had a plastic evidence bag and I put my hand inside it, grabbed the end of the knife, then folded the bag over it as I pulled the knife out of the ground. Sealed the bag, the knife untouched by human hands."

"Smart," Jones said.

"He's really good at this," Virgil observed.

"Everybody in America is good at it," Lucas said, leaning his chair back. "Look at casual street interviews, or fan interviews after a game. Everybody knows what to do when you get a shot at being on TV."

Jones said, "Well, thank you very much, Bud . . ."

Light: "Can I say one more thing? Might be important."

Jones said, "Sure."

"We've been talking this whole interview about the killer being male, calling him 'he.' I'm not so sure. If you read the medical examiner's report, you see that Doris Grandfelt was stabbed in the back, just once, and that was fatal," Light said. "The blade went into Doris's heart. I believe that was the first strike, the first attack. I mean, after you did all the other knifings, more than twenty of them on the front of her body, why would you roll her over and stick her in the back, and only once? No. I think the killer came up behind her and stabbed her, and when she fell, did all the other strikes."

"And you think a woman . . . ?"

"Well, I think it could have been," he said. "A man attacking a woman, especially if he'd raped her, would be facing her, wouldn't he? He'd stab her in the throat or chest or somewhere on the front of her body, just like she was . . ."

"Maybe she tried to run."

"Think about that," Light said. "Doris is running away, it seems like somebody chasing her would be striking down at her, not straight in, like the medical examiner's report says," Light said. "That would be hard to do. I think the killer snuck up on her and stuck her. She never saw it coming."

"I can see circumstances where she could be attacked from behind, and then turned . . ."

"So can I. Of course, I can," Light said. "But a number of investigators thought that the sex she'd had was consensual—no sign of sexual violence, no vaginal tearing, just all the knife wounds. Wounds that appeared to be inflicted in a frenzy. Suppose she'd had sex with somebody, that last man who didn't use a condom, and that guy's wife stumbled in on them, and she's the one who did it?"

"An interesting thought," Jones said, not quite blowing him off. "I'm sure the BCA agents will take that into account as they press on with this investigation. I want to thank you . . ."

"THAT *WAS* AN interesting thought," Virgil said. "That it might be a woman."

"Did you know that she'd been stuck once in the back and that was the fatal wound? Is that in the papers somewhere?" Lucas asked.

"I knew she'd been stabbed in the back, but I didn't think about it," Virgil admitted. "I knew she'd been stuck a lot, but I wasn't paying any attention to which might have been the fatal one."

"Let's look."

They went through the stacks of papers, found the ME's report. "Sure enough," Lucas said, when he'd found the right section of the report. "Once in the back, into the heart, and she was alive at that point."

Virgil, feet back on the desk, pointed a yellow pencil at Lucas. "Okay, let's suppose you're the attacker. You've just had sex, you've ejaculated . . . are you going to be in a murderous frenzy? Usually, wouldn't you be feeling pretty mellow?"

"Depends on the guy. Women get killed by guys *while* they're having sex. Or maybe she wouldn't do him a second time . . ."

"Thin," Virgil said. "If she wasn't up for a rerun, you'd think he'd try raping her before stabbing her, whatever it was, twenty-some times. There'd be some sign of an attempted rape. Vaginal damage, semen on her leg or wherever. Some defensive evidence, skin under her fingernails, blood in her mouth."

Lucas nodded: "True, but you have to keep in mind that we're dealing with somebody having a psychotic break. You can't predict what the killer might do or not do."

"Also true," Virgil said. "But I'm thinking now we can't take women off the table. I'm thinking sixty-forty the killer was male, but forty is a large number."

"I'd agree, except for one thing: size ten-and-a-half Nike shoes," Lucas said. "That's a goddamn big woman, and she was wearing men's shoes. Even goddamn big women wear women's shoes."

THAT EVENING, THEY took Weather to dinner. She disagreed with Virgil's sixty-forty, arguing that it might be closer to fifty-fifty, a woman as the killer. "If you close your eyes and think about the totality of what was done to Doris, and how it was done . . . I can visualize a woman doing it, as much as a man. I think a man could have stabbed her, but I think he'd also batter her, and as I understand it, she wasn't battered or choked."

"A big woman, wearing those ten-and-a-half Nikes," Lucas said.

"What about the man who discovered the body? What was he wearing while he was trampling around the scene?" Weather asked.

"He was eliminated—he was wearing eleven-and-a-half Adidas," Lucas said.

"A smart woman, to get away with this without leaving a single clue," Weather retorted. "She planned it all out, and very carefully. Nothing was spontaneous. You don't know where Doris was killed, or exactly when. The killer didn't leave any DNA, anywhere. The BCA didn't recover a murder weapon, all they knew was that the killer used a knife of some kind. She must have scouted the dump site, must have known she'd leave footprints. Hence, the shoes."

"I could use the word 'hence' in a novel," Virgil said.

Weather: "Shut up."

They talked about it for a while, then Lucas and Weather went home and Virgil checked in to the Radisson Blu Mall of America.

After dropping his luggage in the room, he walked down to the mall, to Barnes & Noble, and found that they had three copies of his third novel and one of his second. They were shelved spine-out, so he surreptitiously moved some books around, then replaced his so the covers were face-out.

That done, he bought a Cinnabon, ate it, went back to his room, tried to work for a while, and talked to Frankie, who agreed with Weather: "You idiots should have figured this out a long time ago," she said.

"We're not the idiots, we weren't on the case," Virgil said.

"Well, *some* idiots should have figured it out," Frankie said.

When Virgil went to bed, he closed his eyes like Weather had suggested, and created the attack in his mind. After a few minutes of that, he got up, dug out the ME's report, and looked at a diagram of the wounds.

The back wound began slightly above the level where the knife tip entered Grandfelt's heart—but only slightly, perhaps a half-inch. Picking up a pen, he tried to replicate how a man would have stabbed Grandfelt, and how a woman would.

Grandfelt was short; a man of any height at all, anything five-eight or taller, would almost always be stabbing downward, assuming an overhand grip on the knife. More sharply downward than Grandfelt had been stabbed.

A woman of average height or slightly shorter would probably have stabbed Grandfelt as shown in the diagram, at a much lower angle. A man or a woman stabbing with an underhand grip on the knife would almost certainly be stabbing with an upward motion . . .

"Holy shit," Virgil muttered out loud. "It *was* a woman."

That decided, he slept like a log until seven o'clock in the morning, when he got a call from the BCA duty officer, who knew a couple of things about a violent change in the direction of the case, but not much, and some of what he knew turned out to be incorrect. One of the things he got wrong was when he referred to Charles "Bud" Light as "Bug Light."

Off the phone, Virgil called Lucas, who groaned and asked, "What now?"

"Somebody murdered Bud Light last night," Virgil said. "I'll pick you up in half an hour."

LUCAS WALKED DOWN the driveway to Virgil's Tahoe, looking sleepy, but otherwise sleek as a melanistic mink in black slacks, black jacket, and white dress shirt, with the top two buttons of the shirt undone. He made Virgil feel like he'd just fallen off a turnip truck.

"What the fuck is this?" Lucas asked when he got in the passenger seat.

"I don't know," Virgil said, as he pulled away from the curb. "I had two thoughts—the original killer is back, or one of the true-crimers is trying to eliminate the competition for the five million. Then I had a third thought . . ."

"Which was?"

"He was staying at the Wee Blue Inn," Virgil said. "Could have been a routine bump and run that went bad."

"The place *is* a shithole," Lucas said. "I went there once to talk to a guy who'd bought a boom box we were looking for, and we were sitting in the café and a cockroach crawled across the table. You know, like it was a pet."

"Whatever. One more thing: the original killer was a woman," Virgil said.

"Tell me," Lucas said, and Virgil told him.

"I'm not a hundred percent on that, but I'll go to fifty-fifty like Weather was arguing for," Lucas said. "I don't think a woman would have thought of those shoes. Some things are just *too* smart."

FOUR COP CARS, a crime scene unit, and a medical examiner investigator's car were parked sideways in the Wee Blue Inn's parking lot, behind a half block of yellow crime-scene tape. A small but growing crowd of true-crimers were gathered on the civilian side.

The Wee Blue Inn had once, long before, been a bad supper club on St. Paul's east side, later converted to a motor-hotel, as the sign outside still read, with an eight-table café at the far end of it. The café came with a beer license, which kept it solvent. A long, low, narrow building, the inn had a rounded roof, like a Quonset hut. The exterior was covered with rough, dirty, once-white plaster that reminded Lucas of a Dutch painting he'd seen in one of Weather's art books.

Virgil had been there a number of times as a St. Paul detective, usually for an assault or rape, but never for a murder. He and Lucas got out of the Tahoe and slipped under the tape. Anne Cash, who was in the crowd, yelled at them—"Marshal! Flowers!"—but they ignored her and walked up to the open motel room door where the cops were clustered.

A BCA agent named Carroll Bayes was standing exactly in the doorway and Virgil, coming up behind him, said, "Move over, C."

Bayes, a tall man wearing a straw-colored Panama hat, looked over his shoulder and said, "Hey, Virgie. Not much to see."

"Got to look anyway," and Bayes made room for Virgil and Lucas.

Light was lying flat on his back, arms stretched out to the side. He was wearing knit pajama bottoms and a white V-neck tee-shirt with a slash of blood down his face and onto the shirt. Another small pool of blood had collected under his head. Virgil and Lucas could smell it, the sticky raw meat odor.

They could see blood trails down the side of Light's face; gravity pulling the blood down through surface veins when the heart stopped beating. If Light looked like anything, he looked sad, rather than angry or frightened.

A St. Paul detective was talking to a medical examiner's investigator, and they both nodded at Virgil and Lucas.

Lucas said, "Not shot."

"No. Looks like he was hit hard with something that had a corner," Bayes said. "A club of some kind. Busted his skull. The blood on the floor is coming out of the head wound—he was hit from behind. His wallet is down on the bedstand, wasn't touched: I could see the corner of a twenty."

"No weapon?"

"Haven't found anything. Looks like he was eating dinner, there's a plastic bowl with a little chili in it," Bayes said. "Somebody came in, maybe he knew whoever it was, he turned his back . . ."

Virgil asked, "Who found him?"

Bayes turned to the parking lot and nodded at a couple of uniformed cops talking to Dahlia Blair. "His partner, name of Dahlia Blair. I understand that you guys met her. The victim worked for her . . . more or less worked. She didn't pay him, he wasn't an employee. He's retired, former post office employee. He volunteered to come along on her *investigations*."

"We saw him on TV yesterday, on Daisy Jones's talk show. Talking about the knife he found."

"Really," Bayes said. "Does that go anywhere?"

"I don't know," Virgil said. "Is Blair staying in the same room?"

"No. She's down at the other end. She says she walked down here to get him this morning, and the door was open an inch or two. Blood on the inside doorknob, like maybe he tried to get away from whoever hit him," Bayes said. "Anyway, when she knocked, the door moved, and she saw a foot. That's what she says. No video cameras on the motel. They have enough trouble here that they don't want to provide evidence against their customers and maybe have to go to court."

"You think she might have done it?" Virgil asked.

Bayes said, "She's on the list, but she didn't do it. We'll talk to her some, but, no. She's harmless."

"All right," Lucas said. He and Virgil had both known Bayes for years, and he was competent. Lucas took a last look around, and said to Virgil, "Let's go talk to Dahlia."

THEY STEPPED AWAY from the door and Virgil paused, looked left and said, "Lara Grandfelt."

"That's all we needed," Lucas said. Grandfelt was behind the crime scene tape with Wise, her personal assistant. "We should talk to her first."

They went that way, told a cop on the crime scene tape to let Grandfelt and Wise through, and took them far enough into the parking lot that the true-crimers couldn't hear the conversation, although they were making movies.

Grandfelt said, "I guess it's true? One of the true crime people is dead?"

"Clubbed to death, it looks like, murdered," Lucas said. "Seemed like a harmless guy. He's the one who found the knife yesterday."

"So my reward wound up getting somebody else murdered," Grandfelt said. She wanted to hear a denial.

She didn't get it from Virgil, who said, "Maybe. We don't know much yet."

Grandfelt turned away from him, staring at the cops around the motel room door, and then said, "I never wanted . . ."

"We warned you that people could get hurt," Lucas said. "Now, somebody has. There's a possibility that he was killed by an addict or a robber, but he had money that was easy to see and it's still there."

"Oh, God. Oh . . . God."

"We don't have anything more to tell you at this point," Lucas said. "We won't be running the investigation, that'll be the St. Paul cops, with the BCA looking in because of the connection to your sister's murder."

"Should we stop this?" Wise asked.

"That's up to you," Lucas said. "The discovery of the knife and now the murder are shaking things loose. We might actually be able to find out who killed Doris, if this murder was done by the original killer. But . . . who knows?"

Virgil plucked at Lucas's jacket sleeve and said, "Let's go talk to the witness. Miz Grandfelt, we gotta put you guys back on the other side of the line."

They did that, and Grandfelt and Wise headed for a waiting car, some of the crowd of true-crimers hurrying after them, cameras up.

AS THEY WALKED toward Dahlia Blair, Lucas asked quietly, "Do you know what a shotgun mike is?"

Virgil half-turned, then shook his head. "Ah, shit."

"Yeah, when I saw it, I thought, Is that a suppressor? It wasn't," Lucas said. "But it might have been pointed at us when we were talking to Lara."

DAHLIA BLAIR WAS a thin, tense brunette with short-chewed nails. She kept reaching two fingers toward her lips like she'd quit smoking the week before. Lucas knew both of the St. Paul cops who were with her, and they said, "Lucas," and "Big guy."

Blair was wearing a short-sleeved shirt and kept rubbing her arms and said, "You know what I can't get over? Charles didn't have anyone. No one. No brothers or sisters and his parents are dead. He was never married. He was like a lonely little church mouse. There's no one in the world who will . . . will, you know, mourn for him, except me and a couple other people who didn't . . . pay much attention to him."

She rubbed her arms and finished: "I don't know."

"Where were you overnight?" Virgil asked.

She pointed: "Down there. Last room."

"From what you said before, you and Charles didn't have a relationship," Virgil said.

"No, no, not at all. He's from the same town I'm from," Blair said. "We're from North Platte. Nebraska . . . it's . . . Ah, jeez."

Tears trickled down her cheeks and Virgil asked, "How did you wind up here? I mean, at the Wee Blue Inn?"

"Cheap," she said. "What with gas and everything, from North Platte, we didn't have much money for other things. Charles used to deliver my mail before he retired, that's how I knew him. He thought I was kind of a big deal because I've got sixteen thousand followers on my blog, but I'm nothing like Anne Cash. All the money I make barely pays for the Wi-Fi. I thought this could be my big break and Charles wanted to come along. He was lonely, I guess, and he had the metal detector and I thought what the heck . . ."

"Why do you think . . ." Lucas gestured toward the room where Light was killed.

"Oh, it's definitely linked to the Grandfelt murder, one way or another."

"Why do you think that?" Virgil asked.

"Didn't that other officer tell you? Officer Baily?"

"Bayes."

"Bayes," she said. "Didn't he tell you about the tip?"

Lucas and Virgil looked at each other, and Virgil asked, "What tip?"

"Somebody called Bud yesterday evening. Six o'clock or so, after dinner. At McDonald's. Said he had important information that would lead to the killer. Bud asked the guy why he was getting the call, and the guy said because he'd seen Bud on TV with Daisy Jones. He looked at our site and found our phone numbers. We listed our phone numbers for tips."

"What was the tip?"

"The man didn't say. He asked if we got the money, if we'd share it, and if we would, if we could keep his name out of it. Bud told him we could try. The man said he had to think some more and would call us back this morning. Bud told him to call either one of us and he said he would. He hasn't."

"Did you actually hear the call?"

"Yeah, I was sitting right across the table from him in McDonald's, he put his phone on speaker."

"And you told all this to officer Bayes?" Lucas asked.

"Yes, all of it. Why didn't he tell you?"

"He told us to talk to you—I guess he wanted us to hear it first-hand," Virgil said.

"If this guy calls you back, don't mess around," Lucas said. "It might be messing around that got Bud killed. Call us. Immediately."

Virgil: "Did you see anything at all that worried you last night? See anything that, you know, might give us something to work with?"

She ticked a finger at him and said, "Yes! I told the other officers.

I saw a white SUV three times, and it looked . . ." She straightened and said, "Like that one!"

She pointed at Virgil's Tahoe. "That's mine," Virgil said.

"Well, it looked like that . . . kinda." She was peering at Virgil's truck. "But yours isn't really white, is it? It's more cream color. This one was white-white, like a business panel van, but it was big like yours, not a small SUV. We were coming from the park and I saw it behind us, and then when we got into town—we weren't familiar with St. Paul so we got off at the wrong place and went across a bridge into downtown and had to circle back—and I saw it again, and I didn't think anything about it, then. But then it passed us, I think it was the same one, when we got here. I was in the parking lot and saw it go past, and that time, I remembered the other times, and I thought, That's odd. Maybe somebody was following us to see where we were going, or maybe if we had contacts with the police or something. I didn't see it after that."

Virgil: "You didn't see any license plate numbers . . ."

"No."

"You think whoever it was might have seen which rooms you went in?" Lucas asked.

"I don't know," Blair said. "After the call from the tipster guy, we came over here and checked in, and I wanted to talk to the desk clerk for a minute about possible . . . amenities . . . and Charles went down to his room by himself. The last time I saw him was when he walked out of the motel office. Just his back. I didn't even say good night because I was talking to the clerk. About amenities." She looked at the motel and said, "I'm such an idiot. We were lucky we got hot water."

WHEN THEY'D FINISHED talking to Blair, they walked back over to Bayes and Lucas asked, "You bag his phone?"

"Yup. It's on the way to the lab. The St. Paul guys got the incoming, but it was incoming from Caccamano's pay phone."

Lucas: "The restaurant? Down on Seventh?"

"Yeah, they actually got a coin-op pay phone, down a hall, around a corner by the back entrance," Bayes said. "St. Paul is telling me they haven't found anyone who saw a guy making a phone call there last night. They're still looking."

"Have to be a regular, to even know the phone was there," Virgil said.

"They probably got five hundred regulars and a couple of thousand casuals, and nobody knows anybody else's name. So . . ."

Lucas said, "I eat there occasionally. I've seen a camera by that back door, coming in from the parking lot."

"There's a camera, but it's on the wall above the phone, and it's pointing at the door," Bayes said. "Doesn't pick up phone users at all."

"That's convenient," Virgil said.

"Yeah. That was our big hope, for a while," Bayes said. "We still got a chance. It was raining pretty hard at the time of the phone call, lot of people coming in from the parking lot. Trouble is, most of them were wearing hats and rain hoods . . . might ID a few of them. The phone call only lasted for about a minute and five seconds, so . . . the guy wasn't on the phone long."

"Fingerprint on the coin? There couldn't be many people using the phone."

"Coins have been bagged. That's our other big hope."

They talked for a few more minutes, and Lucas looked at Light again. He was still dead. "Didn't bleed much," he said.

"Looks to me like he was only hit once," Bayes said. "Maybe the killer didn't actually mean to kill him."

"Dahlia told you about the van?"

"Yeah, St. Paul's got two guys walking the street, looking for cameras. Nothing yet."

They left Bayes in the doorway, and Lucas said, "We should get out of here. All these cameras and microphones are making me nervous."

"I want to talk to Blair again. Just take a minute."

Virgil spotted her on the edge of the crowd, waved her under the tape, and he gave her his business card. "My personal cell phone number is on the back. I want you to post it on your site—ask the tipster to call me."

"Fat chance," Lucas said.

"Yeah, but it's a chance," Virgil said.

She said she would do it right away. They put her back under the tape and walked over to Virgil's truck.

"You're gonna get a million crazies," Lucas said.

"It's my backup phone. Basically a burner. I can throw it away when the case is over."

"Huh. That's not bad. Maybe I'll get one myself."

"What now? BCA?" Virgil asked.

"Let's get some coffee, so we can think."

THEY WOUND UP in a Caribou Coffee in downtown St. Paul, got a coffee for Virgil and a hot chocolate for Lucas, sat at a table where

Virgil asked the key question: why would somebody risk murdering a man who seemed like a nonentity? It wouldn't be the tipster—the tipster wanted to use Light, not kill him.

"I can see three motives—probably the same ones you see," Lucas said. "And they are . . ."

Virgil considered for a moment then said, "One: money. He was the leading contender to get the five million. Somebody killed him to eliminate competition for the money."

"That's one," Lucas said.

"Is this an IQ test? If it is, I can think of *four* possible motives. So, two. Despite appearances and what Dahlia Blair said, Bud actually had a little more on the ball than people knew. Maybe the tipster called him again, and something was said that gave away an identity. Bud stupidly makes a call to the wrong person—the Grandfelt killer."

"That's two. We don't have to worry about that one, because the BCA has his phone."

"Three: his murder has nothing to do with anything," Virgil said. "He was in a bad motel that was used by druggies and street people. Somebody tried to rob him, he fought back, and got hit with a stick or a club of some kind but didn't go down completely—he crawled at least as far as the door. Rather than fight someone who might fight back, or even scream—and maybe he did scream—the killer ran."

"That's my three," Lucas said. "What's your fourth one?"

"He's a true-crimer with a metal detector. What if there's something else out there? In the park? What if Doris's killer knows he—or she—lost something during the attack, and doesn't know where, but it could be used to identify him? A cuff or a ring or something. Or maybe Doris had something he gave her, and when he tried to find it on her body, he couldn't."

"Nah," Lucas said. "That's too TV."

"Yeah, you're right. Forget it."

Lucas took a sip of his hot chocolate and squinted out at the street. The street was empty, a concrete canyon. He said, "I don't like the money motive much. Those women are a little goofy and very competitive, maybe even money-hungry, but I don't think they could do that."

"You haven't met them all," Virgil said. "You haven't even met very many of them."

"True. Still. I don't think any of them could do that. They're a bunch of slightly barmy ladies. And I don't think it's Grandfelt's killer. How would Grandfelt's killer even know about a tip? Even if he did know about it, how would he know how to find Bud? And I have to think that whoever killed Grandfelt would be a lot more lethal than going after a guy with a club."

"A club's quiet," Virgil said.

"So's a hammer or a knife or an axe," Lucas said. "Kill him with one whack, Lizzie Borden notwithstanding." After another moment of silence, he continued: "Street people, a junkie, a robbery . . . A meth freak is a possibility. Maybe the strongest. But that's not what we're doing. Right now. You and I."

Virgil leaned into the table. "I don't see us investigating Bud's murder at all. St. Paul and the BCA got the troops, and we're supposed to be on the Grandfelt cold case and watching the true crime people. I read the interviews with Stephanie Brady . . ."

"Who's that again?" Lucas asked.

"Didn't spend enough time with the paper, huh?" Virgil asked. "She's Grandfelt's last roommate. I'd like to wring her out. See if there's *anything* that got missed."

"That's a thought," Lucas agreed. "Something else. When you look at these true crime sites, they've got a lot of readers. The readers are out there doing their own research, and they're kicking into the whole online discussion. That could be a resource for us. I'd like to get together with the owners of the biggest sites, see if we could set up something."

"Resource for what?"

"Like they could go through a zillion old newspaper and magazine stories, look at pictures and hook people together and see who was talking to who, way back then. Look for Doris. The 'net was already getting big back then. I know AOL was around in the nineties . . ."

"Not a bad idea," Virgil said, "But when and where? We don't want them all, that's a three-ring circus."

"I sort of hate to suggest it, but the kids are still at summer camp and Weather's working until late in the afternoon. We could meet at my place."

"Dahlia Blair isn't one of the bigger ones, but she knows them all," Virgil said. "We could ask her to organize it."

"There's one other thing that I'd like to look at," Lucas said. "Your BCA guys should have a list of every single person who had access to Bee's executive dining room. Including the cooks and the dishwasher guy. I'd like to see the list in case it rings any bells downstream."

"I'll get it," Virgil said. "In the meantime, the true-crimers and then the roommate."

VIRGIL WENT OUT to Dahlia Blair's website, which was headlining the murder of Charles Light, found her telephone number, and called.

She was still at the motel and said eight or ten true-crimers were still there, including Anne Cash.

"Where'd everybody go?" Virgil asked.

"Scattered around. Some went over to the park, they've got two metal detectors now. Some other ones went over to Bee, to see if they could catch employees coming out."

"Stay there. We need to talk to you and Cash. Separately from the others."

"I'll tell Anne, though I don't like her very much. She doesn't like me, either. We stole some of her readers when Bud found the knife and then got killed."

THERE WAS STILL a small crowd of true-crimers and a few locals watching the crime scene processing when they got back to the motel. They pulled to the side of the street, and watched as Blair nudged Cash, and the two women started walking over.

Lucas dropped the passenger-side window and when they came up, said, "Hop in the back."

They did, and Cash asked, "What's up?"

Virgil said to Lucas, "You talk."

Lucas: "Most of the true crime hints and suggestions are going through Michelle Cornell. She's supposed to filter what we get from you guys, find anything that might be good, and send it on to us."

"We know all that," Cash said.

"Shut up and let him talk," Blair said.

"You shut up!" Cash snapped back.

"Both of you shut up," Lucas said. "Michelle hasn't sent us one thing that even remotely seems to be a possibility—she hasn't sent anything that we haven't thought of, or the BCA hasn't investigated already. You guys might be a resource for us, but the present arrangement isn't working. We'd like to get the biggest website owners together at my place this afternoon. Talk about what you could really do for us, and what we could do for you."

Blair said, "A lot of us don't get along that well. We're competitors."

"You could tamp down the competition if we gave you big sites an equal edge against all the little ratshit sites that are starting up," Lucas said. "I looked and there are about a thousand of them."

Cash said, "I'll talk."

Blair said, "I'll come, but I don't think I'm staying here. After Bud."

"Everything you do here, you could probably do from your home," Lucas said. "Standing around behind the police tape isn't getting you anything."

"Pictures. On-the-scene commentary," Cash said.

"All right. But. If you'd be interested in doing this, we don't want a crowd, because a crowd is impossible to talk to. We'd want the owners of five or six of the biggest sites . . ."

Blair and Cash looked at each other, then Blair said, "Ruby Weitz is here. Karen Moss."

"Sally Bulholtz," Cash said. "Everybody else is small."

"Mary Albanese," Blair said. "She was here this morning for a little while, I think she went over to the park."

"She's smart, she'd be good," Cash said. "She used to be a professor or something."

Virgil had been making notes and he said, "That's six, including you two. That's about all we can handle. Could you guys get them together?"

"They'll jump at it," Cash said. "Where do you want us to come?"

Lucas gave them his address, and said, "Don't pass the address around. I'm nervous giving it to you two."

Cash popped the door on her side and said, "We'll see you there. Three o'clock."

WHEN THEY WERE walking away, Virgil said, "Let's go find the roommate. Brady."

"The BCA should have an address for her," Lucas said. "Make a call."

In the truck, Virgil called Jon Duncan and got Stephanie Brady's address, workplace, and phone number. When Virgil called her, she said her office was on the south side of St. Paul, near the airport, and that she was eating lunch across the street. She'd be back in fifteen minutes.

12

The offices of Canton, Domingo and Brady, CPAs, were in a small, freestanding yellow stucco building two blocks from the Mississippi, with an Apple/Mac computer repair service on one side and lactation consultants on the other. Before they went in, Virgil checked his backup cell, and found that he'd already had two calls. He read the voicemail transcripts and deleted them.

Lucas: "Crap?"

"Crap."

"Toldja."

STEPHANIE BRADY HAD a lot of freckles. A lot.

She was slender and tall with red-brown hair, a thin, long nose, wore a greenish suit; Lucas noticed that she had large hands, like a piano player has in the movies.

"I've been trying to forget the murder for twenty years," she said, when she came to the receptionist's desk to meet them. "Come on back to our conference room."

"We saw in the interviews you did at the time of Doris's murder that the investigators came to you three times, for interviews. They also picked up all of Doris's possessions," Lucas said as they took chairs around a circular mahogany table in the conference room. One wall was a bookcase stuffed with tax code volumes that appeared to be unused.

"That's correct," she said. "Doris had an expensive wardrobe and they wondered if she'd gotten gifts from guys she'd dated . . . or if . . . they were wondering if she'd been paid, you know, to have sex with guys and used the money to buy the stuff."

"I take it she couldn't have paid for it with the salaries you guys were on?" Virgil asked.

She shook her head. "No way. Some of those shoes . . . they'd be way more than we made in a week, and she had lots of them. I tried not to be curious about it, you know, because she said she got financial help from her parents. I suspected that wasn't true, because she didn't want to talk about it—but why wouldn't you talk about it, if you were interested in fashion, and the money came from some innocent place like your parents? The investigators told me later that she didn't get money from her parents."

"Did you go out with her? Did you hang out together, go clubbing?" Virgil asked.

"Only once in a while," Brady said. "We'd go over to First Avenue if there was a rumor that Prince might show up. I was a huge Prince fan, so I'd go with, if she'd heard something."

"The source of the money—you didn't inquire or suspect anything about a specific guy?"

"No." She hesitated, and then, "That's . . . why I wondered if she got money from them. There seemed to be several of them. Sometimes she . . . smelled like sex, if you know what I mean."

Lucas nodded: "We do."

"One thing we didn't do was double-date," Brady said. "I didn't date much anyway, I was too busy. I always wanted to be a CPA because they make the big bucks. That takes extra schoolwork and also work experience—a minimum of two thousand hours of work experience—and you have to study for the exam, which is no walk in the park. Anyway, when I wasn't working, I was usually studying and taking classes, not going out to clubs."

"Doris wasn't interested in being a CPA?"

"She said she'd do it later. You know, when she was in her thirties. After she was married."

Virgil: "Huh." He looked at Lucas.

"I got nothing," Lucas said.

"There was one thing, that the original investigators didn't get, and I don't think is important, but I thought later, like, years later, that maybe I should have mentioned," Brady said.

Virgil: "Yeah?"

"I had this old Canon film camera. I think it's called a Rebel. I only had one lens for it. Anyway, Doris used it more than I did. She liked to look at the pictures and she had a lot of them printed. I've still got the photos, in a box, that she took. I looked through them years after she was killed. I didn't see much of interest, but I do have quite a few photos."

Virgil said, "We'd like to see them. Maybe they'd show the people she hung out with; or executives she was talking to?"

"Maybe. I haven't looked at them in forever."

Brady had clients that afternoon, but they arranged to meet her at her house that night in the Highland Park neighborhood, a half mile or so from Lucas's house.

Out in the parking lot, Lucas said, "Photographs. This could be something."

Virgil had turned off his phone while they were talking to Brady, and when he turned it back on, he thumbed through three more voicemail transcripts and at the last one, he stopped, and said, "Oh-oh."

"What?"

"Guy says, 'I was the guy who called Bud Light last night. I was the one who slept with Doris Grandfelt the day she was killed, who used the rubber with the sperm killer. That was the tip I gave Bud. I'm out driving around for a while and if you don't call me, I'll throw this phone down a sewer.'"

"Whoa," Lucas said. "Call him. Put it on speaker."

VIRGIL CALLED. A man answered, a baritone with gravel, and Virgil asked, "Who is this?"

"Never mind. Is this Davenport or Flowers?"

"We're both here," Lucas said. "How'd you get this number?"

"They posted it on Bud Light's site. I heard he was murdered and I was watching the site and called as soon as I saw the number."

"How'd you know that somebody had sex with Doris Grandfelt with a condom?" Virgil asked.

"Because it was me," the man said. "Also, I read all the stuff about the rape, the stuff that's online, the investigation files. They said she'd had two sexual contacts and the first guy had used a rubber with a sperm killer. If they got any details on that, you can tell them that I was *not* using a Trojan which most everybody else did, back then. The ones I used were called Hot Rods and didn't have a sperm killer, so I bought a sperm killer gel and lubed it up myself. I didn't want to knock up some hooker. I bet the gel was different than whatever Trojan used."

Lucas glanced at Virgil and nodded. The guy sounded convincing. On the other hand, that's what hustlers did: they sounded convincing.

"You're looking for a piece of the five million?" Virgil asked.

"How'd you guess? Also, I've always felt a little guilty about not calling the police after I heard about the murder. I was scared. The BCA seemed desperate to hang someone, and I wasn't going to volunteer for the honor. When I was a kid, I had some trouble with the cops. I might have fit a frame."

"You need to come in for a full interview," Lucas said.

"Not yet. I'm still scared."

"Not gonna get five million from what you've told us so far," Virgil said. "No way that a spermicide clue is gonna get us anywhere."

"That was just to demonstrate that I'm not bullshitting you. Here's what you can use: Can you write this down?"

Virgil took out his main cell phone and hit "voice memos," and said, "Yes. Go ahead."

"There was guy who was a night bartender at a strip joint on Hennepin Avenue in the early 2000s. I forget the name of the place. I don't think the name is the same anymore. Everybody called the bartender Inspector Gadget because the guy used to sell these . . . mmm . . . custom dildoes. Anyway, his real name is Roger Jepson. J-e-p-s-o-n. He worked at a bunch of places as a bartender and sometimes as a bouncer, but he wasn't very good at either thing. He now works in a body shop off Highway 13 in Savage, called Loco's. Or he did a couple of years ago, when I saw him there, when I took my truck in. Back in the day, he'd set Doris up with customers. I was one of those."

Virgil: "Jepson was a pimp?"

"Not exactly. He didn't do anything for Doris except make introductions," the man said. "I don't think she paid him anything. Might have rolled him a piece of ass from time to time. Roger was not a looker, wasn't big with pretty women."

Lucas: "But you got an introduction?"

"Right. Doris was fun. She'd fuck right back at you," the man said. "Most hookers, you'd be banging away and they'd be reading their phone over your shoulder."

"So you patronized working girls . . ."

"Not street girls. I was careful, always used a rubber and paid them a lot, to get a classier chick. Doris fit all of that: an accountant, fun, she'd do you for five hundred bucks, which was a lot at the time. And with her, it wasn't just the sex. She'd meet you someplace and dance, and then go back to your place. Like an actual date. I figured that's what got her killed: she went back to the wrong guy's place."

"Did she ever take you to her place, or to her office?"

"No. I never even knew where she worked. Or lived. She told me she was an accountant, but we didn't talk business. I didn't know she worked at Bee until I saw the news stories about her getting raped and killed. I don't think she wanted me to know more personal stuff."

"Somebody murdered Bud Light last night, but we can't figure out how the killer even knew where he was. Did you talk to anyone about making the call?"

"Not a single person. Not a single fuckin' person. I'm talking about how I used to go out with hookers. I don't want anyone to know that. Not now. I'm respectable. Back when I was a kid, it wouldn't have been so bad if people found out. Now I'm in business. So no: I didn't talk to anybody. I got no idea where Bud was staying."

Virgil took a shot: "Where are you right now?"

The man said, "Somewhere in the Twin Cities metropolitan area. Or western Wisconsin. Listen, I been reading up on you two guys, on the crime sites. I think you got a chance to catch the killer. If you think I can help you with something else, put up a note on the Anne-CashInvestigations true crime site that says, 'Big Dave, call home' and I'll call this number. Also, I've recorded this call, in case this info gets you somewhere. I'll want my cut of the five mil."

Virgil took another shot: "So your name is David?"

The man said, "No. And guess what? I'm not big. Now I'm going to throw this particular phone down a sewer. Don't ask me to call unless you're serious—these things cost twenty bucks apiece."

"Wait, wait, wait," Virgil said. "You think it's possible that Jepson killed her?"

"Nah. Not from what I read in those files, all that stabby shit. He was a pretty mellow guy. I think it was real, too, the mellow. Everybody said so."

"Why wouldn't he have called us?"

"Same reason I didn't. Doris's murder was a big deal. I believe everybody who knew her or slept with her was running for cover. She had professional people as customers. Who wants to get his name in the paper as a john? Or as a pimp? Or a rape and murder suspect?"

"Why do you say 'rape' like you knew she was raped?"

"Because that's what the cop files say, and the newspapers said, back when she was killed. That she was raped and stabbed. Listen, Doris didn't have many customers. If Roger hooked her up with someone and she got murdered by a crazy guy that very night . . . and this killer sounds like a maniac . . . then Roger would know who he was. I believe he would have called you. If he didn't, he probably didn't hook her up with anyone. She probably went somewhere private with someone, got raped and murdered. That second sex guy, the guy with the DNA . . . he's the guy you're looking for."

THEN HE WAS gone, a light blinking out. Virgil looked at his phone for a few seconds, said, "Damnit," and redialed. Nothing.

"Down the sewer pipe," Lucas said.

Virgil tried once more, got nothing. "What do you think?"

"We need to talk to Jepson."

"Loco's body shop . . ." Virgil punched it into his phone. "Well, it still exists. We can be there in half an hour. If you want the thrill of lights and a siren, we could cut three minutes off that."

"You're a fuckin' drama queen, you know that? Everybody says so. No lights, no sirens, just . . . peace and quiet. But hurry a little."

"You think this is real."

"It feels that way," Lucas said. "It feels like we got something."

LOCO'S BODY & TIRE was on the frontage road off Highway 13, on the south side of the metro area. If the sign outside hadn't tipped a stranger to its purpose, it might have been reckoned a junkyard. A long, bare-metal building with a corrugated steel roof, it was surrounded by cars sunk in islands of weeds, either in the process of being stripped for parts or waiting for trips to an actual junkyard. The front of the place had two overhead doors, with four hoists visible inside, one occupied by a battered Subaru, the other by a beat-up Ford pickup.

The interior was as junky as the outside: a circle of salvaged car seats sat inside the entry door, around a rickety table covered with empty Coke and beer cans, and an oversized ashtray. Shoulder-high piles of worn tires were stacked against one wall. Red tool chests sat between the hoists, with steel wheels hung from the walls over a "For Sale" sign, on which the local wit had scrawled "cheap" with black paint. The whole place smelled of diesel exhaust, and the metal walls carried a patina of exhaust oil and dust.

Two men were lounging on the car seats, two more were working on the vehicles on the hoists, all four of them in oil-spotted coveralls. Virgil parked at the entrance and he and Lucas got out of the Tahoe and walked to the two men on the car seats.

"Can I help you?" one of the men asked; he sounded doubtful. Virgil's Tahoe was ten years too young for Loco's.

"Is Roger Jepson around?" Virgil asked.

The man asked, "Who's askin'?" while the second man glanced at the guy who was working on the pickup, who'd paused in his work to look at Lucas and Virgil.

Lucas said, "I'm a U.S. Marshal, my partner's with the state BCA . . ."

Virgil asked the man at the pickup, "Are you Roger?"

The man nodded and said, "I guess. U.S. Marshals? I haven't done nothing."

"We don't think you have, but we do need to talk," Virgil said. He looked around, then added, "Privately."

Jepson shrugged and said, "I guess we could go in the office. There's no place to sit . . ."

"That's okay," Lucas said.

Jepson tore a half dozen blue paper towels off a roll that sat on one of the red tool carts, used them to wipe his hands, and said, "This way."

He was a bulky man with a sandpapered face, pasty white, like a prison guard who worked too many night shifts. He walked past them, threw the towels in a trash can, walked to a man-door at the edge of the building. The office smelled the same way as the shop, of diesel fuel with an overtone of hot dogs. A short grimy counter held a rack of tire advertisements, a cash register, and a microwave.

Jepson went behind the counter, leaned on it, and asked, 'What's up?"

THEY TOLD HIM what was up, and he said, "I was afraid that's what it was. One of her clients ratted me out? Wanted that five million?"

"You don't seem too upset," Virgil said.

"I don't even know if what I was doing was a crime—I'd say, 'Bill seems like a nice guy' and Doris would say, 'I'll check him out.' She'd check him out and maybe the guy gets laid and gives her a gift," Jepson said. "Did I commit a crime? If I did, doesn't it fall under the statue of limitations?"

"That does, if it was a crime, and I'm not sure it was," Lucas said. "But murder doesn't fall under the statute of limitations, if you were an accomplice."

"I wasn't. I didn't have anything to do with her business," Jepson said. "When she got to feeling grateful, from time to time, she'd stop over to my place. I appreciated that."

Virgil held up his hands: "We don't think you had anything to do with the murder, Roger. Not at this point anyway. We do think it's possible that you know the killer, even if you don't know that he's the killer."

"Okay. One big problem, though. These guys, I'd get to know them across the bar. Dick, Joe, Mike, whatever, I didn't know their last names," Jepson said. "It was twenty years ago, guys. I didn't know them that well."

"How many customers did she have?" Lucas asked.

Jepson stuck a finger in one ear and wriggled it, thinking. "Maybe . . . three or four at any one time. Maybe not four . . . Some would drop out, some she wouldn't go back to. In the time I was talking to her, maybe for two years or so, probably a dozen."

"Why would they drop out?" Virgil asked. "Do you think one of them might have come back at her?"

Jepson shrugged. "I don't know. I don't think so. Look: she wasn't a hooker. She wasn't like a professional. She was like a college girl who took money for sex, but she expected to enjoy herself. Maybe some of these guys expected more . . . you know, advanced sex. She wasn't going to do anal, she wasn't going to get spanked, no water sports. Anything north of a blow job, she wasn't going to do."

Lucas: "Did you ever see any of her customers later . . . I mean, like years later? Or recently? Any kind of hint of who they might be, or where we might find one?"

Jepson smiled across the counter: "You trying to get me whacked?"

"So you did?"

"Yeah, sorta. Not in person, though. And not recently. A few years back, one of the guys was running for something. A political job of some kind. Not the U.S. Congress, or anything big. Bigger than dogcatcher, though. I can't remember what it was, but I saw his face on TV, and it popped into my head that he was one of them."

Virgil: "Did he get elected?"

Jepson made a tent out of his hands and covered his nose and mouth, looked down at the floor. "You know," he said after a minute, "I think he might have. Let me . . ." He rubbed his nose, then said, "Stan. Stanley, that was his name, and he was a Democrat. If you're a Democrat running in Hennepin County, or around Hennepin County, you probably got elected."

"A Democrat named Stan."

"And he drank rum Cokes. He called them rum Cokes. Republicans don't do that. They call them Cuba libres."

"How old was he when he was going out with Doris?"

"Maybe . . . thirty, give or take."

Lucas: "So he'd be maybe fifty, now. Give or take."

"That'd be about right," Jepson agreed.

They talked for a while longer, then Jepson asked, "If this turns into anything, do I get a piece of that five million reward?"

"Not up to us," Lucas said. "But we will keep track of your name."

"So I have one last embarrassing question," Virgil said. "We were told that you sold custom dildoes . . . what was all that about?"

Jepson laughed. "Man, the guy who ratted me out really *did* know me, didn't he?"

"I guess so," Virgil said. "Anyway . . ."

"You ever hear of these chicks back in the early rock 'n' roll days, called the Plaster Casters?"

Lucas: "Sure. They get to the rock stars, and you know, they'd do whatever they needed to do to get an erection, and then they'd make a plaster mold of the guy's dick. I guess they got quite a collection . . ."

"Bunch of them, yeah, Jimi Hendrix, I think," Jepson said. "So we had this entrepreneurial chick here in the Cities did the same thing with all kinds of celebrities—sports guys, rockers, movie stars, whoever she could get. Then, she'd make silicone casts with a vibrator inside. She'd sell them through us guys on the Hennepin strip, bartenders. You know, you'd get the Vikings quarterback . . ."

"We get the picture," Lucas said. "Did the caster make any money at it?"

"I guess," Jepson said. "I sold probably ten or twenty of them for fifty bucks up to a hundred, depending on who the model was—sort of a novelty, you know? I sold almost all of them to guys, not women. She'd take half. I wasn't the only one selling them. I believe she must have sold hundreds of them."

"Keeping Minneapolis classy, huh?" Lucas said.

ON THE WAY back to the car, Lucas said, "Forget about the dildoes. We got the tail of something here. We need to do a little political research, find this Stan guy."

"You know who'd probably know off the top of his head? Henderson's weasel . . ."

"Mitford."

"Yeah, bet he'd know."

"I'll call him now," Lucas said, as they got into the truck. Virgil looked out the side window at Loco's and said, "I'll be right back."

Jepson was walking back into the body shop and Virgil got out and caught him, took him aside and they talked for a minute, then he turned around and walked back to the truck.

Lucas was on the phone with Mitford, said, "Thanks," and clicked off. "He didn't have a name, but said he'd check around. A pol or former pol or wannabe pol named Stanley. Can't be that many."

"We're operating," Virgil said.

"What'd you tell Jepson?"

"I suggested he call up one of the true-crimers and stake a claim to the money. Or a share of it. Tell them what he had."

Lucas scratched the back of his neck, thought about it, smiled his wolverine smile and said, "Okay. Shit storm. That could work for us. The BCA won't be pleased, but then, I don't work for the BCA."

13

Roger Jepson got hit in the mouth by a squirt of transmission fluid, wiped it away with a shirt sleeve, spitting, got some blue paper towels to mop up around his chin and neck. Nobody laughed, because it had happened to all of them, and it wasn't that funny. Jepson went into Loco's restroom, washed his face with the gritty yellow soap that was all they currently had, looked at his wet face, neck, and tee-shirt in the mirror, and said, "Fuck it."

Five minutes' research on the office computer got him the number of the biggest true crime site working the Doris Grandfelt murder, along with the phone number of a woman named Anne Cash.

He went back outside where one of the other employees was drinking a beer and said, "Roy, borrow me your phone. I gotta make a call."

Roy was sullen, as always, but not a bad guy. "Use your own phone. I ain't got the minutes."

"I'm not gonna make a call. I'm gonna record one I'm making on my own phone."

Still grumbling, Roy fished his phone out of a pocket and handed it over.

Jepson set the phone to "record," tested it once, then reset it to record and called Anne Cash.

Cash answered, sounding harried: "This is Cash."

"I got the biggest break in this murder case. I want a piece of the reward, if you get it," Jepson said.

"How do I know you're not some retard wasting my time?" Cash asked.

"I was just interviewed by two cops named Davenport and Flowers and they went tearing out of here like their asses were on fire. That interest you?"

Empty air, then: "Tell me. You get a chunk of anything we get."

"I want more than a chunk," Jepson said. "I want at least fifty-fifty when this upsets the apple cart."

"We'll see. What is it?"

"I'm recording this call, you just said I'd get fifty-fifty."

"No, I didn't. I said, 'We'll see.' That's not a promise."

"Fuck it, then. I'll call somebody else," Jepson said. "There are lots of you people. What I got is killer."

Cash said, "Okay. Fifty-fifty of what we get, if this leads to something."

Jepson told her everything he'd told Lucas and Virgil, and when he was done, she said, "Holy crap. You sound for real."

"Yeah. When I was on your website, I seen you put up the cops' phone number. Call and ask them. Ask the Virgil guy. What I told you is the whole truth."

"Okay, I'll do that for sure." Now she sounded excited. "I got your phone number. What's your name? And gimme a little background on yourself. This will blow the whole investigation sky-high."

CASH CALLED THE number Virgil had given Blair.

Lucas picked up the phone from the truck's center console, looked at the screen, let it go to voicemail. Anne Cash with a short message: "Call me. Now. Important."

He did, and asked, "What?"

"Is this Davenport? I want to talk to Flowers. I need some answers from him."

"What's the question?" Virgil asked, as Lucas held the phone up.

"Did you interview a man named Jepson who told you that Doris Grandfelt was selling sex at a bar in Minneapolis? A place called the Lite House?"

Virgil: "We can't talk about our investigation at this point."

"So you did."

"We cannot talk about our interviews," Lucas said. "I will tell you, if you go with this, you could get sued by Lara Grandfelt."

"We're not talking about Lara," Cash said. "She sues me, it'll keep the story in the news for months, and in the end, she'll lose out."

"We won't say anything more," Lucas said. "We can't. We don't know any Roger Jepson."

Cash laughed out loud and said, "I didn't call him Roger. So you know him and you talked to him—and you just confirmed it. See you in an hour. Goodbye."

She rang off and Virgil smiled and said, "Shit storm."

"Every time I work with you, I'm amazed by your treachery," Lucas said.

Virgil: "Me? You're the one who said 'Roger.' Made me laugh."

LUCAS TIDIED UP the family room and brought two chairs in from the study, while Virgil lay on a couch, talked to Frankie and then the twins, checked an online newspaper, plugged in headphones and listened to Bob Seger songs.

The true-crimers arrived in a scrum. Lucas sat them in the family room and brought in glasses and a jug of lemonade. Dahlia Blair: "You have a grand piano."

"My wife's," Lucas said.

"Still. This is quite the house."

Cash said, "This is quite a house . . . for a cop."

There was a *tone* to the comment, and Virgil said, "Lucas is rich. Started a computer company back around the time Doris was killed and made a huge wad of money. Also, his wife is a plastic surgeon, and she makes a huge wad of money every year. So they've got lots of wads."

"And you're still a cop?" Cash said, with a slightly different tone.

"I like shooting assholes," Lucas said. "Everybody got a lemonade? Anybody want a mint leaf?"

"Do you have any mint leaves?" Ruby Weitz asked.

"No, but I thought it'd be polite to ask."

Ruby Weitz was a tall, square woman with hair that was neither red nor purple but something in between; Karen Moss had narrow rounded shoulders and blond hair with a gray streak down the part;

Sally Bulholtz was short, dark-haired and -eyed, and was wearing a tennis hat that read "Quiet Please" with an embroidered tennis ball bouncing above the words; Mary Albanese was owl-like, pale, with big glasses and dark hair pulled back in a bun. They all had spiral notebooks or legal pads and pens.

Cash asked, "What's up?"

Lucas explained that the officially routed information coming through Michelle Cornell was basically static, and that he and Virgil were not well coordinated with the investigation being done by the BCA. "We're supposed to be doing something entirely different, and the BCA guys sort of resent us sticking our noses in. We've decided we need a new tactic."

Moss: "That's us?"

Virgil: "Yes. You guys can do things that the BCA really can't, and Lucas and I can't do on our own. We need to use your brighter readers and researchers to hit public information sources looking for anything that might . . . mmm . . . be useful."

"Any online newspapers you can find, public records, that sort of thing. Virgil has a list of all the employees at Bee Accounting back when Doris Grandfelt was murdered. We want to run down everything we can find on all of them. We also have a BCA list of the people they contacted during the investigation. We want those run down."

"We also want somebody to check the newspapers for unsolved murders for a few years before Grandfelt was murdered, looking for similar unsolved murders," Virgil said. "Stabbings, and now with Bud being murdered, people who were beaten to death. It'd probably only be the *Star-Tribune*, they've got everything online. If there's a subscription fee, we'll pay it."

Virgil told them that he suspected the body had been dumped in the park because the killer was intimately familiar with it. "Did he come from that neighborhood? Run all the names we've got, and that we'll get, against property tax records back around the time Grandfelt was killed."

"That's a lot of work," Bulholtz chirped.

"Yes. Guess who'll be in line for big payoffs if you come up with something," Lucas said. "Your researchers could have fun with it. This is, like, a real criminal investigation."

Virgil looked at Cash: "Did you put up anything on Jepson yet?"

"I wrote it and sent it off to one of my editors to look at. She might have put it up—if she hasn't, it'll be soon."

The other women demanded to know what that was about, and Cash said, "Don't tell them—yet. Let me check and see if we got it up. "

She pulled out her phone and fifteen seconds later she was reading the site: "Yep, it's up," she said. To the other women, "Read it and weep."

They did, and that touched off angry arguments, which Virgil shut down: "You'll all have it up in fifteen minutes anyway."

"Yeah, but she got the headline on FirstStabAtIt," Albanese said. "Not fair."

"Fair is something losers whine about," Cash said.

"You're such a bitch," Weitz said.

"Everybody shut up," Lucas said. "Listen to me: Virgil and I are the referees for this whole reward business. If you find anything, we want to know about it. If anyone else gets a tip from an anonymous source, we want to know about it. If somebody does and they don't tell us, and we find out, they'll be automatically banned from any reward and I will personally arrest her—or him—for interfering with a police investigation."

Weitz: "When will we get the names?"

"If you agree to this, you'll have them before you get back to your cars. Leave your emails with Virgil, he'll send them to you."

"And I'll give you all a piece of information that nobody has leaked yet," Virgil said. "It appears that the knife was sharpened immediately before the murder, not with a whetstone or knife sharpener, but on a piece of red stone or red brick. Reddish grains were found in the sharpening grooves at the point of the blade. Bee is a redbrick building. So is the bar that Doris may have been going to. Does it seem likely that a Bee executive—only the executive dining room had metal silverware—would try to sharpen a knife on a brick? Maybe he did. Then again, most of the buildings down there, in Lowertown, are redbrick, and it was also a hangout for street people. Addicts, mentally disturbed guys, like that. We're wondering . . . anyone down there make the papers for violence involving knives?"

"Lots of street people have knives," Albanese said. "Maybe most of them. But would they have a car to take the body to the park?"

"Good point, but who really knows?" Virgil said. "The particular kind of knife found by Bud might be one of the most common knives in the whole country. I've got no idea how many cafeterias and restaurants must have been using them back when Doris was murdered."

Lucas: "So you see why we really need to crowdsource this case, looking for information. I don't know how you could do it, but maybe you could find out what other places used those knives back then. Virgil will send you the exact model."

They talked for another fifteen minutes. At the end, Virgil took a deck of business cards out of his pocket. "The cards have my direct number. For my real phone. The top is an office number, and you won't get far with it. If you have a legitimate tip, or a real need to reach me directly, use the second number. Don't burden me with bullshit or silly questions—this is for real information."

LATE THAT AFTERNOON, Amanda Fisk paused in the process of arranging her husband's funeral to check the major true crime sites, found several that claimed the report on AnneCashInvestigations was completely spurious, while others hinted that Cash's information was probably good, but she must have slept with the witness to get it.

Fisk went to the site and found a story about a man named Roger Jepson, an auto mechanic at a place called Loco's Body & Tire who'd worked as a bartender as a younger man. He claimed to have set up Doris Grandfelt with customers who would pay her for sex.

Timothy had sex with Grandfelt on the evening she'd been murdered, but Fisk didn't know he'd been paying for it—if he had been. When the Grandfelt murder hit the newspapers, he'd been shocked. He lied to her at the breakfast table, saying that his only contact with Grandfelt had come when she'd worked on his tax returns. Now, Fisk wondered if he *had* paid her. He would have been a big fish for Grandfelt. Maybe she had done him for free, hoping to land him.

ALTHOUGH TIMOTHY WAS gone—and with his death, she didn't have to worry about diminishing financial assets—you can't prosecute the dead, even if the cops learned that their DNA belonged to him.

And she was working hard to diminish the chances of that.

Another problem had popped up. She's seen a news report about a man named Charles "Bud" Light, who'd told a local television interviewer that he thought Doris Grandfelt's killer might have been a woman. He was right, but where he came up with that thought, she had no idea.

If that became a hot new idea, the cops could ride it like this: DNA man has sex with Doris Grandfelt, jealous wife, or lover, freaks out and murders her rival. If somehow they tracked down Timothy, even dead, might they then look at his wife, an employee at Bee Accounting at the time of the murder? They would. They would push hard.

She was turning a silver funerary urn in her hands, thinking about it, and unconsciously muttered, "Jesus Christ."

The funeral director had stepped into the room a half-second earlier and heard her reference to Jesus: "The Lord can be a comfort in the most trying of times," he said.

Fisk showed him a shaky grief-stricken smile, thought, *What a dipshit*, and said, aloud, "I often find it comforting to appeal to him. Now that the medical examiner . . ."

"We have a full release, so we can proceed," the funeral director said.

"Thank you. When will it be done?"

"Tomorrow morning. I understand that you are arranging a private home memorial service with our memory manager and would like to have the vase there." He pronounced it *vaz*.

"Yes, thank you again. Timothy didn't want a church service," Fisk said. "He was a believer, but unconventional. Unlike myself. I'm actually an Anglican."

"It's wonderful that you have that to fall back upon, in tragic times like these," the funeral director purred. She was buying a twelve-hundred-dollar solid silver urn, into which she'd put three thousand, five hundred dollars' worth of ashes. The funeral home had to do exactly nothing except some light paperwork and drive the ashes from the crematorium back to the funeral home.

Ka-ching.

FISK WAS TAKING a thirty-day mourning period away from work and was in a hurry.

When she got out of the funeral home and back to her car, she glanced at her watch, drove to the first of the four same-day dry cleaners, and recovered a batch of her husband's suits. She continued to the other three, and recovered dress shirts, golf shirts, sweatshirts, and everything else he wore that might reasonably be taken to a dry cleaner's.

Hurrying now, she drove to Minneapolis and dropped the clothing at four more dry cleaners, then to a Goodwill store where she purchased the five best pairs of size eleven shoes, along with four pairs of athletic shoes. She drove to a St. Paul Goodwill and left the shoes in a drop box.

A sign at the drop box said, "Gently used and new clothing only; no shoes, please."

That's because she knew, from an acquaintance, that the shoes' next stop would be a dumpster, and from there, a landfill; but somebody at Goodwill might remember nine pairs of good shoes, if the cops should go looking for them.

She'd get back to the dry cleaners the next day and drop the clothes off at another Goodwill store, near the house; dry cleaning fluids were generally good at destroying DNA and sending them twice through baths of tetrachloroethylene should get rid of all of it, if the cops should ever go looking for the clothing. As a newly bereaved widow, she simply couldn't stand to look at Timothy's clothes hanging in the shared dressing room . . .

Still sitting at the drop box where she left the shoes, she rubbed her forehead: getting rid of all of Timothy's DNA might be impossible, but she wouldn't make it easy for anyone looking for it. She'd soaked the dogs' collars in rubbing alcohol, then washed them with soap. Timothy watched television from a special recliner chair, and she'd dumped the chair and bought a similar used one from a high-end used furniture dealer all the way across town in Minnetonka.

She'd cleaned the drains in the shower and poured Drano down the trap of the sink he used. She collected all his hats, bagged them, and threw them in a garbage can at a shopping center. Everything he touched got soaked or wiped with heavy-duty household cleaner, including all three of his Rolex watches, his shirt studs, and a turquoise cuff he'd bought in Colorado.

What had she missed? She'd worked sixteen hours a day, getting rid of every trace of him, in the house, in the cars, everything.

And in two days, she'd have at least a hundred people wandering through the house, at the memorial service, leaving behind copious amounts of their own DNA, further confusing things for any possible investigators.

Most likely, none of that work would be absolutely necessary; but she was psychotic and driven and so she did it anyway. She'd keep doing it, over and over again, until any possibility of investigation was gone.

A car drove in behind her at the drop box. She glanced in her rear-view mirror and pulled away.

She was on her way home when she passed the strip mall and saw the red, white, and blue barber pole on the outside of one of the store-fronts. The idea rang in her head like a bell. She slowed, turned into the parking lot.

She had the idea, but how would she pull it off? She got out of the car, walked over to the barbershop, and went inside. There were three chairs, but only one barber; and the barber was sitting in one of the chairs, reading a free newspaper. He looked over the paper, pushed his eyeglasses up with an index finger, and asked, "What can I do you for?"

"Do you give haircuts to children?"

"Sure . . . if they're old enough to sit still."

"He's seven," she said.

"That should be okay."

"Would it be all right if I sat in that chair for a minute?" she asked. "I want to see what he would see, if he could see himself in the mir-ror. He's sort of . . . a sissy. He's afraid of things. If he could see himself in a mirror . . ."

"Go ahead," the barber said.

Fisk climbed into the chair and spun it around until she could look in the mirror. The barber moved over behind her. "That's what he'd see."

"I'll talk to him. Would we need a reservation?"

"Does it look like he'd need a reservation?" he asked.

Fisk glanced around the empty shop, smiled, and said, "We'll drop in."

"Do that. We have a special rate for kids."

"Higher or lower?"

He smiled at her—she was being a little flirty. "Lower," he said. "Come back. Anytime. With or without him."

As she was on the way out, the barber said, "Oh, hey—you got some hair on your jacket sleeve."

She looked and said, "No problem. I've got a tape roll that will take it right off."

In the car, she carefully picked a pinch of gray hairs off her jacket and rolled them up in a piece of notebook paper.

Now: new mattress to buy. Jepson to think about.

Busy, busy, busy.

LUCAS AND VIRGIL said goodbye to the true-crimers and hello to Weather, who said she was going back out with a neighbor to a Pilates class. She changed, came down to say that their daughter had called from summer camp to say that she could extend for a week and take the trail riding option. "I told her I'd call her back after I talked to you."

"Horse riding is dangerous," Lucas said. "I'd worry."

"Ah, trail riding in a summer camp is not going to be dangerous, not any more dangerous than walking around in St. Paul," Virgil said. "If you could see Frankie and her horses, you'd say yes."

"That's what I think," Weather said.

Lucas shrugged: "If you all say so."

Weather left, and they went to the den, where they called up Anne Cash's website and read the Jepson story. She'd spoken directly to

Jepson and had a recommendation for all the other true-crimers: track down all Lite House employees from the early 2000s and interrogate them on the Grandfelt prostitution allegation. Find the names of her customers.

"All good." Lucas tapped the screen with a greasy finger. "She's offering to cut people in on the reward. I bet she breaks some loose."

They were in the family room with the television on the local Channel Three, but muted, when the doorbell rang.

"Better not be Cash," Lucas said. He went to a window and peeked out past the blinds. "Aw, shit; it's Lara Grandfelt. Bet she heard about Jepson."

"All part of the shit storm, man," Virgil said. "Let her in."

SHE CAME IN, trailed by Wise, her assistant. Lucas pointed to easy chairs, but Grandfelt stayed on her feet, distraught, crying, which made the two cops feel a little bad, but not too.

"She was a prostitute," she cried, tears running down her cheeks. "My sister . . ."

"Was more like an escort," Lucas said. "Not a prostitute."

Grandfelt looked at him with anger in her eyes: "Yes? Would you care to explain the difference? Men paid her money for sex."

Virgil said, "Still . . . a prostitute, a hooker, generally will take on all potential customers, unless there's something obviously wrong with him . . . or her. That's always dangerous. Doris was more what we'd call a party girl—she'd go out dancing with these guys, and some she'd go home with. Not all of them. Most of them, but not all, would give her money. I mean, they'd say this was a gift, not a payment. That makes both sides feel better, even if it doesn't seem like much of a difference to you."

"Then how did she wind up with someone who murdered her, if they were just out dancing?" Grandfelt asked.

Virgil looked to Lucas, who said, "That . . . we don't know. This man, this bartender, told us he was careful about who he recommended. Plus, if he knew she was going out with a particular . . . man . . . and she turned up murdered the next day, he said he would have gone to the police. And honestly? We believed him. He said she hadn't gone out with anyone that night, that he knew of. So she was seeing men that she picked up on her own, or former acquaintances. And, I suppose this is a possibility, she was simply going somewhere and was attacked."

Grandfelt shook her head: "You know that isn't true, Lucas."

"Why do I know that isn't true?"

"Because of the knife," Grandfelt said. "The knife that killed Doris came from the place that she worked. We need to track down every man who worked there, when she died, and do DNA."

Lucas shrugged and nodded, conceding the point.

"The DNA search is underway," Virgil said. "Before the knife was found, the BCA didn't have any direction to go. They tested some of the men at Bee, but not all. They'll get as many of them as they can now, but it won't be perfect, unless they find him. The knife came from the executive dining room, and a lot of the men who had access to it were older—in their fifties and sixties. Several of them are dead."

"Shit. Shit-shit-shit," Grandfelt said. She took a turn around the living room, touched the passive Wise on the shoulder. "What happens next? You start hunting down her . . . dates?"

"If we can," Lucas said.

"You don't seem to be doing much right now," she said, looking around the living room. "You're eating potato chips."

"Waiting for another interview, tonight. We're seeing a woman who might have some information—and some of it might go to Doris's dates," Lucas said.

"Who are you interviewing?"

"Can't say," Virgil said. "Or won't say, take your pick. Way too much stuff is leaking out to these true crime sites. But we are seeing someone. The possibilities are thin, but they're still possibilities that nobody has looked at yet."

Grandfelt scratched at her lower lip with her upper teeth, then said, "Okay. I have to trust you. This Anne Cash woman . . . she's vicious."

"She *is* a trial," Lucas said. "But really, if she's vicious, she's yours. This whole thing is not our idea, it's yours."

"But we've actually turned up new evidence," Grandfelt snapped back. "Opened up a whole new path of investigation. Not Anne Cash: you two. And this Bud Light."

Lucas said, "I'll give you that. It's possible that we'll actually catch Doris's killer; or if he's dead, identify him."

Grandfelt turned down the offer of a lemonade or potato chips, and after another minute of meaningless conversation, she and Wise walked out.

14

Stephanie Brady poked her head out her door, eye-checked Lucas and Virgil, and said, "Come in. I hope you're not allergic to cats."

They weren't, and a good thing: four cats, three tabbies and one black as Satan, were either already in the living room, or came strolling in, to inspect the visitors. The house was neat, with minimalist furnishings and a complete lack of knick-knacks. Through a doorway, they could see a kitchen and a man standing by a counter, with his back to them.

"Let's do this in the kitchen," Brady said.

They went that way, trailing her, and the man turned to meet them; he'd been eating a bowl of cereal while he looked at a laptop. He was thin, balding with a modest brown mustache, wearing a yellow Miles Davis tee-shirt. He had a glass of milk in his hand. He said, "Hi. I'm Dan Peltz, Stephanie's husband."

They shook hands and Brady said, "I've got the picture box on the table . . . I just got home. I didn't have time to sort the photos, we can do that now."

The kitchen smelled like cereal and toast and milk, with a faint, but not subtle, odor of cat pan. A brown cardboard box sat in the center of a hardwood table with four chairs around it. One of the cats jumped up on the table, looked in the box. Peltz picked the cat up and dropped it on the floor, where it landed as soft as a sponge.

The box, twenty inches wide and long, and a foot high, with a lid, looked like it might once have contained a cowboy hat. The interior was half-filled with a pile of photographic prints, most of them four by six inches, a few smaller, some larger. They looked like they'd been machine-printed at Walmart or Target.

A small Canon 35mm film camera sat beside the box. Brady picked it up and said, "This is my old camera, but I hardly used it—Doris used it last. I noticed there's still a roll of film inside. The film probably isn't any good anymore. It's been in there for twenty years."

"Where'd you keep this stuff?" Lucas asked.

"Well, at the apartment. Not in Doris's room, where everything else was. Because, the camera was mine. The box was in the hall closet, on a shelf, where we could both get it when we wanted it. When the investigators went through Doris's stuff, I never thought about the box," Brady said. "I stayed in the apartment until I met Dan and never touched the box until we moved here. Then, this was like six or seven years after the murder . . ."

"Seven," Peltz said. He took a sip of milk, leaving a rim of white on his upper lip. He licked it off. He was a type that Lucas found irritating: he was satisfied with who he was and what he had, and always had been. No tread wear on Dan. "Almost eight."

"I didn't think there'd be anything significant in it after all that time," Brady concluded.

"The BCA has a photo lab contact who might be able to save the film," Virgil said. "I'd like to take the camera with me. If we get prints of you, or people you know, we can return them to you."

"That'd be fine, but I can't hardly remember using it," Brady said. "I don't know when phone photos started. When they did, which I think was a little after Doris was killed, I started using my phone and never looked back."

SHE SET THE camera aside for Virgil, reached into the box, pulled out a handful of photos, shuffled through them, and dealt a half dozen out to Lucas and Virgil. "That's Doris in the photos. They're not very good."

The photos were faded, the color gone blurry, as if they hadn't been fixed very well. But they could see Grandfelt as she'd been when she was alive, and her pretty pale face showed the kind of sad defiant vulnerability that both Lucas and Virgil recognized from the faces of women they'd known who sold sex.

They divided up the rest of the box between the four of them, and in the end had a stack of photos of Grandfelt, including twelve with several different men. The photos were poor enough that they were unable to decide how many of the twelve were actually of different men, and how many might be duplicates. With one exception, all the photos were taken in or outside of bars. The exception was a photo taken at Bee Accounting, of Grandfelt and a man standing next to a coffin-sized Xerox machine. Brady recognized the man: "That's George McCallan. I don't think Doris would have had anything to do with him. He was obnoxious and he smelled funny. You notice that they don't look especially happy."

Lucas spread the other eleven photos like a tarot spread: "You don't recognize any of these guys? You're sure?"

"I don't. None of them worked at Bee. Like I said, I didn't go to clubs very much. Except, you know, for Prince," Brady said. "Doris went three or four days a week, Wednesday or Thursday, then always on Friday and Saturday for sure. She liked to get high and she liked to dance."

"Alcohol, weed, coke?" Virgil asked.

"All of that, I think," Brady said. "I talked to her about it, but she said she was okay. She never bought any drugs, she said, sometimes she used when somebody gave her some. I told that to the investigators."

"How many nights a week didn't she come home?" Virgil asked.

"Oh, she stayed out late, but she always came home. Late, I mean, two or three o'clock. A couple of times, the sun was up, but she always showed up."

Lucas: "Worse for the wear?"

Brady nodded: "You could say that. Especially if she'd been out on Wednesday or Thursday, and had to go to work the next day, and then went out Friday and Saturday. On Sunday mornings she'd look like she'd been in a wrestling match. That 'Sunday Mornin' Comin' Down' song . . ."

"Johnny Cash," Virgil said. "Kris Kristofferson."

"Yes. Those. I could see that song in her."

"Did you know she might have been getting paid for sex?" Lucas asked.

She shook her head: "It never occurred to me. She was like the classic good girl. She'd even go to church sometimes. I thought she was having a good time, and if she slept with someone, it was part of that, having a good time."

Lucas: "You didn't think much about it."

"It's not like we were living in the 1950s," Brady said.

"Huh." Lucas picked up the photos and said, "We'll let you know about the camera."

OUTSIDE, VIRGIL SAID, "You know, there's probably a fast way to find out who the guys are, in those photos."

"I don't like what you're about to say," Lucas said. "But I agree."

"I don't like it either," Virgil said. They walked farther along the sidewalk, until they were under a streetlight. "If we post the pictures to the true crime sites, or if somebody does . . . we'd crowdsource their identities. I don't know any other way to do it. We'd probably know some of them by noon tomorrow."

"We'd take some shit," Lucas said.

"So what? The people who'd be giving us shit are the same ones who twisted our arms to do this."

Lucas thought it over, then said, "We could give them to Dahlia Blair, if she's still here. With Bud Light dead, she could use the break."

DAHLIA BLAIR ANSWERED the phone, but said she was planning to go back to South Dakota in the morning. "I can't deal with this. I'm kind of scared—if they murdered Bud, are they coming after me? I'll take your pictures and post them, but I'm *so* unhappy I can barely get off this bed. I shouldn't have come. We shouldn't have come."

"You can't predict what will happen when you start messing around in situations like this," Lucas told her. "None of us could have predicted this."

"Yeah, yeah, I know," Blair said. "It's all fun and games until somebody gets hurt. I've heard that phrase a hundred times. My dad would say that when me and my brothers would be fooling around on the farm. I never thought about what it *really* meant. This was supposed to be fun and maybe some money."

IN VIRGIL'S TRUCK, Lucas put the photos on the center console one at a time, illuminated with his iPhone flashlight, and Virgil used his iPhone to take pictures of them and texted them to Blair. She called back to say that she'd have them up on her website in half an hour and they'd be everywhere by morning.

"People will do screen shots, trim them, and put them up as their own," she said.

"Dahlia, you know we're sad about Bug, but . . . there's a good chance that the BCA and the St. Paul cops will track down the killer," Virgil said. "Maybe it'll be Doris Grandfelt's killer, and there'll be some money in it."

"I don't know if I'd want it anymore," Blair said.

When they ended the call, Lucas said to Virgil, "You called him Bug."

"No, Bud."

"I know it's Bud, but you called him Bug."

"Ahh . . . shit. I think a cop called him Bug and I picked up on it. I'm tired of this. Why don't we both quit and do something else?"

"I've thought about it, and I know why I won't quit. I still get a thrill out of chasing assholes," Lucas said. "Of course, I'm not chasing buck-toothed shitkickers around pig farms for banging their sisters. Like you."

"I've only been on a pig farm once, and not for that," Virgil said. "But I gotta admit, you just gave me the theme for another novel."

"You know what I'm saying."

"I'll take you home now."

AFTER DROPPING LUCAS, Virgil went back to the hotel, set up his laptop, and started working on the novel. His first three books had been praised for the realism of the murder scenes. That was because the murder scenes were real, or mostly real scenes he'd seen and worked himself.

Building a story around the scenes was an entirely different process—creation rather than recall. The problems with creating the stories ate at him—kept him up at night, as his law enforcement chores no longer did.

He was still at work on the book, at eleven o'clock, when Carroll Bayes called. "I knew you stayed up late. I didn't wake you up, did I?"

"I'm up for another hour," Virgil said. "What's going on?"

Bayes was still the lead BCA agent on the Charles Light murder. "People were screaming their heads off about the Bud Light murder. All those true crime sites, the TV stations. The ME, you know, wanted to look good, so he got right on it. He called me about half an hour ago. One of his assistants had looked at some blood tests and called him with the results. Richardson suggests that we not talk so much about murder. It might not have been one."

Darrell Richardson was the county medical examiner.

"What's that? He's saying it's not murder?" Made Virgil stand up.

"Well, mmm . . . Look, do you know how to make crappy chili taste better?"

"Chili? What are you talking about, C?" Virgil asked.

"It turns out that you can make cheap, crappy chili, the only kind you can get at the Wee Blue Inn, taste better by dumping in a scoop of peanut butter. Light had a plastic bowl and a plastic spoon sitting on the room table, mostly empty, but with some of the motel chili still left," Bayes said. "One of the blood tests suggests that Light was suffering from a massive anaphylactic shock, and it killed him. He apparently had a serious peanut allergy. He carried a card saying so and had a box of EpiPens in his suitcase."

"He was hit. His skull was cracked . . ." Virgil started.

"His head was cracked, and he bled some, but he probably wasn't hit," Bayes said. "When the tests results started coming in, the doc sent an investigator back over to the Wee Blue Inn, to look around. She found that the bed had one of those cheap steel bed frames, and a corner of the frame was sticking out an inch or so at the foot of the bed. There was a dark sheet over it, so no blood was visible, but the corner of the frame fits the wound on Light's head. They missed it the first time around. The thinking now is, he gobbled down the chili, laid down, felt the allergic reaction coming on, panicked, got out of bed, staggered, fell, and hit his head. He didn't actually crack his skull. Didn't die immediately. He probably knocked himself out, at least for a few seconds, and the anaphylactic reaction killed him. The blood trail to the door could have been an attempt to call for help."

"Why didn't he inject himself with the EpiPen?"

"I dunno," Bayes said. "Maybe because he was messed up. Concussed, not thinking straight. His suitcase with the pens was on the other side of the bed, so . . ."

"Wow!"

"It's not for sure, yet. Richardson has some more chemistry to do, but that's the way they're headed."

"Thanks, man. Jeez—that's something. I'll tell Lucas."

AS LONG AS he'd been disturbed, Virgil didn't see any reason why Lucas shouldn't be, and he knew Lucas was a night owl anyway. He called, and Lucas picked up on the first ring.

"What are you doing?" Virgil asked.

"I was watching West Coast baseball. You think of something?"

"Not exactly. I did get some interesting news . . ."

THE NEXT MORNING, Lucas walked out to Virgil's truck and got in, shaking his head: "Peanut butter allergy?"

"I'd laugh if I didn't feel so sorry for the guy," Virgil said, as they rolled out the driveway.

"The weird thing is, his getting killed got us some breaks," Lucas said. "Where'd we be if he hadn't got killed?"

"Okay. What are we doing this morning?"

"I got a call from Mitford. That guy running for office, the one Jepson mentioned?"

"The one named Stan?"

"Mitford thinks it's a guy named Stanley O'Brien, who ran for a seat in the legislature, the state house. He actually won and served four terms. Mitford said he quit to join a lobby group and moved on to a couple more after the first one. He's currently the director of the Minnesota Small Manufacturers and Assemblers Association."

"Here in St. Paul?"

"Right across town. They've got an office on University, a couple of blocks from the capitol."

"We should drop in," Virgil said.

"I looked at the biggest true crime sites, they've all got the photos," Lucas said. "You heard anything from the BCA about that?"

"Not yet, but I will."

"I suppose." Lucas yawned, covered his mouth with a fist. "What happened with Brady's camera?"

"Nothing, yet, it's still on the back seat. I called Jon and he says he'll get the film guy working on it. We should swing by the BCA and drop it off."

"After Stan."

THE MINNESOTA SMALL Manufacturers and Assemblers Association offices were in a redbrick building among a bunch of other redbrick buildings squeezed between parking lots north of the capitol. Most of the offices were occupied by lobby groups of one kind or another. The MSMA offices were on the fourth floor behind an oaken-look door.

They pushed through and found themselves standing in front of an unoccupied receptionist's desk. A chime had tinkled overhead as they walked in, and the receptionist showed up a few seconds later, hurrying around a privacy wall that blocked the view to a hallway of offices in the back.

The receptionist looked from Lucas to Virgil and a "cop" light went on in his eyes. He asked, "Can I help you?"

Lucas produced his marshal's ID and said, "We'd like to speak to Mr. O'Brien."

"We have two Mr. O'Briens . . ."

"Stanley O'Brien," Virgil said.

"He's not in his office, he's in the back . . ."

"Well," Lucas said, "show the way."

THE RECEPTIONIST DID, but not enthusiastically. "We're actually having our morning warm-up right now. It's an informal chat that we do every morning . . ."

He ushered them into a back room where four men and a woman were standing around with golf putters, one of them lining up a putt on a ten-foot-long putting carpet. The room had a lunch table, a refrigerator, a dartboard, and a couple of four-top tables with chairs. The man making the putt ignored the opening of the door, but pulled the putt to the left when the receptionist said, "Uh, Mr. O'Brien . . ."

O'Brien turned, irritated, but snapped his mouth shut when he saw Lucas and Virgil. The receptionist said, "These . . . mmm . . . officers would like to speak to you."

"Officers?"

"I'm with the Bureau of Criminal Apprehension and my associate is a deputy U.S. Marshal," Virgil said. "We would like to confer . . . privately."

"Well, of course." O'Brien propped his putter against the wall and said, "Come with me."

As they followed him down the hall, Virgil said, "You have the same putting problem that I do. You're handsy. You jerk at the ball."

"I know that," O'Brien said.

"You can buy gloves that keep your wrists straight and teach you to rock your shoulders," Virgil said.

O'Brien glanced back and asked, "You try them?"

"Yup. And some other things."

"They work?" he asked.

"Not especially."

"Thanks for the tip, then." He said it with a quick smile, friendly enough.

O'BRIEN'S OFFICE WAS spacious, but not ostentatious: picture of a woman with two kids on his L-shaped desk, turned so a visitor could see it. Probably his family, though they didn't ask. Much of the wall space was taken up with plaques, photos with well-known senior politicians, including Senator Henderson. A flag hung from a pole in a corner.

O'Brien settled behind his desk, knit his fingers together on the desktop and asked, "What can I do for you?"

Lucas turned to Virgil and nodded, and Virgil said, "Twenty years ago, Doris Grandfelt, an accountant with Bee Accounting . . ."

Both Lucas and Virgil were watching O'Brien closely, and saw his eyes widen as he took a breath. He knew what was coming.

". . . was murdered, stabbed to death. Recently, the investigation was reopened, and without going into a lot of detail, it was determined that Doris was providing sexual services for pay and that you were one of her customers."

O'Brien looked down at his fingers, then pulled them back and dropped his hands into his lap. He said, "Yeah. I . . . dated her once or twice. I certainly didn't have anything to do with her murder."

"Did you pay her?" Lucas asked.

"I . . . gave her gifts. We went dancing one time, the two other times . . . I gave her gifts."

"You didn't talk to police after her murder," Virgil said.

O'Brien shrugged. "I was married at the time. I had nothing to do with the murder and I had no clue who might have done it. I was running for office, for the state legislature. This was in pre-Trump days, when an . . . affair . . . would have instantly thrown me out of the race. Which I won, incidentally."

"We know," Virgil said. "Would you be willing, now, to take a DNA test?"

"If it could be private. If it wouldn't be spread all over these true crime sites," O'Brien said. "I've been following this whole thing in the papers, on television, and it seems like you guys have pretty much gone to mob rule."

Lucas, sharply: "Not us."

"Bullshit. I saw lots of investigations when I was in the House, and I never saw anything like this," O'Brien said, just as sharply. "Every-body in town is watching it. Every TV news show, and then this poor bastard from Nebraska got murdered."

Lucas didn't bother to correct him, but said, less sharply: "Okay, I know what you mean. I don't like it any more than you do. Now . . . do you know any more of her customers? Anything that could help us?"

"I could give you a name, but I'd hate for it to get out, that the name came from me," O'Brien said. "I'd feel like a rat. I'd *be* a rat."

"This is not a TV show," Lucas said. "We don't think people who help us are rats."

"This *is* a TV show, that's the whole problem," O'Brien said, rapping on his desktop with his knuckles. "Have you seen those pictures of her customers they have on the true crime sites? They're all over the morning news programs. They're hunting those guys down. I don't know, there must be nine or ten of them, and the mob has torches and pitchforks and they're hunting them down."

"I didn't know that they were on TV news," Lucas said.

"They are. It scares the shit out of me," O'Brien said, pushing away from his desk and looking around at his plaques in what looked like desperation. His face was red, and Virgil suddenly feared he might have a heart attack.

"Easy," Virgil said. "We'll have a crime scene woman come over to collect the DNA from you. It's a simple gum scrub, takes only a couple of minutes. If you weren't the last one to have sex with Doris . . ."

"No! No! That won't help if my name gets out there. These other guys, the guys in the photos . . . There must be a dozen of them . . ."

"Eleven," Lucas said.

"Okay, eleven. Even if it's one of them, the other ten are innocent."

"Paying money for sex is a crime . . ." Lucas said.

"Give me a fuckin' break."

THEY ALL SAT in silence for a few seconds, then Virgil said, "Give us the name. We'll call you a confidential informant and we won't give you up."

More silence, then, "Lawrence Klink, PhD."

Virgil and Lucas looked at each other, and then back at O'Brien.

Lucas: "Klink the Shrink?"

"Yeah. Klink the Shrink."

Lawrence Klink had had a long-running call-in show on a public radio network, then, after a while, when the ratings got high enough, he'd moved to a commercial station. He also had a popular blog. He didn't call himself Klink the Shrink, but everybody else did. He liked attention, and every couple of weeks would show up in a *Star-Tribune* gossip column. The columns, as far as Lucas and Virgil knew, were never about his love life, they mostly concerned his discussions of the effects of social media on children; and about his real estate holdings, which included condos in Manhattan, San Diego, Austin, Vail, and Fort Lauderdale.

Klink famously believed that you could determine where investors could make large gains in real estate values through psychological analysis of public comments by artists and the female nouveau riche. His view was encapsulated in a bestselling book called *Paint Me a Riche Bitche.*

"How'd you know Klink?" Virgil asked.

"This was way back when—twenty years ago. We hung out in the same kinda political, academic, media circles. I'd see him in clubs checking out the good-looking women, but never saw him walk out with one. You know about Klink's nose?"

"Yeah, it's somewhat famous," Virgil said.

"The fact is, his nose looks like the fuckin' Hindenburg. This meant that, uh, Lawrence did not do well with certain kinds of women. I was dating Doris at the time, and I mentioned her name and . . . status . . . to him. He picked up on that. We never talked about it, but I saw him with Doris one night and he nodded to me, so I knew. Like he was saying thanks."

"So he had a somewhat *stressed* attitude toward women?" Lucas asked.

"Yeah, but he didn't kill Doris. He . . . you gotta know him. I don't think he'd ever do anything that was physically risky. I believe if he'd attacked Doris, she would have beaten the shit out him."

More silence, then Virgil said, "You'll take the DNA test? We'll send a technician around and she'll do a little gum scrub, in your office, privately. Nobody will know."

O'Brien put up his hands, as if in surrender. "Okay. Bring her on. I gotta tell you, though, I don't believe you. Somebody will leak my name. I don't think the association will fire me, but they might. I'll tell them that I was a kid in an unhappy marriage, that I was drinking, that I met her in a bar, blah blah blah. Maybe they'll let me hang on. But some of these other guys . . . the ones they're hunting down, they're fucked. Am I right? Am I right?"

BACK IN THE truck, Lucas said, "He's right. Some of those guys are about to get their lives wrecked, if the true-crimers find them."

"They'll find them," Virgil said. "That's one thing they can do. We made it possible."

"Yeah, well, we're trying to catch a killer," Lucas said. Then: "You ever nail a hooker?"

"No. How about you?"

"Nope. They kinda scare me," Lucas said. "They are the world's natural nihilists. A lot of them don't believe in anything. Given the way they try to get through life . . ."

"I didn't exactly come close . . ." Virgil started, then stopped.

"C'mon, let it out."

"I was working a guy who did strong-arm robberies," Virgil said, looking through the windshield, remembering. "Good planner. Never carried a gun. Giant guy, spent all day lifting weight out in the barn. Carried a sap, and he'd use it, if he had to. Anyway, he was hard to catch at it. His girlfriend was doing two years in the women's prison at the time, and I drove up to talk to her. See if she could give me something. The place was more like a dormitory than a prison, at least for her . . ."

"I've been there," Lucas said.

"Anyway, there was a woman there, she used to run a high-end brothel down in Rochester, mostly, you know, for the Mayo Clinic docs. She was doing a year and a day inside. So I was talking to the asshole's girlfriend, and this brothel madam came over and asked, like, 'What's up?' She was friends with the girlfriend. I was trying to get the girlfriend warmed up enough that she'd give me something, so I pulled this chick into the conversation, introduced myself. I gotta say, she was very good-looking. Very."

"And, importantly, for a fuckin' Flowers, soon to be available," Lucas said.

"I didn't know when she was going to get out, and I didn't ask. Anyway, I gave her my card, and after I got out of there, I looked her up, saw what her background was, and why she was inside. Running a whorehouse. Like six months later, when she got out, she called me up and said, "Hey, I got a bottle of Cabernet and I'm looking for a get-out-of-prison party."

Lucas snorted.

"I thought about it for a couple seconds. I mean, I did," Virgil said.

"I was unattached at the time. But, I begged off, never heard from her again. She was a very good-looking woman. Close as I ever came, I guess. She wasn't looking for money, but she'd been selling sex whole-sale, even if it wasn't hers. And it might have been hers, as far as I know."

"You're a saint," Lucas said.

"So, what would you have done?"

"The same. I've never met a hooker I really liked. Felt sorry for some. Not for some others." After a moment, "You ever catch the strong-arm guy?"

"Yeah, we decoyed him out with Henrietta Mackey. You remember her?"

"Oh, yeah. I heard she moved to California. Good cop. Had some guts. She was SWAT for a while, when women didn't do SWAT."

"She was," Virgil said. "But, she wanted to learn how to surf. Can't do that on Lake Phalen. She wound up with the Santa Monica PD."

"Good for her."

Virgil nodded and said, "Next topic."

15

They didn't have to create a new topic because Jon Duncan, Virgil's boss, did it for them. Virgil answered his phone and Duncan said, "Did you dickheads give pictures of Doris Grandfelt's dates to the true crime sites?"

Virgil said, "Maybe."

Duncan: "Ah, shit. I knew it! I *knew* it! The first guy they found was the CEO of Earthwise Crypto, which, in case you didn't know, is the fourth-biggest tech company in the state, and they give money to every politician in sight."

"I'm sure you can handle it, Jon," Lucas said.

"Handle it? I'm not looking to handle it. I'm looking for somebody to blame."

"Blame us," Lucas said. "We'll be happy to pass the blame along to Henderson and the governor."

"We could go on *Jonesing on the News*," Virgil said. "Daisy'd be happy to have us. We're both old friends of hers. In fact, she already got in touch, but we put her off."

"Stay the fuck away from all news outlets—YouTube, TikTok, TV, whatever else you can think of," Duncan said. "Stay away until this quiets down. I mean, the guy has like six kids and the TV stations are parked outside the poor bastard's house."

"And you sent a crime scene tech over there to get a DNA sample?"

"I suppose somebody will. That's not my job. My job is to shut you guys up."

"We warned everybody. You were there," Lucas said.

"I'll deny that. Oh. Something else. You're both movie stars on the true crime blogs. And it's 'fuck this' and 'fuck that' and 'fuck you' and the guy who gets his wife to lick the tires of his shiny red car . . .'"

"Tires weren't mentioned," Virgil said.

"You know what I'm talking about," Duncan said. "We need one thing from you guys right now. It's called discretion."

"Too late for that, Jon," Virgil said. "This is a snowball rolling downhill. You say the first guy was a CEO . . . what about the other ten?"

"Haven't found them, but the crimers are out there beating the bushes. Just pray that a minister or a priest isn't among them." Pause. "Or a bishop. What are you guys doing now? Where are you?"

"On our way to the Wee Blue Inn to talk to one of the true crime people," Virgil said. "Have you heard about Bud Light?"

"Everybody has. Peanut butter chili. The woman who came with him is trying to arrange for a cremation, but they're expensive and she doesn't have any money."

"I can handle that," Lucas said.

"You're going to pay for it?"

"No, I'm going to guilt-trip Lara Grandfelt into doing it."

"Ah. Excellent solution. Keep me out of it. I'm going to find the biggest clump of weeds I can find, and jump in. And you guys . . . easy. Easy does it."

They ended the call, and Lucas said, "He was a pretty good investigator."

"Right now, he's a pretty good bureaucrat, as bureaucrats go," Virgil said. "He does try to take care of me. Let's find Dahlia. You can call Grandfelt on the way."

Lucas did that.

THE PARKING LOT at the Wee Blue Inn was almost deserted, but Dahlia Blair's car was parked outside her room, and when they knocked, she opened the door a crack and peeked out, then opened it all the way and said, "Thank you. Lara Grandfelt called. She'll handle the cremation when we get Bud's body from the medical examiner, and she offered to pay for a gravesite and a headstone."

"Or, you could just pour him in the Missouri River when you go back home," Virgil said.

"Nope. He's getting the full deal," Blair said.

Lucas: "What's happening with the photos? Are you staying in touch?"

"Yes. I picked up a lot of readers today, and the other guys are starting to pay attention to me," Blair said. "We got Darius Carmel, he's the CEO of a big tech company . . ."

"We heard," Lucas said.

"And we think we might have spotted another one—people have been getting calls about a man named Elias Johannson, we're pretty sure we've got him," Blair said. "He's a retired pharmacist, which is why people remember him—they looked at him over a drugstore counter for thirty years."

"He's here in St. Paul?"

"No, he's in a place called Golden Valley," Blair said.

"Are all your friends congregating outside his driveway?"

"No, I don't think so. Nobody's put his name up, yet, in case it's wrong and you'd get sued," Blair said. "We're being careful. That first guy, the CEO guy, is kind of a public figure, a publicity hound, so we're safer there."

"Since you got the word about Bud . . . you feel safer?" Lucas asked.

"Yes. Definitely. I'll stay for a few more days, at least, to get the whole Bud thing settled, but now . . . I don't feel so guilty about him," Blair said. "I'm going to keep working on the Grandfelt case. I could use that reward money."

Lucas looked at Virgil, who said, "Golden Valley."

LUCAS USED VIRGIL'S iPad to download DVS—Driver and Vehicle Services—background on Elias Johannson, helped along by the unusual name. He had three cars, registered in his name and apparently in his wife's, Jemna Johannson.

"We might have to deal with a wife," Lucas told Virgil.

"Don't do the crime if you can't do the time," Virgil said.

"That's very empathetic of you," Lucas said. "The guy's got a Corvette Stingray, a '69. That's something."

"Is that a good one?" Virgil asked. "I mean, I drive Tahoes."

"Yeah, a '69 is pretty good. It's not a Porsche, but if you have to drive a Stingray, that's the one you might want. In fire-engine red, of course. Tires licked by Jemna. What kind of name is Jemna anyway?"

GOLDEN VALLEY WAS an older inner-ring suburb of Minneapolis. The trip across the Mississippi and through the Minneapolis downtown took half an hour. Johannson's house was a sixties ranch style, robin's-egg blue, on a comfortable block with overhanging maples, abundant hedges, and one shiny new tricycle. The house had an attached two-car garage, but the driveway split, with a narrow lane going around to the back—"Probably another garage for the Stingray," Lucas said.

When they pulled into the driveway, Virgil saw a curtain move; somebody had heard them arrive and had snuck a careful look outside.

"They know about the photo," Virgil said. "We won't be a shock, but this could be sad."

AS IT TURNED out, it wasn't sad.

The front door was opened by Jemna Johannson, who looked like she'd just arrived from Sweden, a muscular woman, maybe sixty, with a single gray/blond braid hanging down her back. She was wearing a camo shirt, cargo shorts, and hiking boots.

"You look like police," she said; her accent spoke of Australia, rather than Sweden.

"We are," Virgil said, holding up his ID. "My partner . . ."

"Is a U.S. Marshal. We've been reading the blogs. C'mon in."

A black-and-tan dog stood in the middle of the room; some kind of German shepherd variation with a foot-long tongue, and Lucas asked, "Is he friendly?"

"Sometimes," Johannson said, with a grin. "If he comes for you, don't cover your face. He's going for something more delicate."

"Good to know," Lucas said.

A man hurried in from a back room, carrying an oversized backpack and a duffel. He did not look like anyone's idea of a pharmacist: midsixties, two inches short of six feet, wide as a garage door, gray hair and reddish beard.

"You guys going somewhere?" Virgil asked.

"What do you think?" Elias Johannson said. "Getting the fuck out of here. If those true crime people want to interview us, they're gonna need a boat."

"We have to talk," Lucas said.

"Sure thing. I'm gonna keep getting our gear together and packing the truck. And I need a cigarette. C'mon."

They all went out to the garage where the Johannsons were in the process of packing an oversized white Jeep. A red canoe was already on the roof; Virgil read "Common Loon" hand-painted on the side of the boat, though the words were upside down from his point of view.

Virgil: "So you, uh, had a sexual relationship with Doris Grandfelt?"

"Not exactly a relationship; I did take her back to my bed on three different occasions. Cost me fifteen hundred bucks."

Lucas looked at Jemna: "Did you know about this?"

"Not until last night, when we got the first call from the blog people. El was divorced at the time, forty-five years old, and she was a looker, from what I can see from the online photos. I was nowhere about. What was he supposed to do, spend all his nights choking the chicken?"

"Before we leave, I should mention that I didn't kill her," Elias said. "I last saw her probably a month before she was murdered. Didn't know any of her other customers, so I had nothing to say about it that would have been of any use to anyone."

"How'd you meet her?"

"In a bar. I read about that bartender who was hooking her up—I didn't know him, and I never went to that bar. I met her at a place called the Big O. She was friendly right off. Too friendly, but boy, she looked good after a long dry spell. A couple dances, I knew it was going to cost me something."

Jemna stuck her lip out: "You told me you don't know how to dance."

"I don't. I jump up and down and wave my arms around. White man boogie. Honestly, nobody seemed to notice."

Virgil: "You got nothin' else?"

"I got nothin' else," Elias confirmed. "Where the hell are my cigarettes?"

"Front seat passenger side with your lighter," Jemna said. "We need to stop and pick up a couple of cartons."

"There goes the budget," Elias said. He found his cigarettes, knocked a Winston out of the pack, fired it up, sucked up some smoke. "Ah: love the feel of those cancer cells crawling around my lungs," he said.

Virgil: "What size shoes do your wear?"

Elias held up a foot: "Eleven and a half. Why?"

"Just wondering," Virgil said.

Lucas said, "Look . . ."

"You look," Elias said. "We gotta get out of here before those crime kooks start showing up. You got a DNA kit with you?"

"No."

"Okay. Well, it's out of our way, but we can swing by the BCA before we head north. Is it still in that building off Maryland?"

"Yeah, it is," Virgil said.

"You might give somebody a call, tell them that we're coming," Elias said.

"We'd appreciate it if you wouldn't leave town," Lucas said.

"You can appreciate your ass off, but we're leaving," Elias said. "Unless you want to arrest me or get a court order or whatever you do. Here's the facts of the matter: I slept with Doris—nice girl, and she liked my act—but I didn't kill her. I'm willing to do the DNA. What else do you want? You can't want me to stay around here so I can have a bunch of crazies parked in my driveway harassing us."

"No, we don't," Lucas said. "We'll take some pictures of your driver's licenses and your rig and get out of your hair. We do want you to stop by the BCA—and if you don't do that, we will come after you."

"Great," Jemna said. "Listen: there are a couple more big bags upstairs and a dog kennel in the kitchen packed with dog food and some bowls. Could you help us load?"

LUCAS AND VIRGIL took care of the dog kennel, which weighed a hundred pounds with all the stuff packed inside of it. They were paced by the dog, which turned out to be as violent as a chickadee. While they were hauling it out to the garage, and away from the Johannsons, Lucas asked, "What do you think?"

"I believe him," Virgil said. "He's not worried enough."

"Yeah. Hey: don't tip the fuckin' kennel, everything will fall out. We ought to find out where they're going."

THEY WERE GOING, Jemna said, to the Boundary Waters. Lucas and Virgil's help modestly sped up the loading process, but not quite quickly enough. Two compact SUVs pulled up to the curb outside the house as Elias opened the garage door before rolling out.

Two women climbed out of the cars and immediately began filming the four of them. One of the women shouted, "Officers, are you going to let him escape?"

Virgil turned his back to them and said to Lucas, keeping his voice low, "Not a word, okay?"

"Right."

Jemna asked, "What should we do?"

"Step back in the garage," Virgil said. "Close the garage door."

When the door was down, Virgil said, "There are only two cars outside. If you still want to leave, you should go, now, before more of them start coming in. I'll call the Golden Valley cops and ask for their assistance in identifying the occupants of the two cars, who seem to be frightening you. Are they frightening you?"

Jemna looked at Elias, who shrugged and said, "If that would be helpful."

"When the cops show up, we'll get them reading IDs and checking license plates, and you can make a run for the BCA without somebody trailing you. Don't slow down. And don't skip the BCA unless you want to spend some time in an outstate jail."

Jemna nodded: "Let's do it."

Virgil called Duncan, explained the situation, and Duncan said he would talk with Golden Valley immediately, and that he would also get one of the newly assigned investigators on the Grandfelt case to interview Elias Johannson.

Jemna went into the kitchen and peeked out the window. "They're still there, out of the cars, with their cameras."

"On your property?" Lucas asked.

"No, they're staying clear, in the street."

"They know better than to trespass," Lucas said.

Virgil said, "You're going to be interviewed at the BCA. I mean, in addition to doing the DNA scrub. That'll slow you down some, but you shouldn't have these people on your back."

Jemna: "Is this a sneaky way to arrest El?"

Virgil shook his head: "Not unless he decides to confess that he killed Doris Grandfelt. But it'll be a formal interview. You can have a lawyer there if you want to."

"See what happens," Elias said.

"That's what I would do," Lucas said. He said that because he hated to have lawyers sitting in on interviews, because most lawyers understood that the best thing their client could say is *nothing*. Elias seemed like a talker, and Lucas loved talkers, as would his BCA interviewers.

A few minutes later a Golden Valley patrol car pulled up behind the two crimer vehicles, and a cop got out.

"Time to run for it," Lucas said, and the Johannsons did, leaving the true-crimers showing their driver's licenses to the cop.

IN THE TAHOE, Virgil said, "We need to get Stephanie Brady's camera to Jon and get somebody to go over and give O'Brien a scrub."

"Yes. I think . . . Elias picked Doris up on her own, which sort of expands the universe of what she was doing. She was kinda on the street, even if the street was a bar."

"I did notice. That's a little depressing. She was maybe turning pro."

Lucas sighed, and said, "Damnit. The other way was easier. Let's get over to the BCA and make sure the Johannsons showed up."

"And then . . ."

"Klink the Shrink."

16

Jon Duncan caught Virgil and Lucas inside the BCA's back door, pulled them into his office, took possession of Brady's camera and promised to get a DNA scrub from O'Brien, told them that the Johannsons were being interviewed, and, finally, said, "Tell me everything. Don't leave anything out."

During Lucas's time with the BCA, which had ended several years earlier, he'd been more or less the boss of both Duncan and Virgil. As agents, Duncan had persistence, Virgil had talent. Both characteristics were valuable, and a lot of cops would argue that persistence is more important. Lucas generally agreed with that, except on the hard cases, where talent was essential. Virgil sometimes made arrests that, in terms of procedure, baffled his fellow agents.

To say nothing of the fact that he sometimes slept with suspects . . . which was how he wound up as the father of twins.

————

SINCE THEY TRUSTED Duncan as much as they trusted anyone at the BCA, they told him what they'd found.

Duncan: "You're about three laps ahead of everyone else."

"If you tell everyone else what we've told you, we'll be tripping over each other," Lucas said. "Polluting the possibilities. We've already got enough problems with the crowd of true crime people."

"Tell everybody that we're focusing on clues from the true-crimers," Virgil suggested. "Which is almost accurate. Keep them off our backs for a few days and maybe we'll come up with something decent."

"The guys are all gonna know what the Johannsons are saying . . ."

"That's great," Lucas said. "Tell everybody that we sent the Johannsons over here, and they'll all assume that we're one big happy family."

"Won't last," Duncan said.

"No, but we'll get some slack," Virgil said. "Right now, we're gonna go jack up Klink the Shrink."

"Talk to me," Duncan said, urgently. "Call me."

ANOTHER NICE SUMMER day, though with a thunderhead forming its anvil off in the distance; the niceness was something they were having a hard time appreciating inside a Tahoe. They motored back across the Mississippi after calling Klink's office to make sure he was there. Virgil identified himself as a member of the American Psychiatric Association, and the woman who answered the phone said, "One moment please, I'll see if Dr. Klink is with a patient."

She put them on hold and Virgil hung up. "We're on."

———

THE TRIP TO Minneapolis took twenty minutes. They drove around for a while, circling Klink's office but unable to find a parking spot, until finally they left the truck in a no-parking zone. Virgil put a BCA placard—Bureau of Criminal Apprehension, Official Business—on the dashboard where a meter reader might see it.

Klink's building was one of the older ones in downtown Minneapolis, dating to pre–World War II, reinforced concrete and bland as a boiled potato. They rode up six floors in a rickety elevator and walked down the hall to Klink's office; the hallway smelled faintly of mold and carpet cleaner, though it was neat enough.

Klink's office door was both anonymous and locked—a brass plaque said only "621." An LED doorbell light glowed discreetly below the plaque. They pressed the button and a woman's voice, the same one who'd put them on hold, asked, "Who is it?"

Virgil had called, so Lucas responded: "U.S. Marshals Service. Official business. Open up."

The door buzzed, and they pushed through.

On the other side, they found themselves in a small, square room with a desk on one side and four chairs, facing each other, on the other. The room had plastic wallpaper of the kind used in hospitals to make it easier to clean up blood and other fluids. A woman in a purplish patterned dress was retreating down a hallway in front of them, then stopping at an open door. They couldn't hear what she said, but she was apparently talking with Klink. The man himself stepped into the doorway, and gestured them forward with his fingers.

"Can I help you? I'm recording a blog entry . . ."

"We need to talk privately," Lucas said. "Shouldn't take too long."

Klink was a tall man, thin, balding, with warm brown eyes behind tortoiseshell glasses. The glasses were perched on a nose the size of a hot dog bun. His hair was receding and he wore a spade beard, the image of a psychiatrist, although he wasn't one. He appeared to be about fifty. He had a deep voice with a flat Great Lakes accent. "Can you tell me what this is about?"

"Yes, in private," Lucas said.

Klink regarded them warily, tipped his head toward the back of the office space: "We have a consultation room. That should be comfortable."

They followed him down the hallway past a compact recording studio, where another woman, much younger, dressed all in black, was fussing with a video setup and microphone. "What's going on?"

"We have a delay—an urgent consultation requested by the police. We'll be in the consult room. I'm told it shouldn't be long."

"We're running a little tight," the woman said. "We need another six minutes outside the ads . . ."

"I understand. I'll be back," Klink said.

As they continued down the hall, Klink looked over his shoulder and said, "We have a radio deal where the blog entry is first broadcast before we put it up on the 'net. We need to be on time with it. Exactly on time."

"Okay," Virgil said.

The consult room was soft, quiet, a circle of comfortable leather chairs facing each other, with beige-pink walls to soothe the troubled mind. Klink waved them into two of the chairs, sat himself, crossed his legs, and asked, "What's this all about?"

Virgil: "Twenty-three years ago, you were a customer of a woman,

Doris Grandfelt, who sold sex to customers who she met on the Minneapolis club scene. She was murdered, which you must know, and we have some questions for you."

Klink slapped the arm of his chair, half rose, sank back and said, "That is slander, sir! That is slander!"

Virgil: "We have a witness who knows you, and says that you were one of Doris's . . ."

Now Klink stood up: "If you wish to question me, you'll do it in the presence of my lawyer. I'll have to ask you to leave."

Neither Virgil nor Lucas moved, and Virgil looked up at Klink and said, "That's certainly your right. But one way or another, we're going to get some questions answered—or, maybe we won't, depending on how smart your lawyer is, and how guilty you are. We will get a search warrant for a DNA specimen from you, unless you give us one voluntarily. A search warrant, once filed, is a public record . . ."

Klink snatched off his glasses, ran a hand through his remaining hair. "This is a police-state tactic, making threats, knowing that I'm screwed no matter what I do. Even if I talk to an attorney, he'll tell his wife . . ."

Virgil: "And you being a celebrity . . ."

"There's no way out," Lucas said.

"Well, unless you answer some questions privately and do a voluntary DNA scrub," Virgil added. "All that would be confidential . . . as long as you're not the one who murdered Doris."

"I am not!" Klink screeched. He turned away from them, toward a window covered with venetian blinds. He reached out, pulled a cord to open the blinds, looked out at the city, his face gone haggard.

"Ask a question. I can't promise to answer," he said.

"You did know Doris?"

"I knew her, yes. Oh, and I will do the DNA sample if that can be handled discreetly. I am not the man who slept with her the night she was murdered."

"We can have a tech do the DNA right here in your office, or at your home, after hours if you prefer," Lucas said. "She'll keep her mouth shut, you know, because she likes her job."

"And it sounds like you know some of the details of the case," Virgil said.

Klink circled back around his chair, dropped back into it. "I am aware of the renewed media interest in the case, of course. I even looked at some of the files that have been posted online. I was horrified by the photos. As a psychologist, I can tell you that the killer is a very troubled human being . . ."

"We know that," Lucas said dryly. "We need to catch him . . ."

"Or her . . ." Klink said.

"You think the killer could be a woman?" Virgil asked, clearly curious.

"Possibly. If you read the ME's report carefully, you'll see they checked if she was pregnant when she died. She wasn't, but she'd had sexual intercourse shortly before she was murdered."

"Yes, we know all that," Virgil said. "There's an argument about whether the sex was rape or consensual."

"It seems unlikely to me that she was raped, but what I think is neither here nor there. The details of the report say that semen was found in her vagina and cervix, but not in her uterus or fallopian tubes. After ejaculation, the semen passes through the uterus and into the fallopian tubes in a matter of minutes—fifteen minutes in some cases. It never got there. She must have been murdered immediately after having sex. I mean within minutes. Looking at the photos, I thought, this is a crime of passion. Either passion on the part of the male who ejaculated into her, or someone who passionately objected to that."

"An act of jealousy," Lucas said.

"It could be," Klink said.

"This is very interesting, Doc," Virgil said. "How do you know all that stuff about fallopian tubes and so on?"

"Much of my . . . practice, such as it is, involves questions of sexuality. I need to know how the parts work."

Lucas: "Are you married?"

"No. Never."

"Do you still see escorts? Are you out on Tinder?"

"I do not patronize prostitutes, and never have. I have used Internet dating services," Klink said.

"But you did patronize Doris," Virgil said.

"I did, but when we met, when we first slept together, I didn't realize that . . . she would ask for a gift." Lucas glanced at Virgil, who nodded: Klink wasn't being entirely truthful—they already knew he'd been introduced to Doris with sex in the offing.

"A gift. Okay. I'll let that go," Virgil said. "Did you give her gifts more than once?"

"Yes, several times," Klink said. "At the time of her death, I hadn't seen her for a couple of weeks."

"And you had no further contact with her?"

Klink had two fingers pressed against his lips, and then he said, "This, as you say, is confidential."

Lucas nodded, "Yes . . . Unless you admit to participating in some way . . ."

"No, no, no . . . but I have a small piece of information that you may find interesting. A week before her death, perhaps ten days, I called her to see if we might get together again. She said she probably wouldn't be dating for a while. She said she'd met somebody in the medical field and they were very drawn to each other."

"Jesus! Why didn't you tell somebody?" Lucas asked. "Back at the time?"

"Why do you think?" They sat and looked at each other, then Klink added, "I know I should have."

KLINK HAD NOTHING more, though they talked until there was a knock on the door. When Klink said, "Come," the door popped open on the young woman in black. "Dr. Klink, we're getting pressured here . . ."

Lucas said, "One more minute. Close the door."

The woman, a worried look on her face, closed the door and Lucas said, "We'll want a gum scrub. When would that be convenient, like, today?"

"Later. I'll come to your office. Who should I talk to?"

They gave him Jon Duncan's phone number. Virgil asked, "You don't have any more information about the medical guy?"

"No. Well . . ." He scratched his bald spot. "This is supposition . . ."

"I like what you had to say about fallopian tubes. Go ahead and suppose," Virgil said.

"Before I went into showbiz, I was actually a decent psychologist, especially in relational matters. I found Doris interesting, and not just sexually. She was very clear about what she wanted. She wanted a

good time, and whatever it took to have a good time. She liked par-
ties. She liked getting dressed up. She liked alcohol, marijuana, and
cocaine. She would have fit perfectly in a place like Hollywood, or at
least, the idea of Hollywood. And she wanted it right now, before she
got old. For her, old was thirty."

Lucas: "Okay. So what?"

Virgil answered him: "This medical guy, whoever it was, wasn't
just a medical student. He was already making the bucks she needed."

"Exactly," Klink said, jabbing a finger at Virgil. "You're looking for
a doctor. A successful doctor. Follow along here: if a student makes
it through college in four years, starting at eighteen, and then immediately follows that with med school and goes straight through, then
he's twenty-six. Most people can't do that—they're twenty-seven or
twenty-eight when they get out. Then, he's got a few years' post-grad
training, in some specialty or another . . . I mean, a plastic surgeon,
for example, is rarely fully out on his own before he's in his mid-
thirties. Then he still has to build a practice."

"You're saying, we're looking for an old guy," Lucas said. "Not an
old guy back then, but an old guy now."

"Depends on what you call old, but Doris was killed twenty-one
years ago? I'd say you're looking for a doctor in at least his midfifties,
to maybe sixties. Could be seventy. And I'd give you two-to-one that
he drives a Porsche 911 or a Jaguar. Possibly a Mercedes-Benz, but
nothing Japanese. A convertible. He might possibly fly his own private plane. That would pull Doris right in, get her excited. And you
know what? I'd bet that he's still here in the Twin Cities."

"Help me with that," Virgil said.

Klink shrugged: "Because he was established. If he went someplace else, he'd have to start all over. I'd bet he's still here. Especially if he's innocent of the murder."

Lucas: "We'll get Jon Duncan to set up the scrub."

Virgil: "Thank you, Dr. Klink."

BACK IN THE Tahoe, they called Duncan and told him to expect a call from Klink. Duncan said, "You asked for a list of people who had access to the Bee Accounting executive dining room. I've got that."

"Email it to me," Virgil said. "I'll pull it up on my iPad."

"It's on the way," Duncan said. "I'm pushing the button now."

"We need something else from Bee—we need a list of their clients who were in the medical field when Doris was killed."

"More than twenty years ago, man. I don't know what they'll have, but I'll ask."

"They're accountants, Jon," Lucas said. "They'll have it."

Off the phone, and back in traffic, Virgil said, "I gotta say, I was impressed by Klink. I thought the guy was a charlatan, you know, from his radio rep."

"He had some interesting ideas," Lucas said. "But that doctor stuff? That woman killer stuff? We're a long way down the road from anything you might call a fact."

"True, but we're also into new territory. Nobody was ever talking seriously about what we're looking at," Virgil said. "A woman as the killer? A sixty-year-old doctor? Fallopian tubes? I didn't even know you could set a time of death by fallopian tubes."

"That wasn't emphasized in the ME's report," Lucas said. "I remember the word, so it was mentioned. They didn't say anything about the timing, but that now seems critical. We need to check with somebody who'd know for sure."

"Call Weather. She'd know somebody who could tell us."

LUCAS CALLED, WEATHER gave him the name and phone number of a University of Minnesota fertility doctor named Bridget Kenyon. They called Kenyon, and after speaking with her secretary, were put through. They didn't talk long, but Kenyon confirmed what Klink had said about the timing.

Virgil to Lucas: "A doctor has sex with Doris, but he's married, and Doris tells him she's going to talk to his old lady about it. For the doc, it's a fling. For Doris, it's the road to riches. They argue. He has a knife . . ."

"Where are they? If it's a fling, he'd want it to be secret. In his office, maybe, but most doctors' offices have security, and he'd be hauling around a body and there'd be a lot of blood to clean up. A hotel or motel always has people around, you couldn't carry a body out . . ."

"He's a rich doctor and has a cabin on the St. Croix," Virgil said.

"And instead of taking her deeper into the woods, he hauls her back into town to hide the body?"

"All right, that's a weak spot."

After a while, Lucas said, "She was killed in a restroom at Bee. No carpets, easy to clean up the mess. Late at night: the ME thought she'd been dead for eighteen to twenty-four hours when she was found, and she was found at seven o'clock. So, sometime after seven o'clock at Bee. They get it on, she goes into the restroom to clean up, you know . . ."

"Yeah, I know. To avoid the wet spot in her underpants."

"And no little spermies have time to make it up to her tubes because the doc . . . okay, wait. They're on the same floor as the cafeteria. They have their fight about his old lady, the doc goes into the cafeteria and gets a knife, spends a couple minutes honing it on the red brick . . . waits for her to come out of the toilet stall to wash her hands, comes up behind her like he's going to wrap his arms around her, and he sticks her. Because he's got one arm around her, his knife hand is low, and it goes straight into her back, instead of slashing down."

"That's a good story," Virgil admitted. "But you were saying something about being a long road away from a fact."

More silence, listening to the tires. Then, "We do have something like a fact. That she was seeing somebody in the medical field."

"Okay," Virgil said. And, "Let me make a call."

"Who to?"

"Klink the Shrink."

Klink had finished the last blog segment, came to the phone and said, "I was about to call your man Duncan."

"Great, do that, he's waiting," Virgil said. "I have another question. When you said that Doris was dating somebody in the medical field, was it you saying, 'medical field,' or was that Doris? Did she say 'medical field' or did she say 'doctor'?"

Klink said, "Oh, boy. 'Medical field' sounds like something I'd say or think. If she said 'doctor,' I might have remembered that as being in the 'medical field,' because all kinds of people are calling themselves doctors now. But if she'd said 'doctor,' I would have assumed the person was in the medical field, and not some other kind of doctor. I can't answer your question. It could go either way. Memory is a very fluid thing. As you should know."

"Why should I know that?" Virgil asked.

"Because police officers have to talk to people about what they remember about a traumatic event. Quite often, I have read, what they think they saw often doesn't stack up with what actually happened. Even though they're sincere about what they think they saw."

"Fair enough," Virgil said. "Thanks, Doc."

LUCAS AND VIRGIL talked about that, then Lucas recapitulated what they'd learned from witnesses and photos: Roger Jepson, the auto mechanic and ex-bartender, had given them Stanley O'Brien, the lobbyist and former legislator. O'Brien had given them Klink the Shrink.

The Johannsons had—most likely—given them only one useful thing: their cop instincts told them that Elias Johannson probably wasn't the killer.

"He's a pharmacist. That would be considered being in the medical field. If he has a PhD, he might be called doctor," Lucas said.

Virgil: "I don't think so. I didn't smell even a hint of guilt."

"He'd be a psycho, so he might not feel a hint of guilt," Lucas said.

"Yeah, but if he's negative, and I'll bet he is . . ."

"Then he's out of it."

GOING ON THE conversation with Klink, they'd convinced themselves that anyone whose DNA didn't match the DNA taken from Doris Grandfelt's body, probably wasn't the killer—because the timing was so critical, with the fallopian tube clock. The owner of the DNA was either the killer or had been very physically close to the killer at the time of the crime—possibly in the same room, or at least nearby.

"The true-crimers know about Jepson and they might be able to jump from him to Stanley O'Brien. But O'Brien almost certainly won't talk, so they won't get to Klink. What we need to do is to track down anyone in the photos who is in the medical field, or to talk to the guys in the photos who can point us to someone who is."

LUCAS CALLED DAHLIA Blair. "How many of the photos have you identified?"

"Four, now, we think. We got Johannson and Roger Jepson gave us Stanley O'Brien, but O'Brien's not in any of the photos. There are a couple of people over trying to interview him but he's being stubborn."

"Because you're trying to ruin his life," Virgil said. "Anyway, who are the others in the photos?"

Blair read off three names: one was a government employee, one a banker, another one an architect.

"Much more white-collar than I would have expected," Blair said. "It seems like either Roger Jepson or Doris was very selective. Haven't had one truck driver."

"Tom, Dick, and Harry?"

"Not so far," Blair said. "But it's like that."

"A BCA agent will call you for the names," Lucas said. "We'll give him your phone number. If this turns into something, we'll see that you're considered for the reward."

"Thank you. I will talk with him. Or her."

They rang off, called Jon Duncan, told him about three new

names, and Blair's phone number. "I'll pass them along," Duncan said. "Why aren't you looking at them?"

"Too many names all at once," Lucas said. "We'll need a team to get to them before they get a crowd of true-crimers outside their doors."

"I almost believe that," Duncan said. "I'll get some people on the way."

"What about the film I gave you?" Virgil asked.

"Hey. That's something. Rolvaag got right on it, already has some images. He made a set for you, and a set for the team here. You can pick them up . . ."

"Give us the address," Virgil said.

Duncan did that, and Lucas wrote it in his notebook.

Virgil: "And Jon? When you send your guys out, to the people in the photos, consider the possibility that they might be thinking about suicide."

"Ah, jeez . . ."

17

Barry Rolvaag lived in a big house above a ravine called Swede Hollow, which was not a place with a lot of big houses, but his was. Two stories with a front porch, swing hooks but no porch swing, gray shingle siding falling apart from old age. A two-track driveway ran to the back of the house, thirties style, from the days when people drove Model T's. A tiny out-of-kilter garage slumped in the back, at the end of the driveway. An aging Harley softtail sat in the bed of a Ford F-150, pointed toward the street for a fast getaway; the Ford wore a bumper sticker that read "Is there life after death? Fuck with this truck and find out."

Rolvaag came to the door with a cup of coffee in his hand. A bear-built man with a gut, square yellow teeth, and a gray beard that dropped to his chest, he popped the door and said to Virgil, "I know you. How you been?"

"Been okay. Working the Grandfelt cold case." Virgil introduced Lucas and Rolvaag said, "Come on back."

He led them through a kitchen that smelled of spicy drinks with a thin overlay of weed and raw chicken meat, past a woman who resembled her husband except for the beard; she was stuffing something into a dead chicken's butt. She said, "Cheese it, the cops."

"Nobody's said that since 1920," Lucas said.

"Yeah, I know. I humbly apologize," she said, unhumbly.

Rolvaag said, "This way . . ."

While the first floor of the house was somewhat tattered, the basement, at the bottom of a narrow stairs, was spotless, with a vinegary smell of photo fixer hanging in the air.

The basement floor was raised off the original concrete and was now covered with gray, engineered planks, as were the walls and ceilings. The main room was hung with black-and-white photos, cityscapes, and furnished with two computers and three printers. The largest printer was the size of a chest of drawers. A doorway with a red light above it led to a wet darkroom.

Rolvaag said, "The film wasn't too bad. There were seven shots on it. Fuji Superia X-Tra 400. C-41, so a bit of a problem converting to digital. I had to buy some new software. You saw a lot more of that Fuji up in Canada than down here. Was the shooter Canadian?"

"Nope. No idea where she got the film," Virgil said.

"Well, what I did was, I developed it, copied the seven shots with a digital camera. I've had them up on my Studio. And I made some digital prints . . ."

The Studio turned out to be a MacIntosh computer. Rolvaag dropped into a business chair, rattled some keys, brought up the seven shots. Three featured Doris Grandfelt, laughing, with a different man in each one, apparently in bars. The other four were of two different men, probably outside of bars, on urban streets.

"Five guys," Lucas said, peering at the screen.

"Five, but two of them would be tough to identify," Virgil said. "Their faces are mushy . . ."

"She took them in crap light with a crap camera, on a sidewalk," Rolvaag said. "Bar light. That red neon washed everything out. The film was okay, but not great after twenty years. I sharpened them as much as reasonable, any more and you start getting artifacts . . ."

Virgil said, "I don't see much of the red . . ." Virgil had been shooting digital photos for a half-dozen outdoor magazines, but his work was all in natural light, during the day and at twilight.

"Yeah, the red was a problem," Rolvaag said, pushing away from the screen to talk to Virgil. "I went into Photoshop and tried adding a layer and some Caucasian coloring, but it looked like crap. What I did next was I opened up the HSL panel and dropped the red saturation to zero. I didn't want to hit the noise reduction too hard because that'd take out the available detail in the shadows. I wanted to keep that even if it was a little messy . . ."

They talked more about Photoshop; to Lucas it sounded like "blah blah crap blah blah noise blah blah . . ."

"You did a damn good job, looking at that original and then the modified one," Virgil said, still bent over the screen. "I oughta take a class."

"Still can't see the face that well," Lucas said.

Rolvaag: "That's what we got left. That's it."

"I gotta say, we might not recognize the guy if we saw him walking down the street," Virgil said. "But if we crowdsource it, and if somebody knew him back then, and the context . . . I bet we could get some names."

"Maybe," Lucas said.

The actual prints were no better than the shots on the screen; Rolvaag had included sets of both the unaltered shots and the one he'd tried to clean up.

"Anyway, we got three good faces," Lucas said, going through the prints. "And they'd be some of her last dates, so it's something."

"It's a little more than that," Virgil said. "You're missing the interesting part."

Lucas looked back at the images, frowned, and asked, "What?"

Virgil tapped one of the exterior photos, a narrow slice of a car visible in the background. "Remember what our shrink said? About the doctor's car? Does this look familiar?"

Lucas looked again and said, "Holy shit."

"It's just a Porsche. An old 911," Rolvaag said.

"Just a Porsche," Lucas agreed.

ROLVAAG GAVE THEM three sets of prints, an envelope with a glassine sleeve with the original negatives, and a thumb drive with the digital photos. "I will send the bill to the usual, and I have to include the price of the software," he said. "You guys getting anywhere with this thing? I went out to one of the true crime sites, seems like some stuff is coming up."

They talked about that on the way up the stairs, where they said goodbye to Mrs. Rolvaag, who was skinning grapes.

Out in the truck, Lucas said, "I would have seen the car sooner or later."

"Yeah, like next month," Virgil said. "Man, is it possible that Klink called it? A doctor with a Porsche?"

"Possible, if unlikely," Lucas said. "But it was one of her last recorded dates, at the end of the film roll . . . if they were actually dates."

"The question is, what do we do now?" Virgil said. "If we give the photos to Jon, and he passes them on to the main team, they'll never find the guy. They don't have the resources. If we give them to the true-crimers, we could get crucified, but they might find him."

Lucas said, "I think we push Jon into a crack. Tell him we want the one photo. The team can have all of them, but we get to leak the Porsche shot to the crimers. He could go for that."

"What if he doesn't?"

Lucas shrugged. "We give it to them anyway. Fuck a bunch of bureaucrats. If they give us any trouble, we'll have the governor go down and chat with them."

"And what if the governor won't do it?"

"We'll have Lara chat with *him*. The guy would sell his children for a hundred-dollar campaign donation."

Virgil nodded. "That observation might help Jon make the correct decision, without us having to push him that far."

"That's what I'm thinking," Lucas said.

AT BCA HEADQUARTERS, they didn't have to push Duncan at all. He quickly agreed that they could release all the photos to the true-crimers, as long as they did it anonymously—and if they kept the BCA out of it.

"Hell, I'll give it to them, keep Virgil completely out of it," Lucas said. "My real boss is in Washington. He'll never even hear about it."

"Big of you," Virgil said. To Duncan, he said, "I thought you'd resist."

"No. Releasing them makes sense, even if some of the guys won't like it. This is exactly the kind of stuff you might want to crowd-source," Duncan said. "The crimers have shown they could do that. Besides, I *will* blame it on Lucas."

"I was just telling Virgil that you weren't nearly as bad an investigator as people used to say you were," Lucas said to Duncan. And to Virgil, "Let's call Dahlia."

THEY CALLED DAHLIA Blair, who instantly agreed to put the photos up.

Over the next two days, several tips came in, and they identified two of the men in the most recent photos, but not the man with the Porsche.

On the third day . . .

18

Amanda Fisk was running about fifty-fifty on whether to pay the caterer or kill her. The food was okay, though it seemed to focus on the aromatic: sauteed chicken livers in sesame oil? Smoked salmon crostini?

But the caterer, whose name was Joyce, instead of sticking close to the food, seemed to be more focused on the house and whether or not Fisk was going to put it up for sale. Fisk found her wandering through every room on both floors, including the bedroom, where she'd been peering out the window where Timothy had taken his fall. She wasn't trespassing, exactly, because there were a lot of people wandering around, and Fisk had put up a sign, with an arrow, pointing up the stairway, that read "More bathrooms."

Joyce had even asked, "Is this where . . . IT . . . happened?"

Fisk avoided an answer, instead asking, "Do we have another pan of the baked brie bites? There seems to be a demand."

Fisk had begun to suspect that the woman was scouting for a real estate agent; but no matter, there were at least a hundred other people all over the place—from Timothy's practice, from the hospitals where he was on staff, from the county attorney's office, along with, Fisk suspected, gate-crashers there for the food.

She would be expected to give a tearful eulogy in the not-too-distant future, and she'd prepared for it. Could she squeeze out a few tears? She doubted it, but she was prepared even for that. She'd make a last-minute trip to the bathroom, hit both eyes with some Systane eye drops, and with flooded eyes, would make her way downcast through the living room where she'd ring her little bell. With any luck, some of the Systane would trickle down her cheek . . .

In the meantime, the mourners, all of them, collectively, were laying down a blanket of unidentifiable DNA, while mumbling regrets through a mouthful of spinach puffs; the mourning seemed perfunctory, the eating not so much.

Timothy was still present, in his solid silver urn. She planned to dump him over the fence into the Belgian Malinois' yard as soon as the crowd had gone and it got dark. If anyone asked, he'd gone in the Mississippi, where he'd spent many hours happily wandering the overgrown shores with the goddamn Jack Russells.

"You know, the thing I liked about Timothy was his joie de vivre . . ."

Yeah. You could take your joie de vivre and your bad French accent and stick them where the sun don't shine . . .

As for the urn, maybe she could have it melted down? But that was for later. For now, dressed in a dark blue knee-length dress, with a double string of pearls, she wanted to get as many people as possible sitting in chairs, opening doors, handling Timothy's tools—she'd had a lowball offer on the tools, and would accept it before the bidder left the premises.

And from people not gauche enough to actually inquire (yet) there had been noticeable interest in Timothy's 911 and the Range Rover. She'd been hinting to those people that the cars were actually available after she'd given them a thorough cleaning.

All of this was splattering through her mind like random raindrops when she passed a group of prosecutors from the county attorney's office, and heard one of them saying, ". . . a bunch of new photos taken by Doris Grandfelt, supposedly her last dates . . ."

And she thought, *What!*

The caterer, Joyce, was forgotten. She couldn't kick a hundred people out of the house, when they'd barely dented the antipasto skewers, but she desperately needed to look at the true crime sites, and *right now.* She walked back to the library, got her laptop, and locked herself in the guest bathroom.

AnneCashInvestigations had the new photos. Fisk had no idea who the men were in four of the photos, but the fifth one . . .

Timothy. And Timothy's fucking 1998 Porsche, with that funny tail fin thing, the wing. The photo was not a good one and was old and murky. It could be a shot of any tall, slender, sharp-nosed balding man in what looked like a blazer and slacks combination, standing on a sidewalk outside a bar. With a Porsche.

On the other hand, if you knew him at the time . . .

Something, she thought, sitting there on the toilet seat, had to be done. And the only thing she could think of was the elimination of the prize for finding the killer of Doris Grandfelt. The cops, as far as she knew, had made no progress whatever in solving the case. The true crime people had been another story altogether.

Out of the bathroom, she made her Systane-eyed speech about Timothy, reliving some of the good times from Timothy's point of view, even got a few laughs. Cleared the house out, including the caterer and the gate-crashers, and left the urn of ashes for later.

It occurred to her that she ought to feed the dogs, and she did. The dogs were another problem that would have to wait for later. Too many people knew how much Timothy loved the mutts, so she'd have to keep the little fuckers around until any questions about their fate might no longer be asked. Like maybe she gave them to a passing troupe of dog lovers.

But Lara Grandfelt had to go.

FISK WAS THOROUGHLY versed in the theory and practice of murder, having, over the years, sent four dozen murderers to prison as a prosecutor, and having killed six people herself, including Timothy.

Her personal kills included a fourteen-year-old ninth grader, tripped and shoved in front of a moving truck. The girl had been ejected from behind a tree and the driver said he never saw her before he hit her, and even after he hit her, wasn't sure what he'd hit.

When he'd stopped to look, he'd found a horrified Amanda Fisk standing over the body of her crushed schoolmate. Fisk told cops that the girl had started to step out from behind a tree and had tripped and fallen over the curb and under the oncoming wheels.

She'd cried real tears at the funeral. Not because she mourned the young girl, but because she was so frightened for herself—how poorly and impulsively she'd done it. If the girl hadn't died, she would have told everyone about the hand in her back.

But she had died; and that had been strangely satisfying.

Over the following years, at the University of Minnesota and the William Mitchell College of Law, she'd analyzed the ways of murder, and when the time came to kill the second woman, she thought she'd worked it all out. The hardest kind of murder to solve was the random attack where the killer escaped from the scene without being seen. Any murder with an obvious motive would be a problem: cops loved motives.

A second thought: obvious motives could also be misleading.

WITH ONE EXCEPTION, Fisk wouldn't kill for entertainment. That was simply stupid. But any gain on her part had to be non-obvious, as was the situation with Rose McCauley, a very pretty and very smart classmate at William Mitchell. One of them was going to be the top woman in the class, and after making a realistic assessment of the possibilities, Fisk was almost certain that it wouldn't be her. Being top woman meant something at the time.

She killed McCauley one dark night—they went to the Mitchell night school—with a classic lead pipe that she found on a demolition site. She'd decided on the pipe because McCauley's death would be fast and silent.

She hit McCauley as the other woman walked along a sidewalk to her car. Fisk stepped from behind a dense bridal wreath bush on the warm autumn evening and hit the other woman three times: once knocking her down, twice to make sure, crushing her skull. She took McCauley's purse—robbery, the misleading motive—put the lead pipe inside it, and it all now resided safely at the bottom of the Mississippi.

Doris Grandfelt was the third kill.

The fourth kill . . . better not to think about that one. That one was over the top, even for Fisk; but entertaining. Just thinking about it, she could smell the buttered popcorn.

Fisk's mother was the fifth.

Listen: her parents had divorced after her father had an affair with a woman in his shop at 3M. Her mother had never remarried, and ten years after the divorce, Fisk's ancient grandmother had died and left a substantial estate to her daughter, Fisk's mother.

It seemed unfair, somehow, that her mother, then in her sixties, would simply burn through that estate, and the money and house she'd gotten in the divorce, in her declining years. Her mother, in fact, was largely a waste of good air, an inert devotee of social media and streaming services.

Also a diabetic and insulin dependent. A couple of sleeping pills in a cup of late-night tea, followed by an overdose of insulin, moved the two estates right along to Fisk.

She didn't think about her mother. She never had. It never occurred to her that she should, except in the context of a fully stuffed Fidelity account.

The sixth was Timothy.

LARA GRANDFELT.

The problem was right out front: she was driving the research by the true crime enthusiasts, and so far, that research had turned up the only clues in Doris Grandfelt's murder: the knife, the photos of Grandfelt's customers, including Timothy. If the five-million-dollar reward package were to disappear, so would the true-crimers . . . she thought.

She wasn't entirely sure about that. It was theoretically possible that the reward was somehow incorporated in Lara Grandfelt's will. But Fisk thought that idea simply wouldn't have occurred to Grandfelt, who was in her forties. She wanted to *know* who killed her twin. To have the murder solved after she was dead herself wouldn't satisfy that quest, so it wouldn't occur to her to put the reward in a will.

Even if Grandfelt did put it in her will, it would take a while for the will to be settled. Fisk had dealt with enough murder investigations to sense the movement in them . . . sense when an investigation was either moving forward or was dead in the water. The Doris Grandfelt investigation felt as though it were gaining momentum, running downhill.

If she could stop it, even temporarily, gain some time, get Timothy's death well into the past, that could be critical.

WITH THE MEMORIAL service over, Fisk went to her home office and started the basic research she'd need to kill Grandfelt. As a prosecutor, she had routine computer access to driver's license files, and she went out for Grandfelt's license information. That gave her an address: Grandfelt lived in the upscale Lake of the Isles neighborhood in Minneapolis, on a parkway that ran along the east side of the lake.

It also gave her Grandfelt's cars: an older BMW sport utility vehicle, and a flashy, heart-stopping black Jaguar convertible.

From Google, she got a satellite view of the lakeside houses and the garages and parking spaces behind them. Access to the parking was through an alley that ran behind the waterfront homes. There was on-street parking all around the neighborhood, so she could get close in a car. She'd have to check for district parking restrictions. She noted, on the satellite view, a jogging trail around the lake.

In forty-five minutes, she'd worked out a credible approach to Grandfelt's house. She would scout it by car and then on foot. She would pose as a jogger, on the lakeside trail. Why would she be running there when she lived in St. Paul? Because running in St. Paul had begun to frighten her. Any long running loop in St. Paul would take her through some rough neighborhoods, a woman alone, a new widow. She couldn't run during the day because she worked.

Lake of the Isles was quiet, pretty, and very, very safe.

That should work, if the improbable happened, and she was stopped by the police for an ID check.

Her bigger problem was that Minneapolis had a lot of cops. If there was some kind of alarm, the response would be quick. She kicked back in her chair and thought about that. What if there were to be some kind of incident that would pull the cops to another location?

She couldn't help thinking, *Fire?*

Or was that too ambitious? What about a swatting? If there were a swatting on the other side of the lake, another affluent neighborhood, all the local patrol cars would be pulled in . . .

A year before, she'd prosecuted a high schooler who'd had the bad judgment to be over eighteen—a legal adult—when he swatted his physics teacher. Swatting was a bit of a plague: call 9-1-1, screaming that there was a man in the house with a gun, that you'd locked yourself in a closet but he was coming, that you had a gun of your own, call out the address and then . . . *Bang!* The gunshot. And hang up.

You'd have the SWAT squad there in twenty minutes, along with every other cop in the area.

She could easily swat somebody, but if she made a 9-1-1 call, which would be recorded, then, when the swatting call was proven fraudulent and Lara Grandfelt was found murdered at the same time as the SWAT call, she'd be giving away the fact that the probable Grandfelt killer was female.

Was there any way she could make it seem like a male voice calling in?

More online research: yes, AI made it possible to create something that sounded like a male voice saying anything you needed it to say, but the voices she heard didn't sound real. Further, they were flat. She could find no way to make a voice sound panicked.

There were also apps that could change the pitch of a voice, make it lower, but the samples she heard didn't sound convincing.

And to make the call, she'd have to buy a burner phone. She knew as a prosecutor that many of the places that sold burners also had serious video surveillance. She couldn't afford to be on camera buying the phone.

BACK TO THE fire idea—crude, but workable, she thought. The whole Lake of the Isles neighborhood was older, with a high percentage of wooden houses. A gallon of gasoline in a glass jug, a rag for a fuse, and she'd have her fire. If there were any noise to accompany the fire, if it was immediately obvious that the fire was arson, then anyone seen running would be suspect. If a cop stopped her to check her ID, then she'd have two murders to commit.

Would it be possible to spot an empty house? How would you do that?

She turned to Zillow, the real estate website, and began looking at homes in the Lake of the Isles neighborhood. There were many candidates for sale, almost all of them with photos attached.

She quickly found two that appeared to be empty—where the owners had already moved out. Switching to Street View on Google Maps, she saw they looked satisfactorily old and wooden. They'd burn like a circus tent.

ABOUT THE ACTUAL approach: push a doorbell, and when Grandfelt answered, what? Shoot her? What if it wasn't Grandfelt who answered? What if, like more and more people, she had cameras covering her property? What if the neighbors did?

Fisk leaned back in her office chair and ran the approach through her mind, visualizing every step, all the possible booby traps along the way.

And concluded that everything she'd just researched amounted to a fantasy. Too many cops. Too many cameras. Too much exposure— two separate crimes, an arson and a murder? Nonsense.

THINKING ABOUT IT, thinking about what she, herself, did in the evenings . . . She'd go out, sometimes with Timothy, but most of the time without him. She'd run out to a supermarket, she'd play tennis, she'd go to the Mall of America.

Why wouldn't Grandfelt do the same thing? Would she come home from work, lock herself up, or go out with her husband, if she had one? Or would she go somewhere on her own?

She would do that, at least sometimes, Fisk thought. And that was her vulnerability—moving from her car to wherever she was going, and then walking back to the car.

Fisk had already noted the on-street parking around Grandfelt's house. She could wait for her on the street, from a point across from the access alley that ran behind the houses.

From there, unless something had changed, she should be able to see Grandfelt backing out of her garage, from where she'd have to drive past Fisk's parked car. Fisk would be able to see if anyone was in the car with her. If she was alone, Fisk could follow her . . .

All very loose, very random. If she'd had to prosecute a case based on what she was thinking, she wouldn't know how to do it, not unless the killer was actually caught in the act. There would be no intricate planning. There would just be the hit.

Risky, but there was no way to avoid risk. Doing nothing was risky, and the risk was getting more serious every day.

She got out of her chair, walked around the house, and finally out to the garage. The man who was buying Timothy's tools hadn't taken them with him—he'd be back later in the week to pick them up. She opened one of the drawers on Timothy's rolling tool chest and her eye immediately fell on a fifteen-inch combination wrench.

She picked it up and hefted it: excellent. She flashed back to the night she'd killed the law student. Same thing, but with a better heft to it.

Now, Grandfelt would have to cooperate.

She had no real idea of what Grandfelt looked like, but she'd seen something on that website . . .

She went to Anne Cash's website and found a series of videos of

Grandfelt and her lawyers being interviewed on network morning shows, and on CNN. She watched four videos, until she was sure she could spot the woman.

All right, she had that. Next question: When?

She looked at the wrench sitting on her desk. Not that night; she was too tired from the day. Tomorrow?

THE NEXT NIGHT, having had twenty-four hours to plan, she went into the kitchen for vinyl gloves, got the wrench and her car keys and walked out to her Mercedes SUV, bought to match the SL550.

The trip across the Mississippi took twenty minutes. There was still light in the sky when she cruised past Grandfelt's place, where she felt a quiver of house envy. Her own house, on the most prestigious street in St. Paul, was extremely nice. Grandfelt's house was absurd, though she wouldn't have minded living there. If it wasn't exactly at the pinnacle of the Twin Cities housing heap, it was close.

Having spotted the house, and the alley that led to Grandfelt's garage, she circled the block one last time and squeezed into a parking place a half block down from the alley.

And waited, and waited.

And that night, Grandfelt stayed put. Fisk went home at ten o'clock, frustrated, and with an ache in her back from having sat in the car too long.

19

The next night:

Marcia Wise went into the kitchen and chose a set of car keys—she loved the Jaguar, top down, summer breeze blowing through her hair, but she knew that Lara really didn't like her driving it. Subtle, she thought, but a status thing. Lara was the boss; she was the help.

She hesitated, then picked the BMW keys out of the wooden bowl on the countertop. The BMW was a stuffy five-year-old SUV that they mostly used for winter driving and for Wise's errands.

She hesitated again, then called, "Would you mind if I took the Jag? It's a nice night."

She got no response for five seconds, then Grandfelt called back, "No, go ahead. Be careful."

"I will." Wise could tell Grandfelt was put out, but she'd recover quickly enough. Grandfelt was in the library, reading a book on The Eight, a group of early-twentieth-century painters.

Wise walked into the library, kissed Grandfelt on the forehead, and added, "If you want anything else, text me."

"I will, but I don't think I'll want anything," Grandfelt said. "I'll be in the TV room, I'm going to look for a movie. Don't scratch my car."

"Don't start the movie until I get back. Half an hour. I'll add some kettle corn to the shopping list . . ."

"You really shouldn't," Grandfelt said, which meant that Wise really should, while acknowledging that they both could stand to lose a few pounds. Like fifteen. Or twenty.

WISE WENT OUT to the garage, pushed the door lift button, got in the sparkling black Jaguar two-seater, backed it out and dropped the top. Marcia Wise lived a rich life, but she wasn't wealthy, not on her own. Grandfelt gave her a salary barely large enough to max out the Social Security contribution, though she also picked up every other expense in their joint lives. On her own, Wise had a hundred and seventeen thousand dollars in an investment account, and that was it.

No house, no car, no nothing. She was a year younger than Grandfelt, and they were aging into their forties. If Grandfelt should fall for a younger woman . . . Wise didn't want to think about the possibility.

So she didn't. She focused instead on the light, snaky feeling of the F-Type R75 as it bumped down the alley to the street, and then the sense of freedom, and wealth, that the convertible brought to her.

She took a left at the end of the alley and drove a mazelike route to Whole Foods, less than ten minutes away. The supermarket parking lot served several other franchises, a Chipotle, a Caribou Coffee, a Noodles & Company, like that. She parked near the end of the lot, and on the far side, facing a concrete wall probably eight feet high. She did that because she wanted the empty spaces on both sides of the Jag. She brought the convertible top back up, and walked into the store, carrying a reusable grocery bag, jingling the car fob and house keys.

TEN MINUTES TO nine with still some light in the sky, looking west down the street toward Lake of the Isles. Fisk was parked three cars closer to the alley than she had been the night before, in Timothy's Range Rover. She was feeling restless, ready to quit again, go back home. Then the black Jag appeared at the mouth of the alley, paused, and turned toward her, away from the lake, and accelerated past.

Fisk sank down in the car seat, eyes barely above the level of the driver's-side window. This was the opportunity she'd been hoping for, but she hesitated to do a lights-on U-turn right behind Grandfelt. This would be risky, depending on where the other woman was going, but had to be done. Her mind was clear on that.

When Grandfelt was a block away, Fisk made the U-turn and fell in behind as Grandfelt rolled up to a stop sign. Grandfelt took a right, and Fisk waited a beat or two, before following. The Jag would be a hard car to lose, at least while there was a bit of light.

Fisk had never followed anyone before, not in a car, but her frequent contacts with police witnesses gave her some ideas about how to do it. When cops followed someone, and that resulted in an arrest, the defense attorneys were always insisting that the cops swear that they never lost constructive sight of the car they were following. That they couldn't have inadvertently and accidentally lost the person they were following, and might have understandably followed the very similar car of their innocent defendant, while the real criminal took a side street.

Fisk would then lead the cop through their surveillance routine, and exactly how the defendant had been tracked.

So she had that going for her.

EVEN IF SHE hadn't had that, she'd have had no trouble following the Jaguar. Grandfelt stayed on main streets, paying no attention to anything coming up from behind. She drove into the Whole Foods parking lot and parked out on the edge, well back from the store.

Fisk said aloud, "Perfect," while feeling a tickle of apprehension. She was going to do it. But there were other considerations before she did that.

She went to the next shopping lot, parked, got out of her car, and walked back to the corner of the Chipotle and looked for cameras. She spotted them right away and her heart sank: she couldn't be on video, in the Whole Foods parking lot, at the same time that Grandfelt was murdered. Not after Timothy's freak accident.

But wait . . .

The cameras—she thought there might be four of them, aimed in different directions—were housed atop a twenty-foot-high pole with a battery box at the bottom, mounted on wheels so it could be moved to different locations. But there were trees scattered across the parking lot. Not extremely tall, but, she thought, tall enough. She looked at the alignment and thought it possible, thought it likely, that the cameras couldn't see the area where Grandfelt had parked.

Finding out for sure would *not* be risky. If she parked next to Grandfelt, as she had planned, she could get out of the car and look back toward the cameras. If she could see them—and they could see her—she'd simply leave. If Grandfelt returned home uninjured, there'd be no reason for anyone to look at the video.

She considered it, chewing on her lip, walked slowly back to her car, and drove back to the Whole Foods lot, turned in, drove to Grandfelt's car, and parked on the driver's side of the Jag.

Without getting out, she looked toward the camera pole—and could see nothing of it at all. Not the pole, not the cameras.

And she sat for a full five minutes, watching the lot. Watching people come and go. Watching the routes that they walked to their cars.

Satisfied that she could pull this off, if she did it right, she picked up the wrench she'd kept on the passenger seat, got out of the driver's seat, walked around the car, and got in the back seat next to the Jaguar. She didn't quite close the door—kept it closed, but not latched. She pushed it open, pulled it back, did it again.

The door made no noise at all.

Ten minutes later, Grandfelt walked out of the Whole Foods carrying the grocery bag. Fisk was kneeling on the back seat of the Range Rover, scanning the parking lot. Grandfelt was getting closer and closer, and Fisk hovered behind the Land Rover's D-pillar, her eyes flicking again and again toward the camera pole, never catching even a hint of it, as much out of sight as she could be.

Grandfelt went to the passenger side of the Jag, opened the door, put the grocery bag on the passenger side floor, and walked back around the car to the driver's side. As she was doing that, Fisk sank deeper into the back seat of the Range Rover.

Looking up, she saw Grandfelt pass the Range Rover window. She got a firm grip on the wrench, pushed the door open with one foot and slipped out. Grandfelt had the Jag's door open and had one leg thrust out so she could slide into the tight interior . . .

Grandfelt never saw Fisk. Fisk hit her on the back of the head with the eighteen-inch-long piece of steel, and Grandfelt dropped to the ground as though struck by lightning.

Fisk, now caught up in the kill, hit her again, and again and again, and then, breathing hard, teeth bared, ready to fight anyone else who needed it, she half-turned, half-stood, looked around the lot like a wary lion.

No alarm. Grandfelt was dead on the ground. Fisk sat down and pushed the other woman as far under the Jag as she could, using her feet. That done, she walked back around the Range Rover, wiped the wrench with a damp wash cloth left on the driver's seat just for that purpose, and dropped both the wrench and the cloth in a garbage bag.

Two minutes later, she was gone. Saw no cameras.

LARA GRANDFELT GOT caught up in a documentary on global warming, which showed, among other things, a polar bear mired in mud that was once solid permafrost. At some point, she glanced down at her watch: Wise had been gone for an hour. The Whole Foods store was ten minutes away.

She went back to the documentary, glanced at her watch again. Where was she? Joyriding in the Jag? Now worried that Wise had been in an accident, she called her, but got no response. Fifteen minutes and three more calls after that, she was very worried, but didn't know exactly what to do.

She called Whole Foods, and somewhat to her surprise, the call was answered. She told the woman who answered the phone that she was worried about her friend, and the woman said she'd look for Wise and check the parking lot for the Jag.

The same woman called back and said the Jaguar, black and shiny—she read out the license tag number—was still sitting in the parking lot, but as far as she could tell, there was nobody in the store who resembled the woman described by Grandfelt.

LUCAS TOOK THE phone call from Grandfelt. "Marcia's disappeared!"

"What?"

Grandfelt described the sequence of events: Wise's departure for Whole Foods, her failure to return, the unanswered phone calls, the call to the supermarket and the response—the car still in the parking lot.

"Is there a restaurant there?" Lucas asked. "Somewhere she could have gone for a bite to eat or a drink?"

"She doesn't drink and we were planning to watch a movie and eat popcorn," Grandfelt said. "I'm going over there."

"No. No. Lara, I want you to make sure all your doors and windows are locked, and I want you to hunker down there," Lucas said. "If there's actually a threat, I don't want you wandering around helpless. I've got a good friend on the Minneapolis force, I'll call her, get some cops over to the store, and I'll go over myself. I can be there fast. I don't want you exposed."

The fear clutched at her heart: "I'll lock the doors and wait here," Grandfelt said. "I'll keep trying to call her."

LUCAS GAVE WEATHER a one-minute explanation and headed for his car. In the car, he called Margaret Trane, once a lead homicide cop and, after three heavily publicized murder convictions, now a deputy chief. He explained the problem, said he was on the way, and asked her to do what she could to route some cops to the store.

The first Minneapolis cops arrived nine minutes later. They got out of the patrol car and walked up to the Jaguar and one cop said to the other, "Is your phone ringing?"

"If it was, it sure as shit wouldn't be playing 'Tiny Dancer.' Is it coming from under the Jag?"

When Lucas arrived a couple of minutes later, he was told that the woman under the car was definitely dead. Homicide was on the way.

20

Margaret Trane, a Minneapolis deputy chief and one of Lucas's longtime friends, showed up in jeans and a sweatshirt, even as the phone under the car continued to ring every few minutes.

Lucas's phone was ringing, too, alternating with the phone under the car, but Lucas didn't answer.

"You gotta go tell Lara," Lucas told Trane. "I won't do it. I'm terrible at it."

"I'll get someone . . ."

"You should do it. You're important enough to make an impression," Lucas said. He added, "Chief."

"Then you're coming with me."

"Ah . . ." Lucas was dragging his feet, but finally nodded. "Okay."

"You think this is the original Grandfelt killer?" Trane asked as she watched the homicide and first-arriving crime scene investigators crawling around the Jaguar.

"I believe it is," Lucas said. "I can't think who else it might be. In one way or another, the true crime investigation has become a threat. I don't know why it has—if I knew that, I might know who it threatens."

"Where's Flowers?"

"I haven't called him yet. I'll go do that. Didn't you guys work together on that professor case, the professor who got murdered in the university library?"

"Yeah. I kinda like the guy. Flowers, not the professor."

"I'll call him. Then let's talk to Lara."

VIRGIL WAS AT his hotel, working on the novel. He was astonished to hear about Wise. "What have we done?"

"I don't think we're to blame . . ."

"Neither do I. I meant, what have we done to stir this up? We must have done something."

"I was just talking to Maggie Trane about that. I don't know."

"How did Maggie get involved?" Virgil asked.

"I called her to get some cops to look at the Jaguar."

"Good move. All right, I'll see you at Grandfelt's place. I'm still dressed, I'll leave here in five minutes."

LUCAS WASN'T GOOD at death notifications, and he knew it. He became too gruff when he was angry or upset, and sometimes that came out during a notification, putting out a "Yeah, he's dead, get over it" feel.

Trane was far better: straightforward, but bleeding sympathy.

When they rang Grandfelt's doorbell, Lucas saw a curtain move at the side of the stone porch. He lifted a hand, and Grandfelt unlocked and opened the door.

"I'm Margaret Trane, I'm a deputy chief of police for the City of Minneapolis. I'm afraid I have dreadful news for you," Trane said, as Lucas hovered unhappily in the background. "May we come in?"

Grandfelt backed away from the door, leaving it open, and said, "She's dead."

"Yes, she is," Trane said, stepping inside.

"And Lucas was too chicken to tell me himself."

Trane nodded: "Yes. He was."

"Oh, goddamnit." Grandfelt burst into tears and turned away from them, her hands to her face.

Trane went over to her and wrapped an arm around her shoulders as Lucas stepped awkwardly inside the door and closed it behind him.

WHEN VIRGIL SHOWED up twenty minutes later, they were all sitting in the overcooked living room. Grandfelt had a roll of toilet paper sitting on the couch beside her, and she was using pads of the tissue to blot her eyes during sporadic episodes of weeping.

Virgil was also good at notifications, and touched Grandfelt's shoulders as Trane had, muttering comforting cop cliches as he did it.

They listened to her talk about Wise for the best part of an hour, but then Grandfelt asked the question that was most obvious to the three cops: why now and why Wise?

They all agreed that Wise was murdered because she resembled Grandfelt and was driving Grandfelt's car. Several things fell out of that assumption.

The killer had access to a database that gave him Grandfelt's address and the makes and models of her cars. One place that was all available was the DVS. The database wasn't open to the public, but entry was easy for anyone who had the right passwords.

"A lot of people do. Mostly cops and public employees, and I suspect quite a few media people and politicians, so there's that," Virgil said.

Grandfelt: "What if they know me, and have been here in this house and have seen my cars?"

"That's not likely," Trane said. "Marcia closely resembled you. But if they'd actually met either of you face-to-face, they wouldn't have attacked her. We know she'd already gone into Whole Foods because of the grocery bag in the car. That means whoever was watching her saw her in good light . . . and they attacked her anyway. That suggests that they really didn't know you, but were acting on the basis of your address and automobile and the resemblance. They staked out your house and followed the Jaguar."

"Sounds a little like a cop," Lucas said. "Access to the DVS and he could follow her without giving himself away."

"We're pulling video from every camera we can find around the store, that may kick out something," Trane said. "We don't yet know exactly how the killer approached the car."

"He'd have to have a car of his own to follow her," Lucas said. "Maybe there were witnesses at the store who saw the killer or his car . . ."

"Maybe," Trane said. "I wouldn't bet my life on it. It was dark and we have no idea of what car we're looking for, or who might have seen it."

"If we're looking for a motive, I'd say the killer was attempting to complicate the whole reward situation," Virgil said. "If he'd killed you . . ." He looked at Grandfelt. ". . . I would think that the reward offer would be up in the air. Especially if your heirs challenged it."

"My heirs are my parents and a few nonprofits," Grandfelt said. "My folks want to find Doris's killer as much as I do."

"Still . . ."

"That's a good point, Virgie," Trane said. "I would be surprised if that wasn't a motive."

"What are the chances that it was a random killing?" Grandfelt asked.

"About zero," Trane said. "Her purse is under the car, she was hit a bunch of times, not just once. Whoever did it was there to kill her, not rob her."

Lucas said to Grandfelt, "I spent some time talking to Chief Trane at the scene, and to Virgil, and we've sort of agreed that we did something during this true crime situation, the reward thing, that stirred up the killer. We're a threat to him. We suspect that we've posted photos of him . . ."

"I saw those," Grandfelt said. "They didn't mean anything to me."

"We're hoping they mean something to somebody, and we get a call," Lucas said. "Because we think they mean something to the killer. We need to figure out what that is."

"I plan to lobby all the TV stations, get the photos on every news program and keep them up," Trane said. "If the killer is worried about the photos, that means he's worried that somebody might recognize him."

Grandfelt: "I can call the major stations. I could buy ads showing the photos and talking about the reward."

"That might help, but it would be expensive," Trane said. "If you do it, you should press for some extra news time, to go with the paid time."

"I could do that," Grandfelt said. "I'm already in this for five million dollars . . ."

THEY ALL LOOKED at each other: they were finished here. Then Grandfelt suddenly began weeping again, blotting her eyes with the toilet tissue, and Trane said to Lucas and Virgil, "I'll hang around here for a while. I'll stick a couple of cops out front overnight."

Virgil and Lucas stood up, and Virgil said to Grandfelt, "We're so sorry about your friend," which sounded stupid when said out loud, but Lucas nodded: that was all they had.

OUTSIDE, ON THE porch, Virgil said, "Doctor, doctor, give me the news . . ."

"I thought this case was going to be a joke," Lucas said. "I'm not laughing anymore."

"This killer. We know he killed Doris, and almost certainly killed Wise. Is it just those two? Or is he a serial killer? Have there been a bunch of them?"

Lucas said, "When you get back to the hotel, drop a note to our true-crimers. Let's get them together again tomorrow. There are some more things they could do for us. I'm gonna go home and make a list."

"Where do we meet? What time?"

"How about where we started? My place. Say, eleven o'clock."

WEATHER WAS GETTING ready for bed when Lucas got home. She did operations almost every morning and hospitals started early. He stuck his head in the refrigerator, came out with a string-cheese single-pack, and told her about Wise as he stripped the plastic wrapper off the cheese. "It could still be a woman, I guess, but she was battered. You said yourself that's more like something a man would do."

"I'll back off to forty-sixty, woman-man," Weather said.

"Okay. I'll be up for a while," he told her. "This thing is complicated. I gotta stop talking and start thinking."

"Do you have anything at all?" Weather asked.

"That's what I'll be thinking about. We do, but it's all bits and pieces. I'm trying to figure out what we do with them."

"A puzzle. You're good at puzzles."

She kissed him goodnight and went up the stairs to the bedroom. Lucas got a beer, carried it into the den, sat in his favorite chair and stared at a blank TV screen for a couple minutes, then got up, found a legal pad and a pen, and began his list.

- Could Klink the Shrink be right? Was the killer a doctor or another medical worker? Drives a Porsche?
- BCA now has a list of Bee clients when Doris was murdered. How many doctors on the list? Do DVS files go back that far, to Grandfelt's murder, to ID doctors with Porsche 911s?
- How is the research going on those cockeyed murders in the Twin Cities? The ones with no reasonable

motive, in which the killer left no clues, seemed to be
in a frenzy when he stabbed or bludgeoned the victim,
between the Grandfelt murder and the present?

- Do we have anything on the 2000 time-frame tax
collector or assessor lists for neighborhood around the
park where the body was found? Any hits of Bee
employees there?

- Talk to Cory Donner at Bee. The knife was sharpened
on red brick. The killer must have sharpened the knife
there, if the murder had been there, and that would
also have scarred the brick. Could they find the scars?
If so, where exactly?

Lucas spent a few minutes contemplating the list. It was, he
thought, thin. Nothing on it would definitively pin down one person.
They had the DNA of the last person to have sex with Grandfelt, but
after looking at the investigative files, he was feeling more and more
uncertain about whether the DNA actually belonged to the killer.

If they could find the DNA donor, though, they might have a line
on the killer, since the sex and the murder were very close in time.

FROM HIS HOTEL room, Virgil sent out invitations to the six true
crime blog owners who were doing the online research for them.
Two of them got back within minutes—pulling all-nighters, Virgil
thought, which might be their routine.

And the next morning, as a thunderstorm pounded the streets
with a downpour of the kind normally reserved for the tropics, the
six true-crimers settled in with them at Lucas's house, bringing with

them cups of coffee, tea, and bottles of Coke. Virgil had included Michelle Cornell in the invitation, and she'd brought a stack of yellow legal pads from the law firm's office supply cabinet, along with a clutch of ballpoint pens, which she handed out to everyone.

Anne Cash started things by asking, "Is this about the five million?"

"Well, no, not exactly—though I suppose it could be, if everything works out," Lucas said. "Let me start out by saying that Lara Grandfelt's assistant was murdered last night, after apparently being mistaken for Grandfelt herself."

Three of the six true-crimers simultaneously blurted, "What!"

"You can post it—later," Lucas said. "It's not on the TV news channels yet, so you're not getting beaten with the news, but it will be on TV this afternoon. You'll have it first, so let's settle down while I give you some more information."

"But this is amazing," Sally Bulholtz said.

"It's tragic, is what it is," Virgil said. "That woman is dead by mistake. Beaten to death."

"Where did this—"

"We'll fill you in later, okay?" Lucas said. "Right now, and the reason we're here, is we need some more help from you. If you help us out, you're welcome to take credit for it."

"What do you want?" asked Karen Moss. She was wearing a different tennis hat, this one reading "Kiss My Ace," with a yellow tennis ball below the inscription.

"Tell us quick, I want to get the murder on my site," said Mary Albanese.

"We haven't gotten anything good from you guys," Lucas said. "You need to jack up the pressure."

"Everything you gave us was too flimsy . . . too vague," Ruby Weitz said. "I got a couple of friends trying to organize those property tax records, but there are hundreds of different owners and people buying and selling . . . it's a mess, and we really don't know what we're looking for."

"I got the list of year 2000 doctors from the medical association, but there are twenty thousand names on the list," said Bulholtz. "I don't know what I can do with them. There are like ten thousand more medical-type personnel: dentists, pharmacists, like that, not including nurses."

"We're going to get more specific this morning," Lucas said. "In the next day or two, Virgil is going to send you a list of all Bee Accounting clients at the time Doris Grandfelt was killed. Bee is compiling that information now, for the BCA, and we'll have access to the list. There'll apparently be several thousand names. We need to figure out which ones were doctors—"

"You think the killer is a doctor?" Cash blurted. "Can we put that up?"

"Please, not yet," Lucas said.

"We're giving you early breaks on the good stuff, like the murder for Marcia Wise. You'll be able to beat all the other true crime sites on that. Some stuff, we'll talk to you six about, but you have to hold it close," Virgil said. "If you don't, you'll be out. We won't talk to you anymore."

"We need to sort out the doctors," Lucas said. "And anyone else you think might be considered to be in a medical profession. Dentists? Whatever. We need to compare those names against a list of DVS records to see which of the medical people were driving Porsche 911s."

"I don't even know what those look like," Dahlia Blair said.

"You could look them up online, but you don't need to—you just need to look at the record and see if it says Porsche," Lucas said. "I talked to the head of the DVS this morning, early, and they're seeing what they can do about printing out all the Porsche records from the years around 2000. There'll be several hundred of them."

"So you're asking us to compare lists of thousands of people against lists of hundreds of people. You know how long that will take?" Cash asked.

"Not too long, I hope," Lucas said. "I want you to sort out which are the doctors from among the Bee clients and compare those to an alphabetized list of Porsche owners. Once we get the lists, it should be smooth sailing."

"But you want us to sort out a few dozen doctors from thousands of names from Bee—that'll be the hard part."

"Well, that's true," Lucas said. "But that's why we've come to you—you have the juice to do that."

"Anything else?" Cash asked.

"Yeah. We've asked you to look at murders in the metro area reported in the *Star-Tribune*. How is that going?"

"My group is looking at that," Albanese said. "So far, there aren't too many that meet your criteria, but there are some. I'll send them over. We started in 1990 and we're up to 2012. The problem is, the reporting can be thin on murders outside of Minneapolis. We have names and addresses and that sort of thing, but not always exactly what happened, unless the person was stabbed or shot."

"How many cases so far?" Virgil asked.

"Including all the questionable ones—we've marked those out— we have forty-two in the twenty-two years. The ones we think are specifically good, we have twelve."

"Send them to Virgil," Lucas said. "Now, how many of you guys have . . . assistants, or colleagues, or whatever you'd call them, here in the Twin Cities?"

Between the six of them, they had eight associates in town.

Moss: "Why do you want to know?"

"I'm going to talk to the CEO at Bee. I'd like to send a group of people over to their offices, and have people get down on their hands and knees in all the offices with redbrick walls and have them looking for whetting marks. Sharpening marks."

The women looked at each other, and Weitz asked, "Could we film them doing that?"

"Don't care," Lucas said. "It'll get out one way or another. If they find anything, they have to back off and call me immediately and we'll get some CSI people over there. But don't do anything until I talk to the CEO and give you the go-ahead."

Moss: "I can ask my friends to do that . . ."

They talked—argued and speculated—about what else might be done, then Lucas pushed them to get more serious about the research.

"Yeah, we'll push, but this is pretty boring work," Cash said.

"Pretty boring until we nail the guy," Cornell said. "Then it's going to be a five-alarm fire. You'll be the most famous true crime bloggers on earth."

As the meeting was breaking up, Blair asked, "So we can post the Marcia Wise murder? Tell us what happened and how you found out."

Lucas gave them some details, asked that they not be attributed to him or Virgil, and they all left in a rush.

21

When the true-crimers were gone, Lucas and Virgil picked up glasses and carried them to the kitchen. Cornell, who was not in a hurry, followed them and asked, "Are you guys going to sit on your thumbs and wait for the returns to come in?"

"We've got a couple of irons in the fire," Virgil said. "We don't want to talk about them, no offense."

"If you're not going to tell me about them, I want my legal pads back," Cornell said. "And my pens."

When Cornell had gone, Lucas asked, "What irons do we have in the fire?"

"The guy who tipped us about Jepson. We need to put up a note and have him call us, and we need to talk to Jepson again, about doctors. We should have done it before now, but we've been running around."

"We really ought to talk to everybody we've identified as Doris's customers and ask about doctors."

"Of course, we might be a little overfocused on the doctor thing," Virgil said.

"I know that, but what else have we got? I should talk to Maggie, see if the Minneapolis guys came up with anything."

"A license plate would be good," Virgil said.

Lucas frowned: "I don't think we'll get one. The way Doris was killed, the way Marcia Wise was killed—fast, efficient, brutal, without a trace of him. The killer is no dummy."

"You're right. Think about that while I send a note to Dahlia Blair and have her put up a note to Big Dave."

WHILE VIRGIL WAS typing on his iPad, Lucas's phone rang. He took it out, looked at the screen: "Michelle Cornell."

"Why is she calling? She's probably still sitting in your driveway."

"Maybe I should answer the phone and find out." He answered and Cornell said, "We have something for you."

"Yeah?"

"The owner of one of the smaller sites, she wasn't at the meeting, Phyllis Binley, got a wild call a few minutes ago. She says one of her readers down in Farmington told her that her father recognizes the guy with the Porsche. Phyllis wanted to put in a bid for a piece of the reward."

"Whoa. That's serious," Lucas said. "Who's the woman who called?"

"I wrote it all down on one of the yellow pads I took back. With one of the pens."

"Michelle . . ."

"Her name is Rochelle Green. She lives on Walnut Street in Farmington . . . Do you have a yellow pad of your own that you can write this down on?"

Lucas took the address down and asked, "Is Rochelle gonna be around?"

"She says so. She says she's a caregiver for her father," Cornell said.

"Uh-oh."

"Yes, I don't know exactly what that means, but I thought you'd want to check," Cornell said.

"We do," Lucas said. "We'll head down there."

Off the phone, he asked Virgil, "You know everything south of the Cities. How far is Farmington from here?"

Virgil: "If I'm driving, half hour, maybe a little more."

"You're driving."

LOTTA CORN, AND though this was Minnesota, and not Oklahoma, the corn was higher than an elephant's eye, and the soybeans were looking good, too. Highway 3 down to Farmington rolled through farm country, lined with trees and widely spaced farmhouses usually half-surrounded by unpainted steel silos. A light drizzle was still falling out of the overcast sky; the creeks they crossed were overloaded and some of the fields were decidedly soggy.

"This is wet, but down home at the farm, I mean, I've never seen the Minnesota River as high as it is, this time of year," Virgil said.

"Uh-huh. Tell me some more rural shit, I'm deeply interested."

"Making conversation," Virgil said.

More buildings began popping up at the side of the road and Virgil said, "We haven't had lunch. There's a Dairy Queen just before we get into town. I could use a chocolate-dipped."

"You're driving."

"Clever. You want a cone, but you don't want the responsibility for stopping."

THEY BOTH GOT hot dogs at the DQ, which they ate immediately, and then vanilla cones, Virgil's chocolate-dipped, Lucas's not. They followed Virgil's navigation app to Spruce Street, and then, because he was licking his cone and not paying attention, past Walnut Street to Locust Street, and then around the block and back to Walnut, where they spotted Green's house.

While much of the town had older, prewar houses, Walnut was newer, probably fifties or sixties—ranch-styles and split-levels with two-car garages, old enough that many had been re-sided with aluminum or vinyl siding, mostly in tan, gray, beige, brown, or blue. There were sidewalks on both sides of the street, with trees that appeared to be younger than the houses growing from the verge between the sidewalk and the street.

They sat outside the house for another minute, finishing the cones, threw the cone wrappers and napkins on the floor of the back seat. then hurried through the drizzle up to Green's house and knocked.

Green came to the door and opened it without peeking out. Virgil held up his BCA identification and said, "Miz Green. I'm agent Flowers with the Bureau of Criminal Apprehension, and my partner here is U.S. Marshal Lucas Davenport."

She pushed open the door with a smile and said, "You two are just the berries. My goodness, I didn't expect to hear back for hours, and I wouldn't have been surprised if it was days. Come in, come in, Dad is in the porch, where he likes to sit. Can I get you a Dr Pepper or a cup of coffee?"

They declined and followed her through the house, passed a console organ with sheet music, an overstuffed couch facing two La-Z-Boy recliners with a coffee table between them. Pictures on the wall ran to family portraits, yellowed with age, including two young soldiers in what looked like Vietnam-era uniforms.

Green was probably in her late sixties or early seventies, Virgil thought, wearing a blue blouse and lighter-blue slacks, with sandals. Her hair was what might once have been called a beehive, but was lower, and improbably reddish-purple.

She said, "Dad has faded out considerably. He's ninety-two, and he was sharp as a tack until he was eighty-eight or eighty-nine. Drove himself until he was eighty-five. He was watching TV and saw that picture of the man with the sports car and he said, 'I know that fella, the one with the car. He's the one operated on Helen.' Sometimes, you know, he can still pull himself together, and he was like that for a little while this morning. He's been sleeping, I don't know how he is now."

Virgil caught Lucas's coat sleeve to slow him down, and asked, "Who's Helen?"

"Helen was his sister. She died, oh, let me see, eight, no, seven years ago, a year after Ralph. Ralph was her husband. Helen had breast cancer back when she was in her seventies, but they caught it early and she recovered. She died from a stroke. She was a year older than Dad."

"Do you know who Helen's doctor was?" Lucas asked.

"No, I don't. I didn't know her very well. She never lived here in Farmington when I was a child. And when she got sick, I was living in Fairmont with my husband. We divorced about the time Helen got cancer. I didn't pay much attention to her problem because Dad said she was going to be okay, and I had those problems of my own."

"Let's go talk to your father," Virgil said.

She didn't move immediately, but said, "I need to warn you, Dad can be a little stinky. I changed him just a half hour ago, but he doesn't have control of his bowels and he could let go anytime."

"That's fine. Let's go talk," Lucas said. "What's his name?"

"Bradley. Brad. Trimble. Green's my married name. I remarried after my divorce, my husband's up north fishing."

They followed her to an add-on porch at the back of the house, an aluminum-frame structure with windows all around, looking at a backyard with a single tree in it. Trimble was sitting in a third La-Z-Boy, a shabbier one than those in the living room. He was dressed in sweatpants and a blue tee-shirt, the tee-shirt covered by a gray zip-up hoodie.

Trimble didn't turn his head when they walked in, but stared straight ahead through a window at the tree. Forty-five degrees to his right, a small television sat on a walnut table, tuned to the Weather Channel, which was showing color radar of thunderstorms outside of Dallas.

Green touched her father's shoulder. He moved his chin toward her and she said, "There are some policemen here to see you. They need to know the name of the man who operated on Helen all those years ago."

"Helen?"

"Your sister. Helen. You said you saw a picture of a man who operated on Helen."

He sat unmoving, then twitched: "Operated on who?"

"Your sister."

He was silent, and Lucas looked at Virgil and shook his head.

Green said, "You remember, Dad, you saw his picture on TV today."

"Don't remember that," Trimble said.

"It's important, Dad, try to remember."

"I . . ." And the room was suffused with the odor of flatulence.

Green: "Dad, did you just poop?"

Silence for a few seconds, then a shake of the head. "Didn't poop. Just gas." Then he added, "Helen. Medicare saved her ass."

Virgil looked at Lucas and raised his eyebrows: of course she'd have been on Medicare if she was in her seventies. There'd be a record.

Trimble cranked his head around, looked first at Lucas, then at Virgil, and said to Virgil, "You don't look like no cop. Hair is too long."

"I'm scheduled to get it cut, but I've been too busy," Virgil said. "Do you remember the name of Helen's doctor?"

"I talked to him in the parking lot after the operation on Helen. He had a little car. Two seats. Couldn't put nothing in it."

"Do you remember the doctor's name?" Virgil pressed.

"Of course I do," Trimble said. He fell silent again, and his chin dipped to his chest.

Lucas: "Do you remember . . ."

Trimble looked up. "Remember what?"

"The name of Helen's doctor?"

"I talked to him in the parking lot," Trimble said.

His chin dipped, and Green said, "Dad?"

Trimble pulled himself up and said, "Carlson. Dr. Carlson. Timothy Carlson. He had a little car, not practical at all. Have to be a dumbshit to ride around in one of those if you didn't have to."

"I'd have to agree with that," Virgil said.

Green: "Did that help?"

"It might. We hope so. Whatever happens, we're grateful, Miz Green," Virgil said. He looked down at Trimble, who now seemed fully asleep. "When your father wakes up, tell him he did a very good thing."

"I will," she said. Tears gathered in her eyes, and she patted her father on the shoulder.

"We'll leave you with him," Lucas said.

OUTSIDE, IN THE car, Lucas asked Virgil, "Who has the Bee list? Was that Moss?"

"No, it's Weitz."

"Gimme Weitz's phone number."

Virgil found the number and Lucas called Weitz. When she answered, he asked, "Is the list alphabetized?"

"Most of it. Down to the Rs."

"Is there a Timothy Carlson on the list?"

"Let me look." She went away for a minute, then came back and said, "Yup. Is that a big deal?"

"We don't know. We're out of town, headed back. Where are you?"

"We're at a Motel 6 on I-94, a couple miles from the park."

"We'll be there in half an hour or so . . . maybe a little longer. We'd like you and your people to start searching Carlson. Everything you can find out about him."

"Is he the one?"

"We're working on a very shaky tip here. Right now, we want to know as much as we can find out."

"See you in half an hour, then," Weitz said.

Ten minutes later, she called back: "We got a quick piece of important information about Timothy Carlson."

"Yeah?"

"Yes. He's dead. He died in a fall. Give me a phone number, and I'll text you the obituary from the *Star-Tribune*. Like, right now."

"SONOFAGUN. THAT DOESN'T help," Virgil said, after they'd rung off.

"Where's your iPad?"

"Back seat."

Lucas unbuckled, turned in his seat, groped around, and got the iPad. Virgil gave him a password and by the time he signed on, the obituary had come in. He read through it, as Virgil waited impatiently, saying, "What's it say, what's it say?"

"He fell off his roof and killed himself," Lucas said.

"Fell off his roof? When?"

"Lemme see . . . Uh, not long ago." Lucas did some mental calculations and then, "If this is right, about three days after we announced the reward."

"Man. That gives me a little buzz," Virgil said. "A suicide?"

"The obituary says he fell while trying to recover a dog's ball from a roof gutter. I don't think suicides usually set it up that way."

"Still, that's an interesting accident after twenty years of no accidents," Virgil said.

"It does have the smell of bullshit," Lucas said. "But where's the bullshit coming from? We need to find out what happened."

"Call the ME. Find out if there was an autopsy."

"I got a dollar says there wasn't . . ."

"No bet."

Lucas called the Ramsey County Medical Examiner, and after he'd identified himself, got switched to an investigator, Darren Trask, who'd handled the Carlson death.

"No autopsy was needed," the investigator said. "There was a witness who was there at the time he fell. His wife."

"What happened, exactly?" Lucas asked.

"I went over there, the body was still at the scene, on the patio at the back of the house. One of his dogs—he had two—had rolled two rubber play balls, Chuckit!s, under a balcony railing down a slanting roof into a gutter," Trask said. "The wife said the gutter had given them problems in the past, clogging up. When it overflowed, it stained the siding on the house, so Carlson wanted to get the balls out, with all the rain we've been having. The Chuckit!s came with a plastic throwing arm that has a cup at one end . . ."

Virgil jumped in: "I have one, I know about Chuckit!s. . . ."

"Who is that?" the investigator asked.

"Virgil Flowers, he's working with me," Lucas said.

"Hey, Virgie," Trask said. "How you doin'?"

"Hey, Darren. So then what happened with Carlson?" Virgil asked.

"Okay, so you know about Chuckit! balls. Anyway, Carlson couldn't reach the gutter, and instead of getting a ladder or something—this was pretty high up, second story on a big house, a mansion, really—

he taped the throwing arm to a mop handle and leaned way over the balcony railing to try to get the ball in the throwing arm's cup. His wife said he was leaning over the railing, balanced on it, with the mop handle in one hand, and holding on to the railing with his other hand. She said she warned him not to do that, but he did anyway. His hand broke loose and over he went, headfirst. His wife was seriously screwed up about it."

"Jesus."

"Yeah. He was killed instantly, his skull was cracked wide open, both arms broken, neck and back broken."

"Do you have any tissue samples?"

"No, we don't. No autopsy," Trask said. "He was brought here, and the ME reviewed my notes and signed off on the death. Body was moved to a funeral home, I think, I wasn't here for that."

"Well . . . okay."

"Is there a problem?"

"Part of an ongoing investigation," Lucas said.

"I've been reading about you and Virgil . . . I've done a couple of sudden death investigations for Virgie down in Nobles County. Suicides, both of them. So . . . is this related to the Grandfelt thing?"

"We would have liked to get some DNA from the guy," Virgil said.

"Trying to match up with the Doris Grandfelt rapist DNA?" Trask asked.

"Exactly."

"If you've got good reason, you could have him exhumed . . ."

"We will probably try to do that," Lucas said.

"Hang on one minute," Trask said. "I'll be right back."

He put his phone down, and Lucas and Virgil listened to the silence for fifteen seconds, and Virgil said, "I hope he wasn't cremated."

"Even if he was, his house has gotta be full—"

Trask came back. "Okay, bad news. His body was picked up by South Minnesota Cremation Services. He'll be ash, by now."

Lucas: "Goddamnit."

"One other thing," Trask said. "His wife's name is Amanda Fisk, and she's an assistant county attorney here in Ramsey County. A prosecutor. Well known in the business. Maybe if she hadn't been who she was, the ME might have wanted to take a look at him. But the whole cause-and-effect situation with the Chuckit! balls and the fall was so obvious . . ."

"All right," Virgil said. "Listen, thanks, Darren. Take a look at your notes, and if anything occurs to you, give us a ring."

"Will do."

WHEN THEY'D RUNG off, Lucas asked, "Is Trask competent?"

"He's not the brightest star in the Milky Way. You wouldn't want him on a really hard call."

"You're not filling me with confidence," Lucas said. "We gotta nail down Carlson. His house has gotta be full of his DNA. Get some of your BCA people over there."

"We will do that. I worry about the fact that he was killed so soon after the reward was posted," Virgil said.

"So do I," Lucas said. "I'm not that impressed by coincidences."

"His wife was a witness."

Lucas: "Yup."

"Let's talk to her," Virgil said. "Call the county attorney, get her phone number."

"I will. If he's a match for the DNA . . ."

"What does that even mean?" Virgil asked.

Lucas looked out the passenger window and saw some goats. He said, "Goats."

"Yeah. We're in farm country. You can tell by the barns."

"I don't know what it means."

"The barns?"

"No, I don't know what it'll mean if there's a match," Lucas said. "We'll have to review the Grandfelt autopsy down to the last atomic particle . . . not us, but the ME and his pathologists. Was she raped? Give us a percentage call. Seventy-thirty, no rape? Sixty-forty, rape? If she was, then Carlson was the killer and case closed. If she wasn't . . ."

"Then what?"

"If she wasn't raped and we get a DNA match with Carlson, then we've maybe—maybe—still got an unidentified killer on the loose."

"You're saying *maybe* because the sex may have been consensual, but then he flipped out and killed her," Virgil said. "Which would explain a lot, like the tight timeline between the sex and the murder."

"Yes. Let's say they had the sex, and then she confessed that she'd slept with somebody else earlier that evening, which we know she did. There's your motive for the killing. He gets dressed first, he goes to the kitchen and gets a knife, whets it on a brick, and then he does her. But then, damnit, instead of killing her, he kisses her goodnight and somebody else comes in . . ."

After mulling that over, Virgil said, "You're telling me that no matter what the ME says, everything's gonna be up in the air."

"Yeah."

"I can buy some of that, but then who killed Marcia Wise?" Virgil asked. "And why? Carlson didn't, he was dead."

"Shut up."

They sat silently, thinking about it. Finally, Virgil said, "A lot of great goat cheese comes from this part of the country."

"You told me once before about goat cheese," Lucas said. "Remember what I told you what you could do with your goat cheese?"

"I may have repressed it," Virgil said.

They had the satellite radio tuned to an Americana station, playing low, and Ray Wylie Hubbard came on, singing "Drunken Poet's Dream." Virgil turned up the sound and sang along for a couple of verses in a grainy baritone.

When the song ended, he turned the radio down again, and Lucas said, "Fuck me. I don't know what we're doing."

22

Fisk freaked when she read about the murder of Marcia Wise. She'd pulled off a risky killing, but of the wrong woman. Even worse, Grandfelt would now be on guard—might even have guards—and she'd told a true crime site that she would provide an additional one million dollars in reward money if anyone could tie the murder of Marcia Wise to that of her sister.

The story had been dying on the national media, but now was back with a vengeance. CNN sent a former Minneapolis TV anchor back to the Twin Cities to track every move by the BCA and the true-crimers.

When Fisk went out to a true crime site, she found a report that Virgil Flowers believed he'd identified the man who may have raped Doris Grandfelt twenty years earlier. The woman circulating the report—quickly picked up word for word on the other true crime sites—said that Flowers refused to give up the name but said that he was in the medical profession.

Fisk rocked back in her computer chair: "Jesus Christ."

She scraped a thumbnail on her lower teeth until the fleshy back of her thumb began to bleed. She could feel herself coming unglued: if they thought the DNA donor was in the medical profession, it seemed to Fisk that it would only be a matter of time before they identified Timothy. In her various prosecutions, she'd known identities established with less evidence than a profession, a foggy photo, and a car, especially an elite car like a 911.

And, of course, Carlson was a Bee client, and they would have a list of those.

Not knowing what else to do, she got a gallon jug of Drano Max Gel, and walked around the house pouring the gel down drains; it was the third gallon she'd used in the various sinks, tubs, and showers around the house. The stuff supposedly dissolved hair, which was the objective.

With that working for her, she went back out to the various true crime sites for another look. After checking five or six, it appeared that the marshal, Davenport, was not nearly as involved as Flowers, the BCA agent. So what was Davenport up to? Was he up to anything? Flowers appeared to be the lead in the investigation.

Both law officers had gotten extensive coverage at one time or another in the local papers. She checked the *Star-Tribune* website, did a search for both names. There was more about Davenport than Flowers, but Davenport lived in St. Paul while Flowers apparently lived on a farm near Mankato.

She checked the websites of the county tax collectors around Mankato and found nothing under Flowers's name. Another search of the *Star-Tribune* records turned up the name of Flowers's "partner," which meant they weren't married: a woman named Florence Frances (Frankie) Nobles. Nobles had a farm in Nicollet County, a few miles northwest of Mankato.

She had to think about that. She was still thinking when Virgil called her.

"MIZ FISK," VIRGIL said. "I was sorry to hear about your husband's death. I've been investigating the death of Doris Grandfelt, twenty years ago, which has been the subject of a reward . . . I got your telephone number from Russ Belen . . ."

Belen was the Ramsey County Attorney, and Fisk's boss.

"I know about it, the investigation, at least, what's been in the media," Fisk said.

"Okay. There have been some indications . . . well, if you know about it, you know that some DNA was recovered from Grandfelt's body. We've had some indications that your husband may have been intimate with Grandfelt back on the day she was murdered."

"What? Indications? You mean DNA?"

"Yes. DNA. Dr. Carlson was a client of Bee Accounting . . ."

"I know that. I worked there briefly, at the time Doris Grandfelt was murdered," Fisk said. "In fact, I met Timothy as the murder investigation was taking place. He had some complicated legal issues involving taxes . . . I can hardly believe that he was involved with Doris Grandfelt, though. She was a clerk, and I was told that she was not overly bright. I didn't know her myself."

Virgil was astonished, struggled to control his reaction. He took a low breath, and said, "It might not have been her IQ that attracted

Dr. Carlson. If you've been following the investigation, you know that there's been a question about the extent and . . . quality . . . of Doris Grandfelt's sexual activities."

"Yes. There have been reports of sex for pay. That doesn't sound at all like Timothy . . ."

"We've been told that Dr. Carlson was cremated after his death?"

"Yes, he was."

"Well, we would like to come to your house and take some samples for DNA comparisons."

"I have no objections to that, I suppose . . . Or wait a minute. Maybe I do," Fisk said. "I'd really prefer that this didn't become public. Could I get some kind of written agreement, a letter, perhaps, from you, saying that you and the BCA will hold this procedure confidentially?"

Virgil: "If it turns out that there's a DNA match . . ."

"Then, I know, the information would become public," Fisk conceded. "I don't think Timothy would have touched Doris Grandfelt with a ten-foot pole, much less his penis. I would like the . . . mmm . . . examination to remain confidential if you don't find a match. So we don't have the rumor mill spewing its garbage all over Timothy and myself."

"I understand," Virgil said. "I'll talk to my supervisors at the BCA and see what kind of agreement they would be willing to commit to. I don't know what their answer will be."

"Call me when you know. If we can make an arrangement, you will have my permission to examine the house and cars and anything else you might need."

"Thank you. I will call you back."

———

FISK REPLAYED THE conversation in her head and decided that she'd handled it as well as it could be. She'd sounded surprised and concerned by the call, and she'd been cooperative. She had to be, she thought: all the information that she'd given them, they would have eventually found themselves, including the fact that she'd worked for Bee at the time of the murder. If she'd tried to hide that, they would have been curious about why.

She included one critical time change, but she didn't think they'd be able to challenge that: she'd said that she'd started dating Carlson after the murder, rather than before. Was there anything else that she could throw at them that might lead them astray?

More thinking would be needed. She didn't doubt that Flowers would be back in her face sooner rather than later.

"SHE TOLD ME the most amazing thing," Virgil told Lucas and Jon Duncan in the borrowed office at the BCA. "She worked at Bee when Grandfelt was murdered."

Lucas: "What!"

"That's almost what I said. But I didn't. I was nice. But man . . . she said she didn't know Doris Grandfelt."

"We gotta look at her," Lucas said to Duncan. "There's the jealousy motive."

Duncan: "Is she gonna try to keep us out of the house?"

"No. She was cooperative," Virgil said. "She wants a letter from us more or less promising to keep the DNA sampling confidential—she said she knows that we'd have to go public if we found a match with her husband. She doesn't believe there'll be a match."

"Sounds like a win," Duncan said. "We might be able to get a crew over there tomorrow . . . though somebody said something about comp time."

"I'll call her back and ask if tomorrow's okay," Virgil said. "She doesn't believe that Carlson would mess with Grandfelt, not for money anyway. Oh, by the way, she said she met Carlson there at the same time the murder investigation was going on."

"Curious," Lucas said. "Things are beginning to coalesce around Bee."

"If it turns out there's a DNA match, we could get busy," Virgil said. "If you guys don't mind, if we could schedule the DNA sampling for tomorrow afternoon . . . anytime noon or later would be good . . . I'm going to run down home overnight. I can be back by eleven o'clock tomorrow."

"Let me check about the DNA," Duncan said. "Why don't you head over to the hotel, get packed, and I'll call you about the schedule."

"Good for me," Virgil said, standing up.

"I'm fine with it," Lucas said.

"If we can't schedule the DNA, I might stay home an extra day," Virgil said. "Call me."

DUNCAN CALLED HIM, and Lucas as well, to tell them the DNA techs were off the next day, because they'd been working overtime on the men identified through the photos and were being pushed to take comp time instead of overtime, so Virgil stayed on the farm that extra day.

The farm, which rolled across two hundred and forty acres of pasture, alfalfa, and a line of woodland that followed a creek on the far west side of the property, wasn't a major source of income. A hundred and sixty acres was in four separate alfalfa fields, the rest being in pasture, Frankie's garden, and the farm buildings, which included a modest barn, a garage, a machine shed, a newer horse stable built by Virgil and a neighbor, and the house.

On the first evening at home, Virgil had worked through some baseball drills with Sam, Frankie's fifteen-year-old son with an extremely former husband, and picked sweet corn with his own twins, Alex and Willa, and generally got no writing done at all.

When the sun was three finger-widths above the horizon, he and Frankie saddled their two horses and rode the perimeter of the farm, with a nice gallop along the edge of the creek.

On the morning of the second day, Virgil sat glassy-eyed at the kitchen table as Frankie and Olaf Nilsson, a neighbor, discussed the possibility of overseeding two of Frankie's aged alfalfa fields with some kind of grass to rehab the declining alfalfa. They were trying to decide who would do the work with what machinery and who'd pay for the diesel and what cut Nilsson might get of the hay produced by the two still-productive alfalfa fields in return for his work and machines on the older fields.

Virgil eventually asked, "Why don't we just buy the seed and pay Olaf to do the work?"

They both looked at him as though his brain had just rolled out of his ear, and then Olaf said in kindly Scandinavian tones, "Because then Frankie would have to come up with a stack of cash which she'd want to deduct from your taxes, and I'd have to pay taxes on what I get from her. If I do some work for you and get back a few tons of cattle feed, you think some dim-bulb accountant at the IRS is gonna be able to figure that out?"

During the afternoon, they ran farm-related errands and took the twins on a hike around the barn, and Virgil took a call from Duncan: "We're good on the DNA sampling for tomorrow at one o'clock."

"I'll be there."

IN BED THAT night, he told Frankie, "I'm just burning up this August. Burning it up, talking to Internet influencers. I want to be here with you guys, and I want to write, and instead, I'm up to my neck in true-crimers in the Cities. The question is, how many good months like this can we burn and not regret it when we get old? I mean, this is one of the greatest months I've ever felt here, except for a little too much rain."

"Good questions," Frankie said. "No easy answer."

Virgil punched his pillow back so he could lean back on it, half-upright, and Frankie put her head on his shoulder. "I wonder if the BCA would give me a leave of absence," Virgil said. "You know, a year off. I could do a book and a half and then go back to the BCA if the books don't work out."

"You won't find out about a leave of absence unless you ask," Frankie said. "That seems like it might be a temporary solution. But: the books will work out. People like what you write."

"When the new contract comes in, maybe I could build you an arena."

She patted his stomach: "Not a pipe dream, but not a big urgent thing, either. You don't really need an arena with two horses."

"How long are you going to have . . . only two horses?"

She smiled, rolled her eyes, and said, "Rick and I have been talking about this warmblood rescue horse at Connie's. Six years old. He's a beauty, but he's been abused. He'd need a lot of work just to get him to trust us. We could get him for a contribution to the rescue ranch. Maybe five thousand. Maybe a little more."

"A rescue," Virgil said. "A warmblood. I kinda like the sound of all of that."

THE NEXT MORNING, Virgil left for the Twin Cities at nine o'-clock, and halfway there took a call from Lucas.

"I won't be with you at Carlson's house," Lucas said. "We went to a goddamn vegetarian place last night. Asmov's Veggies. I'd stay away from it if I were you. I'm sick as a dog. I can't get more than ten feet from a toilet or I'm in trouble."

"You gonna see a doc?"

"I'm married to a doc and she says I have a mild case of food poisoning and I'll be good again tomorrow. I'm weak as a puppy right now. I get tired when I try to stand up."

"Don't worry about it. I won't be doing anything but watching," Virgil said. "I'll give you a call when we're done."

"Try to lay a little bullshit on Fisk. See what she thought about her old man. Push her a little on Doris."

"I will do that."

"Uh, I have some more news—I've gotta go out to New Mexico, to Santa Fe. I'm being deposed in the virus case, the murders. I'll be gone for a few days. Leaving tomorrow afternoon, so . . . you got it."

"A few days? What's a few days?" Virgil asked.

"A few days," Lucas said. "They're talking about the deposition happening on Friday, but it'll probably slop over until Monday, so I'll be there over the weekend. I'm sorry, but I gotta go."

"Will Letty be there?" Letty, Lucas's adopted daughter, was an investigator for the Department of Homeland Security and had worked the virus case with Lucas.

"No, she's already come and gone," Lucas said. "She was deposed a couple of days ago. Anyway . . ."

"I'll hold the fort," Virgil said.

LUCAS THOUGHT ABOUT getting something to eat, because he was both sick and hungry. When he stood up, he got dizzy, so he sat back down again. His phone rang, an unknown number, and when he answered it, "Hello?" a man said. "This is Big Dave."

"Hey, Big. We've got a question. The guys who hung around with Doris, were any of them doctors? As far as you know?"

"I don't know. I mean, I don't think I met anyone who said he was a doctor, but it was a long time ago."

"All right. Listen, you want to tell me your real name?"

"Not yet. How's the money thing coming along?"

"I think you may be in line for a chunk of it, but we'd need your real name, of course."

"Send the bat signal up when you know for sure, and I'll call you back."

"I will do that."

TWO BCA TECHS were sitting in a car on the street outside the Carlson/Fisk house when Virgil arrived and pulled into the driveway.

They were finishing Subway sandwiches and Cokes, and Virgil waited while they tidied up the wrappers and crusts and put them in a sandwich bag, which they threw into the back seat.

He'd worked with both of them before—Linda Esselton and Carl Smith. Both were easy to get along with, and competent.

"Nice place," Smith said as they climbed the front steps. He asked Esselton, "What do you think? Buck and a quarter?"

"Maybe a little more," she said. "Depends on what's inside."

"You going for a real estate license?" Virgil asked.

"My husband does custom cabinetry," Esselton said. "I've been in a lot of places like this. Mostly over in Minneapolis, or out on Minnetonka."

"Wouldn't have painted it yellow, myself," Smith said, as he pushed the doorbell.

AMANDA FISK ANSWERED promptly, a solid-looking blond woman, pretty in a hard way, intelligent eyes: but she didn't look good, Virgil thought. She looked ragged, tired, stressed, as she probably should, a couple of weeks after her husband died in an accident she'd witnessed. Her eyes seemed to be glittering with tears.

And now the same husband was being investigated to see if he might have paid for sex with a woman who he might have murdered immediately after the sex.

She didn't bother to smile, but said, quietly, "Yes, come in, please." To Virgil: "You're Agent Flowers?"

Virgil nodded. "Yes. Thanks for letting us do this. We'll try not to bother you any more than we absolutely have to."

"I admit that it doesn't make me happy, but it is what it is." She looked past him to the street. "I understood you were working with Marshal Davenport."

"I am. He won't be with us. He's out of sorts today, food poisoning, and tomorrow he's flying down to New Mexico. He's being deposed in a case down there."

"That thing about the viruses? From last year?"

"Exactly. Federal court, they're going for the death penalty. Gonna be a tough deposition."

"Interesting," Fisk said. "I hoped he'd be here. I've never met him, and I'd like to."

"On stuff like this, there's not really much for us to do. It's mostly the lab folks, Linda Esselton, Carl Smith."

Fisk looked at the two techs and said, "You might have a problem . . . we have been cleaning the heck out of the house the past two weeks. Getting ready to sell it. Timothy was talking about retiring and we'd been discussing the possibility of downsizing here in Minnesota and buying a place in Southern California. Santa Barbara, actually. He loved golf. Now, after . . . what happened . . . I've decided to keep going on that. I don't want to be here anymore."

She looked so downcast that Carl shuffled his feet and said, "It must have been awful. We'll find something and we'll try to be quick. Did he have a closet that we could look at?"

"We have a closet, but I got rid of his clothing. Everything. It's all at Goodwill. They might still have some of it. A friend of his bought one of his cars, the other is still here . . ."

Linda: "Did you have separate sinks in the bathroom? A shower he routinely used?"

"Of course. Let me show you."

"Thank you. And we'll need a scrub from you, so we can differentiate your DNA from his. I'm sure you know all about that."

"Of course."

FISK TOOK THEM up the dark walnut stairs, through a series of rooms done in carefully coordinated shades of off-white accented with beige, to a bedroom with a walk-in closet showing a line of empty clothes racks on one side, and the other crowded with a woman's clothes and shoes.

"I had professional cleaners in to do the floors and clothes racks," Fisk said. "Anyway, Timothy's clothes were all along here . . ." She waved at the empty racks. "He didn't have much in the way of jewelry, but what he had . . . we have a safe in his home office, down the hall, and the watches are there . . ."

Linda said to Carl, "Why don't I take a look at the jewelry while you check the bathroom."

Virgil followed Carl and Fisk into an expansive bathroom with two sink basins, but no sign of a man's presence. "All of his stuff . . . deodorant, lotion, shaving cream, razors . . . all gone to the trash," Fisk said. "The left sink was his, I was on the right."

"Let me take a look at the drains," Carl said.

While he did that, Virgil followed Fisk and Linda down a hallway to Timothy Carlson's home office, which featured a desk that must have been eight feet long and four deep. There were four shallow drawers on either side of the leg hole; the drawers were shallow because the back of both sides of the desk were actually concealed safes.

Fisk opened them both, but said one and a half of the two safes were purely her things—necklaces, bracelets, rings, watches—while the top half of one side had a sparse collection of male jewelry, including four watches, a cuff, and two sets of tuxedo cufflinks and studs.

"Okay," Linda said. "Let me settle in here for a bit." She opened her briefcase and took out a box of full of sealed swabs.

THEY WATCHED HER unwrap the swabs, then Virgil asked Fisk, "Is there somewhere we could talk for a minute? I have a few questions about Timothy."

"Sure. We could go back to the bedroom . . . there are comfortable chairs . . ."

They walked back to the bedroom, heard Smith making scraping noises in the bathroom, and then dropped into two matching easy chairs that faced a pair of queen-sized beds. As they sat down, two Jack Russell terriers jumped on the far bed and peered at them.

"They love to sleep with me," Fisk said.

"I've got a yellow dog, does the same thing," Virgil said.

Fisk smiled and said, "Can't get through life without dogs . . . You know I'm a Ramsey County prosecutor, I assume?"

"Yes. I'm not sure, but you may have been an assistant when I was working with the St. Paul police. That would have been twelve years ago, or a little more. When I saw you at the door today, it kind of rang a bell."

She shook her head: "That could well be true. I'm sorry, I don't remember you. Of course, I've seen about a million cops since then."

"I don't mean to be harsh about what I'm going to ask . . ."

She showed a short, curt smile, almost a grimace, and said, "Virgil, I've spent my life listening to what various dirtbags did to women—rape, child molesting, ag assault, murder. Nothing you could possibly ask me would be shocking . . . although I have to say, I'd be shocked if Timothy turns out to be a match for the Doris Grandfelt DNA."

"You don't think Timothy might have paid Doris for sex?"

She looked at the floor, three fingers pressed against a cheek, and looked back up and said, "You know, if a friend had taken Timothy by the hand and led him to Doris and said, 'If you pay this woman five hundred dollars, she will have sex with you,' then I think it's possible he might have done it, at least at the time, a year after a divorce. I don't really remember her from Bee—I mentioned that I worked at Bee at the time of the killing . . ."

Virgil nodded, and said, "Yes."

". . . but I've seen photos of her, and she was quite attractive in a farm-girl way. Blonde, big tits. What I have a hard time imagining is how they might have hooked up. At Bee? That seems impossible, frankly. How would the subject of sex ever come up? She was a clerk, for God's sake, she wasn't in any of the accounting conferences, as I heard it. Timothy was a shy man, but arrogant, and status-conscious. He was hardly the type to be hitting on a clerk, no matter what her tits were like."

"We don't know if Timothy was involved at all," Virgil said. "We're just running down various threads that we've encountered, hoping something will come up."

"Then I may have a thread for you," Fisk said. "Tina Locklin."

Virgil sat up: "I haven't heard that name."

"She was a nurse in Timothy's practice . . . he was in a joint practice with three other surgeons. There were several nurses working with them, uh, and surgical techs, they had their own little crews. I heard way back when that Tina Locklin was somewhat obsessed with Timothy. In love. Eventually . . . what I'm telling you is mostly third-hand, Timothy really wasn't interested in talking about it . . . eventually, she had to be let go. One of the other docs, George Baer, did the deed. Fired her. You should talk to him."

Virgil had his notebook out, and took down the spellings of the two names, Locklin and Baer.

"George Baer is still around?"

"Yes, retired. He's here in the summer, though, he has a place up on Turtle Lake," Fisk said. "Has a Fourth of July party every year, and Timothy and I would go. He was here for Timothy's memorial."

"Thank you," Virgil said. "This is the kind of thing we always look for, maybe it leads to something. I hope Tina Locklin is still around."

"She should be alive, even if she's not around here. She was a year or two younger than Timothy."

"Blonde?"

She hesitated and showed the short curt smile again. "I see where you're going with that. Blonde, big tits? I don't know, I never saw her. Like I said, Timothy didn't want to talk about it."

They chatted for a while, and Fisk told him that she was doing the prep for a murder trial expected to start in a month or so, in September. "It's not much. Three-way argument. A domestic, really, about who was sleeping with who and when, and one guy shot the other one and regretted it about one bullet too late. The interesting part, for me, is that they both had guns. The killer said it was self-defense, the other man pulled first. The only witness, who was sleeping with both of them, has changed her story a few times, so we'll see. He's got a public defender who knows what she's doing."

"You think you'll get him?"

She considered the question, then said, "Yeah, probably. Both men, and the woman, too, were basically white trash, and a jury won't see much downside to putting him away, no matter who pulled first."

"It's an odd business we're in," Virgil said. "There was a public defender down in Watonwan County, good guy, basically, I think he's working up here, now, Eddy something . . ."

"Eddy Webster? He was a PD outstate somewhere."

"Yeah, that's right. I busted a guy, mmm, Donny Herbin was his name. He went after a former friend with a shovel, for no good reason, hurt him bad. He was charged with ag assault and Eddy got it knocked down to simple assault. Herbin's problem was that he was basically nuts. The judge put him in jail for thirty days, and two days after he got out, he shot and killed a grocery clerk over in Faribault because the clerk wouldn't double-bag him."

"I remember that story, the double-bagging thing—didn't know you were involved," Fisk said.

"I wasn't, with that part. I only did the shovel part and told the judge that Herbin ought to get some treatment. The Jackson cops and the highway patrol ran him down after the shooting," Virgil said. "Still. A strange business."

They talked about the strangeness of what they did for another ten minutes, trading stories, and Virgil did a couple of soft probes about Timothy, and Fisk asked about how they'd gotten Timothy's name, which Virgil fended off, and then Carl Smith, carrying his gear bag, stuck his head into the bedroom and said, "I'm good. Got some hair out of the trap in Dr. Carlson's sink. Linda should be finishing up."

And she was.

She had scrubbed all of Carlson's jewelry and bagged the swabs. "If that doesn't do it, nothing will," she said. She asked Fisk for a gum scrub, to separate her DNA from Timothy's, and Fisk agreed.

"I'm a DNA virgin," Fisk told Esselton. "This is my first time."

"I'll be gentle," Esselton said with a smile.

Fisk nodded and they did the scrub.

She wasn't worried about the other samples. The hair in the sink wasn't Timothy's. His jewelry was either gold or platinum, impervious to most chemicals; and she'd soaked them in a household cleaner that the 'net told her would destroy DNA.

You can find anything on the 'net.

On the way down the stairs, Virgil said to Fisk, "Tina Locklin, George Baer."

"That's right," Fisk said. "I have no idea if Tina had anything to do with anything."

"I get that a lot," Virgil said, and he thanked her for her time.

OUT IN THE street, Virgil asked Esselton and Smith about what they thought, and they both thought that a DNA check would be routine. "I got some hair out of his sink, and I got some hair out of her sink, too. Make sure there was no funny business."

"How long for the results?"

"You know we're backlogged. We could be a couple of months out."

"Yeah yeah yeah . . ."

"If you put pressure on somebody to jump the line, maybe . . . two weeks at best?"

"I'll put pressure on somebody to put pressure on somebody else, and it won't be two weeks. Call as soon as you have something."

VIRGIL CALLED LUCAS from his car, told him about the sampling situation, the delay in the DNA results, which was not news to either of them—sometimes, DNA delays ran to months—and about the nurse who may have been obsessed with Timothy Carlson.

"I'll call Henderson and have him talk to the governor either about jumping the DNA line or getting the samples out to a private lab," Lucas said. "I'll get something done."

"Good. How are you feeling?"

"Still wobbly. I'm not on the toilet, though; I don't think I have anything left inside."

"Been there," Virgil said. "Listen, I'm going to see if I can run down George Baer, and then maybe look for Tina Locklin."

"Does that feel right to you?"

"I dunno. I'll tell you what—Fisk is a tough nut. Smart, controlled. I kind of liked her," Virgil said.

"How often do you run into somebody you kinda don't like?" Lucas asked.

"Not that often, I guess," Virgil said.

"You're weird, Virgil, and you have to live with that," Lucas said. "Call me after you talk with Baer."

23

George Baer lived on the tree-lined shore of Turtle Lake, which was north of St. Paul. As far as Virgil knew, and he tended to know these things, Turtle Lake had had a good population of large-mouth bass, of nice size, and also a lot of smaller northern pike.

Which, in his humble opinion, was not outstanding, but was okay. He followed his iPhone app to Baer's house, and found him, after speaking to his wife, Edna, at the front door, in his backyard with a compound bow, shooting at a life-sized whitetail deer target.

When Virgil walked around the house, Baer peered at him, frowning, and barked, "Who're you?"

"Bureau of Criminal Apprehension," Virgil said. "Your wife told me you were out here. I need to chat with you about Timothy Carlson."

"Is there something wrong?"

"Wrong about what?" Virgil asked.

"Timothy died in a strange way, falling off a balcony," Baer said.

He was wearing a blue LA Dodgers ball cap, a blue lightweight Orvis outdoor shirt, and jeans.

"His death was investigated by the medical examiner's office and found to be an accident," Virgil said.

Baer had a bow case laying on the ground behind him. He picked it up, slid the bow inside, and said, "C'mon in the house. Let me get my arrows."

Virgil waited, studying the small lake as Baer pulled a half-dozen arrows out of the plastic deer's target zone and put them in a pocket in the bow case.

"Nice lake," Virgil said, as Baer finished packing up the arrows.

"It's exorheic, so we get a regular turnover in the water," Baer said. "I pee in it from time to time. I like to think I'm contributing to the biological complexity of the Gulf of Mexico."

They walked together through a back porch and into the house. Inside, he yelled, "Edna, me and the cop are in the library."

She yelled back, "Okay."

"She's in her studio," Baer said. "She's a potter."

"Yeah, I talked to her at the front door. She was a little muddy," Virgil said.

"She often is," Baer said.

The library was a large room with a wall of books of all kinds, set on built-in steel shelves that Virgil would have stolen if he could have gotten away with it.

"Great library," he said, looking around.

"Should be," Baer grunted. He was a compact man in the way bears are compact, medium height, thinning reddish hair and freckles, rimless glasses. He pointed at an easy chair and took another one that faced it. "Goddamn thing cost an arm and a leg."

"Worth it," Virgil said. "Good reading lights."

"I spend a lot of time here," Baer said. "So: you have questions about Timothy?"

"About Timothy and a nurse named Tina Locklin."

Baer was surprised by that, and it showed on his round face: "Tina? What does she have to do with anything?"

"You knew her?"

"I still know her. She works over at Abbott Northwestern in Minneapolis. I was on staff there before I retired. Timothy wasn't. He was focused in St. Paul."

"Amanda Fisk told me that there was an episode a long time ago, twenty years or so, when Tina was somewhat . . . romantically obsessed with Timothy. She was fired because of it, left your clinic or partnership or whatever it was."

"That's more or less true, but she wasn't fired. She was encouraged to move along, and she did, with a very good severance from us," Baer said. "Exceptional nurse, one of the best. I'd still see her over at Abbott and we'd chat. She was more embarrassed by what happened, than angry or upset."

What had happened, Baer said, was that Carlson had gotten divorced, and had worked closely with Locklin for several years before that. Locklin may have been in love with him for a while. She was about his age, or a year or two younger or older, was divorced and had hopes . . .

"Timothy wasn't interested. He was looking for something younger and sexier, and said so, to us guys anyway. His first wife was an engineer he met in college," Baer said. "She was at least as smart as Tim, and more creative. She was always getting patents on one thing or another, and never hid her light under a bushel. There was this competitive tension between them, and they got tired of each other—and the tension."

"I spent an hour or so with Amanda Fisk, and she didn't strike me as a low-stress, walk-in-the-park-type," Virgil said. "I mean, if Timothy was looking for a caregiver."

Baer nodded, a jerk of the head. "You got that right. When you showed up and said you were BCA, the first thing that popped into my head was that you were looking at Amanda and the *accident.*" He put some oral italics on the word *accident.*

Virgil leaned toward him: "Wait. You don't think Timothy's death was an accident?"

"Oh, I think it probably was," Baer said. "I do have some respect for the ME's investigators. I have a Fourth of July party here, and was hanging out with Timothy . . ."

"Miz Fisk told me about it . . ."

". . . he told me about a complicated murder case she'd prosecuted and won. He said, 'Amanda's a real killer. *A real killer.*' When I heard that he'd died in an accident, that was the first thing that popped into my head. Honestly, I'll deny this if you tell anyone I said it, but Amanda is a cold-hearted bitch. I mean the lights are on in the kitchen, but there are bats in the attic."

"Is that medical jargon?" Virgil asked.

"Take it for what it's worth," Baer said. "And it is worth *something.*"

VIRGIL CONSIDERED THAT, then said: "Back to Tina Locklin. I am looking at the death, the murder, of Doris Grandfelt. That was way back about the time Timothy Carlson had gotten divorced, and was looking for something younger and sexier, which Doris Grandfelt was."

"You don't think Tina . . ."

"The question is out there," Virgil said.

Now Baer leaned forward, pointed a finger at Virgil's chest: "Tina is one of the softest, mildest people I've ever met. Not timid, but . . . ethical. Kind. She wouldn't hurt a fly."

"Sometimes people break."

"Not Tina. I watched her deal with a hundred very worried patients in our practice. Scared people, sometimes making outrageous demands. We were all surgeons, so when people came to us, they had serious problems. Tina was the most caring kind of nurse. I haven't paid much attention to this Grandfelt thing, but I know what's going on. It seems like Grandfelt was murdered in her workplace. Is that correct? If she was, it had to be in the middle of the night when nobody was around . . ."

"That's one assumption," Virgil said. "I guess it's the main assumption."

"How would Tina even have gotten in the building? You people are looking at DNA recovered from Grandfelt, which means whoever had sex with her must have been there. You think Tina was standing around holding Tim's undershorts while he was screwing Grandfelt?"

"That doesn't seem likely," Virgil conceded.

"If it's a big accounting firm, don't you think they'd lock their doors at night? I mean, I know how Grandfelt got in. She worked there. How would Tina get in?"

"She could have followed Carlson . . ."

"Then what? She stuck her foot in the door as it was closing, and Timothy never saw her?"

"Okay."

"I'm telling you: you can talk to Tina, but you're barking up the wrong tree. She had nothing to do with a murder."

VIRGIL PULLED AT an earlobe, thinking, and said, "You know Amanda Fisk worked at Bee at the time of the murder."

"What!"

"She says she actually met Timothy Carlson during the investigation. He was a client of Bee's, and she consulted on some contract matters."

"So you're looking at two violent deaths attended by the stone-eyed bitch from hell, and you're asking questions about Tina?"

"We're looking at everything," Virgil said. He asked, "You seem to more than dislike Amanda."

"I dislike her. Strongly dislike her, but I don't hate her. She and Timothy were an odd couple. Timothy could be quite cold with some people, warmer with others, and he loved his dogs. He'd loved his dogs from the time he was a child, to hear him tell it. I believe he was sincere. But Amanda. Well, I have no solid reason to think she's a terrible person . . . but I sense that she might be."

"Does she know you think that?"

Baer shook his head: "I have no reason to think so. Timothy was a friend and a golfing partner. We were both members at Turtle Lake Golf. Amanda and I are . . . congenial when we have to be."

"Could you find out when Tina Locklin is at work?"

Baer glanced at his watch. "She'd be getting off about now—she goes in early, her shift would usually be about six to three. I have her phone number, I believe, I could give her a call. She lives down in St. Paul."

"Could you do that? I could meet her at her house," Virgil said. "Don't tell her too much—just that I want to talk to her about Timothy Carlson."

BAER CALLED AND Virgil drove back to St. Paul; Locklin was waiting. She lived in a small house north of I-94, halfway between St. Paul and Minneapolis, flower beds planted with easy care flowers, red and yellow zinnias, marigolds, coneflowers. Virgil parked in the street and she saw him coming up the sidewalk and opened the door.

Locklin: "Virgil Flowers."

"Yes, I just left George Baer. Thanks for talking to me."

"You really think I stabbed Doris Grandfelt to death?" Locklin appeared to be in her early sixties, with short gray hair and oversized plastic-rimmed bifocals. She didn't smile when she asked the question.

"You must have talked to George twice," Virgil said. "One when I was there, and again after I left."

"He was worried about me. George is a good guy. Come in: watch for the cat."

Her house smelled of pasta and bread, and an orange-striped tabby looked suspiciously at Virgil, sniffed at his pants cuff, and then, in the living room, after Virgil sat down, leaped onto his lap to give him a more thorough going over.

"Toss her on the floor," Locklin said.

"She's okay. I like cats," Virgil said. The cat settled on his lap and looked up at him, Virgil gave her an easy stroke from her neck to her tail.

"She's trying to make me jealous," Locklin said. She was wearing a white blouse and blue slacks, crossed her legs and said, "I didn't murder Doris Grandfelt. I was unaware of Doris Grandfelt until this whole hoo-hah blew up, all these true crime people coming to town."

"Did George tell you . . ."

"Some of it. You're wondering if I might have gone crazy after Timothy told me that he wasn't interested in a relationship and stabbed a woman he may have been sleeping with. But I didn't even know about Doris Grandfelt, at the time."

"Did you—"

Locklin broke in: "I wasn't paying too much attention to this investigation until George called. I spent the last half hour reading the *Star-Tribune* online stories and I looked at one of the true crime websites. Here's the thing: Timothy told me he wasn't interested in me, way before the murder. She was killed in the spring, and I was asked to leave the practice, like, six months before that. The fall before, like in October."

"I didn't understand that," Virgil said. "I was under the impression that the two things happened closer together."

"Depends on your definition of 'close.' Anyway, the docs gave me a great severance, which took some of the sting out, and Gary Parsons . . . Dr. Parsons . . . got me fixed up with a job at Abbott. I've been there ever since."

"Never married?" Virgil asked.

"Never remarried. I was married in my twenties and divorced just before I turned forty. Part of my grasping after Timothy was that he was also available after his divorce, and we liked each other. Maybe I just wanted a friend."

"And Timothy's . . . attitude . . . didn't make you angry?"

"A little. It mostly left me depressed. Feeling sort of unwanted by anybody. But I didn't stab Doris. He was seeing another woman when I left the practice and I got the impression, from a last talk with Timothy, that the relationship might be somewhat serious."

"Really," Virgil said. "Who was the other woman?"

She shook her head. "Don't know. He told me there was someone, a professional lady, I think. Could have been another doc. But I don't know. I didn't even have a hint of that when I started nudging him."

"George didn't say anything about that," Virgil said.

"I don't know if George knew about it," Locklin said. "Timothy could be close-mouthed. He was a good guy when you got to know him, but it took a while to get there."

The cat meowed at Virgil, who gave it a couple more strokes, then picked it up and put it on the floor. They both looked at the cat, as it sat by Virgil's feet and began cleaning a paw, then Virgil asked, "Do you stay in touch with anyone at the practice? Anyone who might know who Timothy's girlfriend was?"

"I don't think anyone would remember. I mean, I probably knew Timothy as well as anyone, and I didn't know about it until we had that last chat," Locklin said. "All of it was more than twenty years ago."

"What did you think when you heard he was dead?"

"I was shocked, I guess. He was a healthy man, exercised, ate right, all of that, the kind you think will live to be a hundred. I heard he fell when he was trying to get a dog ball out of a gutter, and that somehow seemed right. Like something he'd be doing. He was huge on dogs. I remember when he had a Labrador that died, and he couldn't talk about it without choking up. Like, for years."

"We think Doris was murdered at the Bee Accounting building, in Lowertown, or close to Bee—her car was found near a bar that she might have been going to. She was almost certainly killed with a piece of hardware from the Bee executive dining room. Were you ever there at Bee, in any capacity? As a client, delivering something to them . . . anything at all?"

She shook her head: "Never. Never even heard of them. I do my own taxes, I've always been an employee of somebody, so my financial life is routine. Never needed any kind of accountant."

WHEN VIRGIL LEFT her, he was convinced that she hadn't had anything to do with the murder. But he was curious about Carlson's unknown girlfriend. Fisk hadn't mentioned a second woman, only Locklin. Would she have known about her? She said she'd met Carlson during the Grandfelt murder investigation, which would have been months after Carlson told Locklin about the unknown woman.

Might Carlson have concealed that other, more serious relationship, from his soon-to-be wife? Or was there even another woman? Might Carlson have simply been lying about that, to put off Locklin?

In the truck, Virgil called Lucas, who asked, "What did you find out?"

Virgil told him about the interviews with Baer and Locklin: "Bottom line, I didn't get much, but I'd like to know who this other woman is."

"So would I," Lucas agreed.

"I'm gonna focus on finding her. And any possibilities the true-crimers turn up."

"What do you think about Carlson?" Lucas asked. "Is he our DNA guy?"

"I'm cautiously optimistic, but I really don't have to be anything in particular—we got hair out of the sink he used, so we'll know for sure whenever the DNA analysis gets back."

"Okay. Something else you don't know," Lucas said. "Henderson called a while ago. The DNA scrubs are being sent to a private lab in Chicago. We'll have the results about the time I get home, early next week."

"Good. See you then. Take it easy, big guy."

"You too, Virgie. Probably see you Tuesday. Listen, call me if anything comes up. Anything."

VIRGIL CALLED BAER: "Tina Locklin told me that Timothy Carlson had a relationship with another woman, back when the problem came up with Tina," Virgil said. "Would you have any idea of who that might have been?"

"None at all," Baer said. "Tina left in October or November, somewhere after it got cold. I quit playing golf in early October, about the time for the first snow squall, so . . . I don't have a lot of social chitchat with Timothy in the off-season. Although . . . it's kind of odd that I wouldn't know."

"Any chance that there was no other woman, that Carlson was trying to let Tina down easy?"

"That's a thought," Baer said. "That's something that Timothy might do."

"All right. If you have any new thoughts, let me know."

Still sitting in the truck, Virgil got out his notebook and made a note about the timing of Carlson's rejection of Tina in the autumn before Grandfelt's death. He finished the note and started the truck, but hadn't yet put it in gear, when Baer called back.

"I had a new thought," Baer said.

"Tell me."

"You said that Amanda told you that she met Timothy during the investigation of Doris Grandfelt's murder . . ."

"Yes."

"Huh. I'll tell you something. Timothy was not impulsive. I'm digging around in my memory, now, but if you look it up, I think he married Amanda at the end of that summer. They were married at the golf club. It's possible that it was the next year after Grandfelt was murdered, but I don't think so. I think it was the same year."

"So . . ."

"So that would be awful fast for Timothy. Awful fast, if they only knew each other from the time Grandfelt was murdered in the spring. I was wondering if it was possible that Amanda was the woman Timothy was talking about with Tina. That he and Amanda were actually dating the autumn before the murder?"

"That's not what she told me."

"I know. You told me that," Baer said.

"You think she was lying?"

"Let's just say that I wouldn't necessarily believe everything that Amanda tells me," Baer said.

"Okay. Thanks, Doc."

"Don't call me Doc. You're not Bugs Bunny, and I'm not Elmer Fudd."

Virgil called Dahlia Blair and said, "I have another search, if you guys could do it."

"What?"

"I need to find out when Timothy Carlson got married to Amanda Fisk—whether it was the year Doris was murdered, or the year after."

"Do you know where he was married?" Blair asked.

"Here, in Ramsey County."

"Okay, that should be easy. But everything is going to be closed in a few minutes, so it'll have to be tomorrow."

"That's soon enough," Virgil said.

24

Amanda Fisk saw the DNA samplers out the door, with Flowers a step behind. She thought about Flowers: he was a convivial sort, easygoing, friendly, either naturally or because he'd consciously trained himself to be that way. She recognized it from other detectives she'd worked with over the years, the better ones. They could talk with anyone and get their suspects talking back.

If you were a criminal—Fisk didn't usually think of herself that way but recognized that technically she was one—talking was one of the worst things you could do. Talking with anyone, but worst of all, a detective.

She'd talked a little too much with Flowers, she thought, though she couldn't actually pick out any missteps. But she'd been talking. And Flowers was smart. She'd done a search of his name, and learned that he was not only known for his detecting abilities, he was a bestselling novelist and a magazine writer. Two of the articles she'd found mentioned he was known in law enforcement circles as "that f*ckin' Flowers" for his unusual insights and nonstandard investigative procedures.

After brooding for a while, sitting alone in the big house, Fisk got up, went to her home office, brought her computer up, and began browsing the true crime sites. The true-crimers were still hunting down the men shown in Grandfelt's last photos.

And she stumbled over the link between the true-crimers, Flowers, and Timothy. Timothy had been recognized in the old photograph by a man who was apparently suffering from dementia. Flowers had interviewed him, and after he'd left, one of the true-crimers had spoken to the man's daughter, who confirmed both that her father had recognized Timothy, and that he was suffering from Alzheimer's disease.

Reacting as a prosecutor, she would not want to put a demented man on a witness stand to confirm a key piece of information. On the other hand, that's not what Flowers was doing—he might not know whether or not the demented man's information was accurate, but it was enough to get him in the house, and a DNA match would stand by itself.

They wouldn't get a match from the hair in the sink, which came from an anonymous donor at a St. Paul barbershop. If they became suspicious of the negative result on the hair, they could go looking for another sample. That might take them to Timothy's clinic office, but that office space was shared, so there'd be massive amounts of contaminating DNA, and she'd already collected and disposed of all the personal clothing and equipment he'd kept there.

But the threat remained. Why would anyone be suspicious of the negative DNA result taken from a man's own sink? Most cops wouldn't be—but Flowers might be.

From what had become her compulsive reading of the true crime sites, it appeared to her that Flowers was leading the investigation. Davenport had been mentioned in the early days of the investigation, but after that, Flowers had come to the fore. Now, Flowers himself had said that Davenport was off in New Mexico.

If she could interrupt the rhythm of the investigation, perhaps get Flowers diverted to something else, a new man brought in, someone more conventional, someone more likely to take any DNA results at face value . . .

How to do that without bringing attention to herself?

VIRGIL FELT HE was working a couple of angles that could actually produce: the DNA samples, the various bits of research being done by the true-crimers, including the Carlson-Fisk marriage date. At the same time, it wasn't what he wanted to do. He wanted to work on the novel. He wanted to do it badly enough that he'd begun to worry about his driving. He'd get in his truck and start off for somewhere, but then he'd start thinking about the novel, and later find himself at his destination without really knowing how he'd gotten there.

He was not, he thought, "in the moment," as the Buddha might have recommended.

He had a laptop with him, but not a printer, and he really needed to see the book on paper, so he could pencil-edit. With the DNA results not available until next week, he decided that if nothing new came up, he'd go home on Friday afternoon and stay through the weekend, and maybe even take three days off.

HE'D MISS LUCAS, for as long as Lucas was gone. He and Lucas thought about the world in different ways. Lucas had the ability to pick up on small, insignificant details in an investigation that were out of sync with how he thought the world worked, and more often than seemed likely, the insignificant turned out to be critical. Virgil tended to think in more global ways, like painting a picture, putting together colors and shapes until he could see an image emerging from the chaos.

And he was starting to sense something. The shapes and colors were coming together. George Baer, for instance, had suggested that Tina Locklin would have had one difficult problem to solve in planning the murder of Grandfelt, if it happened at Bee: how would she get into the building? How would she get a key?

He could think of ways, but they were all complicated and improbable. If Carlson was meeting Grandfelt on a regular basis, at Bee, which seemed improbable all by itself, Locklin might have followed him and perhaps seen him use a key to get into the building . . . and somehow might have gotten his key and copied it . . .

No. Never happened. That same thought applied to all other possible suspects. How would they get into the Bee building after hours? That one simple problem made it more likely that Doris Grandfelt wasn't killed at Bee at all—that she'd been picked up in a bar or on the street and killed elsewhere.

But. Baer's question about how Locklin would get into the Bee building made him consider the fact that at least three people had been regulars at Bee: Grandfelt, who worked there; Fisk, who worked there; and Carlson, a client.

That was odd all by itself, and he made another entry in the notebook, looked at the note, then paged back through his notebook to entries he'd made during the interview with Bee's CEO, Cory Donner. The entry included a personal cell phone number, and Virgil punched it into his phone.

Donner answered on the third ring, and said, "Agent Flowers. I was wondering if I'd ever hear from you again."

"Sorry to bother you so late in the day . . ."

"I work late," Donner said. "How can I help you?"

"When Lucas and I spoke to you, you mentioned a sexual scandal you had at Bee a couple of years before Doris Grandfelt was murdered. You said that the company had instituted a somewhat draconian prohibition about sexual relationships between employees . . ."

"Yes, indeed. Draconian is the right word."

"Did you ever have to enforce it?"

"No, not really. Actually, we softened it. Two of our employees began seeing each other, secretly, and when it got serious, the man, Tom Bergstrom, went to the CEO at the time, told him what was going on, and offered to resign if the company thought that was necessary. Tom was a good guy, *is* a good guy. He's still with us. There was some conversation about it in the upper ranks. We all agreed that the absolute ban had served its purpose, as a warning, and could in some circumstances be inhumane. Both Tom and his girlfriend, Mickey Lee, were excellent employees and that had some influence as well. They eventually married."

"Was that right around the time Doris was murdered?"

"No, no, that would have been later."

"If a senior married executive had developed a relationship with Doris, back fairly soon after the relationship ban was instituted, would he have been fired?"

"Oh, yes, I think so. The original relationship, the one that caused the ban, was quite a shock to the company," Donner said.

"So if Doris . . ."

"I see where you're going with this. Doris develops a secret relationship with somebody who ate in the executive dining room, and then threatens to reveal the relationship unless he dumps his wife and marries *her*. So he kills her. With a cafeteria knife."

"Just considering the possibilities."

"I've got two words for you. Maybe three, depending on how you think of contractions."

"And those are . . ."

"*We're accountants*. If we were going to murder Doris, we would do it carefully, unspectacularly, thoroughly, and a long way from Bee. We wouldn't hack her to pieces."

"Ah."

"Was there anything else?" Donner asked.

"If somebody wanted to get into Bee at night, where would he or she get a key to the building?"

"That would be difficult. Doris had one—among her duties was what amounted to being a mail clerk. All the outgoing things would be collected at the end of the day and parceled out to UPS or FedEx. She would wait for the pickups and then lock up. That was one of her duties. Her friend Stephanie also had a key, and the same duties. We also had two receptionists who would arrive early, and would have had keys to open the building so employees could get in. Several executives had them; I did not, not then."

"So the keys were controlled. They weren't just handed out to everyone."

"No, they weren't. There's quite a lot of sensitive information in our files. For instance, we hold tax returns for a number of prominent politicians and businesspeople. We're responsible for that information, for its security. Right now, I believe there are twelve keys."

"Okay."

"I don't feel like I've been much help," Donner said.

"Actually, you have been. Thank you."

Virgil rang off, looked at his watch. Time to head back to the hotel, get something to eat, read through his notebook, and get himself settled in front of his laptop to knock out some words.

FLOWERS WAS LOOKING at Timothy as a possible DNA match for the last person to have sex with Doris Grandfelt. According to information Fisk found on a true crime site, Flowers had determined that the sex occurred very shortly before Grandfelt was killed. If he concluded that Timothy had killed Grandfelt, then she, Fisk, was safe, except for the possibility that the surviving Grandfelts might go after Timothy's estate with a lawsuit. If they won the lawsuit, that would be a blow to her financial security.

But if an intense look into Timothy's personality and history suggested that he hadn't killed Doris Grandfelt—if they concluded that his contact was a one-time, sex-for-money deal—who would they look at next? If Flowers did a deep dive into her own history, he might find a series of violent deaths.

Even if he did all of that, she doubted that she would be indicted, or could be convicted. All the evidence would be purely circumstantial. But it would be ugly, and in a criminal case, nothing was certain.

She was now deep into pure speculation, but she had the sense that the investigation was turning against her best interests. Getting Flowers off the case, she thought, might be critical.

How to do that?

She went back to the Google satellite views of Flowers's girlfriend's farm. Way out in the sticks. She looked at the roads around the farm . . .

And after a while, she thought, small risk now, or possible bigger risk later? She would have to do an on-the-spot evaluation of risk . . .

She went to bed in sweatpants and a tee-shirt, lay awake for a while, a little too warm, then got up, went to the garage, opened a storage cabinet, and took out the final gallon jug of Drano Max Gel. She took a few seconds to unscrew a stubborn cap and pour the contents down the utility sink. Careful not to let it splash on her, she rinsed it three times, then took it in the house and put it in the kitchen sink while she went back upstairs to dress.

A half hour after that, she was at an all-night gas station. She filled the tank on the car, then without hesitation, the gallon jug. She tightened the cap on the jug and went inside, through a cloud of small moths, to claim her change.

Looked at her watch: 1:30 a.m.

Small risk now?

Faced with the reality of it, it suddenly seemed not so small.

25

Frankie Nobles always slept soundly, even when Virgil was gone. While she didn't believe in the mystical powers of pyramids, she and Virgil did sleep under the canted ceiling of the old farmhouse, which was like being under a pyramid. And it was nice, especially in a thunderstorm, to hear the rain drumming on the roof while they were safe and warm inside.

She was soundly asleep at three o'clock in the morning when Honus the Yellow Dog jumped off the bed and padded to the open window, looked out through the screen, and woofed. Woofed again, and then left the bedroom, running down the stairs, where he began barking frantically.

Frankie struggled toward consciousness until she heard Sam screaming from the downstairs bedroom: "Ma! Ma! The stable's on fire. Ma! Ma!"

Frankie came out of bed as though on a catapult, ran down the stairs barefoot, found the kitchen door open, heard Honus barking frantically, now outside. She looked toward the stable and saw Sam running toward it, silhouetted against the bright light of a fire that was already climbing toward the building's loft.

She shrieked, "Sam, come back, no, Sam! Sam!" and she went after him.

The fire was climbing the stable's side wall, which faced her, and she ran barefoot across the farmyard, driveway stones biting into her feet, and saw Sam disappear through the stable's front door. Honus was running in frantic circles outside the door that Sam had gone through, barking, barking, and as she got there, she could hear the two horses bawling from their stalls, crazed with fear, kicking the wooden stall walls.

She followed Sam through the door. To her left, she could see a fire crawling up a wall of hay bales, which were stored opposite the tack room. There was smoke, not as much as she'd feared, but the flames at the end of the building were ferocious, a blowtorch, a hurricane. Through it, to her right, she saw Sam running toward the opposite end of the building.

She screamed, "Sam!"

The kid turned and shouted, "The horses are crazy. We got to let them out the back."

He disappeared through the doorway and she went after him, knowing without thinking that he was right, the horses were out of control, and they were big, and they were violent. She went out the door behind him, and he was already around the corner of the building.

Each stall had a separate, small twenty-by-thirty-foot turnout at the back of the barn, with a stable door opening into each turnout. The turnouts were contained by six-foot-tall pipe fencing. Sam slipped between pipes on the turnout fence, ran to the first stall door, turned the latch handle on the door, and yanked it open. The rescue they called Rush exploded from the stall, smashing the door back before it was fully open.

The door knocked Sam down and the panicked golden-brown horse bucked in a tight circle inside the fence as Sam rolled toward the building to get away from the horse's iron-shod hooves. Frankie ran around to the outside of the pen and yanked the latch on the pen's gate and dragged the gate open. Rush saw the opening and was through it in an instant, disappearing into the night.

The fire was spreading from under the roof and Frankie shouted, "Sam, get away from the wall . . ."

Sam was already crawling into the second turnout; sparks were firing into the sky, pieces of hay carried aloft, some the size of kitchen towels, and Frankie feared that the house might go until she realized a breeze was carrying the sparks away from the house, but toward the two of them, like flaming, falling kites.

She unlatched the second turnout gate as Sam turned the handle on the stall door, and Bruno, a big black quarter horse, pounded into the turnout and then through the open gate into the night. Frankie felt a spasm of relief as she watched the horse go, then a spasm of terror as she turned back to Sam and saw that one of his shirt sleeves was on fire and he was slapping at it while trying to pull his pajama shirt off, and she ran to him and as he turned, grabbed the back of his shirt and yanked it straight over his head.

As she did that, she stepped barefoot on a wad of burning hay and did a dance away from it, still tearing at the shirt. Flames from the shirt caught Sam's long hair for a second, but she slapped it out and Sam shouted, "You're on fire" and she realized she was, and she ripped her own nightshirt off as they both ran out of the pen and into the adjacent pasture.

The stable, built of wood, except for the roof, was now fully involved. "Gotta call Fire, you get Honus," she shouted at Sam. The entire yard was lit by the inferno, and she ran to the house, ignoring the pain in her feet, and up the stairs to her cell phone and called the volunteer fire department and shouted, "We have a fire!"

"Frankie? This is Clark. We're coming! Stay clear. Olaf called us. You need an ambulance?"

"Sam's shirt was on fire, but we got it off him."

"I'm sending an ambulance, but it'll be coming from town . . ."

"Hurry!" At the back of her brain, she could hear the twins crying in their shared bedroom, and she headed that way.

Inside the house, she hushed the twins, quickly—harshly, she thought later, maybe had frightened them. She ran to her bedroom, her phone still in her hand, pulled on a tee-shirt—it occurred to her only then that she was wearing nothing but a pair of underpants, not that she cared—and she snatched up a pair of jeans and carried them with her as she ran back down the stairs, into the kitchen, where she grabbed a fire extinguisher and ran back outside. Even inside the kitchen, she could hear the fire roaring.

Sam was holding Honus by the collar; the dog was barking at the fire and Frankie stumbled up and shouted over the dog's bark, "Are you burned?"

"My hands and I think my arms, I stepped on some hot stuff," Sam said. "You're burned too, I could see your shirt on fire, I think you're burned."

"Fire is on the way, and an ambulance," she shouted, looking at the stable. The fire had gotten to bales of bedding, which added heat and velocity to the blaze. They could see the steel roof beginning to distort in the heat. She began pulling on the jeans, felt a finger of pain along a thigh, another burn she didn't want to think about yet.

"Got the horses out," Sam said. "I hope they're not burned, but they might be: it was hot outside the stalls, I don't know about inside."

"You stupid little shit, you should never have gone into that stable . . ." She hugged him and started crying and hugged him harder. "Thank you, you saved the horses . . ."

At that moment, a white pickup roared up the driveway, and Olaf Nilsson and his wife Jean spilled out, and jogged toward them: "At least you're okay. I thought it was the house. I called Fire."

"Yeah, thank you. We got the horses out, but we might have gotten a little singed," Frankie said. She'd been too excited before, but now she felt the pain coming on, in her arms and across her back, in her feet. She turned to her son: "Are you hurting?"

"Some," he said. And then, "Yeah."

"I'll call an ambulance," Jean Nilsson said.

"One's already coming," she said. To her son: "When you finished the lawn, where'd you put the mower?"

"Machine shed," Sam said. "When you went inside the stable . . . did you smell gas?"

"Yes! There was no gasoline in there, but I smelled it," Frankie said.

"Did somebody set us on fire, Mom?"

"If somebody did, Virgil will kill them."

They could hear the fire trucks coming, two of them. Frankie had worked with a volunteer fire department in another part of the state, earlier in life, and she knew what they were going to tell her: there was no saving any part of the stable. Their job was simply to keep the fire from spreading to the other buildings.

And that's what the chief told them when the trucks arrived. A tall man with shoulder-length brown hair, his name was Lon Carpenter, and he got out of the lead truck and walked toward them and said, "Not much we can do about it, honey."

"I know, Lonnie," she said. "We got the horses out . . ."

"Thank God for that." The other men on the two trucks were unreeling foam hoses, in case they needed to quench something other than the stable; the stable would simply be a waste of good chemicals.

"When we went inside, we smelled gasoline," Frankie said.

Carpenter: "Gasoline? You didn't keep . . ."

"Not a goddamn thing in there to start a fire," Frankie said, staring at the blaze, which was beginning to slow. "All the wiring is inside conduits. Never a sign of trouble."

"Virgil's a cop," Carpenter said.

Frankie: "That's what I'm thinking."

"Hands hurt," Sam said.

"We gotta get you to the hospital," Frankie said. "We need to wait for the ambulance—my back, I couldn't drive."

Sam nodded and said, "Horses would be dead if it wasn't for Honus. He woke me up barking. Must have smelled the fire."

Frankie leaned down to give the dog a scratch: "Thank you, Honus."

She turned back to the fire and suddenly began to cry again, hands covering her face, the dog licking her arm.

THE AMBULANCE ARRIVED fifteen minutes later. Jean Nilsson said, "You guys go on. Me and Olaf will take care of the twins and Honus."

The EMTs put them in the back, sitting upright, and started for the Mayo Clinic's urgent care center in Mankato.

"It hurts, but it's not getting worse," Sam said, holding up reddened hands.

"I've seen a lot worse that turned out okay," one of the EMTs said. "I'd put on some painkiller spray, but I'd rather wait until you're talking to a doctor. If you can stand it."

"I can stand it," Sam said. "Mom?"

"I can, too," she said. "I'm going to call Virgie."

THREE- AND FOUR-O'CLOCK calls were not everyday events, but they weren't totally uncommon, either. When Virgil's phone rang, he was asleep, but came up quickly. A call in the small hours usually meant a murder somewhere, but when he rolled over and picked up his phone, the screen read "Frankie."

"Oh shit!" He punched "answer" and asked, "Are you all right?"

"I'm in an ambulance with Sam, we're both a little burned, not too bad. We're going to the Mayo in Mankato. Somebody burned down the stable."

"The stable? I'm coming, I'm coming, I'll call you on the road."

"Wait! Wait! We got the horses out, they're in the big pasture, somebody's got to check and see if they're burned . . ."

"I'll check later. I'll be there in an hour . . . You're not hurt bad? Jesus Christ, are you okay, is Sam okay? Where are the twins? Where's Honus?"

"Don't panic on me," Frankie said. "And don't drive fast. Jean and Olaf are with the twins. We're okay, Honus is okay, I think the horses looked okay, I'll call a vet tomorrow morning. They're taking us to the hospital, the EMTs say we're not too bad, but we'll need some painkiller and bandages."

"I'm coming!" Virgil punched off, scooped his dopp kit, laptop, and pistol into his equipment bag, pulled on jeans and a tee-shirt and ran out of the room, down the hotel stairs and out to the garage. He was on I-494 three minutes later, running with lights and siren, headed south.

When he got off the interstate, he called Frankie, but she didn't pick up, and he called Sam, but he didn't either, so he gave up and focused on the road. Fifteen minutes later, he got a call from a highway patrolman named Ezra Ely.

"Ez! I'm running south on 60," Virgil said. "I'm driving too fast, lights and siren." His voice sounded squeaky and panicked in his own ears.

"I figured you would be," Ely said. "I got a call from our dispatcher who said your wife and kid are on the way to the Mayo in Mankato, that there was a fire and you were in St. Paul. Anyway, I'm coming north on 60. When you see my lights, slow down, and I'll turn around and lead you south."

"Thanks, man. I'm running hard. And I'm scared shitless."

"Gotcha."

ELY PICKED HIM up halfway to Mankato and took him all the way to the clinic, lights and sirens on both vehicles; they went through the college town of Saint Peter like twin rocket ships, faster than Virgil would have dared on his own. At the emergency room, Ely turned around as Virgil parked. Virgil slapped Ely's car hood and said through the open driver's-side window, "I owe you big," and Ely said, "No, you don't," and Virgil nodded and hurried inside.

A nurse said, "Are you . . . ?"

"Virgil Flowers, here for Florence Nobles and Sam Nobles . . ."

"They are being done up right now," the nurse said. "I think the doc is through with them. Hang on here, I'll get him."

Virgil hung on at the counter, almost jogging in place out of anxiety, as the nurse went into the back and returned a minute later with a young doctor who was eating a sad-looking white bread sandwich.

"Mr. Flowers," the doctor said, chewing and swallowing. "Florence and Sam will be out shortly. Florence has second-degree burns with blistering on her arms, upper back, and a spot on her left leg, as well as abrasions on her feet and small burns on one foot. I understand she ran barefooted across some sharp gravel, which is minor. For the burns, she'll need to keep the bandages on for two weeks or so. Sam has second-degree burns on one of his arms and one side of his neck and also on both hands. His hands are somewhat more burned than his arm or neck, but he'll be fine, there shouldn't be any permanent scarring or disability. He also has abrasions on his feet. They'll both be uncomfortable for a week or two. We'll want to see them back here on Saturday, and then as needed. I've given Florence instructions on wound care, and she seems to understand."

"She's good at that. When can I go in . . ."

The doctor looked toward the door in the back: "They should be out in a minute or so. They're both barefoot . . . why don't you wait here, and I'll check on the hold-up."

"For God's sake . . ."

Then Frankie walked out of the back carrying a paper sack, and when she saw Virgil, she began crying and Virgil stepped toward her and she fended him off and said, "No hugging for a while, let me hug you," and she hugged him with her one unburnt arm and then Sam came out and said, "This sucks."

They didn't seem desperately injured and Virgil said, "The horses . . ."

"They're in the big pasture, they might have some burns," Frankie said. "It took us a few minutes to get them out, that's how Sam burned his hands. If Sam hadn't gone in the barn, they'd both be dead."

Sam flapped his hands at Virgil: both palms were covered with bandages.

"Tell me . . . Honus . . ."

"Honus is fine, he's in the house, now, he's the one who got us up," Frankie said. She handed him the sack and told him about the fire. "Fire is still there, keeping an eye on it. The stable's gone . . . right down to the ground."

"Fuck the stable, we can get another stable," Virgil said. "I can't get more people like you guys. What in the hell were you doing running into . . ."

Frankie, crying again, "What? You wanted our horses to burn to death?"

"No, no! I didn't want you to burn to death, though. I mean . . . never mind," and he reached out to hug Frankie again and she evaded him again and said, "Don't touch anything with bandages," and he managed to wrap one arm around her shoulder and down her back and squeeze.

Sam said, "We both smelled gas. In the stable. I mean, gasoline, when we went in the stable."

"Gasoline . . ." Virgil groped around the word for a few seconds, then: "In the stable?"

"There wasn't any gas in the stable," Frankie said. "Sam mowed the yard, but he put the mower and the gas can in the machine shed where they're supposed to go, and they're still there. But we both smelled gas."

Virgil looked at the doctor, who was still hovering, and said, "Motherfucker . . ."

"What?"

"Not you. Somebody else," Virgil said.

THEY STOOD TALKING for two or three more minutes, and Frankie told him that the sack contained pain-killing spray, and that they had prescriptions for pain-killing pills should they need them, then Virgil said to the doctor, "I'm going to put them in my truck, but I'd like to come back and talk for just a minute. I'll be right back."

Frankie and Sam could walk easily enough—they were wearing hospital slippers—and Virgil put them in the truck, and then went back inside where he said to the doctor, "I need to know how bad, and what's next."

"What I already told you—they hurt, but they're not hurt bad. The biggest problem is avoiding infection, and we've given both Florence and Sam instructions on that. They've got what amounts to very severe sunburns, but on parts of their bodies that don't usually get sunburned. They both have some blistering, and skin will be peeling off, but they're not in any danger if we can avoid infection . . ."

Virgil thanked him, went back outside, and in the truck, Frankie said, "We'll have to move the big chair up the stairs into the bedroom for a while. I won't be able to sleep on my back or side, and I'll have to have my burned arm across my stomach in a sling or something . . . So I need something where I can sit upright and sleep."

"We can do that. As soon as we get home. You need to rest. Sam, too."

THE SUN WAS up when they got back to the house. A different fire truck was on the scene, the first two had gone; this one a tanker, the two firemen spraying water on the smoldering remains of the stable.

Virgil led Frankie and Sam inside, where they were met by a relieved Honus, as well as the Nilssons.

"The twins are still asleep," Jean Nilsson said. "I gave them cookies."

"Two each, and two for me," Olaf said. "A shame about the stable. That was a beauty."

Sam wanted to eat, Frankie wanted to sit down, and both of them wanted Virgil to check on the whereabouts of the horses. Virgil and Olaf went back outside and walked over to the firemen, who said they were about done. "Don't think it'll reignite, there's not much left to burn," one told him.

Looking out across the still-standing turnouts that the day before had been attached to the back of the stable, and well out into the green grass of the big pasture, Virgil could see the horses looking back at him. What he could do about them, he didn't know; they seemed best left where they were, until they could get a veterinarian to the farm.

He and Olaf went back inside. Sam was eating cereal, Frankie perched on a kitchen chair, talking with him.

"Tell me about the gasoline again," he said.

And when they had, he had no doubt that the fire had been deliberately set. The Nilssons had not seen anybody on the road. After another cookie, Olaf Nilsson said he needed a nap, and the couple left.

Virgil went back outside, Honus tracking behind him, where the firemen were finishing their work. He saw no sign of a gas can in the smoldering wreckage, or any kind of bottle or other vessel that might have held gasoline, so the arsonist had taken it away. All he could smell was wet burnt wood, wet burnt hay, and the stink of burned corrugated steel from the roof, now collapsed in the middle of the cinders.

He walked around the mess for a bit, looked across a field where an arsonist might have come in. There was no track that he could see.

He called Lucas, who was still soundly asleep. Lucas came up and without preamble asked, "Who's dead?"

"Nobody, thank God. I'm down in Mankato. Somebody tried to burn us out last night. Burned my stable to the ground . . ."

"Oh, Jesus! Is everybody okay?"

Virgil said, "Frankie and Sam got second-degree burns getting the horses out, but they're okay. I can see the horses in the pasture and they look all right, but I haven't been able to get a close look yet. The twins are fine. Honus is fine. Both Sam and Frankie smelled gasoline in the barn, and we've never had gas in there."

"So it's arson."

"Yes."

"You got insurance?" Lucas asked.

"Not for arson."

"Ah, shit. This is Doris Grandfelt," Lucas said.

"That's what I'm afraid of," Virgil said. "There are a couple of other possibilities."

"No. It's Grandfelt. I can feel it in my bones," Lucas said. "Somebody wants you off the case. Call Duncan, tell him you're gone until Tuesday. I'll be back and we'll kick some serious ass. Until then, take care of your people."

"I called because I was thinking you might want to take care of your own."

"Ah . . . yeah. You're right, though I don't expect they'd try to burn both of us," Lucas said. "That'd be too obvious. Probably hoping your stable would look like an accident."

"It's a fucking disaster, is what it is," Virgil said.

"Virgil, I'm sorry."

"So am I," Virgil said. "And I'm gonna hang somebody for it."

VIRGIL CALLED DUNCAN, who was horrified: "Take all the time you need. We need to get an arson guy down there . . ."

"Nah. There's nothing left to investigate," Virgil said.

The veterinarian made an emergency visit before her office hours, and Virgil, Frankie, Sam, and the vet chased down the horses, which was harder than it looked in cowboy movies. Virgil wanted Frankie and Sam to stay inside, but they told him to stuff it, and both agreed that they didn't hurt much with the application of a topical painkiller and a couple of pills.

The horses were okay, though their manes and tails were curled with heat, and they were still spooked. The vet recommended that they be put in separate pastures in case they had invisible burns that made them cranky. "You really don't need to have a horse fight at this point," she said.

The vet left and as Virgil was watching her truck turn into the road, he took a call from Dahlia Blair. "We're trying to look up the marriage date, you know, Carlson and Fisk, but there's some kind of computer hang-up. We won't be able to get it until Monday."

"That's okay. I've had a major problem here. Somebody tried to burn us out last night . . ." He kept thinking he shouldn't do it, but he babbled out the story of the stable fire, the smell of gasoline, and after a while, Blair said, "This is good stuff. No, wait, this is *great* stuff. I'll see you down there."

She hung up before Virgil could tell her not to come, and when he tried to call her back, she didn't pick up. He knew why: because this was *great* stuff.

Off the phone, he walked back to the house where Frankie and Sam and Alex and Willa were sitting at the kitchen table, with Honus under it. Frankie had a yellow legal pad and a pen: "All right, what are we going to do about a stable?" she asked.

"I'll talk to the bank on Monday, get a loan for a Morton building or something like it. A stable kit," Virgil said. "Probably get it up before snowfall if we get started. Don't really need a mortgage, just a short-term loan and I'll pay it off with the new contract."

"I liked the one you built," Frankie said. "It was like old-fashioned; it fit the farm."

"Yeah, until the goddamned thing went up like a nuclear weapon," Virgil said. "Wouldn't have happened with a metal building. Might have burned the hay and bedding, but the whole building wouldn't have come down . . . If it weren't for Honus . . ." He gave the dog a scratch. "Anyway, we've got the weekend, we can figure out what we can do, and you can call some of the stable-kit companies on Monday. Probably ought to get something bigger anyway. Maybe eight stalls."

"You think?" Frankie said. Her eyes rolled up to the ceiling, already calculating.

A pickup roared into the driveway, they could hear it but not see it, and Sam got up and looked out and said, "Moses."

Moses was Frankie's hotheaded third son, a big man, dark hair, broad shoulders; a minute later standing in the doorway. "I saw Olaf in town and he said somebody torched the place. Who do I kill?"

Frankie said, "Not funny, Mose," and when Moses stepped toward her with an arm out, she shrank away and said, "No hugs, you big lug. I'm burned, for Christ's sakes."

Moses: "Not funny? Did I sound like I was joking?"

THEY TALKED ABOUT a stable replacement, and any possible further danger they thought the farm might be in. "I doubt whoever it is will try again," Virgil said. "I think this was to pull me off that damn true crime case up in the Cities."

Frankie: "But why?"

"Because we're getting close."

"When I find out who it is, I'm going to kill 'em," Moses said again.

Virgil: "A little pro tip, here, Mose. When you plan to kill somebody, don't tell anyone. Don't tell your mother, don't even whisper it to one of your cats."

Moses nodded. "I see where you're going with that."

They were still talking when a three-car convoy pulled into the yard. They all stood up to look as the cars rolled right past the house to the clump of ashes where the stable used to be, and five women piled out and began making movies. Cash, Blair, and Weitz, along with a couple of women Virgil didn't know.

Virgil said, "Ah, shit," and when he hustled outside, they began taking pictures of him. "Listen, you guys . . ."

"We know what you're gonna say," Cash said. "That's why we went straight through the yard. And you can forget it. You're gonna be a movie star."

Moses came out: "Can I be in the movie?"

The cameras swiveled to him: "If you got anything good to tell us," Cash said.

Virgil said, "Mose . . ."

Moses said, "It was arson. They're trying to pull Virgil off the case. My mom and brother smelled gasoline when they went in the stable to rescue the horses, and we never keep gas in there."

Virgil: "Moses, Jesus Christ."

Moses: "Tellin' like it is."

Cash had to smile, but Virgil said, "Ah, God."

After a while, and a lot of movies, that included Virgil, Frankie, Moses and Sam, Alex and Willa, and Honus, the women packed up and left.

"Talk about clickbait," Frankie said, as the last of them rolled out onto the road.

Later, every true crime site they looked at had the movies. "This is like a fuckin' carnival," Virgil said.

Frankie said, "You know, if we were burned out by the Grandfelt killer, an attack on you by a criminal you were hunting, I bet the state would pay for a new stable."

"Keep dreamin', babe," Virgil said. But he thought about it.

THE FARM HAD a Kubota front-end loader. Virgil and Moses spent the weekend pushing the debris from the fire into a pile. Moses now ran the architectural salvage business that Frankie had started years earlier, and he owned a heavy-duty thirty-foot trailer. They loaded the debris into it, and on Monday made two trips to the landfill.

When they got back after the second trip, another of Frankie's grown boys, Tall Bear, was wandering around the yard. They answered some of his questions, and saw Frankie coming down the road in her pickup. When she was out of the truck, she told Virgil that she'd gone over to the salvage yard to get the drag magnet.

"There'll be a thousand nails and screws laying around and we need to pick them up, or we'll be picking them up with our tires every time we drive around there," she said.

She was correct. Virgil and Tall Bear spent most of the afternoon dragging the magnet and picked up a half-bucket of nails and screws.

At dinner that night, Frankie asked, "You've got to go back tomorrow?"

"I should, but I could probably get another day. I need to get down to the bank tomorrow."

"Call Lucas: see what he thinks."

He did that, and Lucas told him that he'd finished with the deposition that afternoon, and that he was catching a very early flight out of Albuquerque. "So early that I've checked in to an airport hotel. I talked to Duncan, and he said we now won't have any DNA results until at least Wednesday, so . . . I don't see why you couldn't take another day. Or two."

"If we get a match with Carlson, I want to be there when we talk to Amanda Fisk again," Virgil said. "I'm thinking we get a match."

On Tuesday, Virgil went to the credit union in Mankato and found that he could get a loan big enough to cover any of the stable kits that Frankie had been researching, but only if they mortgaged the farm as part of the deal. He could get the loan with a fifteen-year pay period, but with a short-term-payoff option, if he wanted it.

He and Frankie talked about it, stressed about it, and decided to go with it—and to contract for one of the bigger kits.

"Now I've *got* to finish the book," Virgil told her. "And it's gotta be good."

Frankie was most interested in what was called a Belkin Building, which had a local rep; the rep could make it to the farm on Wednesday, and Virgil called Duncan and begged for another day off and got it.

"We've got more of the guys in the photos, six of them now, they're all doing gum scrubs," Duncan said. "Wasn't as bad as I thought it would be, but we dinged up a couple of long-term marriages."

The Belkin Building rep showed up at midmorning, and they spent the rest of the morning and most of the afternoon with him, looking at the site, talking about what had to be done, getting a timeline, and making a tentative deal.

"You're going to have to handle this," Virgil told Frankie. "I'm going to get whoever did this to us, and I gotta focus on that. And the book. When I deliver the book, I'll pay off the mortgage."

"I got that."

"And listen," Virgil said. "This whole thing would be a hell of a lot easier both in terms of getting the mortgage and paying it off with book money, you know, tax-wise, if we were married."

Frankie scratched her forehead, said, "Yeah, probably."

"Let's get it done," Virgil said. "Next week, maybe. See if you can nail down a judge."

"That's so romantic."

"It is what it is," Virgil said. "Gimme a kiss."

26

The Belkin man had been gone for an hour, and Frankie was on-line with a company that sold saddles and other tack—she'd lost everything that had been stored in the tack room—when Lucas called from St. Paul.

"Guess what?"

"We got a match!" Virgil said.

"No. We did not," Lucas said. "We got a good profile from the hair in his bathroom sink that is nothing like the profile from the semen recovered from Grandfelt."

"Damnit! I was more and more sure that Carlson was our guy," Virgil said. "We're back to square one."

"Not quite. We still have some photo guys who haven't been lo-cated. You're coming up tomorrow? We do need to see what every-body has done while we were out."

"Yeah, why don't I meet you at ten o'clock at the BCA?" Virgil said.

"We'll get with Jon, see what's what. I'm wondering why he didn't call me with this."

"Because he doesn't know about it yet," Lucas said. "Henderson arranged for the private lab. He made a call at the end of the workday in Chicago and talked to the lab director. They'll be calling Duncan tomorrow morning."

"All right. Damnit, I was so sure."

"See you at ten," Lucas said.

THEY MET IN Duncan's office, and after talking for ten minutes about the burning of Virgil's stable, and the cleanup over the weekend, Duncan said that the fire was a sensation on the true crime sites. "How'd that happen?"

"I mentioned it to a couple of people," Virgil said. "If somebody is deliberately fucking with me, I'm hoping they think I'm out of the case."

"All right." Duncan admitted he was unhappy that Henderson had called Lucas, without notifying anybody at the BCA about the DNA test. "But I'll tell you what—I'm not so sure about the whole DNA thing anyway. I think Amanda Fisk may have been pulling somebody's weenie. That would be Virgil's."

"What?"

Duncan held up a finger. "Let me get Linda, she's right upstairs."

He made a call and Linda Esselton, the DNA tech who'd done the scrubs of Timothy Carlson's jewelry, appeared two minutes later, carrying a file folder. She took a chair and Duncan said, "Tell them."

"The Chicago lab sent us the results and I printed them out." She took several pieces of printed paper out of the file, fanned them on her lap, and said, "If you look at the results from the seven separate scrubs . . ."

"Linda, just talk to us in English, we're not real big on the science stuff," Lucas said.

She hesitated, then nodded: "Okay. I scrubbed seven pieces of jewelry. I got nothing. Zip. That's not right. That jewelry had been sterilized. I didn't notice anything unusual when I was scrubbing it, except with the gold Rolex bands, you wouldn't be surprised to see an arm hair caught in the links. There wasn't any. Okay, sometimes there isn't—but there's always something, even if it's not visible. Skin cells. Tiny specks of blood. Something. But there wasn't."

"Are you sure your swabs were good?" Lucas asked.

"You mean my technique, or the instruments?" She was prepared to be offended.

"The instruments, we know your technique is good," Lucas said.

Mollified, she said, "I had swabs from two different batches. I believe all of them were good."

Virgil: "So what are you telling us?"

"Just what I said. The jewelry, all of it, was sterilized, and in a way that deliberately removed any traces of DNA. Why would anyone do that? I mean, innocently?"

They all shifted in their chairs, looking at each other and then back at Esselton. Virgil asked, "Are you telling us that somebody deliberately defeated the scrubs?"

"I'm not a detective. I'm telling you I've never seen anything like it. Before we sent the package off to Chicago, we split the hair sample that Carl recovered from Carlson's sink, and after we got the results,

Carl and I looked at our sample again this morning. The hair appeared to have been chopped. It's not hair that would have naturally fallen into the sink, you know, because somebody was going bald and they brushed their hair in the morning and it went down the drain . . . it was chopped. Like haircut hair. The other thing is, we also recovered hair from the shower, but it was all Fisk's hair. There was no other DNA in the shower drain."

"You know for sure it was Fisk's?" Duncan asked.

Esselton nodded: "We got the scrub from her, for comparison's sake."

"I saw that," Virgil said. "She did tell us that they'd been cleaning the house, scouring it, really, getting ready for a sale. You think that would have included cleaning out the drains?"

"Possibly, but . . . that thoroughly? I mean, I've sold a couple of houses and made sure the drains all drained, so we wouldn't get dinged by an inspector, but these were, I mean, there were only a few hairs in the shower, when there should have been quite a lot. And all the hair was from Fisk."

"Interesting. And odd," Lucas said. He smiled. "I like odd things. They're trying to tell you something."

Virgil turned to Lucas and said, "Fisk said she was clearing out the house for a sale, and because she couldn't stand to look at her husband's stuff. Other than the jewelry, there wasn't a single damn thing in the entire house that belonged to him. No clothes. No shirts, no jackets, no socks, no shoes, nothing. She said it all went to Goodwill. I'm somewhat familiar with Goodwill, and if this is high-end doctor clothing . . . it'll be gone by now. It would probably have been gone the day after she donated it."

"Trying not to sound like Captain Obvious, it kinda looks like she was trying to hide something," Duncan said. "We need to go back there."

"Don't do that yet," Lucas said. "Give me and Virgil some time to work it."

"I've got an idea about that," Virgil said. "When I was talking to Dr. Baer, he said they were both members of the Turtle Lake Golf Club. I wonder if she remembered to clean out his locker?"

"Be our first stop," Lucas said.

Duncan: "You guys need to talk with your true-crimers, too. I think a few of them gave up and went home while you were gone."

"We'll get with them after Turtle Lake," Virgil said. "They've been doing research, we need to know where they're at."

ON THE WAY north, Lucas said, "Fisk. You think she could have burned you out?"

"Would have taken brass balls. Guess what: she has them."

"She worked at Bee," Lucas said.

"Yes."

"She married Carlson not long after the murder," Lucas said.

"Yes."

"Interesting series of coincidences; in which I don't believe," Lucas concluded.

"If she killed Doris Grandfelt . . . wait. So she knows, somehow, something is up. She's been dating Timothy Carlson, a rich doctor, and all of a sudden this hot piece of blonde shows up on his doorstep. She somehow figures out that they've been meeting at Bee, and she hides in there after hours to see what's up. She sees them having sex, or hears them, is sideswiped by jealousy, and kills Doris."

"Was Carlson there for the murder?"

Virgil had to think for a minute: "Don't know," he said eventually. "Probably not, but the murder was pretty close to the sex."

"One problem with all of this," Lucas said. "Everything you can blame Fisk for, it's more logical to blame Carlson. He's screwing Doris, not long after an emotional trauma, his divorce, has a sudden spasm of regret followed by a psychotic break, and kills her. I'm not saying that's what happened, but a defense attorney would."

"He didn't kill Marcia Wise," Virgil said. "And we *know* that was connected."

"You're saying we're dealing with a serial killer? Women rarely are, not even one in ten, and not this way," Lucas said. "Maybe with poison, or drugs, but they don't stab people to death, or beat people to death, or throw them off balconies . . . I don't know how big Carlson was, but from what I've seen, I'm thinking a hundred seventy, a hundred and eighty pounds? Could she throw him off, even if she wanted to?"

"If he was stretched out, balanced on a railing, and she just had to tip him over, maybe," Virgil said.

"Maybe."

The Turtle Lake Golf Club was pleasant enough, low rolling terrain dressed in midsummer green, with what appeared to be well-tended greens. The clubhouse itself was of the hybrid Black Forest chalet/Southern plantation style.

Lucas had been at the club once before, not to play golf, but to chat with a member. This time, they located the general manager, Dale Young, who took them to the men's locker room. Two obese, white, naked men were walking out of the shower rooms, talking, both jiggling and shaking like bowls of Jell-O.

When they were out of earshot, Virgil muttered to Lucas, "I didn't need to see that."

"Guys haven't seen their dicks in years," Lucas muttered back.

Young said, "I didn't hear any of that."

Gerry Wint, the locker room attendant, showed them Carlson's locker, which was empty.

"Wife came in and cleaned it out," Wint said. "I had to check and make sure no naked gentlemen were wandering around."

"Well, poop," Virgil said. To Lucas: "Think we should bring in the DNA guys and scrub the locker?"

"Man, I don't know. Maybe," Lucas said.

"Did she get his clubs?" Virgil asked Young.

"Same day she cleaned out the locker," the manager said. "I was there for that because that's when she notified us that she was out. She was a club member by being married to Tim, and she let us know that she didn't want to be a member. Tim, of course, was gone. So . . ."

Wint spoke up. "You know . . . I wasn't here when she came in, Marv was filling in. I wonder if he gave her all his other shoes?"

Lucas: "Other shoes?"

"He had three pairs of shoes in his rotation," Wint said. "I wonder if he left some shoes with Marv? Let me go look . . ."

He walked around a counter and into a back room, reappeared a minute later with some brown and white golf saddle shoes. "These are his . . . We put ID tags in them so we don't mix them up. I guess Marv didn't polish them because, you know . . . Dr. Carlson was dead."

"Gone," said Young.

"Yup, dead and gone," Wint said.

Virgil took the shoes, carefully lifted the tongue, and looked inside. To Lucas, he said, "Ten and a half."

Lucas, worried about the current ownership of the shoes, and what Young might think of that, said to Wint, "Could you put those in a bag? We'll take them with us."

Young said, "I'm not sure . . ."

"It's perfectly okay, really," Virgil said, stepping between Young and the shoes, which he handed to Wint. "We've done this for a long time."

Five minutes later, in Virgil's truck, speeding down the tree-lined driveway, Lucas laughed and mimicked him: "*It's perfectly okay, really, we've done this for a long time.*"

"What I think is, we gotta get back to the office right now, and get these things scrubbed, in case Young calls Fisk and she gets all legal on us," Virgil said.

"Get them scrubbed and get a subpoena sent up to Young," Lucas said. "Not exactly the right order, but it'd confuse things."

AT THE BCA, Duncan wanted to know the odds that Carlson's DNA would match the DNA from the Grandfelt murder.

"I would bet lots of money on it," Virgil said. "Amanda Fisk has scrubbed that house clean. Our own people have never seen anything like it."

"We got the hair from the sink . . ."

"Hundred dollars says the hair from the sink doesn't match the DNA from Carlson's shoes," Virgil said.

"Then let's get it done," Duncan said. "Right now."

27

Duncan took charge of the shoes, and when he asked what Virgil and Lucas were planning to do next, Virgil said, "Okay, we're going to sic a couple of our true crime people on Amanda Fisk. We need to background her. We know she was dating Carlson around the time Grandfelt was killed, and maybe . . . maybe . . . well before she was killed. She could have had access, one way or another, to a key that would get her into Bee after hours. Her husband died a really curious death after Lara Grandfelt offered the five million reward and a bunch of true-crimers showed up. We need to get serious about looking at her."

"Man, she's a county prosecutor. She's sorta like one of us."

"She might be a serial killer, unlike us," Lucas said, rubbing his hands together. "I'm starting to get a tingle here."

"Don't tell me what's tingling, I don't want to hear about it,"

Duncan said. "So: quietly, boys. Carefully. We don't want any of this bleeding out on the true crime sites prematurely."

"Why not?" Lucas asked. "A good way to jack up the pressure."

Virgil: "Yeah, but, Jon's right. She knows everything there is to know about evidence. I'd like to put something together before she has a chance to screw with it. Or to start some kind of PR campaign against us."

BACK IN THE borrowed office, Lucas asked, "With the fire and all, did you ever get back to Dahlia Blair about when Fisk and Carlson got married?"

"No. She called me Friday, there was some kind of computer complication that she was trying to work around. I told her I was out of it because of the fire. The next thing I knew, there were six true-crimers taking videos of the ashes. Haven't talked since."

"I saw the videos," Lucas said. "Who was the hulk in the black tee-shirt?"

"Moses, one of Frankie's kids. By the way, Frankie and I are gonna get married, maybe next week. Or next month. Or whenever Frankie can set it up."

"About time," Lucas said. "We're coming, of course."

"Yeah, you're gonna be best man," Virgil said. "Anyway, we need to call Dahlia."

THEY DID THAT. "We didn't know if you still wanted us around after all the fire videos we did," Blair said.

"Yeah, okay, but when . . ."

"Amanda Fisk and Timothy Carlson got married in September, four months after Doris was murdered."

"Hot damn," Virgil said.

"This is something, isn't it?" Blair asked.

"It might be," Virgil said. "But please, please don't do anything with it. Not yet. We will feed you some really good stuff when we get it, and it should be coming soon. Maybe early next week."

Off the phone, Lucas said, "Let's think about this. Let's suppose that Fisk killed Doris, Carlson, and Wise. She didn't leave any hard evidence behind. Minneapolis got no foreign DNA from Wise's body and there's nothing from her on Doris. Carlson she had cremated and nobody looked."

"If there was anything in my stable, it went up in smoke," Virgil said.

"We're building a case on nothing but circumstantial evidence. Other than that, we got nothing."

"So we've got to pile it up, the circumstantial stuff," Virgil said. "The trouble being, we could be wrong."

"We need to get the best true-crimers off all the other shit they're looking at and have them research Amanda Fisk from the time she was born until a half hour ago."

"I'll call them," Virgil said.

THEY SPENT THE rest of the afternoon and most of Friday talking to true-crimers, but nothing of interest turned up. Some of the true-crimers were anxious to be first with Amanda Fisk's name as a person of interest, and Virgil was reduced to pleading with them to keep it quiet. That wouldn't last long.

Government offices were closed on the weekend, though online sources were still up. With the problems at the farm, Virgil went home Friday night.

Karen Moss called Virgil on Saturday while he was eating lunch and said, "I want a piece of the five million when we hang Fisk."

"We've got nothing to hang her with," Virgil said.

"I got something," she said. "It's good."

"What?"

"Guess where Amanda Fisk grew up . . ."

"C'mon," Virgil said.

"She graduated from Woodbury High School."

"Interesting, but a lot of people went to Woodbury. It's a big school."

"So I looked at the property tax records, for a Fisk," Moss said. "I found one. There was a Fisk family that lived on Hattie Lane in Woodbury back in the nineties. Not recently, as far as I can tell. That was a block from Shawnee Park."

"Holy cats."

"Am I good, or what?"

Lucas, laughing when he was told, said, "Another straw on the camel's back."

VIRGIL CALLED DUNCAN, who said, "Keep pushing. We should have the DNA stuff back from Chicago on Tuesday or Wednesday. If we get Carlson's DNA and it matches what we got outa Grandfelt, we'll need to talk to the Ramsey County Attorney about Fisk—that we're looking at her."

"I don't think we're just looking at her, Jon," Virgil said. "I think she killed all of them—Grandfelt, Carlson, and Wise, and I think she burned down my stable to get me off the case."

"None of what you have is definitive. Keep piling it up. We need to catch her in a misstep."

"She's smart."

"Not that smart. Instead of scrubbing everything clean in her house, she should have let us ID Carlson as the person who had sex with Grandfelt. Nothing illegal about that, they were both single adults. Scrubbing his DNA is what a guilty person would do. At least, somebody with guilty knowledge."

"We'll push."

"One more thing," Duncan said. "How old is she?"

"I don't know."

"Hang on . . . I'm going out to the DVS." Duncan put his phone down and Virgil could hear him rattling keys on his home computer. "Okay. She's forty-eight. What I'm wondering is, are her parents still around? If they are, we should interview them."

"Huh. You're right."

"As always."

LUCAS AGREED THAT they should interview Fisk's parents, assuming they could find them. "We need their names. They should be on those old tax records, if that actually turns out to be Fisk's family. Then we can check driver's licenses . . ."

Virgil called Karen Moss back, got Harlan and Alma Fisk as the owners of the Hattie Lane house, but Moss said that the house had now been sold at least twice since the Fisks lived there. Driver's licenses showed Harlan renewing until 1994, and not after that. Alma Fisk renewed until 2018, and then no more.

Virgil: "Are they dead?"

"One way to find out . . ."

An online search of death records turned up a death certificate for Alma Fisk issued in March of 2017; a check with the *Star-Tribune* obituaries found a brief paid obit that listed survivors as a daughter, Amanda Fisk. There was no mention of Harlan Fisk, or death certificate or obit for Harlan.

"We got the right family—and Fisk lived a block from Shawnee Park. She'd know how to deliver Doris's body there. We're beyond coincidence now," Lucas said.

"Wonder where Harlan Fisk went? Divorce?"

"That seems likely," Lucas said.

"If Harlan Fisk is alive, then he's gotta be in his seventies, at least. So—Medicare, Social Security," Virgil said.

"I don't know how you get the records, but I know somebody who can. Let me make a phone call."

The call went to Elmer Henderson, and that was the only call Lucas needed: Henderson got back in an hour and said, "There's a Harlan Fisk in Eau Claire getting Medicare. He's seventy-seven. I've got an address, but no phone number."

"Thank you."

To Virgil: "I think we interview him in person. First thing Monday. You want to come along?"

Virgil shrugged: "Why not? It's an hour and a half from your house. I'll be up there at nine."

———

MONDAY CAME UP rainy, and Virgil didn't make it to St. Paul until nine-thirty. Lucas wanted to drive, which was fine with Virgil, who'd been up since five o'clock, and he dozed on the way over. At eleven o'clock, they were on Badger Avenue in Eau Claire, a neatly kept street of green trees and postwar houses, some with detached hutch-like garages in the back.

They spotted Harlan Fisk's house, which had a rain-soaked American flag hanging from a short flagpole set next to the front door. They parked, pulled on rain jackets, and walked up the front walk, through the smell of sidewalk night crawlers, and pushed a doorbell.

Harlan Fisk pried the door open a couple of minutes later, as a woman called from the back, "Who is it, Harlan?"

"Don't know." He peered with pale-blue fighter-pilot eyes at the two men on the porch. "Who are you?"

Lucas had his ID out: "U.S. Marshal. We'd like to speak with you for a few minutes."

"About what?"

"Well, about your daughter."

"Amanda? I haven't seen Amanda in years. What did she do?"

Virgil edged Lucas out of the way and asked, "You mind if we come in? It's a little damp out here."

Fisk backed away from the door and the woman, who'd come in closer, said, "We don't speak to Amanda."

Virgil glanced back at Lucas, who nodded: this was a good thing. They didn't like her. They followed Fisk and the woman into a small living room, and Fisk went to the eat-in kitchen and brought back two kitchen chairs to supplement the two easy chairs that looked at the television. When they were all sitting, Virgil said to the woman, "We didn't get your name?"

"Ruth Fisk," she said. "Harlan's wife. What about Amanda?"

"We're trying to put together a history on Amanda. There were some . . . irregularities about her husband's death."

Harlan sat back: "Timothy is dead? She push him out a window or something?"

"Good guess. He fell off a balcony of their house," Lucas said. "He died instantly."

"He fell? That doesn't sound like Timothy. He was a cautious guy, far as I could tell," Harlan said. "Didn't know him all that well. And I wasn't really guessing. I was thinking of all those guys dying around Putin. On the news, they're always falling out of windows."

"Well, his death was investigated by the county medical examiner, we're just doing some checks," Virgil said.

"On what?" Harlan asked. "Like I said, I haven't seen her in years. We had problems after the divorce—I did see her a few times when she was in college."

Virgil: "What kind of a person is she? Outgoing, friendly, tough, what?"

Ruth: "Mean. She's mean. She never really gave Harlan and me a chance."

"Well, you can kinda understand that," Harlan said to his wife. To Virgil and Lucas: "Anyway, I don't think she really was against us. She just didn't care. Didn't care one way or the other. We were not important to her."

"She looked at me like I was a bug," Ruth said. "Really, she looked at everybody like they were bugs."

"She had a tough run in life, that's gotta affect people," Harlan said. "After that thing with Becky Watson . . . You marshals know about that?"

"No . . ."

Harlan crossed his hands across his ample stomach. "Well, let me see if I can remember it all. There used to be a big movie theater in a shopping center in downtown St. Paul. Mandy and Becky went to a movie after school, they were in . . . let's see . . . ninth grade? Anyway, I was supposed to pick them up after work, and they were standing on the curb downtown, waiting, and Becky stumbled on the curb and she fell in front of a delivery van and was killed. Mandy was right there with her, saw the whole damn thing. I guess Becky's head was squashed . . ."

Lucas said, "Oh, boy."

Harlan frowned: "What? It was an accident."

Virgil said, "Okay. What we're trying to do here is build a little history. Tell us about her."

Harlan pushed out a lip, then, "Like I said, she had a tough row to hoe. Alma had a bad time in her pregnancy, and right after Mandy was born, she took off. Went back to her family and wouldn't take Mandy with her, so I had to put her with a neighbor lady to take care of her, because I had to work. That went on for almost two years and then Alma came back but she and Mandy were never right. And then, oh, must have been seven or eight years later, Alma's brother Don moved into what had been Mandy's room, and Mandy moved down the basement. It was finished, and everything, with her own little bathroom, so we thought it was pretty good. Mandy called it 'the dungeon.' I don't know for sure, but I think Don might have messed with Mandy."

"Messed with . . . what does that mean?" Lucas asked.

"Messed with her. You know, while I was working. I don't know what he did, and Alma said he didn't do anything, and Mandy said he didn't do anything, but I didn't believe them. Still don't. He did *something*."

Virgil: "And you knew that . . . how?"

"Just the way she acted around him. Like, sometimes, she acted scared, and sometimes, she was a little too friendly. I finally told the sonofabitch that he had to get out of the house. That was the beginning of the end for me and Alma, when I threw her brother out. We started fighting . . . Then, in there, I met Ruth, and we got it together, and Alma and I got divorced. Alma got everything I had. I had to start over, but 3M gave me and Ruth—we met at work—a transfer to the plant in Menomonie so I got to keep my pension. Ruth's folks come from here in Eau Claire, so that's where we settled. We commuted to work until we retired."

"Did Amanda live with Alma until her mother died?"

"Oh, no, she was long gone before that happened. She moved out when she went to college, never looked back. That must have been in the mid-90s. She was born in '76, so she would have graduated from high school, I guess, in '94."

Ruth: "We paid for her college."

Harlan: "Part, anyway. She got good grades in high school, she's a smart one. She got scholarships to cover her college tuition, but her mother wouldn't help, so we chipped in—mostly for a room in St. Paul, you know, and some extra bucks along the way."

Ruth snorted: "Extra bucks? Like a hundred dollars a month besides the room, and that was real money back then."

"Yeah, and she had part-time jobs, too," Harlan said. "Then she wanted to go to law school, and I told her we couldn't help much with that, so she got a full-time job working in a supermarket and went to law school . . . it took her like an extra year, but she went to one of those schools that were flexible about it, so she graduated and got a good job. Then, she went to work for the county. That's the last I heard."

"What happened to Alma?" Virgil asked.

"Well, she got all our savings and the house, and the savings was considerable. I had to give her all that to save my pension, but she had rights to part of my Social Security if she'd lived. But, she didn't. She had diabetes. She died real sudden. I got involved because there was a termination of her share of the Social Security benefits."

"Was there an autopsy? Do you know?" Virgil asked.

"I guess, because we were told that she might have gave herself too much insulin. That's all I know about that."

THEY TALKED FOR a while longer but got nothing more that was substantive. They said goodbye, and as they pulled on the rain jackets and stepped out on the porch, Harlan said, "Whatever you're doing, remember that the kid had a hard time growing up, a hard time, especially with that sonofabitch Don."

In the car, Lucas said, "She had a hard time growing up. She also had a classic serial killer childhood. The Don guy. Messing with her? He was probably fucking her. She was around a lot of early death: the girl hit by the truck, her mother, her husband, Doris . . ."

"And still: not a single piece of hard evidence that implicates her."

They drove in silence for a while, then Virgil asked, "Who do we know who could get a look at her credit cards? Without a warrant, without tipping her off?"

Lucas said, "Letty knows a woman at the National Security Agency who can look at them in real time. It would probably be illegal. If anybody ever found out. Why do you want to look?"

"I want to see when she last bought gas before my stable burned."

"I could ask Letty to check with her source. Then we'd know if we should go after her with a subpoena, all legal-like."

"It would be worth knowing," Virgil said.

"I'll make the call, tonight, when she's not at work," Lucas said.

THEY STOPPED AT a McDonald's in Hudson, Wisconsin, for lunch, then drove the rest of the way into the Cities. On the way, Virgil called Duncan to ask about the DNA samples, and Duncan said that he'd checked, and the Chicago testing firm was still saying it'd be the next day.

"Grandfelt has been calling, she wants to talk to you guys. Where are you?"

"I-94 coming into St. Paul. Did she say if she was at home?"

"Yeah, she is. You gonna stop over?"

"That would be best," Virgil said. He added, "Hey. We talked to Fisk's father. Thank you. Good stuff. She's a serial killer, and more than we even know yet."

"Great balls of fire. You're sure?"

"Yeah, we are," Lucas said. "Get the suits together, maybe tomorrow, we'll lay it out for everybody."

"You want Russ Belen?" Belen was the Ramsey County Attorney, and Fisk's boss.

"I don't know. Ask Rose Marie or Ralphy." Rose Marie Roux was the Minnesota commissioner of public safety; Ralph Moore was the BCA director.

"I will do that. You go talk to Grandfelt."

A TALL BLACK man wearing an earbud met them at Grandfelt's front door. He was wearing a blue suit, the jacket open so he could get at the cross-draw pistol on his left hip. Lucas held up his ID and the man said, "I'm Jim Nelson, with Wright Security. Let me call Miz Grandfelt."

He stepped back from the door and a bit to one side, where he could call to Grandfelt while he could still keep an eye on Lucas and Virgil. They heard Grandfelt call back, "Let them in," and he waved them in.

Grandfelt, Lucas thought, did not look good. She'd lost weight since the murder of her companion, skin sagging around her eyes and jowls. "Any news at all?"

"We need to sit and talk . . ." Lucas said, glancing at Nelson, ". . . privately."

Nelson smiled and said, "Well, that was impolite."

"No offense."

"None taken. I'll go out on the porch." To Grandfelt: "Stewart's outside, in back."

She nodded, "Okay. Thank you." She even sounded older. To Virgil, she said, "I was shocked to hear about the fire at your farm. Is everybody okay?"

"Everybody is now . . . my fiancée and her son got second-degree burns, but . . . they'll be fine."

"Wonderful," Grandfelt said.

Nelson was outside, pulling the door closed behind himself. The three of them sat in the overstuffed living room and Lucas said, "Lara, we have some things to tell you, but you can't pass them on. You know . . . you have to keep your mouth shut."

"I can do that," Grandfelt said. "Do you know who killed Doris?"

"We think we do," Lucas said. "Unfortunately, we don't have any single piece of hard evidence. Everything we have is circumstantial, but it's strong. The person we're looking at, a woman, is a lawyer and a county prosecutor who we think didn't only kill Doris, but is a serial killer. We think she killed Marcia as well, and her husband, and probably set Virgil's stable on fire. It's possible she killed her own mother, and there was another curious death involving a young girl . . . when they both were young. If she killed that girl, she's been murdering people since she was in high school."

"My God. Who is it?"

"Her name is Amanda Fisk. She was an employee at Bee when Doris was killed. We believe the man who had sex with Doris is the man that Fisk married a few months later, and probably murdered a couple of weeks ago."

They outlined the case against Fisk, and the problems with a possible indictment and prosecution. At the end, Grandfelt shook her head and asked, "I believe you . . . I think. But I'm not sure I believe you beyond a reasonable doubt. What do you think the chances of a conviction might be?"

Lucas tipped a finger at her. "Hard to tell. Maybe we'll find some more evidence: this has all come together in the last couple of days," he said. "Tomorrow, we should know if her husband was the one who had sex with Doris. That would be significant because it would provide us with a serious motive—jealousy. Not only that, she lied to Virgil about her relationship with Carlson. She said she only began dating him after Doris's murder, and we have reason to believe that he actually began dating her much earlier than that."

"Does she have any money?" Grandfelt asked.

Virgil: "She does. She lives in a mansion—I think you'd call it a mansion—on Summit Avenue in St. Paul. Carlson was a successful surgeon for at least thirty years, so there is money around."

"Then if she's taken to trial, and I'm convinced beyond a reasonable doubt, even if she's found not guilty, I'll sue her for wrongful death," Grandfelt said. "Then all we need is a preponderance of evidence, and I think we'd get that, from what you've told me."

"And that would satisfy you?" Lucas asked.

She had to think, then said, "Yes. I wanted to know who killed Doris and why, and I want to know who killed my Marcia and why, and I want that person punished. You are almost there. If you get all the way there, if you indict her, even if you don't get a conviction, I'll be satisfied, and I will go after her myself with a civil suit. I'll take her job, her savings, her houses, and her cars. She'll be living in a basement and riding in buses."

Virgil told her about the help they'd gotten from the true-crimers, and Grandfelt said she understood, and that she was prepared to split the five-million-dollar reward, and the one-million-dollar add-on, between all the people who had helped.

28

Tuesday, the day everything turned.

The day began for Lucas when he got a call from Senator Henderson, who spoke in hushed tones. "Jesus, Lucas: I jacked up the DNA guy in Chicago. He took a look and said we got a match. The DNA in the shoes is a match for the DNA taken from Doris Grandfelt. We got him. Or her."

"All right. This is good. We've got to keep it to ourselves for the time being. I'll talk to Jon Duncan at the BCA and tell him to keep it to himself until we can meet with . . . the big dogs at the BCA and the Ramsey County Attorney. You might want to be there."

"I do. What about Lara?"

"Are you in St. Paul?"

"Yes."

"Why don't you pick me up and we'll both go talk to her. She knows we have a suspect. I'll fill you in on the ride over."

"I'll see you in twenty minutes. I'll have Neil drive us over."

Lucas called Virgil, told him about the match.

"We've got to have the big meet," Virgil said.

"Yeah. I'll call Jon. I'll tell him to go ahead and set up the meeting for late today. Henderson and I are going over to Grandfelt's to talk to her."

"Okay. I'm talking to all the true-crimers this morning to see if they got anything else . . ."

Lucas called Duncan and told him about the match. "That goddamned Henderson . . . it's about time he got his nose out of this."

"He won't do that," Lucas said. "Grandfelt is one of his big donors, and besides, this kind of thing gets him excited. Makes him feel like he might be a cop."

"Right. Well, fuck it, water under the bridge. I'll call Chicago and confirm it, the DNA, and I'll set something up for late afternoon. You and Virgil better be on good behavior."

A HALF HOUR after Henderson called, a black Cadillac SUV pulled into the driveway; the sky was overcast, and the weather had turned cool, a hint of the oncoming autumn. Lucas got a rain jacket and carried it out to the car, got in the back.

Henderson was in the front passenger seat, his aide, Neil Mitford, behind the wheel. Mitford said, "Tell us everything."

Lucas told them everything. They both had law degrees and took it in, until Henderson said, "I'm convinced. I'm not sure a jury would be."

"I'm not, either," Mitford said. "It'd be nice if we had a couple more sticks to throw in the fire."

"Virgil's out looking for sticks right now," Lucas said.

———

ANNE CASH HAD been looking for records of a probate proceeding on Amanda Fisk's mother, Alma. She found them in an hour, printed them, and called Virgil, who was in his hotel room, pacing, reading snatches of his new manuscript, watching a rainstorm coming in from the west.

"Yeah, Anne."

"There was an informal probate, but we have a record. Alma had a much bigger estate than you'd think. We couldn't figure that out so we went back and found another probate under the name Schmidt, which was Alma's maiden name. Rhonda Schmidt, Alma's mother, died seven months before Alma and left Alma a house in Stillwater, plus sixty-seven thousand dollars from investments with Vanguard and twenty-five thousand dollars from a life insurance policy. We looked on a real estate site and saw that the house was sold by Alma for three hundred and seventy thousand dollars two months after Rhonda died."

"And that wouldn't include any money Alma had on her own?" Virgil asked.

"No. It doesn't look like she originally had much of her own, before her mom died. We can't figure it directly, because by that time it had been absorbed by the money she got from her mother, but it looks like it was less than forty thousand dollars, total. But she owned her house outright, and Amanda Fisk, her only heir, sold it a month after Alma died for three hundred and nineteen thousand dollars. And Alma apparently bought a new car with the money from her mom, and we don't know what happened with that, but it was valued at forty-six thousand when she bought it."

Virgil was doing the numbers in his head, and he said, finally, "Jeez, Anne, you're telling me that Fisk got eight hundred thousand dollars when her mother died?"

"Something like that."

"We need to look at an autopsy. Get everything you're looking at in print. Everything, and your source for it. I'll be in my car heading over to the Ramsey County Medical Examiner's Office."

"We got her? Fisk?"

"Not yet, but . . . keep quiet for another day. Please."

"Pressure's building up. Something's gonna blow."

"Hang on for twenty-four hours."

VIRGIL CALLED LUCAS, who was still in Henderson's Cadillac, and told him what he'd gotten from Cash.

"That's another stick," Lucas said.

"What?"

"Mitford's with us, said we needed another stick to throw on the fire."

"I'm on my way over to the ME's office, see if they did an autopsy and if they did, what they found."

"Must have been one, sudden unexpected death with no witnesses," Lucas said.

When Virgil rang off, Lucas told Henderson and Mitford about Fisk's double inheritance.

"She's starting to sound like a bad, bad person," Henderson said. He had been looking at himself in a visor mirror and smiled in the mirror at Lucas.

———

DARRELL RICHARDSON, THE medical examiner, met Virgil in his office and a clerk brought in the autopsy report. Richardson looked at it, frowned, and said, "Before my time . . . There's not much to it. It looks like an accidental overdose. She was insulin-dependent, and the chemistry says she overdosed herself on insulin and also had a pretty heavy dose of zolpidem in her bloodstream. Zolpidem's a sleep aid . . ."

"I know, it's Ambien," Virgil said. "How big a dose?"

"She apparently took two ten-milligram tabs. The usual dose for a woman is seven and a half milligrams, but she had a prescription for ten-milligram tabs. We did recover the pill bottle, there were still seven tabs left. So, she'd been using them right along, apparently. From what we could tell, it seemed likely that she'd done her insulin, then a tab of Ambien, or two tabs, and that may have left her confused about whether she'd taken her insulin, and she took another shot. It happens . . ."

The two of them went over the investigator's report, and there was no indication that she'd had visitors the night of the overdose, but to Virgil's eye, it didn't appear that anyone had looked very hard.

VIRGIL CALLED LUCAS with information about the autopsy. Lucas, Henderson, and Mitford were in Grandfelt's living room, and Lucas passed the information on to the others.

"This is now a case," Mitford said.

"I think so, too," Henderson said.

Grandfelt, who had been wandering around the room with brief perches on one of her high-fashion chairs, asked, "Can we tell the true crime people to go ahead and use her name? That would put pressure on her. We might see if she's inclined to do something precipitous."

"Well, I can tell you, from what Virgil said, his impression of Fisk and from Dr. Baer, she's not going to kill herself," Lucas said. "If we manage to indict her, she'll fight it. She's got the money."

They all thought about that, then Grandfelt asked, "Do you really think she burned down Virgil's stable?"

Lucas nodded. "We do."

Henderson said, "If she drove all the way to Mankato and back, she probably bought gas."

"We're trying to get a person to look at her credit cards," Lucas said.

"If I were going to burn down Virgil's stable, and needed gas, I wouldn't put it on a credit card. Maybe you should check some gas station security videos," Mitford said.

"Lot of gas stations," Lucas said. "And everybody buys gas."

"Not many gas stations near her place," Henderson said. "My house is a mile down the street from hers. There are two Speedways and a SuperAmerica that are handy. It would be interesting to see when she last tanked up."

"We'll look," Lucas said. "I'll call Virgil and get him started."

He did that.

THERE WERE THREE gas stations that were more or less handy to Fisk's home. Virgil reasoned that if she were to tank up the car, she wouldn't have gone to the closest one. Of the other two, one would require a turn away from a main route to Mankato and the farm; the other would put her on the main route.

He'd gone to that one.

The assistant manager at SuperAmerica said they did, in fact, have video of the pump area, but he didn't know exactly how to rewind the video and display it, but he knew it went back thirty days. He also knew a woman who worked for TC Surveillance who could do all that, but would charge for it.

"She's not cheap, she'd probably want two hundred bucks to come over right away."

"The state of Minnesota has two hundred bucks," Virgil said.

"They should, what with the taxes here," the manager said. Virgil didn't answer, but stared at him, and when it was about to become awkward, the manager said, "I'll call her."

Virgil was waiting for the woman to show up, and eating a bag of peanuts, when Lucas came through the door: "Got anything?"

"Not yet."

"Big meeting at four o'clock. We could use another thing. As many things as we can get."

Virgil was telling him about waiting for the woman from TC Surveillance when a call came in on Virgil's burner. Mary Albanese, another of the true-crimer researchers. Lucas listened in.

"We've got something weird, could be nothing," Albanese said. "But it's curious. We found a cold case in St. Paul, a woman named Carly Gibson, who was beaten to death in 1998. With a lead pipe, if you can believe that. I mean it's such a cliché. Anyway, it was never solved. The murder wasn't."

"And . . ."

"She was going to law school at William Mitchell. She was in the same class as Amanda Fisk."

Lucas peered at the phone, then at Virgil, then asked, "What's the woman's name again?"

He got it, and asked, "How'd you find this?"

"We were reviewing murder reports in the *Star-Tribune*. When we saw the date and the law school thing, it rang a bell."

Lucas: "You're a genius."

"I certainly think so."

Off the phone, he said to Virgil, "I'm going downtown. I'll get with the chief and pull the case file. Then I'll be over at William Mitchell."

"While I wait here for the Surveillance chick."

THE WOMAN FROM TC Surveillance, Jane Gou, was short, heavy, harassed, late. Before she'd done anything, she wanted to know who to bill. Virgil gave her Jon Duncan's name and phone number at the BCA, and she took Virgil into the station's tight back room and a small video screen.

She rolled the memory back to the night before the fire, then ran it forward at double speed. At one o'clock on the morning of the fire, Amanda Fisk drove into the station in her Mercedes SUV and gassed up the car. The car was parked sideways to the camera, so he couldn't see the license plates. Fisk was dressed for the country in jeans, a jean jacket, and a Twins baseball cap. She kept her head tilted down, under the ballcap bill, so the camera couldn't see her face, but Virgil was certain that it was her. The surveillance tape showed a running total of gallons dispensed. Toward the end, the total stopped for thirty seconds, and then started again, dispensing exactly one gallon.

Virgil said, as calmly as he could manage, which wasn't entirely calm, "I'm going to need a copy of this."

"You'll need an AVI app to see it," Gou said.

"I got one of those," Virgil snapped. "Give it to me. On a thumb drive. If you don't have one, I've got one in my car."

He took a fast circuit around a junk food rack and came back to Gou, who said, "You're scaring me a little. I'll get the video for you."

"Now," Virgil barked. "Get it."

He did another trip around the junk food rack, and Gou was downloading the video. Two more trips and she handed him the thumb drive, and she said, "You gotta chill."

"I'll chill when I'm dead," Virgil said, and he went out the door.

LUCAS GOT THE cold case file on Carly Gibson and skipped through it. Gibson apparently had been walking to her car, a block and a half from the law school, when she'd been attacked and killed. Traces in her hair indicated that she'd been beaten with a lead pipe—old-school, but effective, her skull crushed. Her purse was missing, but a gold necklace was still in place around her throat, and a gold-look bracelet around one exposed wrist.

Robbery was mooted as a motive, but if so, the killer was in a hurry, having missed both gold items. On the other hand, it was dark. He, or she, may never have seen the gold.

The killer left behind exactly no spoor.

Lucas read through it again and was struck by the similarity to the murder of Marcia Wise. Again, no spoor: not a single trace.

WHILE HE WAS there, he pulled the report on the death of Becky Watson. According to the reporting officers, a witness—Amanda Fisk, a ninth-grade student at Woodbury High School—said that she and Watson had been at a movie in Galtier Plaza. They were waiting to be picked up by Fisk's father. Watson was standing behind a street-light pillar when she apparently stumbled over the edge of a curb and fell into the path of a UPS truck.

The truck driver had not been drinking and had a good safety record. He said he only saw Watson a split second before the impact and she "looked like she was doing a racing dive into the street."

Watson was a good student and had no reason to commit suicide. The witness, Fisk, said she didn't know exactly what happened, but agreed with the driver that Watson had lurched into the street, possibly stumbling over a raised curb.

The case was closed as an accident.

Lucas made notes and headed for the law school.

VIRGIL CALLED AND before he could say anything, Lucas blurted, "Fisk killed her law school classmate. Killed her exactly the same way as she did Wise. I talked to the dean, and we went back through the records. Fisk finished fourth in her class and was the top woman student. She would have been number two among women, if the woman who was leading her hadn't been beaten to death. And man, I've been reading the Becky Watson file. If she didn't push Watson in front of that truck, I'd be astonished. And you—did you find anything?"

Virgil's voice grated like a trashed transmission: "That bitch burned down my stable."

29

Russ Belen was a handsome man, a trifle short, with wide shoulders, curly russet hair, a generally cheerful attitude, and smiles for everyone. A firm look-you-in-the-eye handshake. Whether it was all real, nobody but Belen knew. What *was* known was that he didn't consider a county attorney's job as the high point in his political career.

Which was probably the reason he went on alert as soon as he spotted Henderson and his aide, Mitford, in the back of the room. The party included Rose Marie Roux, the state commissioner of public safety; Ralph Moore, BCA director; as well as Duncan, Lucas, and Virgil.

A step inside the door, Belen stopped, looked around, and asked the room in general, "Am I the last one to arrive?"

Roux said, "The rest of us have been meeting for an hour, Russell. Do you know Lucas Davenport and Virgil Flowers?"

"Sure, Lucas and I go back a way . . . Virgil I only know by reputation. You're starting to scare me. What's going on?"

They were meeting in a BCA conference room around a long faux-walnut table. Roux said, "Sit down, Russ. Over there, where you can see Lucas and Virgil."

He took a chair, continuing to look quizzically at the participants. To Henderson, he said, "You're unexpected in whatever this is, Senator. Am I happy to see you again?"

"You may not be shortly," Henderson said.

Belen: "What's the problem?"

Roux said, "Lucas? Virgil?"

Virgil said to Lucas: "Go."

Lucas looked at Belen and said, "We've been investigating a member of your staff. Amanda Fisk. We have serious reason to believe that she may be a serial killer."

"What!" Belen was wearing dark-brown horn-rimmed glasses, and he fumbled at them, knocking them skittering onto the tabletop, where he left them. "What!"

He was shocked, his mouth open, turning to each of the people in turn around the table. "What in the hell are you talking about?"

Lucas laid it out:

"Amanda Fisk has been associated with a number of violent and tragic deaths, and has directly benefited from some of them, although benefits in others are not so clear."

Reading from a legal pad, he listed them: the death of Becky Watson, a young schoolmate when she was in ninth grade. The murder of Carly Gibson, a law school competitor. The murder of Doris Grandfelt, a marriage competitor. The unusual death of her mother, which resulted in a near million-dollar payoff. The death of her husband, which she actually witnessed, and which also provided her with an extraordinary inheritance benefit. The murder of Marcia Wise, probably mistaken for Lara Grandfelt, which was apparently an effort to eliminate the reward package. The burning of Virgil Flowers's stable was an attempt to move him off the case, and resulted in injuries to Florence Nobles and her son Sam.

Lucas provided some details for each of the deaths and gave Belen a printout of additional details, including the fact that Fisk had grown up a block from the obscure site where Doris Grandfelt's body had been left, her employment at Bee, her lie about the timing of her courtship with Timothy Carlson. Virgil had brought his laptop to the meeting and played the video of Fisk buying gasoline in the early morning hours before the stable fire.

In the end, Belen rocked back in his chair and said, "I believe you. I think she's guilty as sin. I hope you all see the problem with a prosecution."

Roux nodded and said, "Unfortunately, we all do. The lack of specific evidence. Though in the case of the nonexistent DNA from her husband, that would suggest a guilty knowledge that she was trying to erase."

"But it's an effort to erase information that could have led to a prosecution of her husband, not of Amanda," Belen said.

"WE STILL HAVE some ground to cover," Lucas said. "In the case of her mother, we need to speak to her doctor to find out whether there had been any other overdose issues. We need to go back to Fisk's house to nail down the DNA evidence. She might very well have gotten almost all of it, but we'll find some."

Belen said, "She's currently on compassionate leave. I suggest we don't change that, for the time being. When we've compiled everything in an . . . executable form, I'll formally suspend her from her job and ask for a search warrant to go back in her house for DNA. Then the cat will be out of the bag."

Henderson: "Russ, I've never been a prosecutor, but I can't see any possible way that your office could handle this, if it's prosecutable at all."

Belen nodded. "There's *no way* we could handle it. I know the guy down in Dakota County, he's good. I'll talk to a judge and request that the case be sent to Dakota for a grand jury investigation."

Moore, the BCA director, said, "I think we should pull Virgil off the case. I don't want to, but since he believes he's been directly attacked, by Fisk, I think it would be best."

"I think it would be mandatory," Belen said.

Virgil: "I agree."

Belen turned to Lucas: "How soon could we get all the material compiled as a complete investigative report that we could act on?"

Lucas said, "We've got a bunch of clerical work to do. You know, names, dates and places, motive and opportunity, medical examiner's reports, all that. It'll probably take a month to get all that done. I would like to keep that process as secret as possible, although a number of true crime bloggers have Fisk's name. It will leak. And soon."

He explained how that had happened, and Belen slapped his forehead and said, "You used the true crime people to do investigative work? You leaked some of the progress of the investigation? That's . . . that's . . ."

Lucas leaned in hard: "Nonstandard. We asked these people to do paper research that the BCA wasn't equipped to do," Lucas said.

"With the exception of the discovery of the knife, they didn't do any actual investigation."

"It's worse than nonstandard," Belen argued. "It could be contaminating."

"I don't see why," Lucas said, leaning away. "What they found for us was basically material available through open public records. Anybody could have found it. For the BCA to do it, it would have had to assign twenty investigators with no surety that there'd be any kind of positive outcome, while the bureau's regular work would have been effectively sidelined. That simply wouldn't have happened."

Moore, the BCA director, said, "Lucas is correct. We couldn't have done that, unless . . . well, we could have assigned two people to work it, I guess, but it might have taken months. Or years."

Belen, fuming, said to Lucas, "I don't like it. I'll give you the fact that you may have needed these people, but you know when Fisk is indicted, if she is, she's going to argue that the jury pool is poisoned by all the publicity and by your leaks . . . and we'll wind up having the trial in Cornbread, Oklahoma, or something."

"You won't, Dakota will," Henderson said.

"I'm speaking on behalf of any prosecutor, Senator," Belen snapped.

"I know that, Russ, and I see the problem. We all do. We do have to consider that without the work by Lucas and Virgil, you'd have a serial killer on your staff until she retired with a nice pension. And she might not yet be done with the killing."

AS HE SAID that, there was a soft knock at the conference room door, which popped open and a young woman stuck her head in. She had a sheet of paper in her hand, and she said, "Agent Flowers asked me to do a computer search and to report here if I got a result."

"What'd you get?" Virgil asked.

"Don Schmidt renewed his driver's license up through 2009. He was unemployed and living in a mobile home park near Harris, off I-35. I talked to the son of the man who owned the park at the time, and he said he remembers Schmidt talking about going to California, and one day, he did. I can find a lot of Don Schmidts around the country, hundreds of them, but none seem to track back to our Don Schmidt. None with the same birth date and location. I need to do more work on that, but so far, I'm not finding him. We need to talk to somebody about Social Security contributions. That might locate him."

"I can help with that," Henderson said.

"Who is Don Schmidt?" Belen asked Virgil.

"A man we think might have sexually abused Amanda Fisk as a child," Virgil said.

Belen groaned: "Great. That's just great. We really didn't need to create any sympathy for the woman."

Virgil: "Yeah, well. I think that's one more item in the hit list. I'll bet Don Schmidt hasn't contributed a nickel to Social Security since he went to California. Because he's in a hole in the Northwoods."

"Prove it," Belen said. "Is there anything else ongoing that might provide some direct proof?"

Lucas said, "One thing. We were going to ask some of the true-crimers to take a look, but now that we're at this point . . . We want to get a couple of crime scene people to go back to Bee and crawl along the wall where Fisk apparently had an office, and the other walls around there, and see if they can find any evidence that a knife had been sharpened on the red bricks."

He explained about the red grains found in the point of the apparent murder weapon.

"If you could match grains, that would be important," Belen said. "Maybe even critical. It'd be something physical, instead of circumstantial. Though it could still be blamed on her husband, I suppose."

There was a long silence, and then Henderson said, "Well, Russ. Now you know our problem."

30

Amanda Fisk woke in the morning to the sound of people shouting in the street, not a common occurrence on Summit Avenue. She put on a robe, went to the front balcony, and looked out. A cluster of compact SUVs was parked illegally in front of the house, and a group of women, and one man, were making movies, and the man pointed at her and shouted something that might have been, "That's her!"

"What the hell?"

But she had a feeling that she knew. She'd locked the dogs out of the bedroom, but the little fuckers were waiting for her to emerge and began ricocheting around her feet as she hurried down the stairs to her home office. The office had only a small window that looked out to the back of the house; she peeked, and none of the people at the front had ventured around back. The yard was empty.

She opened Anne Cash's website and there it was: "Prosecutor Investigated for Murder of Doris Grandfelt and Others, Including Husband."

She scanned the attached story, her lips moving with the words: Becky Watson, Carly Gibson, Doris Grandfelt, Alma Fisk, Timothy Carlson, Marcia Wise.

The story mentioned the burning of Virgil Flowers's stable, and injuries to his girlfriend and her son, and to two horses.

"There'll be more jackasses mad about the horses than about the people," she muttered to herself. "You really want to get me, you should have focused on the horses."

She stared at the screen for a moment, calculating, brushed past the caroming mutts, ran back up the stairs, showered, did her makeup, dressed carefully in a blue-checked dress and low heels. She packed clothes and a lot of underwear, got her business purse, and headed down to the garage.

The dogs were barking at her; they wanted breakfast, and she couldn't remember if she'd fed them the night before. She dumped about three days' kibble into their two dishes, gave them a full bowl of water, and left them. The garage, though attached, was partly behind the house, so she was out, turned and rolling down the driveway before the true-crimers spotted her. She hit the street and turned right and in the rearview mirror, saw true-crimers running for their cars. She had a good lead, made several turns, then headed downtown.

RUSS BELEN WAS in his office, saw her coming, and half stood, crouched over a pile of papers on his desk. She banged inside and shouted, "Have you seen what they've done to me?"

Belen pointed at a chair, said, "Some of it," and "Sit down! Sit down!"

"The goddamn cops are framing me for Harrison," she shouted at Belen, saliva spraying across his desk; she didn't sit down.

Harrison was a cop who shot a Black woman at exactly the wrong time, in exactly the wrong place, and without anywhere near enough justification. Fisk had sent him to prison.

"I've seen what they've got, and it's strong, Amanda," Belen said, in a trying-to-be-reasonable voice. Two assistant county attorneys were pushing through the door but he waved them back. "I've got no choice but to suspend you. I can't pay you during your suspension, but if this turns out to be nothing, you'll get your full salary."

"Suspending me? You're suspending me all right. You're lynching me," Fisk shouted at him.

"Not me, not me," Belen said, a notch quieter. "The BCA is taking the information to Dakota County. Bob Christianson will be making the decisions."

"Christianson? You know what I think of Bob Christianson? He's a goddamned right-wing fool and he's already said he wouldn't have prosecuted Harrison."

Belen held his hands up, a blocking gesture. "Look. I can see you're angry, and if you're innocent, I can certainly understand why. But this doesn't have anything to do with Harrison. And I'm going to have to ask you to leave. If you need anything from your desk, I'll have Clark escort you . . ."

"Escort me? You sonofabitch . . ."

In the end, she was back on the street with two banker's boxes full of personal effects. She carried them across to the Victory Parking ramp where she'd left her car. She thought about the Saint Paul Hotel, which was around the corner, but decided against it. She needed somewhere a little more anonymous, a traveler's hotel, a Holiday Inn or the equivalent, as a bolt-hole if she needed it. She'd go back to her home after dark, feed the dogs again. The dogs. The little fuckers would probably be shitting all over the living room carpet . . .

She wrenched herself straight again. She had to think, and not about the dogs.

One thing: they didn't know about Don.

And for just an instant, a smile flickered across her face. Even Don hadn't comprehended what she was going to do to him, until she'd already done it.

BELEN MANAGED THE transfer to the grand jury investigation to Dakota County, which would be done under the supervision of a longtime assistant county attorney named Dick Roller. Virgil knew him and said he was very good.

Lucas and Duncan coordinated the data collection on the case, pinning down times, dates, autopsies when they were available, interviews with people who'd known both Fisk and the victims. They attempted to document the links between them, and possible motives.

Roller pushed hard for any physical evidence of a murder that could be connected to Fisk. The video of Fisk buying gasoline was good, but not definitive, because she did have a gasoline lawn mower at her house.

A BCA AGENT named Evelyn Harvey was placed in charge of tracing Don Schmidt. She visited his last known residence in a manufactured home outside Harris, Minnesota, north of the Twin Cities, and called Lucas from there.

"The house is a wreck. I mean, literally, it's collapsing. It hasn't been lived in since 2008. But: it's not really in a trailer park. It's in a wooded area, with a few more of these homes scattered around, originally on four-acre lots. Most of them are wrecks, now. If you're thinking that Fisk might have come up here and killed Schmidt, it would have been a heck of a lot easier to kill him and bury him right here, than to haul him away and bury him somewhere else. Plenty of privacy."

"I worked a case down in Louisiana where we used ground-penetrating radar to look for grave sites . . ."

"That was exactly my thought. We can do that, we've got the GPR gear. I don't think it'd be a big problem here, unless she actually buried him under the house. There are little clearings and openings in the trees where I think she'd have put him. In the heavy woods, there are so many roots that digging would have been really hard, so there's a limited amount of area where we'd have to use the radar."

"Good. See if you can get that going, Ev, and I'll talk to people here to support the request."

"Great. I'll tell you what happens."

THE COMPILING OF the available information took a month. In the middle of the month, Harvey called Lucas at home, and said, "You better get up here. We think we've got a grave, or at least a burial of some kind. We're printing radar images now, but there appears to be a lot of junk on top of what could be a body."

"Are you excavating now?"

"We've got a crime scene crew on the way . . ."

"Those guys know this stuff better than I do, but emphasize to them that if there is a lot of junk, that's evidence. If she killed him and buried him there, she may have wanted it to look like he left voluntarily, so she piled personal effects on top of the body before she filled the grave."

"I will mention that to them. When can you get here?"

"I've got some stuff I'm putting together right now. I can leave in an hour. How long does it take to get there?"

"Forty minutes from the BCA office."

"I'll see you in two hours, then. Or less."

Lucas had typed up interviews with several former William Mitchell law students who had known Fisk and Carly Gibson, and who remembered the competition between the two. He was doing a precise editing to make sure the transcripts were exact. The work was tiresome, but had to be done.

When he finished, he got a jacket, some bottles of Diet Coke that he put in a cooler, left a message for Weather, found his son, who was with a male friend and about to go scouting for female friends, told him where he was going, and headed north.

He wasn't too worried; the kid would have a driver's license in a year, and then he would worry.

Although it was almost impossible to get lost, Lucas got turned around for a few minutes after he left I-35 and got to the site a little more than two hours after he left home.

The abandoned house itself was only partially upright; the roof had collapsed to the inside, though the back and one side wall were still standing. A broken sink was visible in what would have been a bathroom, but the toilet seemed to be missing, and the towel racks and medicine cabinet had been pulled off the walls and taken away. There were long slashes in the wall where somebody had pulled out the wiring.

The house was set on a wooded lot with a stake out front, and a rusty chain attached to the stake, apparently for a long-gone dog. Trees pressed close around the wreckage, mostly oaks and sugar maples, but here and there were grassy openings. Evelyn Harvey and a three-person crime scene crew were working in one of the openings.

Harvey was a tall, dark-haired jock-o woman wearing a plaid shirt and jeans; she looked like she could run down a coyote. And she was excited: "First time for me, pulling a body out of the ground."

The crime scene crew, dressed in now-filthy white coveralls, were removing dirt from the possible grave site with trowels and sifting every trowelful. "The GPR guys say that the first of the junk is about a foot down, and we're about there. They think the body, if it is one, is down at least another foot."

The GPR crew had already left, taking their radar with them. Lucas asked, "Why do they think it's a body? Can they see bones?"

"There's some kind of metal thing down there, they think it's part of some cooking equipment, pans or something, but under it, one of the printouts—I could show you . . ."

"Tell me, that's good enough."

"Under the metal thing, they can see something hard and curved and they think it's part of a cranium. Only problem with that is, it's in the middle of the grave, instead of at one end. And there's so much junk down there . . ."

"And we're getting to it," said the woman who was running the CSI team. "We're right on top of . . . mmm . . . could be the cuff of a jean jacket."

A van pulled into the lot, and a Ramsey County medical examiner's investigator got out, walked over, introduced himself, and looked in the hole. "How long has it been there?"

"Probably fifteen years or something like that," Harvey said.

"With that kind of dirt, the dampness, won't be much left," the investigator said.

Over the next three hours, enough junk came out of the hole to partially furnish a house: clothing, cooking equipment including a cast iron skillet, a toaster and a microwave, glasses, cups, silverware.

"Tried to prove he'd skipped out on rent, rather than disappeared," Lucas said.

They found a plastic wallet, and inside, Don Schmidt's driver's license.

Eventually they cleared away enough junk to see the remains of the body. That's when they found out why the head was not at the end of the grave: the killer had cut it off and placed it between the body's slightly splayed legs.

They found a pair of handcuffs, which were no longer quite fastened around the wrist bones, which had collapsed in the damp earth; and a plastic rope, around the ankles.

"Bag the handcuffs, don't touch them," Lucas told the CSIs. "It'd be nice if they came out of the Ramsey County Attorney's office."

"Why would they have?" Harvey asked.

"They wouldn't have; it'd just be nice," Lucas said.

There was leathery skin around some of the bones and the spine. The investigator had a laser pointer and pointed it at the groin area. "Seems to be missing a penis and testicles, but not the skin on the thighs around them. See those straight edges on the skin that's left? It looks to me like he was castrated."

The investigator was fascinated; Lucas was repulsed.

"So now we know," Lucas said to Harvey, as the ME's investigator handed down tools to begin lifting bones. "I'm out of here. You should put in for overtime."

"I will do that," she said. They were standing side by side, and she squeezed his arm. "Thanks for coming, Lucas. Honest to God, I'm kinda getting off on this."

Lucas called Virgil at home, and filled him in.

"Not just a bitch; a witch," Virgil said.

"A line you could use in a novel," Lucas said.

"Yeah, and I probably will, sad to say."

31

A month after the big meeting, all of the investigative material was turned over to Dick Roller, a Dakota County assistant county attorney who either would, or wouldn't, present the material to a grand jury.

Two weeks later, he called Lucas and said, "We'll send you some paper, but I wanted to notify you and Virgil that you'll be called to testify before the grand jury next week."

"You gonna indict her?" Lucas asked.

"That would be up to the jury . . ."

"C'mon, man, the jury does what you tell it to do," Lucas said.

"They do tend to follow my advice," Roller said. "Finding Schmidt's body made things easier."

"So are you going to indict her?"

"It'll take a couple of sessions to get through it all, but, yeah, we'll arrest her sometime during the week after next. I gotta get my boss to sign off on it, but he will."

"I will see you next week," Lucas said.

THE JURY MET for four days, in the evenings. Lucas and Virgil testified on the same evening, went out for beer when they were done.

"What happened with the search at Bee? Knife-sharpening marks?"

"Not that anyone could find, but they might be there somewhere," Lucas said. "The problem is, the whole floor where her office used to be was remodeled ten years ago. There's drywall where there used to be brick, and nobody can pinpoint exactly where her office was. So . . . we'd have to demolish the place. That won't happen."

Virgil went on south, and Lucas turned north to home.

And they waited.

A WEEK AFTER they testified, Roller called: "We're going to arrest her this afternoon. First-degree murder in the case of Doris Grandfelt. Ramsey County sheriffs will serve the warrant and haul her butt to the jail. We'll hold her until she makes bail. You want to be there for the bust?"

"Sure."

"Why don't you call Virgil and tell him? If he's in Mankato, he'd have enough time to make it up here. If he wants to."

Lucas called Virgil, who said, "I'll be out of here in ten minutes. Don't let them do it without me."

"We don't have a precise time, yet," Lucas said. "I don't think you have to hurry."

"I'll hurry anyway. I don't want to miss it."

"Come to my house. Her place is only ten minutes away. Maybe fifteen. We can wait until Roller calls."

"On my way."

THE ARREST ATTRACTED a crowd. Roller, a tall, too-thin man with an extra-high forehead, thin black hair, rounded shoulders, and a small, firm pot-gut, stood on the curb and watched, with Lucas and Virgil. Fisk answered the door, invited the sheriff's deputies inside: they were close enough to hear her ask if she could call her attorney before they took her to the jail.

The deputies looked back at Roller, who nodded, and the deputies and Fisk disappeared inside.

"She's already lawyered up," Lucas said. "Wonder who she got? And what she told him?"

"I'll bet she told him she was being persecuted by cops who are getting even for the Harrison prosecution. And her attorney will use that," Roller said. He smiled at Lucas and Virgil: "You guys are gonna get roasted. Guilt by cop association."

Fifteen minutes later, Fisk emerged with two deputies. She was carrying nothing at all and hadn't been cuffed. She said something to the deputies, and they all swerved toward Roller, Lucas, and Virgil. To Roller, she said, "Thanks for not cuffing me up. That was nice of you. And for giving me a chance to feed the dogs."

Roller nodded. "You're welcome."

To Lucas and Virgil: "As for you two, I hope you get cancer, die, and roast in hell."

"You already tried that with my family and it didn't work," Virgil snapped.

The deputies took her off to jail.

"That was pleasant," Roller said, smiling again.

"Fuck her," Virgil said.

Lucas didn't say anything. He was looking up at the house. "Can I go around back? I mean, I'm investigating."

"There's nobody here who says you can't," Roller said, as the sheriff's car carrying Fisk disappeared down Summit Avenue.

Lucas went around back, with Virgil and Roller trailing. He stood on the patio, looking up at the balcony from which Timothy Carlson had fallen. They could hear the dogs barking inside.

"Interesting," Lucas said.

FISK'S ATTORNEY, EARL Gray, had offices a few blocks from the jail. He was waiting for the sheriff's car transporting Fisk and was present for the booking. Fisk found the time spent overnight in the Ramsey County jail to be unpleasant, but tolerable. Fisk told Gray that she would post any reasonable bond.

The next day, Roller argued against any bond, arguing that Fisk was a multiple murderer and should be held in jail. Gray, a broadshouldered, white-haired man, argued that his client was a well-known lawyer, that all of the evidence presented by Roller was purely "speculative." He didn't use the word "circumstantial," because circumstantial was perfectly good evidence, while speculation was not.

Duncan, Virgil, and Lucas had been sitting in the courtroom during the bail hearing and when Gray entered, Lucas leaned toward Virgil and Duncan and groaned, "Earl fuckin' Gray. You might know it."

"You surprised? They've gone up against each other, gotta be a dozen times," Duncan said. "Fisk is good, but she was batting about .300 against him. I mean, who you gonna call?"

"I don't have to like it," Lucas said. And then, "Whatever you think of Gray, you gotta admire that suit. Wonder where he gets them?"

The judge decided he wanted a million and a half dollars to free Fisk, and when told by Fisk that her wholly-owned home on Summit Avenue had recently been appraised at one-point-seven million by a reputable real estate agent, agreed that the house would do as bond. There was paperwork, but Fisk and Gray were on the street shortly after noon.

THE NEXT DAY, Lara Grandfelt spoke to Lucas. "I want to do something about the reward."

"Well, that's up to you, Lara. Fisk hasn't been convicted," Lucas said.

"No, but I'm convinced. I know who killed Doris and that's all I wanted. Who should I talk to?"

"I'll give you some names. There are maybe twenty of them, who ought to get something, some big, some small," Lucas said.

"Send me a list," Grandfelt said. "And phone numbers."

The discussion about the reward went on for a while, mediated by Mason, Tono, Whitehead and Boone, Grandfelt's law firm. Big Dave called Lucas about the reward. His actual name was Derrick Mc-

Bride, and Lucas passed that on to Michelle Cornell and to Roller, should Roller think it necessary to get McBride on the witness stand. Lucas and Virgil were involved in a half-dozen phone calls about the reward, but that was all.

In the end, Dahlia Blair got five hundred thousand dollars and went back to Nebraska a happy woman, with an urn full of ashes in the back seat of her car. The reward distribution made headlines on every true crime site in the world, and was mentioned in the *New York Times*, *Washington Post*, and *Wall Street Journal*, as well as all the cable news stations.

THE FOLLOWING WEEKS were marked by jousting over disclosure of the state's evidence, which was released in a trickle and leaked to the media at the same time, causing Gray to go to the media himself charging that the jury pool was being deliberately poisoned.

On the other side, in a move that the state didn't immediately discover, Gray sent an investigator north to poke around Don Schmidt's former home and grave site. Schmidt's mutilated body, unfortunately for Fisk, was a serious danger, when combined with her father's statement to Lucas and Virgil that Schmidt may have abused her as a child.

Gray's investigator talked to the few people who remembered Schmidt—his original landlord had died—and then, tracking down a rumor heard by the landlord's son, found a retired Chicago deputy sheriff that the BCA hadn't managed to uncover.

The deputy remembered Schmidt quite clearly. He'd been a member of a low-rent biker gang that called themselves the North Woods Mercs . . .

"For mercenaries," the deputy said.

"Yeah, I got that," the investigator said.

"The thing is, there was a rumor that Don was diddling the daughter of the gang leader, Rufus Bends. The kid was about . . . twelve, I guess. You could talk to her, she's around, must be in her twenties, now. When Don took off—until the BCA dug up his body, we assumed he'd took off—we thought it was because Rufus said he was going to cut off his head and his cock and put his head on a stick with the cock in his mouth. Uh, penis."

"Thank you, thank you, thank you," the investigator said.

Gray passed the interview to Fisk. They'd hold it close as long as possible, but they'd eventually have to cough up the information to Roller, as part of the discovery process.

"What do you think the odds are?" Fisk asked him then.

"Of an acquittal? I hate to guess. It's bad luck."

"Come on, Earl. I'm a prosecutor. I'm thinking less than fifty-fifty for a conviction, now that we got the biker."

Gray nodded: "That's about right. Less than fifty-fifty. Not a lot less."

LUCAS CALLED ROLLER that week and said, "I need to get into Fisk's house."

"What for?"

"I want to make a movie."

"About what?"

"You'll see. You're invited."

A week later, they served the warrant on Fisk. One of Roller's assistants had called Fisk to warn her of what was coming, because they didn't want to kick the door. They were met by Gray, while Fisk stood in the background. The dogs ran around their feet, yipping.

They gave the warrant to Gray, who passed it to Fisk, who asked, "What the hell are you doing?"

"Making a movie," Lucas said.

Lucas led the way up the stairs, carrying a small mover's box, normally used for books, followed by a BCA cameraman, then by Roller, Virgil, Gray, and Fisk.

Lucas walked down the hall to the master bedroom and across the bedroom to the windows leading onto the balcony. He opened the windows, stepped out on the balcony, and knelt. When the cameraman was in position, Lucas opened the box, revealing three dozen rubber Chuckit! balls, in three different sizes, all brand new. The dogs could smell them, and went berserk, running around the bedroom like furry balls in a pachinko machine.

Lucas: "Ready?"

Cameraman: "Rolling." He wasn't actually rolling, of course, because he was shooting video, not film, but cameramen still said "rolling."

Lucas released the three dozen balls, one at a time, down the slanted roof toward the rain gutter. By the time they hit the gutter, they were moving too fast to drop into it—they went shooting off into space, as Timothy Carlson had.

"You got that?" Lucas asked the cameraman.

"In the can," he said. It wasn't in any kind of can, of course, because it was on a memory card, unlike film, which would be in a can, but cameramen still said that.

Virgil looked at Fisk and asked, "You're telling us that the dogs rolled two balls into the gutter, so that your husband had to lean over the balcony to get them out?"

Gray: "Don't answer that."

"I'm going to answer that," Fisk said. She checked to make sure the camera was no longer recording, then said to Lucas: "Fuck you."

Lucas pulled back: he was looking into snake eyes that were far harder than his.

THE FOLLOWING WEEK, after some experimentation, Gray brought his own cameraman to the balcony, and rolled five old Chuckit!s, recovered from the dog beds and the bushes around the yard, down the roof. He didn't roll them straight down, but diagonally, letting them bounce off the extended side of the balcony. They had to make three trials, fifteen balls, to get two to stick in the gutter.

"They're moving slower because they're partially deflated and chewed up, which of course they would be, after your husband bounced them off the back wall for months," Gray told Fisk. "If there were a situation where the dogs had fun recovering the balls in the backyard, then running them up here to roll them down the roof again, eventually some would probably catch in the gutter."

Fisk lied easily: "We did that all the time. It was one of the dog's favorite games. They might have been rolling them down over several days, and we didn't notice they'd stuck in the gutter."

"Really," Gray said.

AFTER GRAY AND Fisk had to disclose the video as part of discovery, Roller went back to Fisk's house with used Chuckit! balls and made a video that suggested the dogs couldn't simply roll the balls to hit the side of the balcony—they would have to spit the balls at the side, to defeat the force of gravity enough to get them to roll diagonally.

He also presented the balls to the two dogs. The dogs happily grabbed them and ran off through the house. Brought back repeatedly, and given the balls, the dogs never attempted to roll them under the lower balcony rail.

FISK MADE A valuable but serendipitous contribution to the defense, as the result of going to her dentist. There was a wait, and she picked up an older *New Yorker* magazine that had a long story about a British nurse convicted of killing seven neonatal babies with a variety of injections. The main evidence against the nurse was her presence at the time the babies died—a statistical cluster of deaths matched to her work shifts. (The defense claimed the cluster was artificially constructed by the prosecution.)

She showed the article to Gray and said, "I did some research. There are all kinds of random, unexpected clusters that don't seem to make any sense. Crimes, diseases, all kinds of stuff. If you have a big enough sample, the clusters not only occur, they're inevitable. There are probably thousands or even tens of thousands of people in the United States who have been close to death clusters as big as the one Roller is trying to hang on me. They're unusual, but they occur all the time—and the key thing is, they're inevitable."

Gray read the article and said, "We need a statistician. One who speaks English instead of mathematics. If we can get the judge to throw out the cluster of deaths around you and all we have to worry about is Doris Grandfelt . . . That would be excellent."

"I think we can do that," Fisk said.

———

IN THE MIDST of the maneuvering around the upcoming trial, Virgil married Frankie. Lucas was best man, and Moses gave away his mother. Weather cried, as did Virgil's mother for the fourth time. By mid-November, the new stable was up. Frankie thought it looked quite handsome.

Despite the reconstruction of the stable, and continuing work with Roller on the Grandfelt case, Virgil finished the novel, spent a week agonizing over the question of whether it was good enough, and sent it off to New York. His editor accepted it two days later and his agent started pushing on the new contract. He asked her if it would be large enough to quit cop work, and she said, "Oh, yeah."

IN THE END, the prosecution and defense disclosed information and witnesses each planned to use in the trial. Virgil, Lucas, and Duncan met with Roller on a cold winter day before Christmas to review it. The trial was set for late January.

"Fuckin' Chuckit!s," Lucas said.

"I think the jury is more likely to believe our videos than theirs," Roller said.

"Are you even going to be able to get Carlson's death up there?" Lucas asked. "All this bullshit about clusters . . ."

"I know the judge fairly well. He's a smart guy," Roller said. "I think he'll let us put up all the deaths, but he'll allow Gray to put up his math guy to talk about clusters and explain how they can happen. Then we'll put our guy up there to explain how clusters often *do* point to a single cause. Not always, but frequently. The jury will have to sort it out."

"You think Earl will put her on the witness stand?"

"I've been wondering about that myself," Roller said. "She doesn't appear to have any emotional range at all. If you asked her whether she was molested, if you ask her if she pushed Carlson off the balcony, I doubt that she'd break down and cry. From what Virgil says, and what the people who know her say, I'm not sure she's capable of that. But if she did . . . that's sort of a gusher of sympathy for her. Down in the dungeon, getting raped while her mother lets it happen? Seeing her husband fall to his death? But if she can't do that, if she can't cry, if she lapses back into her stone-eyed-killer act . . . that would work for us. So, I don't know. Maybe she's sitting up at night, practicing her best weeping hysterics act."

"Getting raped and killing the rapist is one thing, but doing what was done to Don Schmidt, that's a whole different thing," Virgil said.

"It is," Roller agreed. "The photography in the Grandfelt and Schmidt and Wise murders is going to be important. If the judge lets the jury see it, they'll want to punish someone. Gray will challenge it as unnecessarily prejudicial—I don't know what the judge will do. He might ban the pictures but allow detailed forensic testimony, which is not the same. Not the same impact. We'll have to see what he does."

"What about the biker guy?" Virgil asked. "Rufus Bends?"

"Turns out he's a Christian biker, and was, before the murder. In fact, his whole gang was Christian, you know, they supposedly turn the other cheek," Roller said. "He denies doing anything about Schmidt, which is good for us. His daughter was molested, but not raped. She'll testify to that, that Schmidt kissed her and put his hands all over her, skin-to-skin, including the vaginal area, but she says there was no penetration. There was mutual masturbation, no oral sex. Bends took her to a doctor at the time, and the doctor agrees that there was at least no deep penetration. But: the key thing is, she shows that Schmidt was a predator and a pederast, which may convince a jury that he messed with Fisk, as her father believes. There's your motive for his murder and mutilation."

"Is the jury going to believe Bends? That he didn't do it?" Virgil asked.

"Don't know," Roller said. "I believe him. The jury might think otherwise. 'Cause he is a biker, and he looks and talks like a biker."

"You're making me unhappy, here," Lucas said.

"It's gonna be tough. But we've got all the other stuff. That Fisk was at Bee, had access to the knife, that she was dating Carlson at the time of the murder and lied about it, that she lived next to the park. We've got the law student battered as Marcia Wise was . . ."

"They got those fuckin' shoe prints," Virgil said.

Roller: "Yeah. They got the shoe prints."

They talked about all of it for a while, until Virgil asked the question: "What do you think?"

Roller considered, then said, "Fifty-fifty."

"I don't want fifty-fifty. I want ninety-ten," Lucas said. "She killed them all."

"Get me the hard evidence, and I'll use it," Roller said.

"I promised Frankie I'd hang her," Virgil said. "Now I'm afraid it's the jury that's gonna get hung."

ON ANOTHER FRIGID December evening, Fisk welcomed Gray to her yellow house. Snow was falling outside, big slowflakes drifting sideways across the street. Gray brushed off his parka and stamped snow off his feet before entering. Fisk had been reviewing all the information that came out of the discovery process and had built a fire with white-barked birch logs in the living room fireplace.

The smell of the burning birch, the snow flurry outside the window, was like an old-fashioned New England Christmas by Robert Frost or somebody else literary . . . maybe Dickens?

The snow globe scenery didn't fit the occasion.

When Gray sat down, Fisk pulled her feet up under her and asked, "What do you think?"

"Not that again."

"C'mon. I want to know."

Gray looked into the fire, the crackling logs.

"Gonna be complicated, Mandy. I can only tell you one thing for sure. We're gonna take your husband's size ten-and-a-half shoes, which were all over the site where Doris's body was found, and stick them so far up the prosecution's ass that they'll need a winch to get them out. We're gonna hang Timothy. You might find that upsetting, but we don't have a choice."

"Well, you know . . . Timothy's dead. So I'm okay with that. But we're not in a great place, Earl—it's not all good."

Gray sighed, and said, "No, it's not. They've got quite a list of dead bodies. We'll challenge them, and the judge might eliminate some of them, but I don't think he'll throw out all of them."

"The dead bodies have nothing to do with me, Earl," Fisk said. "Give me a number."

"If I gotta . . . sixty-forty for a hung jury," Gray said. "No better than forty percent for an outright acquittal or an outright conviction."

The goddamn dogs were sitting there, looking at her expectantly, maybe with indictments in their beady eyes, canine accusations. It occurred to Fisk that if the prosecution had been able to call the dogs as witnesses, she'd be done.

She turned and held out two hands toward the fireplace, feeling the heat.

Gray: "Feeling the heat?"

"A little," she admitted. "But I'll tell you what, Earl. Sixty-forty for a hung jury? I'll take that. I'll take that. I got faith."

She stood up and reached behind a mantel clock that Timothy had inherited from his mother, and that she planned to throw in the trash as soon as she was clear of the trial. She'd hidden two of the Chuckit!s there, and she took one in each hand and threw them over her shoulders.

The two Jack Russells went careening down the living room rug, jumping, tumbling, chasing the bouncing blue-and-orange balls.

"Sixty-forty," Fisk said, as she and Gray turned to watch the dogs. "Sixty-forty, you little fuckers."